THE WINSTONS

BOOK ONE 

BECKA'S AWAKENING

&

MATT'S DILEMMA

ROWENA DAWN

SCARLET LEAF

TORONTO

2018

This is a work of fiction.

Names, characters, places and incidents are products of the author's imagination and are not to be construed as real. Any resemblance to actual events, locales, organizations or persons, living or dead, is entirely coincidental.

SCARLET LEAF

TORONTO ONTARIO CANADA

COPYRIGHT BY ROWENA DAWN

ISBN: 978-1-988827-53-7

For information address Scarlet Leaf:

scarletleafpublishinghouse@gmail.com

BECKA'S AWAKENING

BOOK I

I dedicate this novel to two couples that fell in love at first sight and whose love is always as strong as ever after many, many, many years of marriage:

Dafinka and Giampaolo Scatozza

Diana and Aurel Botorog

8

THE WINSTONS

Rebecca's children

Adam (m. Anna)

Evelyne (deceased)

Adam's children

Marjorie (Twin, m. Jonathan) – children: Matt (34), Maggie (28), Jay (28)

Michael (Twin, m. Amelie) – children: Josh (26), Lily (26)

Gabriel (m. Emilie) – children: Ariel (32), Alex (32), Becka (19)

PROLOGUE

"Come on, man, this is so not right!" Josh exploded.

He threw his fork back onto the plate and made his aunt, Marjorie, frown. She loved that set of dishes and feared that the young man's frustrations would sooner or later put a crack in them.

"You're complaining, huh?" Maggie waved her fork at him in mockery and rolled her eyes. "You're still fairly young compared to some of us and you have enough time ahead of you, so you shouldn't be the one complaining!" she retorted angrily.

"He has the right to complain, Maggie, as well as any one of us!" Becka replied in support of her cousin. "So what if we are younger? We're all in the same boat!" she punched the table with her little fist. "Auntie, can't we do something about this?"

"I know you want to, pumpkin, but there's nothing you can do about it," Aunt Marjorie stroked her arm in an attempt to soothe her. "What must be done, must be done!"

"So, we have to pay for something that happened a hundred years before we were even born? How does that make any sense at all?" Alex snapped and joined the others in voicing his outrage, though it didn't stop him from scarfing down another piece of pie.

"It's less than a hundred, you nitwit!" Lily replied with disdain and punched his arm.

"Who the hell cares?" Alex retorted with his mouth full.

He never did learn not to talk with his mouth full, try as his parents might. Anyway, he wouldn't have given a rat's ass on such things, anyway, especially at home.

"One hundred, two hundred, same shit, pardon my French. You know what? I don't feel like paying for some jackass's mistakes!" he ended his heated speech, his finger still pointed at Lily.

"So, what do you propose to do, then?" Matt, who had kept his mouth shut until then, asked with nonchalance.

He had been sipping from his glass of whiskey quietly, with a detached expression on his face that suggested that nothing they discussed could affect him.

"Don't tell me you're okay with this!" Alex answered back in disbelief. "Come on, Matt!

You're the oldest, man, and you've only got one year left. You've got to be as angry as I am, if not more! Don't pretend it doesn't bother you because that's not possible!"

Matt took a few moments of silence, sipped a little more from his glass, then looked at Alex and shook his head.

"Angry? Maybe. Can I do something about it? I don't think so," he replied to his cousin with his usual coolness, his eyes gazing steadily at him. "So why should I bother?"

No one had anything to say to that. They were all aware there was one stipulation they had to fulfill and only then they could get their trust funds and also reach their full potential.

The worst part was they had to do so before turning thirty-five, because once one of them turned thirty-five without fulfilling that condition, their share of the fund would be divided among the remaining younger ones who still had time to succeed or fail.

"You know what? I don't really care about unlocking my powers," Ariel said pensively, without addressing anyone in particular, "although, it would be nice to see what you can do if you use your full potential..." she continued, lost in her thoughts as always.

Her cousins gave her time to get to the point. They knew she had the bad habit of rambling on and on or getting lost in her own thoughts only to leave everyone hanging. Yet, sometimes, if not most of the time, she could come up with some very interesting solutions if they had the patience to listen to her.

"But I do care about doing something for myself. I'd like to open a little business..." Ariel finally said longingly.

"Keep dreaming, girl," Maggie snapped, already bored with the way Ariel always liked to drag things out. She wasn't one for patience and, unfortunately, that trait had had some unpleasant results in her daily life. "Till you take care of your part of business, Ariel, girl, you won't be able to open a shed."

"Why are you always so mean to her?" Alex snapped at Maggie. "If she wants to dream, let her dream away. What else can she do? What else is there for any of us?" he asked, his infuriated gaze scanning each one of them to see their reactions.

"Beat the curse?" Marjorie asked softly, trying to defuse a potentially explosive situation.

"Not so easy, auntie," Ariel said sorrowfully. "I tried, you know... Do you remember? I thought that guy, Eric, the one I met two years ago, would be the one. It wasn't meant to be, you know... It's not so easy, and you know it very well. You see how things are. There's no real romance left in this world, I'm afraid. If there's no romance left, where can one find true love?"

Marjorie nodded. She did know it. Finding true love wasn't easy-peasy. She'd been in the same situation when it was her turn and she'd almost lost everything because of her own stubbornness and her family's meddling.

"It's never easy, my dear, I know," she answered and stroked the young woman's arm with love again. "But, Ariel, sweetheart, you have to keep trying. You can't simply give up. Think about it! You will be able to use your powers and get your money, but only once you find your true love and commit to it. You'll be truly happy then!"

Ariel turned her eyes to her plate on the table. She knew her eyes would show everyone she'd already resigned herself and she was sick of hearing platitudes and encouragements whenever her family got wind of something like that.

Everybody around the table remained silent for a few moments. Jay helped himself to some more of his mother's amazing pie.

Marjorie was the best cook in their family, which was why they always chose to meet at her house. Everything was easier to swallow if there was a good pie or cake on the table. At least, in Jay's opinion.

"I think we should see if there's any legal way to get out of this situation, guys. We need the money now, don't we? It's not like we can wait around forever!" Alex broke the silence, when the idea came to him suddenly. His eyes analyzed them carefully and saw them nod their assent. "Look," he continued, "I'm already thirty-two. I don't have time for stupid things and games and all sorts of idiotic attempts at love! I want to do something for myself like Ariel said. Now, while I still can."

Although almost everybody found themselves in agreement with him, they still looked at Matt.

He was known to be the smartest guy in the family and they knew that any kind of solution should have come from him. Matt's eyes shifted around the table, feeling their expecting gazes on him and finally shook his head.

"There's no way out, buddy," Matt put his glass on the wooden table at the same time and stood from the bench. "If you called us here just for this discussion, then I'm out of here. I've got real things to do, places to see…"

"You don't even want to try," Becka cried out, jumping out of her seat. "You've just given up because you have so little time left and you don't care anymore."

"I tried, sweetie," Matt told her with a sad smile on his lips.

Becka was his favorite cousin. Maybe because she was the youngest or maybe because she was unspoiled and funny and had a very big heart. His fingers stroked her cheek in a loving, yet sad caress, and he kissed her forehead.

"Becka, I tried hard to find any kind of loophole in the wording of the trust funds papers. Believe me, there's none. If I couldn't find one, sweetie, then no one can, and you know it. There's a reason I'm one of the best attorneys in the country, and all of you know this isn't just my vanity talking. Anyway, honey, these days, I content myself with making my own money the hard way and enjoying as much as possible the little spare time I have left. I've stopped chasing such dreams. It's not in the cards for me and that's it."

All of his cousins looked at him in shock. Only his sister, Maggie, understood him very well. She didn't have any patience, especially with fools, but Matt was something special.

She'd always looked up to him and she knew he wasn't the kind of guy to give up on anything without a fight. Hearing him say he'd resigned himself made her understand the depth of his anger, even though he hid it from them.

She felt like taking him into her arms and never letting go but she knew he wouldn't like that. He wasn't very big on displays of affection, her brother, so she just lightly petted his hand and left it at that.

"Matt, you should try to use that time you have left to find a girl," his mother said reproachfully and everyone's attention turned to Marjorie, who continued, "You still have a chance, son, and I'm not talking about the money here, you know it. I know that sad affair with Velma's left you afraid to commit again and I don't like that in the least. That's not the Matty I know. That wasn't love, son, and you know it. Had it been true love, you'd have had your full powers by now even if you hadn't gotten the money."

"Mother, Velma's been out of the picture for a decade already. She's in the past. What's the point in bringing her back into the conversation?" Matt retorted curtly, shaking his head. He couldn't understand his mother's reasons for bringing up bitter memories.

"Because she was the reason you stopped looking at women with hope," Marjorie pointed out, shaking a scolding finger at her first born. "You think all women are like her and that's why you just take everything you can from them and move on. Another woman on the list! It's like you're keeping a score: how many women can Matt score?" she reproached acidly, which wasn't something that they'd witnessed before. Everyone's eyes were riveted on her. "It's not good for you, Matt! Even if you've already given up on the trust fund, which is stupid, by the way, you're still alive and you still need a reliable woman in your life, like I've already said over and over again. You'll grow old and alone and bitter!" Marjorie ended her unusual tirade by punching her son's chest with her finger.

"Thanks for the heads up, mom. It's always good to know what your future will look like!" Matt replied sarcastically and removed himself from the path of her pointy finger. Yet, he didn't leave. He seemed undecided and glance back at his cousins.

Marjorie shook her head bitterly, but chose not to continue that line of discussion. She knew her son quite well and she knew there was no way to make him change his mind when he was like that. It was like talking to a rock.

The silence stretched for a few minutes. Everyone was busy either eating their pie or playing with their drinks, pretending nothing out of ordinary had happened between Marjorie and her eldest son. But mostly, they were busy avoiding each other's eyes for fear someone might say something hurtful again.

In the end, Alex, the most outspoken of all, couldn't stand the awkward silence anymore and looked around the table, gauging everyone's mood. Uncertain whether it was even worth it, he shrugged and decided to try a new line of conversation.

"You know, you are the old lady's favorite great-grandson, Matt. Can't you persuade her to end this foolishness? She can change the papers if she wants to. It's not like the words are carved in stone!" Alex anxiously waited for his answer.

"Tried that too, Alex." Matt sighed, shaking his head. "She said she did it for our own good, whatever she means by that. So... I can say I've tried everything and it's time to limit my losses."

Again, no one said anything for a few moments and, again, they couldn't bring themselves to look each other in the eye and the silence stretched on.

Encouraged by the unusual silence, since such get-togethers were normally a very chatty and loud affair, Matt took his leave with a simple wave of his hand and started down the path to the kitchen door, whistling softly to himself.

Ariel, pensive as always, looked after him until he was out of earshot, and said dolefully, "It's sad... It's really sad. He's the oldest and he's already given up."

For a few moments, everyone stared at her absolutely speechless. It was like she'd grown a second head during the last hour.

"Well, we're close to that too, Ariel," her brother Alex retorted angrily after a moment of disbelief. "It's not like we have too much time left, is it? Just about three years, you dimwit! Once we turn thirty-five, everything will be gone: the money, the powers, everything. And we can't do a single thing to stop this!"

"We can't even cheat," Jay intervened bitterly for the first time and the others burst into laughter.

"Oh, yeah, I remember," Lily said. "You tried to pose as a fool in love and came with that simpleton. Camilla, I think her name was?"

Jay nodded smiling. He had already forgotten the ridicule he'd suffered at the time. His easy-going nature didn't allow him to keep a grudge for long.

"Yeah, but it didn't work, did it?" Josh said very matter-of-factly. "Those two fossils sniffed you out."

"Well, they can read minds, so it was a piece of cake to sniff him out," Aunt Marjorie pointed out with an enigmatic smile on her lips. "That's why they've been appointed trustees, you know. No one can fool them. You shouldn't have tried to cheat, Jay. The old lady hasn't forgiven you for that yet."

Jay shrugged. He knew very well where he stood with his grandma those days. He didn't think she would ever forgive him.

The old bat was a real piece of work. She was resentful and bitter.

Just a few of them could steal a smile from her and lately he hadn't been part of that group. After the stunt he had pulled with that woman, grandma didn't even acknowledge him at the family dinners anymore. She pretended he didn't even exist.

He looked around and noticed all the others had gone quiet, each of them thinking about the implications of what had happened to him.

He truly hoped he wouldn't go through a new period of veiled mean jokes or even innocent teasing. At which Becka was a master. He even flinched when she started speaking, expecting the worst.

"So, we only have to wait for them to die…" Becka tentatively began to say, her gaze passing from one to the other.

"Not so fast," Marjorie interrupted her hastily. "The rule says that if they pass away, two others will take their place. Same type of power, pumpkin, so no way to fool them either. You have to understand there is no way around this. You have to play by the rules."

"Damn it!" Alex swore. "All this drama only because great-grandpa had the nerve to abandon great-grandma for another woman and then another idiot left aunt Evelyn at the altar and she killed herself!" he shook his head as if everything was inconceivable for him. "So, now, generation after generation has to pay for those two idiots! Where the hell is the justice in that?"

"Well, I think it was a radical conclusion from my grandmother, as well," Marjorie replied conciliatorily, "but there's never been a way to change grandma's mind, unfortunately. I know my father tried hard at the time, but she wouldn't listen to him. He tried again when my happiness was at stake and still nothing. He didn't have any success. She wouldn't give in. Not even a bit. Since the money was still hers, she had the right to decide what she wanted to do with it."

"But why the curse on our powers? I really don't understand that," Becka wondered.

"Same reason. Grandpa was a witch himself and he used those powers to entice a very young woman and leave grandma. And the man who left Evelyn at the altar was also enticed by a witch. She didn't want any other witch to misuse their powers."

"I wouldn't!" Becka cried out.

"I know you wouldn't, pumpkin," Marjorie patted her hand tenderly. "Not all apples are rotten, I know that much. But grandma didn't want to hear a thing, so... Here we are: now, everyone in my generation paid for that and yours has to pay, as well. However, if you succeed in finding your true love and get your trust funds, then at least the money problem will end and the next generations will have only the curse to defeat," Marjorie tried to lift their moods, but with little success.

"Oh, just that," Lily sighed and put her chin in her hand, fixing her dreamy gaze somewhere in the distance.

"I really wanted to open that nursery," Ariel whispered inconsolably and her brother stroked her fingers, his eyes shining with deep concern for his sister's dreams.

"Nothing is lost, sweetheart," Marjorie said and stroked Ariel's hand at her turn. "You'll see.

You'll find your soul mate, Ariel. Everything will be fine."

"Where? Where could I find my soul mate, auntie? The people I deal with every day are not even lover material, believe me. I wouldn't let them touch me with a ten-foot pole, so finding a soul mate is quite out of question. There's no chance for me out there! I've looked around for years and nothing!" she said, this time with tears in her eyes.

"Wait and see, Ariel. These things have a way of working out," Marjorie whispered to her, then started picking up their plates to show them that the conversation ended.

There was no point in debating something they couldn't fix. There wasn't anything more to add and whining wouldn't help. The older woman knew it well. Whining never helped. You had to roll up your sleeves and do something.

Although the others jumped out of their seats to help her, they were all still thinking about the conversation and a none-too-rosy future, which looked pretty hopeless for them at that very moment.

CHAPTER ONE

Becka left the coffee shop in a hurry. She was holding a hot coffee cup in one hand, while, at the same time, she was trying to stick a muffin and a toasted bagel in her handbag with the other.

She'd forgotten to ask for a hot sleeve for the cup and on top of that, she'd also forgotten to take a napkin. Her head was deep in the clouds that morning, and now, the searing heat burned her fingers through the paper cup.

She couldn't go back to the coffee shop. She was already late for her morning classes and the last thing she wanted was to miss the entire lecture on her favorite subject.

Becka kept struggling. She tried to make the muffin and bagel fit in her handbag, at which point she wondered why she'd left the house with such a tiny purse.

The people and things around her became a blur the more she wrestled with the bag and the more she rushed toward the bus stop.

No more than a moment later, just as she turned around the corner, her eyes still on the tiny handbag that wouldn't cooperate with her, she ran into a tall man and as luck would have it, the lid of the coffee cup came loose and all the hot liquid spilled all over the giant's pristine, white shirt.

Of course, Becka thought, things couldn't get any worse! Not only did she scald him but the damn shirt had to be white! Why not black? No one would notice a coffee stain on a black shirt!

"Oh, my God, I'm so sorry! Really, really, sorry!" she blabbered and tried to clean his shirt with her bare hands, forgetting about the cup lying on the pavement, discarded like yesterday's news, all but empty. She'd also forgotten about her coveted breakfast, which was leaning precariously on one side of the handbag, ready to fall out as well.

Her hands shook the man's shirt as fast as she possibly could. Her meager attempts hoped to limit the burns at the very least.

Becka knew the hot coffee must have already penetrated his shirt and she didn't even want to think of what had happened to the skin beneath it, badly burnt by the freshly boiled brew.

"I think you'd better take your shirt off!" she cried out, without taking her gaze off the task at hand.

Remorse drove her actions. Images of the emergency room flashed at the back of her mind. Focused to a frenzy on her nearly catastrophic mistake, Becka never noticed the rest of the man to whom the chest belonged, much less the eyebrow which shot up as soon as she ordered him to strip.

"May I ask what exactly you're trying to do?" he finally asked in a deceptively mild tone.

Until then, he'd simply looked at the top of her head, completely shocked by the actions of the little woman before him.

Hearing his voice, she finally looked up and blinked. Not once or twice, but three times. The man she had in front of her wasn't the regular polished and polite man she'd encountered in her life before. He was a far, far cry from that.

This man's rugged face was set off by a long, pale scar on his left cheek that began somewhere close to the corner of his eye and continued to nearly the corner of his mouth, giving him a dangerous allure. He looked like one of the mercenaries she had seen in one of the documentaries about the civil war in former Yugoslavia. It wasn't reassuring.

His eyebrow was still raised scornfully and for a moment there, she asked herself how he did it. It wasn't easy to pull off that move for so long, she imagined. The young woman just about forgot her curiosity when she met his eyes, colder than the Arctic Ocean. She almost shivered.

She blinked again, swallowed hard and tried to find her voice. She forced herself to be brave, refusing to even consider the thought of being a scaredy-cat. She'd always tried to face any danger, not run away from it, and that wasn't the moment to change her ways.

"Hmm…. I was thinking… you know… your shirt…"

"I heard that bit about my shirt, don't you worry, but I really don't know what difference you think it would make if I took it off now. With or without the shirt, my skin is still scalded, my morning's still ruined and I'm still pissed off…" he said in a level tone, which didn't show the slightest hint of anger and that made her even more fearful.

While it was true he didn't sound mad, the complete clash between his words and his tone made her nervous. Becka couldn't even begin to think of how to talk to him.

She swallowed again and bravely said, "Yes, I know that, but the coffee is mostly on the shirt, so if you take it off…"

"Now?" he mused, when he saw she stopped without finishing her sentence.

"Well, yes," she nodded and stressed her words, in an effort to lend them more confidence than she had.

She pretended she knew what she was doing, although her face was burning in absolute embarrassment and shame.

It was the first time she'd ever asked a man to take his clothes off, even though it was only the shirt. On top of all that, his tone and attitude made her terribly uncomfortable and she was afraid that everything showed on her face.

She couldn't say she had a poker face worth a damn. Every time she played cards with Jay, he would laugh at her best, yet failed efforts to bluff.

The man looked at her for a few seconds, but then, with a bold move, he took his shirt off.

"Do your worst!" he said and handed her the all but ruined piece of clothing.

However, Becka didn't take it. She didn't even notice he was holding anything for her to take. She couldn't even find her voice to answer back. Her eyes were too busy taking in the expanse of a chiseled chest peppered with curly coarse hair, still wet from her coffee. She'd forgotten what she wanted or was supposed to do entirely.

"Earth to the moon?" he mocked her in his grave voice and waved his hand before her eyes.

Finally, his gestures pulled her out of her reverie and Becka's eyes shot up to meet his in an instant.

"Sorry, just lost in thought for a moment there," she mumbled more than a little disappointed with her silly admiration of the male figure. She'd thought herself above such trivial endeavours.

Finally, she took the shirt from his waiting hand and used it to dry his chest more vigorously than it was necessary.

The coffee was already a dry sticky stain, but that wasn't on her mind and neither was the fact that she might take off a layer of vulnerable, burned skin, too.

None of those things dawned on her because, to be truthful, Becka was brimming with embarrassment, upset with herself for her carelessness and every reaction that followed.

Not only had she poured her coffee all over a stranger but she'd been caught staring at the man's chest like a lustful, simple-minded woman.

"Yeah, I noticed," he replied amused, watching her expression while she cleaned his chest.

The man enjoyed her train of thought. He could read it on her face with no effort whatsoever.

It was refreshing to see someone so unspoiled like the woman before his eyes. He was tired of all the games played in society and wanted something new.

After a few moments, he decided to ask, "Does any man's chest have this effect on you or just mine?"

There was a little malice in his voice and that made her straighten up and look directly into his eyes. Then, she replied sulkily, "I'm just trying to help, you know! Why are you acting like a jerk?"

When she snapped at him, his eyes became colder than they had been before and he yanked the shirt out of her hands.

"Yeah, with such help I wouldn't be surprised if I'm dead tomorrow!"

She tapped her foot in frustration, raised her voice a notch, and replied to him with her usual self-confidence, "You're just pissed off because I ruined your shirt."

Her voice mustered all the determination she could and she added a nod, for good measure, in the hopes it would give her more of a knowledgeable air.

"But it was just an accident, you have to understand. It wasn't like I wanted to spill my coffee all over you! I'd have preferred to drink it, you know," she scoffed and shrugged her shoulders.

She was standing tall before him, matching his confident, dominant attitude with her own, but spoiled everything when she continued in the tone of a stubborn and willful child, "I really could have used that coffee!"

Fascinated with the sudden change in her attitude, he looked at her more attentively. Only now, he noticed her chocolate eyes and especially her little mouth, arched like a bow, with rosy lips. A part of him was almost begging and pushed him to grab her already and just have a taste of her sweet, sensual mouth.

The longer she talked, his interest in her lips only grew more and he got to the point of an agonizing need urging him to lean in and claim what he wanted. He found them more tempting when the tip of her tongue came out and nervously licked her upper lip. Something stirred inside him and, suddenly, his interest changed completely.

"You owe me," he said so abruptly that it charged the atmosphere in an instant.

Becka opened her mouth in shock to reply. Yet, she couldn't make a sound for a few moments. She was too stunned by his sudden outburst.

The man didn't clarify his statement or expand on it. He just waited for her to process his words and get back to him with a bold retort. From what he'd seen so far, he was sure to get one. He didn't have to wait for too long.

"What are you talking about?" she finally managed to say, with a touch of thinly veiled indignation, and her wide eyes held his own intently.

"What you heard," he brushed off her harmless furor and continued, "You owe me."

"For this shirt?" she asked incredulously, showing him the shirt she held in her hand.

"Among other things."

His wolfish smile ran shivers down her spine, as her mind started dreading the worst and conjured unsettling scenarios.

"What other things?" Becka asked, although more than a little hesitation and uncertainty delayed her question.

Her eyes seemed to grow wider still and the tip of her tongue again touched her upper lip nervously, to torment him and make him more aware of his increasing desire for her.

He couldn't understand that irrational, unlikely desire for a clumsy woman he'd just laid eyes on, but something in him wanted her. He actually needed to have her, just like that.

She looked a bit young, maybe too young, that was true enough, but he knew that looks were sometimes deceptive. He still made a mental note to ask her about her age. He didn't want to fool around with jailbait even though he was agonizingly drawn to her.

He had a strict policy about going to jail. His policy was simple enough. Jail wasn't a place he ever yearned to see on the inside. He did once and even once in a lifetime was more than enough.

"You scalded me, ruined my shirt, and obviously, I can't go to my appointment half-naked. And, please, note, it's an important appointment, and I'm already late because of you," he explained patiently, as if he'd been talking to a small child.

Of course, it was all just a ruse. He was only trying to see what kind of reaction he could draw from her.

She felt the blood rush to her face and she cursed her pale complexion that revealed too much and in the most inappropriate of moments.

No matter how much she tried to appear sophisticated or cool-tempered, she always failed because her skin betrayed her. It was the curse of her life. Maybe not the only curse she had to contend with but it made the top three.

Becka thought of going a different way with him, to get herself out of the trouble that seemed to be brewing, and, very politely, said, "I'm very sorry for scalding you and for ruining your shirt. Of course, I'm sorry about your appointment as well, but I don't see how I could…"

She never finished her sentence because she saw a naughty smile flourish on his lips. That made her lose her train of thought again. This time she was afraid of what he'd say.

"I think you owe me something and you can set it right by going on a date with me," he finally specified his conditions in a tone implying too many things that would better remain unsaid.

"A date with you." she repeated automatically as if she weren't able to grasp the concept.

"Yes, princess, a date," he repeated in a tone that showed he meant it. "You know, that thing where we go somewhere, have something to eat, talk, that sort of stuff. It's usually called a date. So, that's what I want. A date with you... Today. Not right this moment because I obviously can't go anywhere without a shirt, but right after you go into that store over there and buy me another shirt. Don't worry about it, though, I won't ask you to pay for it. I'll give you the money," he waved his hand magnanimously, as if the price of the shirt had been the problem.

"That won't be an issue. I'm the reason you need a new shirt, so I can buy it," Becka replied, offended by his condescending attitude.

"No need," he dismissed her concern, took his wallet out of his back pocket, and pulled a few bills out.

"Here, that should be enough," he said giving her the money. "Now, go in, buy me a white shirt – keep in mind, white shirt, not blue, not black or green, or striped or whatever. Just white. Then we can go on our date."

"No, I can't," she said stubbornly, with a shake of her head.

"Why not?" he asked, his face so rigid and serious as if it had been set in stone. He didn't seem to take her rejection too well. "As I said, you owe me. I can say you attacked me, you know."

"Ha, good try!" she scoffed at him. "Attack by coffee! A deadly weapon! Don't make me laugh. No one would believe that stupid thing and you know it full well. Everyone will see it was a simple accident and nothing more."

"So then, am I to understand you're too good for the likes of me?" he frowned.

Becka scoffed again, and dismissed his silly, inconsequential words with a wave of her hand.

"Get serious! I haven't even considered that. But since I don't know a stitch about you or your life, it would be difficult to make such assumptions, don't you think?"

"Is it my scar?" he asked peevishly now. "Do '*stiches*' make you uncomfortable?"

She scoffed at him again, but refused to answer a question she thought to be quite stupid and not worthy of her attention.

"You're not legal, is that it?" he tried again, determined to get her to admit to something.

He didn't understand why but he couldn't just let go.

"No, I am legal enough. I'm not jailbait, don't you worry about that. Three months over nineteen already," she replied, this time smiling warmly at him, which puzzled him a little more than her former, vague refusals.

"So? You have a boyfriend, then, and you won't cheat on him," he tried again.

He'd already reached the point where he just wanted to find out the reason, end the conversation and walk away if she kept rejecting him. He had no explanation for that, but finding out why she wouldn't go out with him was still a priority.

"No, I don't have a boyfriend. However, I do have a class right now and more later on. The point is I really don't want to miss any of them and I'm already so very late... But, if you still want to, I can see you in the afternoon..." she said and saw he was astonished that she actually agreed to go out with him. "And not because I owe you or anything stupid like that, but because I'd like to see you again. I don't owe you a thing! Just so we're clear!"

His eyes searched her face thoroughly. He wanted to make sure she wasn't trying to string him along, but brushed it off after a second of thought. He was almost certain she wouldn't show up, but he didn't have anything to lose, nor could he force her to date him. Anyone would have laughed at him if he'd pretended he was attacked by a girl with a Styrofoam cup of coffee.

"All right," he accepted. "When?"

"If you want it to be today, then it will have to be after four," Becka answered cheerfully, visibly keen on the unexpected date.

"Dinner, at six?" he asked her.

"Why not? I do need to eat dinner."

"This spot here, where we are now?" he asked again.

She nodded, a little amused by his way of asking questions, and turned to leave.

"Hey, you forgot my shirt!" he cried out after her.

"I'm buying it now," she turned her head back to him.

"Take the money, then," he insisted, stretching his hand out to her. "I don't want you to pay for it."

She was stubborn enough to go against his wishes. She did want to have it her way and leave him with his hand outstretched, but took note of the dogged expression on his face and realized he wouldn't give up so easily. He was much more wilful than she was. She gave in and took his money.

CHAPTER TWO

The man paced back and forth impatiently on the corner of the street. In the beginning, when he got there, about five minutes earlier, he'd decided to wait patiently, although he was almost sure she wouldn't show up. He was convinced she had used her classes as an excuse just so she wouldn't have to go on a date with him at all.

The young woman seemed delicate and sheltered. That led him to believe she would avoid any further contact with him.

He had seen that type of woman before, those sheltered flowers, living in a polite world, where everything was covered under several layers of paint to deflect reality. Well, in his experience those innocent flowers would run away like scared rabbits once they took a good look at him and his scar. None ever stuck around for a second chance.

He didn't harbour any illusions about romance or anything of the sort. That was some baggage he'd left aside sometime in his past. He was aware he wasn't the type of man about whom a girl like her would ever dream. He didn't fit the mould of a man she would bring back home to meet mom and dad.

Thank God, he didn't have such aspirations! He was too much of a realist for something like that and even though he didn't want to admit it, he was too terrified to put himself out there in the open, to reveal what was in his soul. It wouldn't have been a smart move. Someone would certainly stomp on it.

He glanced at his watch as he continued pacing around and was surprised to see that he'd actually arrived too early for their meeting. There were about three minutes left until six and he knew he would wait, not only until six o'clock, but probably even ten or fifteen minutes past six, even though he didn't expect her to keep her promise.

Somewhere, at the back of his mind, there was the knowledge he'd partly set up that date with her only to punish himself. He was very good at teaching himself over and over again not to reach for someone as innocent and wholesome as the girl from that morning.

He'd been warned against such wishful thinking many times in the past, but he still found a sort of masochistic enjoyment in challenging fate as if his turn would certainly come one day and then he would win for once. He liked beating the odds.

He was striding on the sidewalk nervously when, suddenly, he saw her rushing towards him. She was pushing past the moving crowd in a hurry, much like she had that morning.

It occurred to him that, probably, being late was one of her habits. It wasn't the worst habit in the world, anyway. He'd seen worse things than that. This was one bad habit he could live with.

This time, at a second, more appraising, glance, the first thing he noticed was her honey-colored hair flowing over her shoulders, thick and full of curls. In the morning, she had it gathered in a thick ponytail. He'd liked her hair that way too. That mass of hair was too rich and vibrant not to like it. However, right then, with that wild mane set free, the young woman was much more enticing than he remembered.

A slow smile flourished on his lips and he wasn't even aware he was smiling, although such an endeavour was something out of the ordinary for him. The longer he watched and admired her, the more he realized he could fall for that girl and in a bad way. The thought troubled him enough and made him frown for a second, erasing any trace of his earlier smile.

The young woman stopped abruptly a few steps away from him and smiled shyly. Her smile reached her eyes and colored the chocolate of her iris in a warmer nuance than the one he'd relished so much just hours before. In that very moment, he was sure he would give her anything she wanted just to enjoy her sweet eyes a little more.

"Hi!" she was out of breath by the time she reached him and her lips arched a little more, tentatively. "I'm really sorry I'm late but I had a bit of a problem at home and I had to take care of that. That's why I couldn't leave earlier. My kitchen flooded. Again."

"You're not late, it's okay. It looks like you're not having a very good day today, though," he replied with a smile, amused with the way she talked.

Her voice had a lower pitch than the voice of some of the women he'd dated and he appreciated it didn't chime like tiny bells in his ears every single time she opened her mouth. He hated the high pitch of an all too sweet, dishonest voice.

"I think we should introduce ourselves for the beginning. I'm Bryan, by the way," he said and his uncharacteristic smile lasted surprisingly long that time.

"Becka," she extended her hand to him enthusiastically, which made his smile grow wider.

She didn't seem reluctant at all to go out with him and that got his hopes up. His perpetual smile hinted at his changing expectations and opinion of her.

"Hello, there, Becka. Nice to meet you." He took the narrow hand in his and shook it lightly. "So, aside from nearly sending a complete stranger to the hospital this morning and the flood this afternoon, how was your day?" he continued, and turned her towards the strip of shops without letting her hand go.

"Well, I was too late for my first class this morning, which annoyed me. Immensely." She rolled her eyes in frustration, as she fell into step with him. "I really like that class, you know. Worse, now, I'll have to figure out everything I missed by myself, which means a lot of work and at least an entire afternoon wasted," she complained.

"So now you resent me," he replied in a low and flat tone.

"Why would you say that?" Becka turned to him surprised at his strange reaction. "I was late even before I bumped into you. It's not your fault at all. It's just I didn't sleep much last night, too many thoughts, you know how it is, and this morning I had a bit of a slow start to my day, that's all."

He nodded once. He understood she didn't blame him or begrudge him for it, but he was more content because she still let him hold her hand than anything else.

"What kind of thoughts could keep a young girl like you awake?"

She scowled at him because of his condescending tone and said peevishly, as she turned her nose up, "The kind of thoughts I can't share with you."

"Hmm," Bryan mumbled but let the subject drop once he saw she was determined not to say anything. He didn't want to push his way in too abruptly and scare her away too soon.

"By the way, I know an Italian restaurant by the lake", Bryan told Becka, squeezing her fingers.

"They have a nice terrace overlooking the lake, a gorgeous view … Not to mention, they serve original Italian food. I've heard it's an unforgettable experience."

"I'd love it!" She looked up at him and a wide smile appeared on her lips. "But are you sure we can get a table at this hour? If the view and the food are so great, wouldn't it be packed now?" Becka worried.

"Don't worry, sweetie," he waved her concern off. "I've already made reservations for us."

"So, you were very sure on you… or rather on me… You were sure I'd come…," she murmured to herself, but Bryan heard her anyway.

"No, not at all," he contradicted her. "Actually, I didn't even think you'd show up, but I'd have gone out for dinner anyway so…"

"Do I seem so unreliable?" Becka asked touchily, pulling her hand out of his and making him laugh.

He liked those little, illogical contradictions in her nature and found her funny.

"No, Becka, you don't, but you do look too sweet and too young for a man like me," Bryan answered unapologetically even if amused. He chose to be direct whenever he could.

"I am not so young," she frowned at him. "I've told you I'm already nineteen, haven't I?"

"Yes, you have. I know. But I'm almost thirty-two, almost a lifetime away, and more importantly, I've seen much more of this life than you and not all of it good."

He took her hand back into his and entwined his fingers with hers, making her shiver for a moment.

Both of them felt something like an electric shock run through their intertwined fingers, but neither dared to say anything. They glanced at each other briefly before Becka looked away, trying to mask what she was feeling.

After a few moments, she looked back at him, "I wouldn't have thought you were so old."

She saw his eyebrow rising doubtfully and she hurried to correct herself, "Not that you're old. You aren't. But…"

He started laughing heartily and she stopped her explanations, turning her nose up childishly again.

"You're so funny, and your fuse is so short! It's amazing you get upset so easily. It's refreshing to see someone so natural, not faking every emotion," he said and squeezed her fingers gently.

"You should know it's not a good idea to annoy me," she started in force, but left her statement at that.

"Or what, sweetie?" he asked a bit steely.

She stopped suddenly, glanced behind them, then back at him again with nervous eyes, and whispered, "I can't tell you."

"Now, you've made me curious. Really, really, curious. Are you with the mob or something?" he asked her, only half-joking.

Nothing truly shocked him anymore and he'd learned to take everything in stride, but he liked to know what he was up against and the sooner, the better. He might have had a worthless hide, but it was his, and he had some sort of attachment to it.

"What?" She cried out and stopped in her tracks for a second. Her eyes widened to what seemed the size of small saucers in incredulity at his outrageous idea.

Becka couldn't believe her ears. She wouldn't have ever imagined someone would ask her such a question and she was afraid Bryan was making fun of her.

"Well, you just threatened me…" he started speaking, only to be interrupted.

"I didn't threaten you, you blockhead! I just warned you," she replied with real anger in her voice this time, but he didn't seem to care.

"Same thing," he shrugged nonchalantly.

"No, it isn't," she insisted. "That's not the same thing. And I haven't said anything about the mob. Where did you get such an idea?" she asked in a biting tone.

He glanced at her and saw her face was turning purple.

"But you warned me not to annoy you," he tried to approach it logically and calm her down at the same time, as he felt her temper rising.

"Yes, but that doesn't mean…"

"I understand a threat when I hear one, Becka," he interrupted her forcefully this time. Any kind of playfulness was gone from his voice. "So, what are you going to do to me? Murder me in my sleep?"

"Are you mocking me?" she scowled at his questions and the tone of his voice.

"No, I'm dead serious. I might have a worthless hide, but it's still attached to my back, you know," Bryan replied in a matter-of-fact voice, echoing his earlier thoughts.

"Wait, what do you mean, you have a worthless hide?" she asked confused, completely forgetting the line of conversation for a moment.

"Just something I've been told...," Bryan replied softly, avoiding going into details.

"You know you shouldn't trust people who say things like that," she advised him wisely. "I might not know you, but you don't seem worthless to me. At least, this is one thing I can do well. I'm a good judge of character. I can tell you're much more complicated than you seem and I would guess you have a very speckled past, but you're not worthless at all," she said pensively, more kindly than she had been in their argument just moments ago.

"Wow, you do like to talk." he exclaimed, hearing her delivering a lengthy speech.

Mostly, her words humbled him and he didn't want to let her see it.

"You want me to shut up?" she replied upset. "I can shut up. If it bothers you so much, I can stop talking altogether! It's not a problem for me!"

"No, not at all," he pulled her closer to him and squeezed her fingers tenderly. "I actually like the sound of your voice. It's not one of those voices that sounds like a chime and grates my ears. It's got a low pitch, almost throaty, sexy, I could say. Although, I'm pretty sure that mouth of yours would be good at other things, too, not just talking," he added with measured nonchalance, watching her carefully to see her reaction to such a blunt suggestion.

Shocked, Becka looked up at him for a few moments, her eyes wide again, then she started walking faster, to leave behind what was just said, but forgot about their laced fingers that wouldn't allow her an easy escape. He laughed and matched his stride to hers.

"Come on, don't act like a little virgin. No one is so innocent these days," he tried to smooth her ruffled feathers.

"It's not about being innocent, you ass! It's our first date!" Becka snapped back and rolled her eyes.

"So? You follow the rules? A kiss on the first date, a longer one and first base for the second and sex on the third?"

"I don't follow any rules. I don't know any rules! But if there are any, then you might just forget about getting any kiss today or tomorrow or the day after," Becka replied furiously.

"Why? Am I being punished?" he asked, a quiet chuckle betraying his teasing interest.

She scoffed at the simple suggestion, "Like I'd care to. It's about what I feel and what I want."

"And you feel nothing when it comes to me, is that what you're saying?" he asked her, more curious about her opinion of him so far than at all disappointed with the thought.

It wasn't as if he'd gotten his hopes up for a relationship only to find out he didn't measure up.

"I didn't say that, so, please, don't put words into my mouth!"

"Then what did you say?" he insisted.

"That it might be a possibility. I actually don't appreciate what you said… It was crass and you know it… I think you did it on purpose only I don't know why…"

He waited to see what else she had to say. He found her more fascinating than he ever thought she would be, especially for someone so young.

"You know what, let's have dinner, change the subject and maybe you'll get that kiss," she replied cheerfully trying to appease both of them and save the evening.

"I'm not a child to bribe me with a candy, Becka," he replied evenly, scowling at her.

"Ugh!" she growled. "You're impossible! You choose to misunderstand everything I say."

"Why, because I don't let you treat me in the way you would treat the children you normally date?" Bryan retorted.

Becka stopped and turned to him, in disbelief yet again, "You know what, Bryan? I think you've got a complex, and it's a big one. You have a big chip on your shoulder, don't you? I don't understand though. If you're so stressed out by our age gap, why did you ask me out? You should have played it safe and spared yourself the trouble of putting up with a *'child'*!" she ended her tirade almost shouting.

A slight breeze ruffled the leaves in the trees.

Bryan didn't say anything for a few moments but thought to himself, *well, damn. She's got a point there!* However, he decided not to let her see she touched a nerve or she'd guessed what he thought and kept staring her down, which didn't have the desired effect. She didn't back down.

"I don't have a complex," he replied stubbornly in the end. "But I don't like to be patted on the head like some five-year-old either. I don't like to be told if I'm good I'll get a cookie."

"Oh, really? And you think I'm going to believe you?"

The man let her comment hang in the air for a few moments, unsure what to believe of her behavior. It was like she'd tried to provoke him and it didn't seem plausible.

"You're a little hellion, Becka. I'm almost twice your size…"

"What's that got to do with anything? Unless you intend to fight me?" she asked as if she wanted to know how that would end, half challenging him, half warning him off.

Bryan laughed heartily, brought her hand to his lips and kissed her fingers.

"Of course, not. Don't be silly. You just astonish me. Usually, women are more careful around me," he replied amused.

"How come?" Becka asked.

"Well, if you want to know, they avoid me. Most of them. But no woman has ever threatened me or provoked me like you do…" he said, watching her as if she had been an odd exhibit in a museum.

"Oh, for God's sake!" Becka snapped, throwing her hands into the air dramatically. "I haven't threatened you! Can't you get it through your thick skull?"

He opened his mouth to say something, but she reached up and covered his mouth with her palm, shaking her head at the same time to stop him from adding anything else to what he'd already said. He obeyed mutely and just watched her.

"Could we leave it at that, Bryan? Believe me it was not a threat, okay. Maybe, one day, I'll tell you what's all that about but not today, okay?"

"Okay, not a threat," he said after she took her hand off his mouth.

***

The hostess showed them to a table close to the lake, where Bryan courteously pulled her chair and helped her to sit at the table. After she was seated, Becka looked at the lake wistfully.

A dozen boats had set sail out on the lake that day and the shiny surface of the water was peppered with white sails, canoes and all sorts of other boats.

Becka was crazy about sailing and yet she'd rarely had the chance to go out on the lake lately. Matt was the only one with his own boat and he hadn't had enough time to take her out sailing that summer because he'd been so busy with his work all the time.

Bryan sat down at his turn and gazed at her. It wasn't difficult to spot the wistfulness in her eyes and he understood what she wanted.

The man took her narrow hand in his broader one and stroking the back of her hand tenderly in a comforting gesture to distract her from her yearning, he said softly, "If you want we can go sailing on the lake tomorrow morning or in the afternoon. I understand the weather will keep so we'll have another nice day. Not a spot of clouds. I have access to a little pocket cruiser you might like."

"Really?" Becka's entire face lit up with excitement. That meant the summer might not go to waste after all.

Bryan was fascinated again. Yes, he'd liked her beautifully arched lips enough to ask her out on a date, but now, he saw much more than that.

Becka was a beautiful woman indeed. She didn't have any use for artifices, and that puzzled him. Most women would wear a lot of makeup to be attractive, especially when they were very young and wanted to appear sophisticated.

Becka's makeup was subtle to the point of nonexistence. She might have used something on her eyelashes, but he couldn't be sure. He could be sure, though, that she didn't wear any lipstick and not even a trace of perfume. And yet, she smelled like wild flowers. Leaning in closer to her, he realised it was her hair that smelled of flowers.

"Hmmm…"

"What?" she asked startled.

"Nothing, nothing," he waved her worries away. "I was just wondering what shampoo you used because I've never smelled anything like that," Bryan explained to her.

"Really? My shampoo? We were talking about sailing," she chided him for such a silly side-note and he could tell she was disappointed.

"Yes, we were," he reassured her. "My offer still stands, even if you don't want to go tomorrow. My question about your shampoo was just curiosity. That scent is amazing," he specified.

"All right, then, let's satisfy your curiosity. It's a shampoo made especially for me by one of my cousins, that's why it's so unique. She chose some flowers that go well with my skin and hair. But that's not important now, Bryan. Yes, I want to go on the boat with you tomorrow. I'll skip my classes, not a problem."

"Just like that?" he wondered.

He wasn't ready to accept it had been so easy to get her to go out with him again. It wasn't usually that way with other women. He had to work a little more.

"Yep, just like that," she replied smiling at him. "I'm truly crazy about sailing, you see, and I haven't had any chance to go on the water this year. That's why I actually took classes this summer because I knew I'd die of boredom otherwise. At least, having to go to school takes my mind of what I've missed," the young woman explained to him.

"Who takes you sailing usually?" Bryan asked, feeling the sting of jealousy rising in his throat. He'd known he must have had some competition but he'd preferred to push the thought aside.

"Matt, but he seems to be busier than ever this summer and every time I tried to ask to go sailing, he never had the time," she said with regret in her voice.

"Who's Matt?" Bryan asked now truly envious of the unknown man. "You said you didn't have any boyfriends, sweetie," he pointed out.

"Oh, no, Matt's not a boyfriend. He's just one of my cousins," she answered to him hastily, but she didn't add anything more when the waitress interrupted them to take their order.

Bryan waited patiently until the waitress left with their orders and asked, pretending to be absent-minded, "You have lots of cousins?"

"You might say that," Becka replied turning to him. She'd been watching the lake again. "I have five cousins and two siblings. You?"

Bryan shrugged and replied, "I might have a cousin somewhere in the west of the country, but I haven't seen him in ten years at least. No siblings."

"Oh, that's bad. Aren't you lonely?" Becka asked, feeling sorry for him.

She couldn't imagine how it would be like not having someone to plot or quarrel with. She'd always counted on having someone to turn to if she needed company or help.

"Not really," he mumbled and leaned back to let the waitress who had returned with their drinks to put the glasses on the table.

The beer was cold and felt good after the hot afternoon they'd had. After a few moments of idle silence, while she watched the boats on the lake and he gazed at her, he continued, "We can leave in the morning if you want, and return in the evening, take a picnic with us…"

"I'd love to!" she jumped at the idea and continued speaking quickly in an excitement she couldn't even begin to contain. "Let's do it! How early do you want to leave? I hope it won't be at the crack of dawn. I can't function so early in the morning," Becka said playfully.

She was serious though. She avoided waking up early every time she could.

"No worries, not so early," he replied with a smile in his voice. "We can wait till eight-thirty or nine... What do you say if I come and get you at eight-thirty? ... Or are you afraid to tell me where you live?" Bryan asked when he saw her reflect upon his words.

"Ah, no, no, it's not that," Becka waved his concern away as not important. "I don't mind if you know where I live. You don't give off that serial killer vibe ...," she said, making his eyebrows instantly go up at her strange ideas. "I was just thinking whether eight-thirty would be too early or not, but I think I can survive getting up at seven."

For a moment, Bryan just stared at her. He wasn't even able to think of a reply as he was still stumped about the serial killer reference.

The man didn't even know or could have imagined that there was such a thing like a vibe specific to a serial killer. After a few moments of shock, he shook his head trying to clear his mind and only then registered what else she said.

"You really like your sleep," he laughed.

"You don't even know the half of it," Becka merrily replied. "I'm a bit of a night owl, you see.

I like to go to bed late at night so it's no wonder I can't get up early in the morning," she shrugged.

"How do you manage with school?" Bryan asked taking another sip of his drink.

"Oh, that's another story altogether," she waved her hand dismissively and sipped from her beer as well. "Actually, it's not that much of a mystery," she suddenly decided to answer. "I simply choose my courses with two things in mind: they can't be too early in the morning and, of course, they have to be interesting... You know," she said with a conspiring air, "I can't even declare a major because I don't really know what to focus on. I like too many things, you see, and..."

"So you're undecided about your future," he concluded, stroking her long fingers with carefully manicured, short nails.

Bryan didn't think that her indecision was too much of a problem at her age. She still had the time to decide what direction to follow in her life.

"Actually, I do know what I want to do in the future," she corrected him. "Not that it would do me any good...." Becka mumbled grudgingly.

His strokes were playing havoc on her sensitive nerves and confused her thoughts, stealing away her senses toward a drowsy concentration on the soft, pleasant caresses. It wasn't as if she'd never met a guy who tried to play doctor with her, but this one was different.

Bryan was totally unlike the guys who asked her out before. She'd been completely indifferent to her dates in the past and she'd even convinced herself it was her fault she couldn't feel anything because probably she was a cold person. What happened now contradicted her beliefs. Her body reacted very strongly to this man and without the usual annoyance she felt whenever someone wanted to touch her.

"Why not?" he asked, mesmerized by the chain of emotions passing over her expressive face.

He was certain she had to be the worst poker player in the world. Almost everything she thought was clearly visible on her face for all to see.

She looked at him startled, as if she hadn't expected him to talk. Then, she realized that she had said too much in her pleasure-induced near-trance.

"It might not be possible to do what I want," she said after a while. "There are some conditions… and even people that are much better than I didn't succeed… so…."

"Don't sell yourself short," he cut her hesitation short. "You might succeed even if others have failed. You want to elaborate though so that I understand and probably help…"

"Oh, no, I can't," she interrupted him. "It's not something I'm supposed to say, you see?"

"Why not?" he frowned. He never liked foggy matters and, apparently, the young woman was involved in a lot of such things.

"Because I can't," she pleaded for his understanding.

"Are you mixed up in something?" he scowled at her, not because he didn't want to get involved with a woman involved in nefarious affairs, but because of a sudden urge to get her out of trouble.

Bryan wasn't the helpful type of man but she'd wormed her way into his heart. That troubled him.

"Oh, no, not that, of course, don't be silly," she laughed with easy cheerfulness, dispelling his dark thoughts. "It's just a family thing... Can we talk about something else?" she waved the subject away.

"People date so they can get to know each other, Becka. If you keep secrets...." Bryan tried a different way to get to the heart of the matter.

"Oh, come on, like you've told me your secrets!" she cried out frustrated. "I won't fall so easily for that sort of thing."

"You haven't asked me anything," Bryan answered with a smile tugging at the corner of his mouth. "But I have asked, you see, so, of course, I expect answers," he nodded to put more weight on his words.

Becka traced the contour of the glass with a finger pensively. She was trying to figure out some way to turn his expectations against himself.

"But why do you get to ask first and not me?" she glanced at him with suddenly sharp eyes.

"All right, ladies first," he generously gave in, as if he'd been doing her a favor. "You ask your questions first and then I'll want my answers," Bryan said with a finality in his tone that promised he would offer her no escape from holding up her end of the deal.

Becka took a few moments to think about it, but finally admitted with disappointment, "I don't know what to ask or... how to ask," she said, glancing back at him.

"Then I don't know what answers you want," Bryan mused at her unwilling to say anything without being specifically asked.

She frowned for a second, then smiled as if she had just discovered the secret of life, "All right, tell me everything about you."

"Huh, you don't ask for much, do you?" he laughed at her ingenuity.

"I think my question covers everything, so start talking," Becka gesticulated. "I'm afraid you might not even finish today and you'll have to continue tomorrow and the day after tomorrow...," Becka laughed, happy that she found the perfect solution to elude his questions.

"You're something else," he said through laughter and took her hand again.

He looked at her fingers, stroking each of them slowly until he realized she was shivering.

"Did I make you uncomfortable?" he asked, glancing at her eyes.

"No... no, you don't. I'm just not... used to... that..." she tried to explain.

"Hmm, you make me wonder how many boyfriends you've had and how clumsy they were," he mused under his breath, but she still heard him.

She took a few seconds to think, tilting her head to the side in a gesture he'd noticed about her earlier and found endearing, before she said, "I think there were four and yes, they were clumsy and went directly for the kill."

"And what did you say?" he asked, holding her gaze with interest, imagining his little hellion crush the laughable attempts of horny teenagers.

"Of course, I said no," she answered haughtily.

"But not always," he surmised. He was a realist after all.

"Why not?" she shrugged. "Believe me, it wasn't worth the trouble," she replied and frowned, at the same time.

Becka didn't understand where he was going with his line of questions. She wasn't very comfortable with them.

His sharp gaze held hers before he let go of her hand. Leaning back on his chair, Bryan analysed her for a few moments. His disbelief was palpable.

Then he asked her in a voice full of awe, "You want to tell me you've never been with a man… or a boy before?"

"It's not that I want to say so, but it seems I've already had. Is that a problem for you, Bryan? You prefer experienced women and you don't date little bookworms like me?" Becka asked him snappily. She hated labels especially when they were attached to her.

"Where did that come from?" he asked, puzzled by her sudden outburst.

"You said…"

"Wait a minute, sweetie! I haven't said anything about you being a bookworm," Bryan interrupted her by putting his hand up sharply to stop her from talking over him.

She waved his concern aside and replied, "It's not a big deal. There were others who said so, so I'm not surprised that you might think the same way too," she shrugged his excuses off.

"Don't lump me in with the others, Becka, all right?" he leaned towards her, stressing his words so she could get his message loud and clear. "I'm not a stupid teenager who's looking to score with a different girl every night and add notches to my belt. And besides, you don't strike me as a bookworm," he clarified, always fixing her with his determined eyes. "Not even a little."

"Well, truth be told, I am sort of a bookworm," she admitted sheepishly, her gaze trailing to the side to avoid his own.

Despite it being the truth, it was a particularly sensitive button for her.

"I prefer reading to spending time with my classmates. Some of them can't share a thought between them and..." Becka shrugged again. "Look, I tried, okay... but it was so damn boring to be around them all the time," she protested with large gestures.

Bryan burst into laughter and said, "Let's hope I'm not as boring as them and you won't get sick of me too soon."

"You know I've never said anything like that," Becka said reproachfully, a little concerned about them being at odds all the time.

She'd never been so snappy and contradictory with anyone before. She didn't understand what made her react so strangely when it came to Bryan.

"No, you haven't, I admit it," Bryan agreed with a nod of his head. "Anyway, I'm sure I can show you some things neither of those kids could," Bryan replied with a wolfish smile that made a shiver trickle down her spine.

His words, as well as his meaningful smile, took her aback for a few seconds.

Bryan was as blond as a Viking or rather, the way she'd always imagined Vikings. His icy blue eyes seemed to shoot arrows her way now and then, and she felt each one of them somewhere in her belly. It was like a constant attack on her senses.

Whenever he would touch her hand, and stroke her skin with those long, thick, and calloused fingers, little sparks ignited in all her nervous endings. It made her feel strange. She found herself wanting something more from him and at the same time, she was afraid of what she might get in the end.

Becka was aware Bryan wasn't the kind of man with whom she could play games and hope he would stop if she said no in the end. He didn't seem like the kind of man who would take any sort of games kindly. This man was too intense and too seasoned for that. One thing was very clear to her, there were risks involved in such a relationship and yet, she didn't want to back out of it.

Becka also had the unsettling feeling Bryan was aware of what he was doing to her and he enjoyed the results immensely. Since she wasn't sure yet if he was serious or just having a little fun with her, she hated herself for being so transparent and offering everything to him on a silver platter.

What bothered her more was the fact that she was painfully aware of what was going on. That didn't mean she could do a thing to change the way she reacted.

Becka was simply stunned that she could experience such intense sensations just because he was stroking her fingers. It wasn't like she had never dated and she hadn't had any kind of experience on the scene. However, she was positive none of the guys she had gone out with in the past could make her feel a tenth of what she was feeling now, and that without too much effort on Bryan's part.

The young woman took her glass and sipped slowly from the cold beer, just to give herself time to come up with something to say. She thought hard and well but she couldn't find anything worth mentioning.

At the same time, she was staring at the tablecloth as if she could find some inspiration there. However, her mind was blank, which only made her more furious with herself. She was acting like a fool.

She couldn't bear the thought that a man could make her forget everything in a matter of seconds. That woman there wasn't anything like her. Where was her witty spirit and her deflective skills?

Bryan touched her hand gently again and made her snap out of her thoughts and look up at him. He was smiling at her.

"Don't try too hard," he advised her in a soft voice. "It's not rocket science, it's just a date. We can talk about anything and everything. It's up to you. No one can make you say or do something you don't want, all right, Becka? Let's find a neutral subject. For instance, why don't you tell me about those classes you're taking," Bryan suggested.

Becka pulled her hand away and let it fall into her lap to cut off the flux of emotion. Then, she cleared her throat before saying, "I'm taking some art classes this summer. They're just optional courses, you know. I just needed something to do," she said shrugging her shoulders and Bryan noted that the gesture seemed to be defining for her.

Becka continued, unaware of his thoughts, "Everybody in the family is busy with something right now and I was feeling a little… left aside, if you know what I mean."

Bryan, who knew very well how it felt to be left aside, nodded and, glancing at her left, said, "It looks like our food is here."

They both kept silent while the waitress laid the food on the table, and then they said their polite *'thank you'* and attacked their plates.

Happy she finally had something to do, Becka started cutting into her juicy steak with enthusiasm. It looked exactly as she wanted it. She hoped it would also taste as good as it seemed.

She hadn't had too much to eat that day. She'd lost the muffin and the toasted bagel when she went to buy the shirt for Bryan. With the flood in the kitchen at home, she hadn't had time to prepare anything to eat that afternoon. Now, she was famished and didn't need to fake her enthusiasm.

"It was refreshing to hear you wanted a steak and not a salad with the dressing on the side," Bryan told her after he swallowed his first bite. "I hate seeing women go hungry just because fashion says they have to be skinny with no curves. I, for one, can't understand why anyone would want a woman with no curves."

"Huh… you won't see me doing that," Becka replied, glancing at him and at the same time, cutting another piece of the steak. "Skipping meals, I mean, or eating only salad," she specified. "Of course, I enjoy a salad as much as the next person, don't get me wrong. But, especially, if I didn't have time to eat all day, like today, I do enjoy a good meal. It's not like I'd ever be skinny anyhow and I don't think it's worth crying about something you can't have," she said and this time she shrugged only one shoulder.

His eyes lingered on her for a few moments. Then he said very matter of fact, "I don't think you have anything to complain about. You're just the perfect size."

"Thank you, you are so kind," she retorted sarcastically.

Becka was sure he was either trying to be polite or was making fun of her in a covert way.

"No, really, you are. Believe me, I can't wait to trace the shape of your body with my hands."

At his words, she simply dropped the fork onto the plate, not even registering the clank, which resonated far enough to make people turn their heads towards their table. Her mouth formed a perfect 'o', which prompted him to laugh heartily.

"Come on, don't tell me you didn't expect me to go in that direction," he said on a playful tone, trying to make her feel at ease. He failed.

Becka tried to say something, swallowed hard, and tried again. Nothing came out. She was speechless.

"Are you all right?" he asked her, concerned by now.

If the situation amused him for the a few seconds, now it worried him and seriously.

Bryan was afraid he'd pushed too soon because she seemed completely overwhelmed. He would hate himself if he had pushed her away with his impatience. She was the first woman he had been attracted to in months and he didn't feel like losing her before having a chance to start something.

Becka nodded hesitantly and then, standing up abruptly, she said, "Will you excuse me for a moment?"

He stood too, setting his fork and knife down on the plate. Now the man was worried and his worry showed in the frown between his eyebrows.

"You're coming back, aren't you?" he couldn't help but ask her.

"Yes, of course, I will. Where do you think I'm going? I'm just going to the ladies' room not fleeing the scene," she glanced at him and nodded.

Then, Becka hurried in the direction of the ladies' room without looking behind. Inside the ladies' room, after checking to see if she was alone, she leaned heavily on the first sink, which didn't seem wet, and looked carefully at herself in the mirror.

Her face was flushed and there was a new shine in her eyes, which worried her a little. Becka closed her eyes for a moment, breathed deeply and thought, "*All right, this is the one, I think. Maybe not tonight, but soon, definitely. The very first one who made me feel like doing it. It makes sense...*"

With the decision finally made, Becka splashed some water on her face, then straightened up and dried her face and hands carefully.

She weighed her decision for a few seconds more before leaving the washroom to go back to the table, where Bryan was waiting for her, sipping slowly from his beer.

His eyes found her at once, and he watched her until she got to the table. When she was close enough, he stood up respectfully to help her sit down.

That was something she hadn't seen anywhere else but in movies until then, and she felt flattered he would go through all that trouble. Becka also admired the fluidity of his movements, which showed he was a man who would go through rigorous training, maybe every day.

She sat down with an encouraging smile and took her own glass of beer to wet her lips in the bitter liquid. Her smile still showed over the rim of her glass, a little more boldly now, and the look in her eyes made him feel that pull towards her stronger.

His cock stirred in his pants and drew his attention to the sudden uncomfortable tightness. Bryan became aware of two things. First of all, he was happy he was sitting down and the tablecloth hid his awkward state. He wouldn't have liked for her to notice how far she pushed him, especially because of how she had reacted earlier to his suggestion of a less than innocent nature. The second thing was he would definitely have her, sooner or later, Bryan promised to himself. That wasn't a woman he could just let pass by and out of his life too soon.

He needed her at a visceral level and not only in his bed. He needed to spend enough time with her to see exactly what that pull between them meant and he was determined to steal that time if it was necessary.

"Are you up for a stroll along the lake after the meal?" he asked her, nodding towards the promenade busy with people. "It's not too windy and it's still warm out for this hour of the evening."

Becka nodded and added in a playful tone, "I hope you'll buy me some dessert as well, though."

Bryan laughed heartily and shook his head as if he couldn't believe her.

"I have to say you're the first woman in years who's asked me for dessert. I wasn't even sure women ate cakes or ice-cream anymore."

"This one does," Becka told him, leaning towards him as if she was confessing a sin. "If possible at the same time, the better. You know, a hot chocolate cake with a scoop or two of ice-cream on top… However, for future reference, it's not a good idea to mention your previous relationships to a woman," she winked at him as if she'd parted with a secret. "We have this thing, you know," Becka waved her hand. "Maybe it's a quirk, but we prefer to think we're the only one that ever existed in a man's life."

"Dully noted," Bryan replied with amusement and grinned. "I'll refrain from making comparisons from now on, although I'd have thought you'd be flattered by the comparison."

She shook her head at him and with a large wave of her hand, she replied, "Not really. You're far, far from the truth. You see, I might conclude you think I'm a glutton, and that won't do. No, it won't do at all."

"Oh, no, baby, I wouldn't think something like that. I've always wanted to see a woman with a healthy appetite and here you are. It seems I've finally found one. You might be totally unique," Bryan retorted as he enjoyed some more of his beer without taking his eyes off her.

"Of course, I'm unique. Everyone's unique, Bryan. There aren't two people alike," Becka said a little too loud and a head or two turned to them. Neither Becka nor Bryan noticed.

"If only you knew…," he said wistfully shaking his head. "Too many people try to emulate someone else and in the end, you just end up with so many copies of the same person that you're sick of them," he continued and something like regret registered in his voice.

"Wow, Bryan, I don't even want to know what kind of women you've dated if you have such a good opinion about my sex," Becka replied with awe in her voice. "Luckily for you, I'm here now. And as you mentioned, I'm one of a kind," she joked.

"Yeah, you are, Becka, and I mean to keep you," he answered back, suddenly with a serious tone.

His words sent a shiver down her spine. His seriousness showed he wasn't a man she should trifle with.

"Should I be worried?" Becka tried to joke, but he could see in her eyes a little glimmer of concern because of the intensity of his statement.

"I'm not a stalker, Becka, don't worry about that. I meant only to say I want everything between us to go just fine so I can have more time with you, that's all," Bryan explained patiently to ease her concern.

"Ah, all right then. We'll see then, won't we?" she stated very matter-of-factly.

Bryan nodded and seeing she'd already finished her steak, he waved for the waitress.

"So, what would you like for dessert?" he asked her, as he handed her the dessert menu, which had been left on the table.

Becka opened the menu and perused the dessert choices at length until she found something to suit her desires best.

"I think the triple chocolate brownie with ice-cream. Told you, already. I love chocolate cake and ice-cream. My favorite. You?"

"Decadent, I like it. I'll take the same. Something more to drink?"

Becka looked at the lake, then at the approaching waitress, and only then, found the courage to meet his eyes and say, "I don't really drink, Bryan. Even this beer was too much, I think."

"Damn it, you're only nineteen. You're barely legal to drink. I'm sorry, Becka, it's slipped my mind. Maybe you want a soft drink?" he asked, troubled that he hadn't noticed something so important.

He kicked himself mentally for letting himself so engrossed with her that he would make such a mistake. Usually, he would let nothing slip past him.

Bryan knew he couldn't afford to make mistakes if he wanted that relationship to last. It wasn't as if she hadn't had her choice of men. He was just one in a sea of tens, probably.

"Yes, I'd like a soft drink or maybe just sparkling water. I think sparkling water is perfect."

"Sure?"

When she nodded, he gave their order to the waitress. After the waitress left, he took her hand and kissed her fingers. He seemed obsessed with her fingers and she didn't know what to believe.

"I'll keep in mind not to have alcoholic beverages around you, all right?"

She laughed merrily and eased his worries.

"Come on, Bryan. You can drink, it's not like the law forbids you to drink around me," she laughed. "I like a glass of champagne now and then. That I like when there's something to celebrate. I'm not too fond of anything else. The taste is not for me."

"So, I'll buy you only champagne, Becka. The best kind, of course. I'm sure I'll be able to afford it if you drink only on special occasions," he said laughing.

They spoke of everything and nothing in particular for the remainder of the dinner and after he paid, he took her hand and led her to the shore of the lake for a romantic evening stroll.

The sun was setting, but the promenade was still bustling with people, which Bryan resented deeply. He wanted to have her only to himself and the people milling around intruded on his time with her.

Becka felt the shift in his mood and wondered what could have possibly brought on such a change from the light-hearted, content mood from just mere minutes ago. He was almost brooding.

"Is something wrong, Bryan?"

"Too many people, that's all, Becka. I'd have liked to be alone with you," he admitted openly.

Becka just seemed to have a strange effect on him, making him reveal things he wouldn't normally tell women, especially on a first date. His preservation spirit was strong enough to stop him doing such mistakes.

"Well, this place is full almost all the time, you know," Becka dismissed the people around with a large wave of her hand. "It's a favorite place for strolls, especially in the evening," she said, trying to appease him.

"I know, of course. That doesn't mean I have to like it, do I?" he replied tersely, even though he was aware it wasn't her fault the place was so popular.

"Well, if we go sailing tomorrow, we'll be alone for some time," she pointed out, in another attempt to cheer him up.

"We are definitely going," Bryan said. "I hope you haven't changed your mind," he turned to her to see the answer in her eyes.

She shook her head and squeezed his fingers reassuringly, a gesture he enjoyed. In the spur of the moment, he leaned towards her and kissed her lips softly.

That first kiss didn't last more than a few seconds, but the pleasant, electric tingle he felt when he touched her lips was stronger than he'd expected.

Both of them stopped, still close enough to feel the warmth of each other's lips and Becka stared at him with eyes full of wonder. It was barely a kiss, but she felt it as if it had been much more than that. The tingling she had felt earlier seemed like a pale reminder now.

When he pulled her to him tightly, she went along. She didn't even think of resisting. She was impatient to taste more of those low vibrations which made her body hum. She found herself completely stretched along his body, every hard plane of his chest and abdomen burning through her dress.

Bryan kept her very close as if he'd wanted to leave his mark on her and she didn't mind. His lips touched hers, traced the shape of her mouth unhurriedly. His mouth was trying to learn the texture of every cell in the sensitive skin he was tasting. His hot tongue touched the delicate surface of her lips, stroking them slowly, as if they'd had all the time in the world to indulge in each other.

The world outside ceased to exist for both of them. Deeply immersed in their own world, nothing else mattered but only what they could get from each other.

The people strolling around them became invisible and any kind of noise drowned in the background as they listened to the rhythm of their hearts and to the blood pulsing in their ears.

Their lips touched harder and sought a way to become one. Their tongues dueled and caressed one another, at times slowly, unhurriedly, tasting one another, exploring one another and creating sensations. At times, they duelled violently, as if they'd feared they had no time left and every second mattered.

Bryan bit sharply on her bottom lip, making her exhale with a whimper, then sucked her abused lip into his mouth to lavish and nurse it with strokes of his tongue, swallowing the moan escaping from her throat and making it part of himself. His voracious fingers played with the skin covered by the flimsy cloth of her dress and pressed harder whenever he expected more from her.

Her fingers dug into the hard muscles of his shoulders, trying to find support and keep her balance. Becka was caught in the middle of a violent storm and was teetering on the edge of the unknown. Her mind was caught in a whirl of sensations and that made her unable to think about anything else but the greedy demanding mouth, teaching hers ruthlessly what a true kiss meant.

The young woman had the feeling she'd finally left her teen years behind and she was on the brink of maturity. She was in the arms of a man able to show her what she'd longed for, over the last few years when she felt so restless.

That wasn't just about the conditions her great-grandma had put on the trust fund. It was much more than that.

When they finally came up for air, Becka was panting heavily and she was trembling. Even Bryan had to gulp a mouthful of air. Then, he smiled wolfishly at her, with that smile, which seemed to belong exclusively to him, then tilted his head and bit the spot between her neck and collarbone, stroking it quickly with his tongue when he heard her sharp intake of breath at the sudden pain. He suckled on the skin, making her forget about the sting she'd just felt, thrusting her from a world of pain and fear to one of bewitched pleasure.

Becka was throbbing everywhere. She knew now that she wanted his touch all over her body. She needed that ruthless mouth of his on her, on her most sensitive spots.

Becka opened her mouth to say something along those lines, but Bryan put a finger over her lips and stopped her.

"Becka, we have an audience," he said and pointed to the left.

He glanced at the left as well and when she turned her eyes in that direction, she noticed several teenage girls clustered together, watching them with curiosity and laughing like they'd never seen a woman and a man kissing before.

Becka couldn't hear what they were saying but she imagined it wasn't something she'd have liked to hear. At a loss for words, she looked up at Bryan, waiting for his opinion.

"I think we should move on," he said softly and after stroking her cheek with his rough, calloused knuckles, he took her hand in his and slowly started towards the other end of the promenade, where the lake was shimmering in the sunset light.

CHAPTER THREE

Bryan arrived at Becka's house five minutes earlier than the time they'd agreed upon. He decided to wait until eight thirty before ringing her bell.

He remembered very well how particular she'd been about the time of their date and how much she loved her sleep. He assumed she would also need time to get ready and he was determined to give it to her.

Bryan didn't want to start his day with Becka on a sore note. Spending his entire day with Becka, as well as developing a relationship with her, seemed very promising and he wanted to cling to his chance.

On top of that, he had his own expectations for their second date. He knew he was probably hoping for far too much and his expectations were maybe too high, but he still wanted to fulfill them or at least a part of them.

At eight-thirty precisely, he rang the bell at the door. The sound of her doorbell stirred the butterflies in his stomach to life and they churned with anticipation and anxiety. At the same time, a grin flourished on his lips as the theme from *Jaws* beamed in his ears.

Bryan wouldn't have expected to hear that song playing on her doorbell. Had it been something else, like *We Wish You a Merry Christmas* or the theme of *Love Actually*, for instance, he'd have understood. Every time he discovered that there was more to Becka than met the eye and that was what made him so adamant not to lose her.

Bryan could hear the echo of the thrilling theme fill the house. That sound made him more anxious to see Becka open the door and beam widely at him with that bright smile of hers, which always reached her chocolate eyes.

Unfortunately, that didn't happen. The man strained his ears and listened attentively, eager to hear the sound of her hurried steps coming to the door or even the noise of a shoe thrown into the wall or anything at all. To his disappointment, no sound came from inside the house and his hopes plummeted hard.

When it flashed through his mind the thought that she might have just made a fool out of him and had no intention of seeing him again, Bryan frowned and gritted his teeth.

He was convinced he'd walked her to her own door the previous night. He'd even watched her go inside. He hadn't seen her use a key to open the door, but she'd waved at him and closed the door behind herself.

It wasn't like he'd left her standing on the steps of a house of her choice so she could walk to another door after he'd left.

The thought he'd been duped was unbearable. He'd been there before and didn't have any desire to revisit the experience. This time, though, the hurt ran deeper because he had truly thought they had had a great time together and it worried him that that impression might have been one sided.

Bryan didn't want to travel down that path, but he had to admit that, although she'd gone inside that house the night before with that air of an owner, it didn't mean she couldn't have just visited the house of one of her friends, who would have left earlier that morning, before he arrived, or who just kept quiet like a mouse, waiting for him to give up and leave.

His anger increased more at the thought of having been played like that. Bryan choked under the pressure of his fury. He wasn't mad only at her because she'd made a fool out of him. He was furious with himself, as well, for falling for her act.

Furious, he punched the door frame with such force that the hardwood scraped his knuckles and he started bleeding.

He swore and cursed himself viciously. Damn it, he wasn't a green, young man and he should have known better. Much better.

Becka had seemed too nice and too beautiful for the likes of him and he shouldn't have pinned any kind of hopes on her because he didn't have that right.

After all, he'd been told that enough throughout his life and he thought he'd learned that lesson. Yet, it seemed that he was only lying to himself.

The man glanced at his watch again and noticed that almost five minutes had passed since he rang the bell the first time. Still there wasn't any sound coming from inside the house.

That was the last drop. It convinced him he'd been wrong and his worst fears had turned out to be true. He'd just been played.

Bryan turned his head and glanced at the car he'd parked in the driveway that morning. He hesitated for a few moments, but then thought he'd better leave since there wasn't anything else for him to do there. If she didn't want to see him, then he couldn't do anything to force her.

In that instant, something hardened inside him and shaking his head, he stubbornly decided to try his chance again. He rang the bell once more.

He listened again to the musical sound bouncing off the inner walls of the house, but he still couldn't hear any kind of movement from inside.

That was the final straw. Bryan had to admit defeat. He leaned in and pressed his head on the front door in a moment of weakness. His shoulders stooped.

A slip of a girl had tricked him and he had to live with that. Well, it wasn't the first time and it probably wouldn't be the last. Weak consolation!

Furious, he gritted his teeth, clenched and unclenched his fists and then, finally, he turned around and made a beeline to his car. His stride was determined and his anger showed in every heavy step he took.

He was just opening his car door when he heard her shout breathlessly, "Bryan, wait! ... Just give me the time to get there... Don't leave now!"

The man sharply turned to the sound of her voice and astonishment glimmered in his hard eyes. His puzzlement increased more when he spotted Becka running down the street towards him on wobbly legs.

Her face was almost blue because of her effort and he could see she was close to exhaustion. That didn't stop her and she still tried to smile at him.

Becka held her hand on the right side of her body where a stitch had been bothering her for the last ten minutes. She hadn't thought she'd be there in time, even though she ran as fast as she could.

He waved at her to slow down and stop running. A bright, wide smile spread on her lips. She was grateful that she could finally stop. That was the smile he'd been waiting impatiently for that entire morning.

She stopped abruptly and bent, her hands pressing desperately on her knees. Then she started panting, gulping noisily for air. It was clear she wasn't trained for jogging.

Becka was only about three houses far away from hers, but Bryan hurried to her and reached her in no time. Worried, he slipped his arm around her waist to support her and brushed the heavy hair away from her face.

"What have you been trying to do?" Bryan asked Becka, seeing the traces her sustained effort had left on her face and feeling her tremble in his arms. "Are you training for the marathon or what? Don't you know you should take it gradually?"

"I… had… to… do… something…," she replied with difficulty, wheezing the words as she tried to draw her breath.

Bryan allowed her to recover and didn't press further. He was content just to have her there with him. For the moment, it was enough. It was much more than what he'd had a few moments before when he thought he'd been deceived.

"When I saw I was going to be late for our date… I had to run to make it here in time," Becka finally said when she could breathe easier.

There was still a strain in her voice and Bryan stopped her, touching her lips gently with his fingers.

"Okay, baby," Bryan told her, "just breathe now and you'll tell me everything later."

Becka nodded and started to walk towards her door, but her legs chose that very moment to start shaking violently and she almost fell on her face. Luckily, Bryan was still there and had one arm around her, ready to save her from taking a dive on the hard pavement.

He shook his head, then picked her forcefully up into his arms and without a word, he carried back to her house. His long strides were eating the distance with ease. With a faint yelp of surprise, Becka slipped her arms around his neck.

"How long did you run?" he asked when they made it in front of her house and he stopped to look at her.

Becka had her head comfortably nesting on his shoulder and her nose was close to his neck. She was just enjoying the smell of his skin when she heard him speak. His voice startled her and she felt a faint trace of guilt, but pushed it aside without too much concern. It took her a moment to process his words once she broke from her reverie.

"Well, about ten blocks, I think, or maybe more...," she answered uncertainly. She couldn't remember exactly.

Bryan looked down at her with astonishment.

"Why the hell would you run such a long distance? Especially if you don't have the training? What went through your mind?"

"How do you know I don't have the training?" Becka pouted, choosing to deflect only a part of his questions.

"Well, the shaking legs and the cramp you have on your right side were clear indications, Becka. I don't need to be an expert to see you don't normally run for so long," he replied laughing, although his concern was far from appeased. "If you run at all," he specified and his right eyebrow shot up inquiringly.

"Ah! Right...," her voice trailed off, as she lost herself in thought.

"Still with me, baby?"

She looked up at him and smiled.

"Yes, still here, of course. I was just thinking."

"Yeah, I noticed that," Bryan replied amused gazing into her eyes. "What were you thinking about?"

"All right, then," Becka said. "I was wondering whether I should come clean or not."

At that, Bryan's left eyebrow rose. He didn't expect a confession from her. He didn't expect her to have something to confess.

"I don't have any training and I actually hate jogging," Becka continued, making him burst into laughter.

He had expected to hear something else and the innocence of her confession was music to his ears.

"No, you see, I had to leave this morning and since I didn't get your phone number to let you know I wouldn't be here when you came, I had to hurry back," she explained after she slapped his shoulder for laughing at her.

"That's very considerate of you," Bryan answered quietly after a second, uncertain of what he should say.

It was the first time in his life that someone had thought to show him any kind of consideration. People either feared him and avoided him from afar or didn't give a damn about him. Either way, no one had ever taken his feelings into consideration before that day and he felt humbled.

The cynic in him was a bit stumped and didn't know how to react. He was deep in uncharted territory there and he felt as if he'd had to act out a part in a play, but he didn't know his lines.

"If you want, you can put me down so I can open the door," he heard Becka's voice and turned his eyes to her, taking in her dishevelled appearance, bright eyes and her cheeks still violently red.

"If you give me the key, I'll open the door without putting you down," he said with a hint of playfulness and a smile to match.

"Oh, fine by me," she answered. "No need for a key, though. The door is not locked."

Stunned, Bryan could only stare at her. He couldn't form a sentence or even move. He'd never heard of someone who didn't lock their doors.

"What happened?" Becka asked him. "Why are you staring at me like that? Is there something on my face and I should know about?" she asked and touched her face to check for herself.

"You didn't lock your door," he said in a flat tone, which clearly conveyed how foolish he believed that to be.

"No, I didn't. Why should I?" Becka asked baffled both by the suggestion and his reaction.

"Why should you?" he asked in disbelief, then repeated more forcefully. "Why should you?"

"No need to get so upset over such a little thing," she patted his shoulder and continued in a tone meant to calm him down. "Believe me, there's no need to lock the door," the woman reassured him.

"Are you for real?" he burst out. "This is not a small village where everybody knows everybody, Becka. Even in small villages things happen. We're in a big city, for God's sake!" he finished his speech almost shouting. "People lock their doors, Becka."

"Come on, Bryan. What's the worst that could happen? You know what's meant to happen, it will," she said wisely.

"Spare me that bullshit. Don't go quoting shit to me!" he replied angrily. "You have to be more careful and start locking the damn door!"

Furious with her foolishness, Bryan kicked the door open with his foot as if he wanted to emphasize his statement.

Becka looked at him in silence, unsure of what to say, seeing how worked up he'd gotten. She thought to diffuse the tension and spoke calmly, hoping that that would make him calm down as well.

"Are you upset because I said what I said or is it because you think something might happen to me?"

"What the hell do you think?" Bryan barked again. "If you start locking the damn door and you're more careful from now on, you can quote me as much crap as you wish and whenever you feel like it!" Bryan snapped at her.

"Okay..." Becka dragged the word out. "So, you're saying you're concerned about me?"

"What kind of question is that, Becka? Of course, I'm concerned. What's wrong with you, woman?" he inquired with a grown and frowned at her.

"Nothing, nothing...," she said quickly to take his mind off his anger. "By the way, you might get tired holding me, Bryan. I'm not so light. So, either you put me down if you want to continue the conversation on the stairs or we could go inside… It's your choice, really," she said while looking at him, as if completely glossing over his mood.

Bryan felt frozen in place as if he couldn't believe her levity. He shook his head, closed his eyes in defeat before the strangest woman he'd ever come across, and then, carried her inside the house, closing the door with his foot.

Once inside, he looked at her questioningly, waiting for her directions.

"I suppose we could go to the kitchen first and have a cup of coffee," she answered his silent question. "I'm dying for a cup of coffee after the morning I've had," she groaned and continued, "I understand you don't feel like letting me stand so… The kitchen is right ahead, through the living room. It's the last door on the right," she pointed.

Bryan nodded curtly and carried her to the kitchen where he put her on a padded chair in her breakfast nook, which overlooked the garden. The entire wall to the garden was an expanse of glass framed by yellow curtains bound with thin silk ribbons.

Her garden sported an explosion of colors. Patches of all sorts of flowers bathed in the morning sunlight. They were plainly joyful and full of cheer.

At first sight, Bryan had the feeling that a madman had designed that garden. It was the oddest garden he'd ever seen. He couldn't remember to have ever seen so many colors and such undefined shapes in a garden.

His mother's garden displayed perfectly rectangular flowerbeds of petunias or roses, each with a well-defined spot for itself.

That strict setting was a far cry from Becka's otherworldly garden. It was nothing like those whirls of all sorts of flowers, tumbling off the pots, scattered throughout, without a distinguishable order to them. Many of the specimens were probably wild flowers because he hadn't ever seen them in a garden before.

He shook his head in disbelief at first, but after a few moments he finally understood that that garden was Becka entirely. It was wild, unpredictable, with sudden moods and unexpected surprises.

"So, what do you think of my garden?" he heard her soft voice from behind.

Turning around, he saw her standing a few steps behind him with an expectant light in her eyes. Despite her curiosity about his opinion, the glimmer in her chocolate gaze told him how attached she was to her garden.

"I think it suits you," he answered honestly. "It's exactly like you, Becka."

"Don't you think it's just crazy and I should change it, maybe tame it a little?" she asked, never taking her eyes off him.

He wouldn't have been the first to find the disorder of her little garden unsettling.

"What for? It's exactly how it should be, I think," Bryan answered her with a shrug of his shoulders. "I don't think you should change anything, baby. It really suits you," he said, stroking the side of her face with his thumb.

She beamed at him with happiness. Becka was pleased that he saw her garden the same way she did. She squeezed his hand appreciatively, before she turned to the kitchen counter where she started to prepare the coffee.

"I suppose you'd like to have a cup of coffee with me," she asked him while she was busying herself with the cups and saucers.

"Yeah, I'd like a cup of coffee," he replied, watching her small hands arrange the cups and saucers on a tray. "Becka, who told you, you should change your garden?" he asked curiously.

Becka shrugged it off as inconsequential, but answered his question to satisfy his curiosity. She remembered well they'd decided to get to know each other better, after all, even if it was about such small matters.

"Well, actually, everybody but you. At least my sister Ariel is a real pest about that garden. She has a knack for gardening and she thinks I should take every piece of advice she has in stock for me when it comes to it. She doesn't understand that I want to express myself, not some rule book. I don't want a geometrical garden with straight rows of flowers and individual flowerbeds... Anyway, that's a sore subject between the two of us, so I prefer to avoid it."

The man came up behind her, slipped his arms around her, and pulled her gently to him.

"You're a smart girl, Becka. You shouldn't change for anybody," he said, kissing the crown of her head first, then resting his head on the top of hers.

They stayed like that for a few moments that stretched on in silence. None of them wanted to pull away and end it.

Becka felt content in his embrace, as if she'd always belonged in those strong arms, which had carried her all the way to the house and inside. She wondered if she could make him stay and give her more time to discover the contradictory man hiding behind those sometimes-abrasive words, but who, in truth, was generous in his gestures and made her feel contented and cherished.

The shrill of the coffee maker startled them apart and both burst into laughter at their silly reaction.

"Well, it seems we both spaced out," Bryan tried to joke, but the humor didn't reach the serious, longing gaze he kept trained on her, as if he didn't want to let that moment end.

She smiled at him, her thoughts still on the comfortable, dreamlike embrace, but finally pushed him away, "Go and sit down. I'll bring the tray to the table."

"No, you go and sit down and I'll bring it to the table," he refused, giving her a little nudge to make her move. "You've just run the better part of a marathon, Becka, and you need to rest. Do you still feel up for going on the lake today?" he asked, worried about the intense workout she'd had that morning.

The woman nodded and went to the table, enjoying the fact that he didn't expect her to wait on him. She could still feel his eyes on her and wondered what he actually saw, if he liked the way she moved or how she looked.

Realizing the path of her thoughts, she admonished herself and almost shook her head. She never considered herself a simpleton who put a lot of stock on her looks. She wanted to be liked for more than that, but had to admit that there was some vanity there, inside her, which inspired a need to be appreciated for her appearance as well, and not only at an intellectual level.

The distant sound of Bryan's words snapped her out of her daydreaming and she realized she'd nearly missed what he was asking.

"Do you take your coffee with sugar and milk, Becka?"

"Oh, yes, I forgot to put the sugar bowl and the milk on the tray," she jumped out of her chair, ready to go back and correct her mistake, but he stopped her with a gesture.

"No need to bother yourself with that. Just tell me where you keep the sugar and milk and I'll take care of that," Bryan assured her.

"The sugar dish is in the cupboard above the coffee maker and the milk is in a little spout in the fridge," she told him, happy to sit tight and let him serve her.

Becka couldn't stop thinking, happily so, about his concern for her well-being and his willingness to make coffee in her home. It made a smile tug at her lips every time she thought of it.

Bryan opened the cupboard and took the sugar dish out. He examined it for a moment and noticed how small and delicate it was, a white piece of thin porcelain with small, dainty, blue flowers painted here and there, so lifelike that they seemed almost real, yet almost a blur at the same time, much like an illusion. He shook his head imperceptibly.

Taking out the milk spout from the fridge, he discerned the same delicate and thin porcelain and the same painted motif, which made him smile.

He had the feeling he'd uncovered another side of Becka that seemed to lean towards the fragile and artistic in her dishes. He'd already seen the lacy rims and the motif of little fairies dancing on the coffee cups and saucers, with their veils flying in the wind.

Bryan liked that side of her. As a matter of fact, he hadn't found anything he didn't like about her. Even her moods were refreshing.

The wild garden couldn't be more at odds with the elegant tea sets in her cupboard, but he couldn't help but feel that the contradiction was perfect for Becka, who wouldn't fit in one category alone. She was a free spirit, ready to express her opinions and didn't let anyone intimidate her, or at least she didn't let him intimidate her and that said something. He had a real talent to intimidate women.

Becka was fresh and young, but she wasn't rambling on and on about irrelevant things, which just made him feel old and left behind or which would put him to sleep. He'd been afraid she would bore him to tears the other evening and he'd been surprised when it didn't happen.

She'd been so lively and interesting that he hadn't wanted the evening to end. He only regretted he'd had to let her go inside her house and close the door behind her when he saw her to her house the night before.

The man loved she didn't try to pass for a fairy, just nibbling on some green leaves, enough not to lose consciousness. She wasn't obsessed with reaching the size dictated by the fashion of the time and that was something. He'd encountered that rare quality only in some women past sixty.

All the others were determined to be a size two and they were doing everything they could to get there, including starving to death.

He couldn't understand what was wrong with a size six or even eight or twelve. It wasn't as if the size had mattered. What was inside the package was more important.

He eyed Becka and appraised her to be a size ten, but that meant only she was the way the nature intended. She was gracious but with curves in the right places, especially in the areas he appreciated most.

Bryan had been drawn to her appearance at first, but now he kept discovering new things and his attraction to her deepened. He liked the Becka who was inclined to the fantastic and used the *Jaws* theme as a doorbell, but he also liked the Becka who created a garden out of a fairy tale.

The man brought the tray to the table where he placed it in front of her. He let his fingers brush a strand of hair away from her face, then he sat down, too.

"I was thinking I'd take a shower after we drink the coffee and then we could leave for our sailing adventure. What do you think?" she asked, smiling at him in excitement and poured the coffee in her whimsical cups.

"Works for me," he shrugged.

After a few moments of comfortable silence, he asked, "Where did you have to go this morning?"

She waved it off as unimportant at first, but then realised it was important for him and decided to tell him the truth.

"I told you I have some cousins … Well, my cousin Jay is a sort of a… gambler, you could say," Becka said hesitantly. "Last night he got involved in a game with some shady guys and apparently, they thought he was cheating and they roughened him up."

Bryan looked at her in disbelief.

"It's not like that," she specified seeing his thoughts reflected in his eyes. "Jay doesn't cheat but he has a… certain talent, let's say," she explained with wide gestures.

"What kind of … talent?" Bryan asked her staring at her intently.

"Well… he knows what cards the opponent has in his hand," Becka rushed with the explanation, hoping she wouldn't have to say more than she was prepared to reveal.

"So, he's counting the cards…," Bryan started to say, but she interrupted him with a shake of her head.

"No?"

"No," she answered.

"Then what?"

She hesitated for a few moments, then replied uneasily, "He just knows what cards you have in your hand. Just never play with him. He doesn't cheat, but … you wouldn't stand a chance."

"It's not possible, Becka," Bryan retorted. "Either he counts cards or he cheats."

She shook her head vigorously again.

"No, he doesn't. I'm sorry, it's not really for me to say, but just don't play with him, okay?"

Bryan shrugged, convinced she didn't want to admit her cousin was a cheater, who got beat up for it.

"So, you went to take care of him or what?" he asked, sampling his coffee.

"Well, when I got there around 3 a.m., he was in pretty bad shape and didn't want to go to the hospital… God, he hates hospitals more than I do."

"So, you played Florence Nightingale for him or what?"

She nodded and poured some more coffee in her cup, adding plenty of milk and sugar, which made Bryan smile. It wasn't coffee anymore. It looked more like milk with a touch of coffee.

"So, you slept only a few hours last night," the man concluded.

Becka nodded, but rushed to say, "Don't worry, Bryan, I still want to go on the lake. Maybe I'll sleep a little on the deck… Who knows?" she shrugged.

Bryan didn't say anything for a while. He sipped his coffee, watching her and assessing the shadows under her eyes.

"We can go out on the lake some other time, Becka, if you don't feel well enough. It's enough for me to see that you want to go."

"No, no, no," she jumped up from her seat. "No way! You promised we'd go today," she shouted at him.

"Easy, love, easy! Of course, we'll go if you want to. I was thinking you looked too tired...," Bryan said but stopped when he saw her shake her head. "We're going, we're going. Go take your shower and then we'll go," he rushed to mollify her.

Becka enthusiastically kissed his lips and rushed out of the room only to be stopped by his question.

"Becka, do you have a travel mug or something? Your coffee's great, and I think we could use a batch with us."

"Oh, yeah, there's one, I think... You know what, you check those cupboards there," she pointed to a row of cupboards, "and you might have a chance at finding it. When I get back, I could prepare some food to take with us," she told him joyfully.

"No need, Becka," he shook his head. "I've already taken care of the food. I told you we'd have a picnic on the lake so I have everything we need in my trunk."

"All right, then. You take care of the coffee and I will go shower. See you in ten minutes?" she said and he could hear the joy in her voice.

He started laughing heartily.

"What's so funny?" Becka asked.

"You're funny, Becka. Ten minutes? Come on. I've never seen a woman ready to leave the house in ten minutes and you still have to shower."

"Yeah? All right, let's make a bet," she challenged him, putting her hands on her hips.

He grinned and accepted her challenge.

"So, you like to bet even when it's not smart to do it?"

"You'll see, mister," she scoffed. "I bet you ten bucks that I'm back here in ten minutes, ready to go."

He stared at her, thinking the joke had gone on long enough, but saw the mutinous expression on her face and found himself nodding.

"You have a bet, Becka, then. Now, go, scat," Bryan push her along and smiled seeing her fleeing the room as fast as she could.

CHAPTER FOUR

Bryan steered the yacht carefully with an eye out on the lake, where lots of sails crowded the horizon. He wanted to avoid any problems and close calls due to inattention.

He kept his other eye on Becka, who was sleeping soundly under the canopy he had mounted on the deck that morning for her before setting sail.

A gentle breeze soothed his warm skin. The sun was high in the sky and the air was hot. Now and then, the echo of a shout or a laughter over the water reached his ears. Otherwise, everything was silent. He felt wrapped in another world, all by himself. He enjoyed it every time he went out on the lake.

When they left the harbour, they worked together, although he didn't need anyone's help to sail his small yacht. Yet, he found out that he enjoyed working in a team with Becka, whose enthusiasm was contagious.

The woman knew her boats and she wasn't afraid to get a bit dirty and use her muscles. She might have been small, but she was a bolt of energy.

Bryan admired her knowledge about sailing and navigation, but more so her determination not to let her small size stand in her way. For such a slip of a girl, she had enough strength in her arms. Even though she was tired because of what had happened earlier that morning, she was still energetic enough to work shoulder to shoulder with him before falling asleep under the shade he'd created for her.

They'd been sailing for about two hours already and his mind was still on the bet he'd lost to Becka. Anyway, it wasn't like he had too much to do while she was sleeping. Minding the yacht wasn't too big a deal since he knew the drills by heart and could drive the boat and let his mind wander somewhere else at the same time.

That bet was bothering him and not because he'd lost money to Becka. The amount was ridiculous, even though Becka had jumped up and down with glee when she took the money from him. The thought made him smile again. It was a moment Bryan had enjoyed immensely.

The man couldn't explain why, but he felt a certain sense of fulfillment whenever he knew he was the reason behind that beaming smile on her face. It was as if her joy had been his own and he felt the need to give her more reasons to enjoy herself.

What puzzled him though was the fact he'd never seen a woman getting ready to go out under ten minutes flat, even if it was only about going sailing, rather than clubbing or something else.

Women, in his experience, needed much more time before setting foot out of the house. He'd had his share of waiting over the years and, of course, his share of the frustration that came with that.

To his astonishment, Becka hadn't even needed the full ten minutes she'd requested. She'd needed precisely eight minutes. Bryan had timed her, and how stupid did that seem now? In exactly eight minutes, she'd already been downstairs, ready to go.

Her hair was still wet from her shower. That was true. Becka had only taken the time to pass a comb through the thick locks of hair in a rush and she'd put on a pair of khakis and a t-shirt. That was the sum of her efforts. She hadn't wasted a second of those pesky eight minutes.

Bryan was bewildered. The young woman had the gift of continuously surprising him and he was sure she would still surprise him in his old age even if he'd spent a lifetime with her.

Becka was a bundle of contradictions. Altogether, she was shy and daring, whimsy and realistic, with a penchant for the horror, while living a fairy-tale in her eccentric garden with shapeless flowerbeds and the explosion of colors and wild flowers.

He kept discovering new things about her and everything made him shake his head in wonder. There were layers over layers still to be discovered and he hoped to have the time of his life to do just that.

Bryan was overjoyed he'd been so lucky to have her stumble over him and pour that hot coffee all over his shirt. It had been a chance he wouldn't get more than once. He wasn't afraid to admit it to himself, despite the tinge of desperation he felt crawl into his heart, because he lived with the constant fear she would disappear one day and his life would go back to what it had been before he met her. It saddened him. He knew his life would be bleak again and he didn't even know if he could go on as he'd done before, whenever things occurred and changed his path.

It was one thing when he didn't know what he was missing, and another to have a great thing in his life and lose it. He was sure he wouldn't be able to forget her the same way he'd forgotten the string of women before her.

In less than twenty-four hours, Becka had touched him like no one before and that was scary. Bryan was a realist and he couldn't discount the possibility that something so good wouldn't last forever.

Bryan was deep in his thoughts, but he still paid attention to Becka's every movement. He just couldn't take his eyes off her for very long, so he noticed when she woke up.

She rubbed her eyes like a child and the gesture made him grin. The woman looked very innocent and young. She hadn't put any make up on and there were no smudges under her eyes. He liked that. He dreaded seeing smudges under women's eyes in the morning.

Becka's hair stuck out in every direction and she looked like a porcupine. Bryan had to stifle his laughter, afraid she might misinterpret his amusement. She was very young and very touchy.

The man slowed the yacht down and kept his eyes always trained on her. He saw her look around with a faraway look on her face. She didn't know where she was and she was taking her bearings.

He noted when she finally took everything in and became aware of her surroundings, understanding sinking in. Then, she turned to look for him. When she saw him, her face lit up, as if she'd been truly happy to lay eyes on him.

That happy smile on her lips touched him profoundly. It was completely unexpected. It squeezed his heart and made him hope for impossible things.

Bryan believed she liked to be with him, at least for a while. She acted that way. Yet, he hadn't even dared to hope she would beam at him with so much joy just because he was still there. The contentment her gesture gave him winded him like a punch in the gut.

He wanted to say something, to let her know how much everything meant to him, but words couldn't pass the knot in his throat. Had he been a lesser man, he'd have cried of joy, and that would have spoiled everything. No woman could stand a man crying, no matter what she said. And why the hell would he feel like that? He gave himself a stern nudge to put himself back together.

"You have a good sleep, Becka?"

Becka stood up with a nod and walked over to him with a dreamy light in her eyes. He watched her lazy stride and admired her long unclad legs covering the spread of the deck.

When they got on the yacht, she'd taken off her capris and t-shirt and was left with only a two-piece bathing suit on. Bryan couldn't stop himself from noticing again how the bathing suit hugged her curves enticingly. He felt his pants tighten a little more.

She wasn't tall by any means. She reached only to his chest and that with her shoes on. Despite her height, her legs were long and her ankles were supple and gracious, even though her thighs were not on the thin side.

In Bryan's opinion, she couldn't complain about anything. The entire package was there and it was tempting like hell for a man who lost more ground every minute.

Becka stopped next to him and leaned on him. She slipped one arm around him and let her head fall on his chest with an easy gesture as if she'd been doing it for ages.

Bryan looked at the crown of her head for a few moments and then, he brushed some of the strands around, trying to bring some order to her dishevelled hair. He abandoned her tousled hair and raised her chin with his thumb. He looked at her for a couple of seconds and then, he leaned down to kiss her.

He lingered for a few moments, just a hair away from her lips. He wanted to give himself the time to inhale that sweet and fresh scent, which was definitely Becka's.

It was only after a few moments of panting expectation that Bryan took her mouth into a searing kiss. The man put into that kiss all the longing, churning inside him for the last two hours, while he'd been watching her sleep there in the nest he'd made for her on deck, and thinking of how it would feel to have her in his arms and know that she belonged only to him.

When Bryan raised his head, and looked down at her, her eyes were still closed. Becka was still clinging to his arms as if she couldn't find her balance.

Her mouth was rosy and her lips were slightly swollen and satisfaction welled up in his chest. It was gratifying for Bryan to see he had such an effect on her because, he had to admit it, the little woman held his thoughts and heart in her little fist.

Her mouth still beckoned to him, and he found himself unable to refuse it. Bryan leaned in again and brushed his mouth over hers flittingly. Then, he bit her bottom lip lightly and made her moan, which increased his desire a notch. His mind was already racing ahead, thinking about taking her right there on the deck, when he heard her whisper.

"I'm hungry, Bryan."

Her words were like a blow to the head. The man just blinked and stared at her. Becka didn't even open her eyes and her fingers were still digging into his arms. Bryan was fired up like a rocket, and Becka seemed oblivious to everything. He shook his head as if he couldn't believe her.

"Are you sure?" Bryan asked her, squeezing her hip, unaware his fingers were digging strongly in the soft curve and could have marked her.

His actions made her nose twitch and she opened her eyes wide. Her mouth formed a perfect 'o' and just looked at him for a few seconds. Becka seemed unable to say anything, but she regained her gumption soon enough.

"I said I'm hungry, and that means I'm pretty sure, Bryan," she scowled at him.

"We were just kissing, Becka…" Bryan started to say with reproach, but she interrupted him, pressing a gentle finger to his lips.

"So? Can't I kiss you and be hungry at the same time? Or everything must be on a specific timetable with you?" she raised her voice a little, which made him look at her with stunned eyes.

"Wow, that's a good way to ruin romance, baby," Bryan chastised her.

He was hurt because he had hoped she would feel the same way as him and her reaction was like a cold shower over his feelings.

Becka shrugged with indifference and finally let go of his arms. She stepped back and looked him straight in the eyes.

"Romance is great, Bryan, even for me, but I can feel romance even if I eat, you know," she replied with practicality.

"Okay, Becka, hold your horses, we'll eat soon enough," Bryan conceded with resignation.

He put aside his dreams of a little lovemaking on the deck. Becka was full of surprises and he needed to adjust his thinking to her if he wanted their relationship to survive, and he did.

"Soon? Why not now? I'm hungry now, you know," she insisted with defiance in her voice.

"Because I was thinking of sailing over there," he explained patiently and pointed to an island not far away. "I was thinking we could have our picnic on the shore of that island, Becka. I'm sure you'd like to eat there instead of here on the deck," he continued drily. "I know I would," he muttered under his breath.

Becka looked toward the island, shading her eyes from the sun with her hand. Then, she looked at the covered portion of the deck with indecision.

"It's tempting, I won't say no," she murmured, turning back to him, "but you won't be able to moor there, so that point is moot," she said louder. "So, we can eat here, even though it is not so idyllic," she concluded, all too eager to eat. She hadn't eaten since the night before and she'd already used up a lot of her energy.

"Not really," Bryan said, still steering the yacht full speed to the island. "There's a dock there and I can moor my boat just fine."

His voice was always dry and that was a sign he was just a bit pissed off with all that fuss. He understood Becka hadn't had breakfast and she'd already made a lot of effort that morning, but he was sure she wouldn't die if she'd waited for a few more minutes.

The woman shrugged again. That seemed to be one of her habits, and one he found very endearing. Then, she went to sit on the bench near the steering wheel, watching the horizon.

"Are you upset or something?" Bryan asked a little unsettled by her sudden change of mood.

He didn't deal very well with women's moods and he would usually try to get out of the line of fire when something like that happened. However, this time, he felt compelled to understand where everything went wrong. He had invested a lot of himself in that fragile relationship and didn't want to let it go to waste.

"No, why do you ask?" Becka asked, fussing around with the blanket on the bench.

She pretended she was busy folding it so she could avoid his eyes.

"I don't know," Bryan replied matter-of-factly. "It's like you're upset. You're not happy like you were earlier and you seem in a mood. You raised your voice," he pointed out.

Becka looked at him shocked. She had no reply for a few seconds but then she retorted, "I'm not in a mood."

Bryan didn't say anything back. He thought he'd better give her some space, hoping she'd be her usual self again after a while.

"All right," she jumped off the bench upset. "Now you know!" she cried out throwing her arms in the air dramatically, and stomping toward the other side of the yacht out of his line of sight.

Bryan looked after her bewildered. He even craned forward to see her better and only after a few moments dared to ask, "Know what?"

Becka came back with small and hesitant steps, her hands knotted behind her and her head down. She was biting her lower lip, preoccupied with how to formulate her answer.

"I'm not at my best when I wake up, Bryan. You need to give me a little space for a few minutes, and then everything's fine again," she confessed with a small voice as if she had admitted to a capital sin.

Bryan grinned, relieved there was nothing else the matter and he had worried for nothing after all. He reached out to Becka to pull her to him.

"Come on, baby, that's not such a big deal. As long as I know that, I can cope with it and I can give you all the space you need."

She took his hand and came closer to him.

"I know I'm a porcupine whenever I wake up, Bryan. It's not like I want to be, you know, but... that's how I am."

"In more ways than one," Bryan said under his breath, but she heard him and looked up at him with a frown.

"What do you mean?"

He tried to avoid saying anything more. He didn't want to aggravate her more than he had already done it, but her eyes were trained on him and demanded an answer.

The man fidgeted for a few moments, trying to buy some more time so he could come up with something less offensive, but there was no way out of it, so he decided to tell her the truth.

"Your hair," he waved around her head. "It looks like... you're a porcupine," he finally expressed his thoughts.

Becka gasped in distress and both of her hands shot up at her hair to tame it, but to no avail.

"Damn it, I shouldn't have skipped the conditioner this morning," she wailed.

Bryan laughed when he heard her dramatic wail. Becka did like her drama and that should have turned him off. Instead, he found her more and more loveable with every moment and that seemed odd.

That wasn't him, the one from before he had met her and that was disquieting. He shook his head and abandoned that train of thought afraid of the conclusion he might reach.

"So, if I understand correctly, you skipped using your conditioner so you could be downstairs on time?" he remarked and not without malice.

"Okay, laugh as much as you want," she retorted fisting her hands on her hips. "I wasn't sure I'd be ready in ten minutes, I admit. The conditioner takes about three minutes to apply," she snapped, and began patting her mane of wild hair in an attempt to tame it.

"Yeah, you'd have been a minute late, that's true," Bryan replied, always smiling. "Would that have been so bad?" he inquired.

For a moment, Becka stopped her frenzy movements and looked up at him. After a couple of seconds, she replied with serious eyes. "Yes, Bryan, very bad. I don't like to lose…" she wrinkled her nose. Then she thought to add, "I think you'd better learn now I'm a sore loser, Bryan… Still want to have that picnic with me?" she inquired in a small voice.

Bryan reached for her again and pulled her into a bear hug, making her gasp in surprise. He didn't let her go, but gathered her tighter to him and whispered in her hair.

"You're perfect, Becka, just perfect. Of course, I want to picnic with you, baby," he continued, touching his head of hers. He inhaled the fresh scent of her hair and felt content to let the moment flow.

Becka could hardly breathe though. Bryan didn't seem to know his strength and his hug was very tight. Yet, Becka started smiling in the folds of his shirt, happy because he wasn't put out by her mood or by her confession.

Bryan held her for a few more moments before he found the strength to let her go and return to the helm. She welcomed the reprieve and filled her lungs with fresh air.

"In a few minutes, we'll be there, Becka," he said and pointed toward the dock that now appeared to be very close.

Becka looked over the expanse of water and saw that they were headed toward a dock which appeared in a very good shape. From what she could see, someone had taken good care of it. It wasn't one of the docks left there to rot in the sun and under the rains.

"I think that dock belongs to someone, Bryan. Won't they complain if we moor there?" she glanced at him and inquired.

He waved her concern away and explained the dock belonged to a friend of his, who let him use it whenever he wanted.

"The best part is, he's not even here, so we have the place to ourselves. No one will bother us for the entire day."

He kept paying attention to his driving as the shore was near now.

"He also let me use his house now and then, so if you have enough of the sun and the lake, we can go there and sit on the porch or even go inside and lie down on a bed."

Becka looked at him with doubt in her eyes, but shrugged. She decided to let him entertain his illusions. She didn't enjoy ruining anyone's hopes, yet, she was sure no one would be so generous and let their friend come and go at their will.

She was close enough to her cousins, but she didn't think any of them would welcome her in their house whenever she wanted if they weren't there as well. She was pretty sure they would frown upon her bringing a friend with her and inviting him into their bed.

"Should I get dressed, you think?" Becka asked. She didn't know what to expect once they got off the boat.

Bryan shook his head. He reassured her that they were alone there, and she didn't need to fear they would meet anyone.

He slowed down when he approached the mooring and handled the boat with a professional's ease, which made Becka beam with pride. That, he liked. He liked to see she found pride in what he did, even though it was something as insignificant as mooring the boat.

Bryan enjoyed basking in her attitude toward him. He even cherished the moments when she got angry with him because, in his mind, it meant she took the time to see him, the man, however strange that sounded even in his ears.

CHAPTER FIVE

Bryan helped Becka off the boat, balancing the food basket and a small cooler in his other hand. It wasn't a small basket by any means and Becka's thoughts started racing when she saw it. She was trying to guess what delicious things he had hidden in there.

Becka couldn't wait to partake in the picnic he had prepared. She also wondered why Bryan wouldn't let her help him carry anything. From the look of things, he had too many things to take care of at the same time.

The man had even draped a blanket over his shoulder and with the other hand on the small of her back, he guided her towards a cluster of trees a short distance from the shore.

"I remember there's a nice meadow there, right in front of those trees," he explained to her.

"It's a good area for a picnic, Becka, you'll see. We can see the lake from there and if I remember correctly, you like watching the boats, although not many sail past here, I must tell you. This island is quite secluded. It's not in the way of traffic. We'll also have cover from the sun. Those trees over there," he took his hand off the small of her back and pointed in the distance, "make for a great shade. I think it's a perfect spot for our picnic. And later, if you don't want to go to the house, we can stretch out on this blanket and no one will be the wiser," he prattled on.

Becka listened to him and smiled. She couldn't help but wonder why he was talking so much. He didn't look like the type to chatter at length about insignificant little things. He seemed somewhat nervous, and she couldn't understand why.

She suspected something wasn't what seemed to be. Yet, she didn't feel she was in any kind of danger, so she pushed the thought aside.

Bryan didn't let her help him with laying down the blanket or arranging the food either. He just directed her to lie down under the shadow of a tree and wait for him to prepare everything.

Once he started unwrapping the food, her taste buds went in overdrive. The smell of the juicy chicken surrounded by a mound of French fries made her mouth water and she sighed with anticipated pleasure. The Caesar salad, coming out of the basket afterwards, looked tasty as well, but didn't hold a candle to the casserole of homemade chicken with fries covered by grated cheese. The man had overdone himself.

Bryan laughed when she licked her lips, while eyeing the food with excitement.

"Come on, let's dig in, sweetie, and keep in mind, I also have dessert and you definitely need to save some space for it. You'll love it, Becka, I promise you," he said and reached out to her.

Becka sat on the blanket and playfully slapped his arm. Then, she reached for one of the plastic plates he had put next to the basket on the blanket. She topped the plate with chicken and fries. She'd just finished filling the plate up when he also uncovered a container with Greek salad, which was her favorite. She forgot about the Caesar salad instantly.

"Oh. I haven't left any space for that on my plate and I want some," she pouted in disappointment, eyeing the salad, which was beaconing at her.

"Don't worry, we can both eat directly from here, can't we?" he reassured her and put the container between them.

He crossed his legs, copying her stance and spooned some of the chicken casserole on his plate.

Becka nodded and attacked the food with fervour. The aromas had made her hunger rise to new levels. Bryan took a moment or two to watch her eat, then, with a smug smile on his lips, he dug into his food, as well.

"Do you cook?" she asked, tasting the chicken flavored with butter, lemon and some herbs she didn't even bother to identify.

The taste was exquisite and that was all that mattered. She was very curious where he had found it but she decided to go with her first guess. He must have made it.

"Yes, I do. I had to learn how to cook since I like to eat and I got sick of so much take-out," he replied with a nod. Then, he asked her, "Do you like it?"

"Oh, it's great. Amazing even… I can't cook, Bryan," she suddenly said with regret.

Bryan glanced at her a little taken aback by her sudden confession. She was indeed upset with her admission. That genuine disappointment with something so unimportant made him smile.

He stroked her arm and comforted her, "It's not a problem, Becka. You probably can do other things. It's not like I'd want you in front of the stove cooking away…," he said and let the words linger between them. "I want you somewhere else anyway," he mumbled, but her keen hearing didn't fail her this time either, and Becka burst into laughter, light-heartedly slapping his arm again.

"You're a naughty boy, Bryan," she managed to say through peals of laughter.

Bryan glanced at her and decided to try his luck, "Naughty, naughty, but are you against what I'm thinking?"

She looked at him for a few moments, seeming to consider his question and finally she shook her head. A faint blush spread over her face and made him grin. He liked to see her blush. Her innocence was refreshing and made him feel manlier, which he didn't mind at all.

After a little pause, the conversation tittered around insignificant things with long stretches of silence. That didn't bother them. They felt comfortable enough together and didn't need to fill the quietness with meaningless chatter.

Being together, sharing the good food and enjoying the air of the lake was enough for both of them. They enjoyed each other's company and that was what mattered.

The day was growing hotter, but the shadow of the trees offered them a respite from the hot air. The infrequent breeze cooled them even more.

In the distance, the sails of the boats spotted the surface of the lake, but the noise of the town didn't reach them. They had the feeling they were secluded in their own paradise, just the two of them, free to talk about anything and everything, free to kiss each other, whenever the mood struck, or to feed each other pieces of succulent chicken now and then, bursting into laughter when one of them would drop some food.

Once they filled themselves with the main course, Bryan revealed two big slices of triple chocolate cake and Becka's eyes widened. She had a weakness for chocolate cake, especially when it came in three thick layers of chocolate. She attacked the cake with renewed gusto even though she was already full.

Becka had never been able to say no to chocolate cake. It was the curse of her life or at least one of them. She couldn't pass on such a delightful dessert and she expressed her appreciation for his taste in organizing picnics.

After a while, Bryan leaned back on the trunk of a tree, with her snuggled up tight in his arms, his chin resting on the top of her head.

Becka closed her eyes and, with a content sigh, she let herself drift into sleep once again, feeling safe in the strong arms wrapped tightly around her.

Bryan felt her chest rise and fall under his arms and her soft breathing lulled him to sleep as well, making him forget about the food left there on the blanket.

A black squirrel had been watching the feast spread out on the blanket for a while now. It was on a branch above their heads and, when it considered it was safe enough, because the humans were out for the count, it came down and stole a piece of the chicken and ran away with it. No one was the wiser.

***

Becka slept for about an hour and a half and woke up refreshed and ready to attack the world again. She realized she was still in Bryan's arms, and she turned her head to look up at him. He was already awake and met her eyes squarely.

The change in Becka's breathing had woken him up and he had been waiting to see what she wanted to do. He also remembered what had happened on the yacht earlier and he didn't want a repeat of the stupid quarrel they had.

All their squabbles seemed unsubstantial. Most of the time, they were the result of misunderstandings. He found them to be a waste of time and he'd proposed himself to avoid any quarrel if possible. The stakes were too high for him and he didn't want to miss on the chance he had been given when he met her.

Becka raised her arm and touched his face with hesitant fingers. She let them skim over the beard shadowing his face, and touched his scar fleetingly. She felt him tense for a second, but when her fingers continued to trace the contour of his face, he relaxed. Then, she turned in his arms and faced him on her knees.

Both watched each other intently. No words were exchanged. Becka leaned in slightly and put her hands on his chest. From there, her fingers started exploring the hard planes beneath.

Bryan left his hands rest on her hips and waited to see what she had in mind, although her wandering fingers had a maddening effect on his system. He could feel the fire stoking inside him.

Hesitantly, Becka leaned forward and pressed her lips to his for a brief kiss and looked up at him afterwards. He was looking down at her, his eyes half covered by his lashes.

She decided to be more forward and kissed him again. This time, her tongue traced the contour of his lips thoroughly, learning their taste and shape.

That spelled the end of her initiative. Bryan couldn't take it anymore and he pulled her forcibly into his arms to lower her on the blanket. He covered her body with his and kissed her with all the longing he had gathered in his heart since the day before.

It was the first time he'd ever felt so much excited at the thought of holding a woman in his arms and so impatient to have her. Not even as a teenager, had he ever been so edgy at the idea of making love as he was now.

At first, Bryan tried to control himself and focused on exploring Becka's lips with his own. Only after he learnt their texture and felt them tremble, he moved on, and started exploring her entire mouth. His tongue slowly slid past her parted lips and danced against hers, filling himself with her unique flavor and texture.

Bryan took his time and tasted her leisurely. He wanted to enjoy every second and immerse himself in the pleasure she offered him.

His gestures were measured and slow, designed to entice and seduce. His calloused fingers stroked the side of her face and went up to mingle with her mane that still stuck out in a frenzy of honey.

Bryan pushed himself onto her hard and the shock of his move made her gasp, but the sound got lost in his voracious mouth.

Far from satisfied, he continued to make love to her lips while his hands started wandering along her neck and arms, leaving behind little shocks and shivers.

Bryan's caresses shook Becka to the core. She trembled against him and in one last lucid moment, Bryan raised his head and looked at her.

"If you don't want me to continue, say it now. I don't know if I'll be able to stop later, Becka," he admitted in a husky voice.

Becka nodded to let him know she wanted him to continue with that torture of her senses. Shyness shone in her eyes and tugged at his heart.

The young woman couldn't find the words to make her wishes known to him. Becka wasn't even sure if there were still words somewhere in her mind. She was immersed in a sea of sensations. Even if she wanted to say anything, her throat felt somewhat constricted and she couldn't utter a sound beside the moans that didn't even register in her ears.

Something odd was going on inside her body but it felt good, so Becka wanted him to continue touching her with all that incensed passion she could read in his eyes.

Bryan's eyes had lost that icy shine she had seen before. Now, an unusual light had lit and darkened those cold blue irises and she basked in that light. Becka felt proud of herself because she was responsible for putting that hot light in there.

Bryan stared at her a moment longer, to make sure she was all right with what was going to happen between the two of them, and then he gathered her into his arms.

He wanted to let her feel his strong desire for her and to let the tension, which had seized his body, sip into hers.

He kissed her lips again and nibbled on them a couple of times before he deepened the kiss some more to satisfy his overwhelming need to become one with her.

Becka wrapped her arms around his neck and welcomed the heat of his body. Her skin tingled and longed for his touches. When his teeth nibbled at the soft skin of her neck, she sighed and let go of any coherent thought.

She had completely forgotten they were outside in the open, lying on a blanket and, maybe, a boat might sail close enough, and people might see them. She was only aware of her strong desire to have that man fulfill all her fantasies and step with him into her womanhood.

She abandoned everything in Bryan's knowledgeable hands and let him mold her body with his touches.

Bryan took off the upper piece of her swimming suit and filled his hands with her full breasts. He held them for a few moments, shaping them with his fingers, and then, he rubbed his cheek on the soft skin of one of them.

Becka shivered when she felt the roughness of his beard on the sensitive spot. She arched, needing to feel him closer, and that encouraged him to be bolder. His tongue flicked out and licked at the little tip, which rose timidly into his touch. Bryan licked it slowly, teasingly, and she felt like her body was on fire. She moaned, closing her eyes. Satisfied with her response, he took her nipple into his mouth and started sucking on it hungrily, to fill himself with her scent and taste.

The first flick of his tongue triggered deep vibrations in her lower body. Her body was strung like a bow, and every fiber of her body was impatiently waiting for release.

The sensations were sharp and pleasantly painful. Her yearning increased tenfold. When he started sucking on her breast in earnest, she cried out keenly, unable to control the tautness bottled up inside her. All the sensations assaulting her senses were strong and overwhelming. She couldn't control them. She felt like she'd been thrust into the eye of a tornado.

Bryan let go of her breast and she breathed with relief. The tension became more bearable. It lasted only one moment though. He moved to the other breast, and the sweet agony started all over again.

Now, his fingers were playing with the little hyper-sensitized nipple he had already tormented with his mouth. He was rolling it between his fingers, now and then, pinching it and tugging at it suddenly.

Becka couldn't discern what happened to her anymore. She couldn't focus on a specific feeling. Her skin tingled all over, and the ocean of sensations in her lower belly had turned into a volatile storm, which shredded her to pieces. The intensity of her feelings was so high now that she was moaning constantly and she started writhing uncontrollably underneath him.

She didn't know whether she wanted Bryan to continue with his ministrations or she wanted him to stop so she could escape the multitude of bombarding feelings, which had turned her into a mass of sensations and erased all reasoning from her brain.

After he sucked at her breast until she was close to delirium, his lips started their journey down and his tongue flicked and swirled here and there, his teeth nibbling at her skin and sending piercing shivers through her entire body.

Becka laced her fingers in his hair to feel more of him. She also needed some support through the storm of sensations, ravaging her body.

When he dipped his tongue into her belly button, she almost jumped off the blanket. Immediately his fingers dug into her hips to keep her there, prisoner to everything he had to give her.

By now, Becka was lost completely in a sea of piercing and coiling sensations. Her eyes were closed. She moved under him unconsciously.

Her movement made it harder for him. It was difficult not to plunge in and take what he wanted the most.

When he reached the edge of her bikini, he lowered it slowly and lavished every uncovered inch of her skin with his passionate attention. His tongue was swirling over spots she had never thought sensitive before.

Becka let his hair go and propped herself up on her elbows. With wide, shocked eyes, she watched him attentively, biting her lips nervously. She didn't want him to stop, but she wasn't sure she wanted him to continue his journey south.

Bryan noticed her move. He thought she might back off then. Becka was excited. That was true.

Yet, she was also new to all of that and she was teetering on the edge of uncertainty.

Bryan removed her bikini with a hasty move and, then, he looked up at her, questioning her intentions.

At first, she didn't say anything, but stared back at him. After a few seconds of hesitation, she nodded her agreement slightly only to receive a ruthless smile in return. That grin of his made her feel fearful and unsure of what was about to come.

It wasn't as if she hadn't known what was supposed to happen next. She had a general idea about how that worked but she didn't know what to expect exactly. What she knew was that she couldn't say 'no' to Bryan.

Becka did want to make love to him. She'd already made her mind up the day before and her body had followed suit the moment Bryan kissed her that afternoon.

Bryan pushed her gently back onto the blanket and his head lowered over the intimate place he had just uncovered. When she felt that his face touched her thigh, and became aware that he was taking in her new and strong scent, Becka blushed violently.

She was happy he couldn't see her face. She was ashamed because she was behaving with such lack of sophistication but there were some things she just couldn't control.

Bryan's fingers hovered over her body for a few tense seconds. His hands slid up and down her thighs, in a slow and maddening movement, his searching fingers leaving newly awakened tingles in their wake, whenever they squeezed and stroked her muscles.

When he felt that her arousal augmented, he pushed her legs apart gently, and stroked the inside of her thighs, starting from the back of her knees and sliding up, excruciatingly slowly, until his fingers reached the top of her legs. There, he let his fingers slide over her womanhood like an illusion and she shivered again.

This time, the urgency of her need was much higher. Becka locked her fingers on the sides of his head, ready to pull him up to her.

Yet, he had something else in mind. Bryan didn't care for her intention of bringing him back to her mouth. He burrowed his nose in the one spot he had wanted to touch all day and breathed her scent deeply. His tongue followed and started making love with her and drive her crazy.

Becka was already teetering on the edge. She felt as if electrical shocks sensitized every nervous ending in her skin and the flickers of his tongue didn't make it easier at all.

Once more, Becka lost any conscious thought and she could only chant breathlessly, "Please, please, please!" over and over again.

She wasn't aware she was begging him. Becka didn't know if she wanted him to stop doing those maddening things to her because she couldn't take it anymore or if she wanted him to continue his arousing torment.

Becka had already reached a point where she could just feel. Thinking was something remote. Instinct and pleasure had already replaced reasoning and, somewhere in her subconscious level, she feared she was losing herself in that uncontrollable mass of emotions.

Whenever his talented tongue reached that sensitive nub, which his fingers had been caressing and rolling for a time that seemed a small eternity already, Becka felt small explosions everywhere inside her lower body.

Bryan's thumb stroked over that ball of sensory endings unexpectedly and, at the same time, he sucked at her already swollen little clit throwing her in an ocean of new sensations.

When the explosions inside her became all too violent, she cried out and her fingers pulled his hair. Her lower body rose completely off the blanket instinctively, seeking more of the attentions he lavished on her.

Bryan raised his head and glanced at her. At the same time, his thumb pressed her core. He was satisfied to see she had abandoned herself to the pleasure he could give her. With the same ruthless smile on his lips, he returned to the throbbing nub, which he stroked tenderly with his tongue, until she calmed down.

When he felt the tension had left her body, Bryan looked up at Becka's reddened face and quivering lips. He continued to touch her thighs and abdomen with long and appeasing strokes, his fingers massaging and burrowing gently in her skin here and there.

Bryan dipped his head once more, and his lips trailed up her body with feather-like kisses and nibbles at a few choice spots. He locked on one of her sensitive breasts with his lips and sucked it in his mouth, while his fingers played with the peak of the other.

She exhaled deeply and moaned. Her eyes opened wide at the shock of the new sensation. Bryan continued to feast on her breast for a while longer and made her arch her back to reach deeper in his mouth.

He sucked her nipple deeper and, at the same time, his fingers shaped her breast and pushed it higher to his mouth. After a few more moments, he released her nipple and a breeze of air on the wet and sensitized nipple made Becka shiver.

Bryan traced more kisses up her torso until his feverish lips reached her neck. There, he decided to make a halt for a few moments and play with her skin, which was already oversaturated with sensations.

She quivered again but he still continued with his sensual trail of kisses and nibbles up to her ear. When he licked the whorl of her ear, the knot inside her coiled again.

Becka turned her head to kiss him and she was startled when she tasted not only him but also herself on his lips. The mingled scents aroused her even more, even though she didn't think it would have been possible to feel anything more.

She kissed his lips at first and bravely nibbled at them as he had done to her, and rejoiced when she felt him quiver. Payback was only fair.

Becka stroked his strong arms and tried to learn the shape of his coiled muscles. She wrapped hers around him with a sense of possession she didn't know she had. A vixen smile formed on her lips and that uncharacteristic smile incited him to grin at her, as well.

Bryan took her mouth again in a scorching toe-curling kiss. He rubbed himself of her, enjoying the feel of her skin.

"Should I take my clothes off, sweetie?" he asked in a husky whisper.

"Yes, please," Becka moaned and patted his arm, more to encourage herself than him.

Bryan stood in a split-second and with hasty movements, he yanked his clothes off. He couldn't wait any longer. He couldn't take his eyes off her body.

Becka was stretched out on the blanket and she was waiting impatiently for him to touch her again. Her skin wore the marks of his beard and greedy fingers, and her lips were red and swollen from their passionate kisses.

Becka looked very well-loved, but he still wanted to give her much more and take his own pleasure at the same time. Bryan lowered himself onto the blanket and over her.

He braced himself on his left elbow and the fingers of his right hand skimmed over her silky skin. He dipped his head and his lips played with her mouth before trailing down to her neck where he marked her again with a mild bite. Her moan amplified his desire.

Bryan hadn't thought it was possible to want a woman more than he already did. Yet, desire knotted in his belly, making him ache at a new level. He was painfully hard and he needed her badly. He needed his release but didn't want to rush her.

His fingers closed on one of her breasts again, playing with it, ready to tease more, when she wrapped her arms around him and pulled him over her with a strength he didn't know she had. Bryan understood her quiet message to hurry and make love to her, yet he didn't want to steal anything from her first experience.

Determined to make her enjoy their lovemaking as much as he did, Bryan leaned forward and started to suck on her breast again, as his hand brushed down south and played with the little tense nub between her thighs.

"Now, Bryan, now!" she cried out. "I want you, now. Enough with all that torture," she demanded, at the same time pulling at his hair savagely.

Bryan laughed and hugged her, gathering her body to him. Then, he covered her, pushing her legs apart so she could cradle him. He kissed her lips with a tenderness that was in direct contrast with the wild kisses he had given her before.

"I've never been with a virgin, Becka, my sweetie, so, you're out of luck here," he whispered with regret over her lips. "I'll try to be gentle, but…"

"You're doing just fine," she whispered back, reassuringly, "but hurry now, Bryan. I need you now," she continued with a tense voice.

He laughed nervously and found his way inside her, raising her hips with his hands. He started pushing slowly forward because she was very tight, but Becka had lost all patience by then and pushed up with force to meet him, just to cry out when he was all the way in.

Becka felt he was stretching her beyond her limit. The pressure she experienced inside was painful and delightful at the same time.

"Are you all right?" Bryan asked with concern.

He was afraid she had been hurt because of the sudden invasion.

"Just perfect," she whispered and smiled at him. Her eyes were wide with wonder. "I'm pretty sure there should be much more than this," she said in a conspiring voice, and flexed her inner muscles.

Her reply prompted Bryan's laughter again, but the squeeze of her inner muscles turned the laughter into a growl.

"Yes, there is, baby, there is," Bryan said through clenched teeth.

Then, he started moving inside her more forcibly, making love to her in earnest.

Becka gasped when she felt him move inside her. He stretched her and the sensation was painful and agonizingly pleasant at the same time. She clung to his arms. She was afraid she would get lost in the storm of sensations.

Becka loved feeling his weight on her. She loved that he was a part of her. She might have had a twinge of pain for a few seconds, but that was soon forgotten.

She relished in the pressure and pleasure he was giving her with his body. Unconsciously, she started moving in rhythm with him. Pushing against him made her feel much more. The sensations were more intense.

She slid her fingers along his back to the top of his thighs and both of them gasped, even though for different reasons.

Bryan lifted one of her legs and wrapped it around his waist. He stroked her thigh from behind her knee up to the hip, using just the tip of his fingers and awakening nerve endings that had relaxed. His rough-skinned palm slid further and touched the roundness of her backside. Then, he pressed on her rump and brought her pelvis closer to his. The change in position ignited sparks through her veins and she felt the tension coiling inside her unbearably painful.

Now Bryan could push deeper and she had the feeling he was connected to her in ways she had never imagined possible. Bryan bowed his head and bit gently one of her nipples.

Becka cried out as her skin tingled everywhere. Then, Bryan pulled the nipple inside his mouth and sucked hard on it. The tautness inside her exploded and, for a moment, she felt pulled apart in a multitude of directions, only to uncoil into a sphere of sensations that set her skin on fire.

Becka cried out again and louder this time. Before she fell into the abyss of sensations and lost any coherent cognitive functions, Becka felt Bryan give in to the ultimate pleasure. She collapsed having the vague feeling that she heard him groan but it was something remote and uncertain.

Becka didn't know how long she had been out, but when she came back to the real world, she felt Bryan's lips brush along her neck tenderly. He was breathing hard and his hands were shaking, but he still took care of her and stroked her lovingly.

"Are you all right, baby?" he whispered in her ear, taking her earlobe between his lips and biting it delicately.

Becka shivered as the aftermath waves were still present, and his bite intensified them more. She tried to say *'yes'*, but she didn't seem to find her voice anymore. Her voice was lodged somewhere in her throat and she couldn't get any words out. She nodded and hugged him tighter.

Bryan rolled on his side with her nestled tightly in his arms and kissed the crown of her head. He covered her legs with one of his, unwilling to let go of her and pull away yet. He continued to stroke her back and her upper thighs, while rubbing his chin on the top of her head affectionately.

"Was it okay for you or...?" Bryan asked without even thinking about what he was going to say.

He didn't want to ask. He didn't want to hear it had been bad for her and he had behaved like a man who'd thought only of his pleasure and hadn't paid any attention to hers. He didn't want to hear the lie in her voice if she'd said *'yes'*, but she actually hadn't felt anything.

Bryan failed to understand his insecurity around Becka. It was probably because he wanted much more from her than he had ever wanted from another woman or because he had had the chance or bad luck, depending how she felt and what she thought, to be the first man who had made love to her.

Bryan, for one, couldn't complain. He had never been with a woman that had belonged only to him. He might have liked to think he was above such caveman's thoughts, but he had to admit it felt good to know he was the only man she had known in biblical terms.

Whatever the case, Bryan was beside himself with anger, especially because he knew his insecurity could ruin the best thing that had ever happened to him.

Becka kept silent and kissed his chest while her fingers brushed the curly coarse hair that peppered his skin. Then, she looked up at him with a dreamy expression in her eyes and nodded staring at him.

A smile started to flourish on her lips shyly and the sweetness of the moment hit him like a fist in his gut. Bryan pulled her tighter into his arms, making her protest.

"It's too tight, Bryan. I can't breathe," she said in a small voice.

Bryan became aware he had been too rough with her and loosened his hug to let her breathe. Yet, he didn't let go of her completely. He still needed to feel her body against his.

Actually, and that was quite astounding, he needed her again. Bryan even thought about the possibility of making love to her once more, but he decided against it. It had been her first time and he didn't want to hurt her. He could have her tomorrow again if she wanted, too.

They remained entwined, both content to be close one to the other and to rest in each other's arms.

CHAPTER SIX

Bryan nudged her chin up with his thumb and kissed her.

"We can go up to the house and clean up if you want," he whispered in her ear.

She looked up to the hill where the big white house with blue-framed windows stood amongst trees and shook her head.

"No, I don't think so. I don't want to be an imposition."

"What are you talking about?" he frowned, not understanding what she meant.

"I know your friend said you could use the house, but that doesn't mean he'd have wanted you to bring friends in there as well. We can clean up when we get to my house, all right?" she said.

She patted his hand without even being aware of doing it. It was the kind of pat one would use to calm a disappointed child when he didn't get any ice-cream.

Bryan knew she doubted someone would let him use their house like that, but he had decided not to let her know the house belonged to him. He had chosen to play things close to the vest because he wanted her to like him for himself and not for his possessions.

He had had more than his fair share of gold-diggers and was sick of them. They wanted him for what his financial possibilities would offer them and once he refused, they had always walked away.

Bryan hoped Becka wouldn't be like that and he wanted to impress her with other things than the size of his bank account or his material possessions. He wanted her to like him for himself and he felt she did like him.

However, he was painfully aware things could change in the blink of an eye. He had met two or maybe even three women who seemed like they had been somewhat into him, but once they had found out how much money he had on his name, they fell head over heels in love with him. It hadn't lasted though. They proved afterwards they loved what he had in his pockets, and they had no interest in his mind or soul.

Becka was too important for him to let the same scenario play out, so Bryan didn't know what to do. He didn't say anything for a moment. He felt guilty because it was his fault that she felt she had to go all the way back home and clean up.

For a few seconds, he was tempted to leave it at that. His sense of self-preservation advised him not to open his big mouth and say something that might not turn too good for him. Yet, he thought better and decided to come clean, so he told her, "Becka, I have to tell you something."

His serious tone made her look up at him again. Becka didn't like where that was going. His tone made her fear the worst and after everything that had happened between them, she hoped she hadn't been wrong about him.

Becka could usually tell right away what kind of person she had before her eyes. That was one of her unique talents, even if it was raw and unrefined.

Up to that point, Bryan hadn't made her believe he was a jerk. Nothing he had done had made her doubt him.

Bryan saw the uncertainty in her eyes and it didn't sit too well with him. He wanted to alleviate her fears because he guessed what she was thinking. He still hesitated for a few moments because what he was going to tell her was against what he had decided on the yacht. Despite all that, he thought she deserved to know the truth and, besides, until then, she hadn't shown any kind of inclination towards material things.

Bryan felt a little tight squeeze in his heart thinking he could nip the relation in the bud if it turned out she was a little fortune hunter. He would suffer, in more ways than one. He had just realized he wanted her more now after he had had her than he had wanted her before. He was almost sure she was the perfect woman for him, but he was determined not to accept another relationship based only on his material status.

Bryan accepted there might not be much to him. Yet, he stubbornly clung to the thought he deserved to be with someone who wanted him, the man.

"Look, the thing is...." He started but he couldn't continue, suddenly more afraid of what she had say about his previous lie than of what he had just thought. He tried to think of the best way to explain his reasons for lying to her in the first place.

"What is it, Bryan?" Becka inquired calmly, as if the anger rising in her throat hadn't existed.

She had too much pride and didn't want to show him how much she would have cared if he had dumped her after she had fallen into his arms like a dummy, not even twenty-four hours after their initial encounter.

"You can tell me anything, it's not a problem, you know. I can take it."

"Well, there is a problem, though... I lied to you and..." he began, but he couldn't continue because she literally jumped up and stood above him like a vengeful goddess.

"Damn it, Bryan, are you married or what?" she almost screeched.

Her gaze narrowed with anger, as threatening as a snake's narrow slits, ready to kill him just with that glare.

His eyes widened and, for a few long moments, he could only stare at her. She was magnificent.

He had expected her to get upset, but he didn't expect that powerful display of anger or that she would jump to unfounded conclusions in a matter of seconds.

Becka understood he found her question way too crazy and he was rendered speechless. She slapped herself in her mind for uttering the words but she didn't know what she could say to make it right.

It took him a few more seconds to recover enough to answer to her. He stood up as well, just as angry with her accusations now, as she was with him. He looked at her incredulously with his fists on his hips.

"Of course, I'm not," he retorted with anger in his voice once he found his speech again. "I wouldn't sleep with another woman if I had been married. What the hell? What kind of a monster do you think I am?" he snapped at her, even though her hard breathing made it hard to focus.

Her generous bust was making it difficult to look anywhere else, even if he knew it was important to look only into her eyes since he didn't want to give her the wrong idea.

She calmed down then. "Well, if that's not the problem, then what is it?"

"I lied to you about that house," he said, pointing to the house on the hill with a nervous gesture.

She looked at the house and then at him, as if she hadn't understood what was going on.

"What do you mean?" she asked him after a few moments of pondering over his statement and not making any sense of it.

"That's my house, Becka. Not a friend's, but mine. I lied to you when I said a friend let me use it," he specified again, to be sure she understood him clearly.

"Oh, okay," she said, utterly appeased, and turned around to look for her bathing suit, pleased that it had nothing to do with her and that he didn't intend to let her go.

Suddenly, Becka turned back to him. Her eyes were sparking with so much fury now that he took a step back involuntarily. If he thought she looked majestic in her anger earlier, now her fury was much more than that.

Apparently, his statement had finally sunk in and she realized what he was saying. One thing was clear though: she didn't like it at all. All the implications seem a little too ugly for her to stomach them.

With a very even voice, deceitfully contradicting the wrath in her eyes, she asked him, "So why did you find it better to lie to me? Why was it so important that I didn't know the house belonged to you?"

Bryan knew her tone was deceptive and he was expecting to be hit with a full blow of her fury soon. The atmosphere was charged with electrical currents and he could feel the twinges of tension ripping in the air.

"I had a thought, you see…," he started, but stopped when he saw the mutinous stance she took.

She did look glorious in his eyes. That fury shining in her eyes, the straight back, like a poised arrow, and her small hands fisted on her hips turned her into a true piece of art.

He knew she had forgotten she didn't have a stitch of clothing on her and he appreciated her forgetfulness. His eyes betrayed his hunger while they swept over her full figure, taking in the heavy breasts and narrow waist, her lush hips and rounded thighs.

"You had a thought," she repeated, but this time her voice dripped with sarcasm.

His eyes snapped back to hers, suddenly aware he was in the middle of an argument and he shouldn't lose sight of that, if he wanted to solve the situation and leave the battlefield in one piece. She was pissed enough to take it out on him.

"Okay, I understand how that might have upset you, but you also have to understand I had my reasons…" he said, dragging the sentence away when he saw she wasn't mollified by far with his attempt to explain himself.

"Of course, you had your reasons," she snapped, throwing her hands into the air. "How could I forget that? That makes everything all right, doesn't it?"

"Becka, come on, just listen to me. It's not easy to explain what I thought," Bryan tried to reason with her.

Becka looked straight at him and said with all the sarcasm she could muster, "I'll tell you what you thought, Bryan. It's a no-brainer. You thought I was a stupid bimbo, interested in a man with money and you didn't want me to stick my greedy hands in your pockets. That's what you thought," she finished her tirade in a shout.

It sounded bad. The way she put it, it sounded very bad. Bryan felt a tinge of guilt because there was something true in her words, even though she framed his entire train of thought in an ugly manner.

"Not really, Becka. But I had my share of women who showed interest in me only because I had money and..."

Becka stomped her foot and groaned and her behavior stopped him from continuing. He waited to see what else she had to say.

She glanced at him, then she averted her eyes as if she couldn't look at him anymore. She moved to gather her swimming suit pieces and in a very quiet voice said, "I want you to take me home now."

"Please, sweetie..."

"I said now," she repeated, emphasizing her words. "I don't want to spend another moment with you. You lied to me! You thought horrible things about me!" she shouted and turned her back to him to get dressed.

He felt the pang of guilt nagging at him again, but then another thought popped into his head suddenly. Taking his pants to get dressed as well, he said sarcastically, "And you were very open with me, weren't you? You were Miss Open Book and Open Heart, weren't you?"

"What do you mean?" Becka turned back to him, stunned to hear his words. "I didn't lie to you."

"Yes, you did. You said some things yesterday and you didn't want to expand on that. Don't you remember? When you said you didn't advise me to upset you, and when you said there were things you couldn't tell me… Well, I also had things I couldn't tell you, so we are square," he concluded.

She looked at him, simmering inside. She felt her rage rise like magma inside a volcano and she couldn't hold back her anger anymore and threw her hands in the air.

A whoosh of wind swirled around him and he felt icicles on his back. The basket flew into the nearest tree trunk and the cooler followed shortly after, as if an unseen hand had lifted them and thrown them away.

Bryan felt like he was in the middle of a hurricane and watched Becka with stunned eyes. He couldn't believe what he was seeing.

Her lips started trembling and she had tears in her eyes all of a sudden. When she closed her eyes, and lowered her shaky arms, everything went back to normal. The wind stopped and the warmth of the day chased away the chills he had felt on his back.

She didn't look at him and he couldn't do anything more but stare at her in shock. He refused to think about what had happened or to find an answer, but he knew she had a hand in it and he didn't feel comfortable near her anymore.

It was sort of creepy and he couldn't find a reasonable explanation for what he had experienced and felt, and what popped into his mind didn't really make sense, but only freaked him out more.

"I think I'll take you home now," he said quietly, unwilling to go into the why's and how's right then.

Becka nodded, defeated, and started getting dressed in silence. When she finished, she went to gather the basket and the cooler. His cold voice came from behind and stopped her.

"Don't worry about those. I'll take care of everything when I come back."

Becka nodded subdued. She felt dejected and walked with small steps toward the dock. She didn't know what to tell him and she could tell he didn't want to hear anything from her right then.

She was sad because she had been having a great day with him, but that day had been built on lies and deceit and she didn't know how she felt about it anymore.

Bryan helped her on the deck of the boat with total detachment, as if she had been a woman he had just met and he had extended a customary politeness to her. Any kind of closeness they had experienced before was now gone. They felt like strangers and uncomfortable ones as that.

Once on the boat, she went under the canopy and put on her t-shirt and pants, while he went to the helm and started the boat, speeding up as soon as it was possible.

Bryan didn't feel like being with her anymore, at least for the moment, but he imagined his feelings would go back to normal once he had time to think about things. The man felt some guilt over his omissions, but he considered she was much more at fault for the situation than him.

He didn't want to dwell on what had happened because he didn't like what he read into the facts. Despite all that, he also felt regret because he felt something for her, even though their relationship had developed only in the span of a day. He had thought she was the one for him and it was hard to think it was just an illusion. He needed time to think about all of that.

Becka was upset with him and with herself at the same time. She was upset he had felt the need to keep his wealth a secret, fearing she would be more attracted to that than to him. She would have liked for him to trust her and to think differently about her.

She could understand past experiences might have made him fearful about people's reasons. However, she thought she had been open enough and she normally didn't make people think she was a person who would take advantage of a man. She didn't seem a woman with greedy little hands ready to grasp everything in sight.

Becka was also mad at herself because she had no control over her powers. Whenever she would get mad, she would unleash them and she couldn't stop anything.

Becka knew people didn't take it lightly when someone made things float in the air and brought icy swirls of wind around them. Her mother had told her that over and over again since she was a baby and she was famous for throwing serious tantrums. Luckily, she had learned her lesson before going out into the real world.

Unfortunately, she had forgotten all those lessons today. She hadn't walked away from the fight with Bryan, and she had put herself on the spot. She had chased Bryan away because he had to be too freaked out now to want to stay with her.

She didn't like how cold and detached he behaved then. After that wonderful afternoon, when they shared those precious moments together, for which she had been waiting for a long time, his demeanour had the effect of a cold shower. His present cold attitude tainted everything.

Becka wasn't sorry she had made love to Bryan. She would have lied to herself if she had said that. However, she was sorry because the aftermath had turned out so bleak and left her feeling so empty.

Becka didn't realize she was crying already, but Bryan heard her sobs and turned to her. A claw squeezed his heart.

For a fleeting moment, he thought he would better mind his business and let her cry. He wasn't very good around a crying woman. He should let her sort things out first and then try to approach her, but he couldn't let go.

That woman had already had a huge impact on him and regardless what he was feeling that very moment, he couldn't stand idle by and let her cry without offering her any kind of solace.

When she felt his hand on her shoulder, Becka looked up. Bryan saw the tears running down her cheeks. He dried them with his thumb and pulled her up and into his arms, rubbing her back. He rested his head on hers and just held her, softly stroking her back to calm her down and make her feel better.

"It's all right, baby, you don't have to cry. It's not the end of the world, you know," he murmured.

His words made her cry harder and through hiccups she said, "It's the end of us, Bryan, and that's the end of the world now."

He smiled, slightly amused and raised her head to look into her eyes and kissed her lips softly, longing to feel her close to him again.

"I don't know if it's the end of us, but both of us have some thinking to do, Becka, and then we'll see," he said evenly.

"You want me to explain?" she asked with hesitation in her voice.

He shook his head, "No, not right now. I must think for a while and then we can talk. It's better not to talk about anything right now."

"Why does it have to be on your timetable?" she snapped at him, forgetting about her sadness for a moment.

"It's not on my timetable," he tried to be reasonable. "It's something I have to do, though. I do have to think. You can't think I'll just put everything behind and go on without any questions, sweetie, because, believe me, it doesn't work that way," he said in an even tone, although he felt like strangling her for being so dense.

It wasn't like everything that had happened was everyday stuff. He had already come up with an explanation, but he didn't like it, even though that possibility was nudging more and more at him. More importantly, he didn't know if his feelings were strong enough for him to continue being in a relationship with a woman who could create a small storm. He liked to have a certain balance in everything and his relationship with Becka wasn't balanced by far.

Becka pulled away and turned her back to him. She understood her show might have freaked him out, but she didn't understand why he didn't want to talk about it.

She had been told never to show her heritage to strangers, but she thought she would have a chance at a real relationship with him and she had to show him what she could do. It happened earlier than she had hoped, but she didn't think it was such a bad thing, quite the opposite.

She tried to console herself with the thought that, at least, she didn't invest too much in a relationship with no chance of survival.

"Becka…" Bryan started to say but she put her hand up to make him stop.

She didn't turn back to him when she said, "Everything is fine, Bryan, don't worry. I understand your reluctance. Let's just go home and forget we've ever met."

Her voice showed more determination than she felt but she didn't want him to stick around only because he felt sorry that she cried. If he couldn't be with her for what she was, then she didn't see a point in continuing with the charade.

"It might not be so simple, Becka. I didn't say we should forget we've met. I just asked for a little time to process what happened. Maybe that time would work for you, too."

"Whatever you say," she shrugged and went to the other side of the boat to get away from him.

In a way, Becka knew Bryan was right. It wasn't as if he had had to get over a bad habit like talking with her mouth full. Yet, she felt cheated because she had jumped into an affair with him without thinking it over.

She didn't like he had lied to her, either. Everything was too much for her to forgive right then. She didn't even think it was worth the trouble.

The rest of the trip was made in total silence. They stole glances at each other, but neither one of them wanted to talk anymore.

When they got to the harbor, they moored the yacht and went to the parking lot where he had left the car in the morning.

The tension grew more during the car ride. The car was too small to contain both their resentments and heartaches. They started to dislike each other immensely and couldn't wait to get to their destination and part ways.

Bryan had hardly stopped the car when Becka jumped out, throwing a quick good-bye over her shoulder and ran to her house. As soon as she was inside, she shut the door behind her with a resonant bang.

Bryan looked after her and even five minutes later he was still there, in front of her house, staring at the closed door. That bang had sounded like a bad omen to him.

Bryan didn't feel as relieved as he had previously thought. While on the boat, on their way back to town, he had wanted just to drive Becka home and be done with everything for that day. Now, though, it felt like Becka had slammed the door over the only good thing that had happened in his life.

The man thought about going to her door and demanding she talked to him, but he nipped the thought in the bud. It wasn't the right moment. Even he, with his limited social skills when it came to love relationships, knew that.

Bryan needed to give her room to cool off and he needed time to mull things over and find a better way to deal with what had happened. That decision made him turn his key in the ignition and drive his car away.

CHAPTER SEVEN

Becka was in the garden, staring into the distance. For a few days now, she couldn't find any peace there, although it used to be her realm of tranquility before.

She hadn't even gone to classes anymore and she couldn't seem able to do anything. She couldn't even read one of the books she loved to read or chat with her cousins. She would chat with one of them at least once a day and now it had already been a week and a half and she still couldn't pick up the phone and call any of them.

Becka had avoided seeing anyone over the past week and a half since her falling out with Bryan. She hadn't felt able to go to the regular dinner with her parents. She had made up a party she couldn't miss, only to get out of it.

Her father hadn't been too happy about it, but her mother had exulted hearing that her daughter finally had a social life befitting a young girl of her age. She'd always thought Becka was too introverted when it came to making friends and she didn't like it.

It was Friday again and, this time, she knew that next day she wouldn't be able to avoid dinner with her parents anymore. Her great-grandmother would be there and not even her mother would find the words to apologize for Becka's absence. When great-grandmother came to dinner, everyone had to attend. Only being bedridden in the hospital would have been a valid excuse.

Becka didn't know what she should do. She was sure everyone would immediately see that something had happened to her and she was heartbroken.

She'd seen her face in the mirror when she brushed her teeth day after day. She knew she looked exactly like she felt, as if her very life had been crushed out of her.

Becka couldn't get over what had happened with Bryan. She had fallen for him hard and no matter how much she rationalized what she felt, she couldn't make those feelings go away.

She knew it was just less than two full weeks, but she was afraid she would always think about him and it would be difficult for her to find another man who would complete her so well.

Now, with a cool mind, she realized her outburst about the house shouldn't have happened. They had known each other for a day only and he had the right to protect himself if he had been burnt before. Hadn't she reacted to that lie so strongly, everything would have been fine and she could have revealed the truth about herself to him later when he could have accepted who she was.

Unfortunately, it was too late to think of that now. She had managed to find a great guy and lose it in two dates. Probably that was a record.

***

Bryan rang the bell and waited for Becka to open the door. He had taken residence in hell since their break up over some stupid words and a little magic.

He had chosen to think of what she had done in terms of *'a little magic'* because it just seemed easier to understand and accept. Bryan knew they would have to talk about that too, but he had already decided to keep an open mind and not just give up because of what she was.

Initially, the man had tried hard to forget her. Owning a dojo helped him spend the days in excruciating effort. He tried exercising and lifting weights. Then he progressed to boxing. He made a point in having a date with the boxing bag every day for hours, but that didn't work.

After the first few days, he left his friend in charge and he progressed to drinking. After the first hangover, he remembered why he had hated drinking. He had always disliked not being in total control and drinking had that power over him.

After the first bottle of scotch, his reactions would slow down and he would hate himself.

In the end, he had just wasted hours after hours thinking of Becka and what he should have done differently or how he should have reacted to get a different result.

Even though their relationship had had such a short span of life, it marked him deeply. He would hear her voice all the time and he would dream of her when he finally could fall asleep.

After a week and a half, Bryan decided he had had enough. He had to go over to her and try to fix everything so he could bring her back into his life. He knew he couldn't go on like that. She had become too important to him and he couldn't just forget her.

Bryan was sure she had something to do with magic, but in the great scheme of things, that didn't matter to him anymore. He was willing to put up with that if she would find it in her heart to take him back.

That was why now, he was waiting patiently for her to come and open the door.

The echo of the bell had already faded away and she still hadn't come to the door. Bryan was stubborn enough though and, with determination, rang the bell again. He resigned himself to wait with his hands in his pocket, rocking on the balls of his feet.

When a few minutes passed and still there was no sign of Becka, Bryan shrugged and instinctively tried the knob of the door. Of course, as expected, the door wasn't locked. He swore under his breath, thinking of the worst, and entered the house, closing the door quietly behind him.

Bryan felt like an interloper for a moment and thought of the consequences of his venture. Yet, he was determined to see his quest had a happy ending so he called her name.

The silence of the house weighed down on him. He didn't hear steps coming down the stairs and decided to go into the kitchen. The room was empty, but then again, he could see Becka through the window, sitting under the gazebo, at the other end of the garden.

The woman looked small and lost, with her hands folded in her lap. There was a faraway look on her face that tugged at his heart. Happy because he had found her, Bryan went out in the garden and walked towards her.

Becka didn't seem to notice she wasn't alone anymore. When he got closer to her, he saw the signs showing she had cried and he felt like a jerk.

She seemed tired and defeated and his heart ached a little more knowing he was the one who put that expression on her face.

"Becka," he called her name softly when he stepped under the canopy.

She sighed, but didn't say anything and didn't glance at him. That wasn't a good sign. Bryan panicked at the thought she had decided to ignore him, shut him out of her life and not to talk to him anymore.

"Becka," he called her more forcefully and only then, she turned to him with a soft gasp.

Her eyes grew wide and he could see she couldn't believe he was there.

"I rang the bell twice," he said to explain his presence in her garden. "I tried the door only because I saw you didn't answer and I thought you didn't lock it."

"I can't hear the bell from here," she said quietly. "It wasn't intentional," she continued. "I mean it wasn't like I didn't want to open the door for you."

He shook his head to chase her worries away and said, "I didn't think about that, sweetie. I just told you why I came inside so you wouldn't think I'm some damn stalker."

Becka gave him a small smile, but her face didn't glow as it used to do before and that didn't sit right with him.

"But why are you here, Bryan? Nothing changed from the last week as far as I know. You still think I'm a gold digger, I know you're a liar and we both know what I can do."

Bryan didn't like her resigned tone, nor did he like the sadness he read on her face. He didn't like her accusation either. He knelt before her and took one of her hands in both of his, and stroked them gently.

"I don't think you're a gold digger, baby, and I never thought that. Maybe it was stupid of me to wait and see if you liked me for me at first, but I really had some bad experiences in the past and I guess... I just needed some reassurance. I hope you can forgive my stupidity."

"And what about what happened when we argued?" she asked with hesitation. She was afraid to hear his answer.

Bryan stood up and sat on the bench, pulling her into his lap.

"Well… That was something else, Becka, I must say… Nothing I've experienced before, I am sure. Maybe you can explain it to me because… It freaked me out, Becka," he admitted in a grave voice. "I've never seen something like that and, of course, the first thing I thought was that you are… a…" Bryan started to say but he couldn't continue and say exactly what he thought.

"A witch?" she asked matter-of-factly.

Bryan didn't answer immediately. He pondered on what he remembered first.

"I don't know… I thought of a poltergeist or something like that," he confessed in the end, staring at her.

"Oh, gosh, I haven't thought you'd think that," she exclaimed. "I'm not anything like that, Bryan, be serious."

Bryan narrowed his eyes and asked, "So what are you exactly? Not that it would matter, to be honest," he rushed to add.

"What do you mean it wouldn't matter?"

He took a few moments to consider his answer. He looked over the garden, absently stroking her hip.

"All right, I'll be honest with you," he said looking back at her. "I can't function. I can't sleep and I can't do anything, as a matter of fact. I've tried and nothing works. I'm thinking only of you.

So, no matter what, I want to be with you. So you know."

Seeing her eyes trained straight on him, he amended his statement, "If you want the same thing too, of course. I can't force you, I know that. But I hope you do want me too."

Becka stroked the side of his face with tenderness and leaned to kiss him on the lips.

"I want to, but I think you do need to know everything before going any further," she said with sadness.

"Just tell me," Bryan said. "I'm sure it's not so dramatic and anyway, I think I can live with what you are. Considering I can't live without having you in my life, the point is moot, as you say. I know it sounds pretentious, but then again you should know the days we've been apart were a living hell for me."

"All right, Bryan. I'll tell you then," Becka started and then stopped.

She couldn't make the words come out as, too afraid he would run away again.

"Come on, baby, just say it. I promise everything will be fine."

"Huh!" she scoffed.

Her distrust was evident and he knew he deserved that. He had already run away from her once. He chose to look at her with insistence and make her talk. She held his stare and finally went on with her explanation.

"So, how can I tell you this, Bryan? I think I should be direct," she murmured and he made efforts to hear her. "All right, here it is," she started again. "I'm a witch and unfortunately not a very good one. I still have to learn to control the gift. You saw what happens if I get angry," she told him and he nodded. "In general, I try to walk out of confrontations because of that, but with you, then, I didn't have the space to do it. You see, when I get mad, all those intense feelings turn into icy gushes of wind and things start flying around and that's something I can't stop. I don't have the knowledge to do it," she explained to make him understand.

"All right, fair enough," he said. "What else can you do?" he asked in a conversational tone, although he didn't feel very at ease hearing his worst fears voiced out, and knowing he didn't have a choice in the matter.

"Not much. That thing and... I can tell if people are all right or not. I can't tell if they're felons or killers or anything like that. I can tell though if they give me a good vibe or not," she shrugged.

"And I gave you a good vibe, I understand," Bryan assumed and she nodded. "So, let's sum it up, Becka. You're a witch and I'm wealthy. Is there anything else that should be said?"

She shrugged again and shook her head. They stayed silent for a while, when she decided to ask, "Should I tell you everyone in my family is a witch?"

He looked at her surprised and said, "Really? Everybody? And all of them do the same things as you?"

She laughed, seeing he looked so bewildered, and answered.

"No, not everyone can do the same thing. Some can read minds, some can heal. Everyone has their gift. Of course, we all can do basic stuff, but some of us chose not to do it anymore. I don't. It's not like I can get very far right now, so…"

"Why?" he asked completely surprised to hear all she had to say.

"This is the part I can't tell you… Or at least not now… Not if there is a chance to be together… And if we are meant to be together, you'll find out when the time is right. I hope you'll understand and don't pressure me to…"

Bryan stopped her with a finger on her lips.

"You don't have to tell me anything now if you can't. We passed over the first hurdle, let's keep it that way. When you're ready and you can, you'll tell me, okay?"

Becka looked at him with hope, but she didn't dare to hope too much. Her heart still ached and she didn't know if she could take another rejection from him. The first time had been enough.

"Will we be together, Bryan?"

Bryan gathered her to him and hugged her. She felt he didn't want to let her go anymore.

"Yes, if you want to be with me and you can forgive me for the way I reacted that day at the lake, yes, we can be together, sweetheart."

She nodded and, smiling, hugged him back as hard as she could. She cuddled as close as possible to him and sighed with content.

Bryan was happy to see her so willing to get over the argument they had had and get back together. He was satisfied to sit there with her wrapped in his arms and just listen to the silence of the garden.

The light changed and the evening came with a pale wind, which hushed through the multitude of flowers populating Becka's garden. They were still cuddled together and none of them felt like letting go.

Becka's head rested on Bryan's chest and Bryan held her tight. He rested his chin on the top of her head and enjoyed the unusual scent of her hair.

"Do you want to come inside with me?" Becka whispered after a while. "Maybe spend the night with me?"

Bryan smiled and lifted her head to see if she blushed. He wasn't disappointed. A faint blush had already colored her cheeks and her eyes were twinkling in the twilight.

He couldn't resist and took her mouth in a kiss that held all that desire he had felt for her during the days he couldn't see her.

Still kissing her, he stood up with her snuggled up in his arms and started towards the house. Only when they got to the kitchen door, he raised his head and looked at her again, then, balancing her on one knee, he opened the door and took her inside, closing the door with his foot behind them.

"So, where's your bedroom?" he asked her, crossing through the kitchen.

"Upstairs, the last room on the left," she answered breathless, unable to believe he would carry her all the way upstairs. It was so romantic that her little heart sang.

He kissed her again for good measure and carried her to the bedroom. Once inside her bedroom, he let her stand and looked for the switch to turn the light on but she beat him to it. The strong light burnt his eyes and he blinked a few times.

Once his eyes got used to the light, Bryan swept the room with his eyes and had to grin. That room spoke loud and clear about Becka. It was a room with the air of the turn of the century, cluttered with pillows and comfortable armchairs on one side. On the other side of the room, a big, antique chest of drawers took most of the wall and was covered with photos showing groups of people, some young and some old, and knick-knacks, all of them fairies, etheric and whimsical. Behind the armchairs, a wide window showed the garden he still could see although it was already dark outside. The window had a large bench built in, covered in thick colorful pillows and he could imagine Becka lying there, reading.

He turned back to Becka and saw she was observing him carefully, as if she had wanted to guess what he was thinking.

"I like your bedroom, Becka. It's got you written all over it. Too many pillows for my taste, but, what the heck, it works for you."

She smiled brightly and advanced towards him with her lazy stride. Her summer dress covered her legs only up to her knees and he enjoyed the sight of her shapely legs in her slow journey towards him. The two straps, holding the dress on her shoulders, didn't cover much and he found her more enticing than if she'd been modelling a sexy nighty.

When she reached him, Becka leaned in and kissed him softly on the lips. That fleeting kiss made him burn even more for her.

He pulled her into his arms and kissed her soundly, molding her lips to his, nibbling at her lower lip, all the while stroking her shoulders and arms and her back.

He gazed into her eyes again to see if she really wanted to make love to him. He needed to be sure because he couldn't go through another fight and another break-up.

When he saw she was on the same page with him, he unzipped her dress and lowered the straps of the dress to reveal her generous bust. He licked his lips in his hunger to feel her nipple in his mouth and lowered his head to satisfy his craving. She sighed and moaned and tried to keep her balance while he started the sweet torture she enjoyed so much.

He led her back to the bed and helped her lie down, then showed her how much he needed to make love to her.

CHAPTER EIGHT

Bryan got out of the shower, whistling. He was in a very good mood that day. He had had a beautiful night with Becka and he had enjoyed her lack of shyness in bed, even though she was timid out of bed.

The young woman was something else, indeed. She had proved she was everything he needed during the long night they had spent together, but also during the first part of his shower, ended with a shared passion.

Bryan realized he was happy. That was a feeling he hadn't had in such a long time, he couldn't even remember when he had been happy before, if he had ever been.

It wasn't just their lovemaking, although it was an interesting experience to make love to Becka. She was open to learn how to make love to him and how to enjoy the pleasures with which he showered her.

Besides that, there was also the pleasure of talking to her. She was not a woman to prattle away about fashion or other things men didn't understand. She could touch an eclectic group of subjects and kept surprising him with her insight.

Bryan had told her a few things from his past. Of course, he kept silent about the worst ones, because he didn't want to scare her away. He hoped he would be able to share those with her in time. However, he had told her about some of the things he had done, because he wanted her to know that nothing about him was just in white and black.

Bryan thought she needed to know the man she got involved with, because, ultimately, all his experiences had had a hand in making him the man he had become and she loved. He told her about his dojo and she showed interest in seeing it and she even wanted to train with him, so he told her that he would take her there the following week.

She had also revealed her dreams and she had told him stories about her childhood and teen years. He had heard a few things about her cousins and siblings, and it made him understand that Becka's family was a close-knit one.

They were close to each other, not like his own. He had admitted he hadn't seen his father in over twenty-five years, since he took off. The old man couldn't live with his mother anymore. Her sharp tongue had weakened his will to keep his marriage together and strengthened his wish to live as far as possible from her. Once he left, he didn't look back anymore, not even to check on his son.

His mother was another story altogether. She was still present in his life, if only to make his life a living hell whenever they would get together. She considered it was his duty as a son to visit her at least once a month and she took great pleasure in cutting him to size, as she used to say, during those monthly visits.

Now Becka knew he didn't love his mother anymore. He had probably stopped loving her when he was five. She was verbally abusing everyone with an odd pleasure and she considered everybody was beneath her station. Her son had been good for various things along the years, but he hadn't been good enough to love.

Yet, he had taken care of her. She had her own house and a monthly alimony for a comfortable living so he didn't feel guilty at all for not looking after her, even though she tried to make him feel that way every chance she got.

Bryan dried himself with a towel and got dressed in a rush. He knew Becka was in the kitchen. She had promised him to cook breakfast for him and he was a little concerned. He had proposed to cook breakfast for both of them, but she insisted. She said it was the only meal of the day she could cook, so she wanted to show off her culinary talents.

Bryan smiled remembering the way she had sounded. He had promised himself to praise her efforts even if her cooking lacked any skill.

He went downstairs still whistling and headed directly to the kitchen. His sweet Becka was swearing loud. He heard her all the way from the hallway and grinned. He hadn't thought she would know some of those words.

Something had happened with the eggs apparently. Becka had wanted to make sunny-side up eggs, but the eggs had refused to cooperate with her.

The grin on his lips grew wider. Bryan didn't care if he ate scrambled eggs or sunny-side up eggs or whatever. He cared she had gone through all that trouble to make breakfast for him. He couldn't remember any woman who had made him breakfast.

Bryan entered the kitchen and for a second there, the man couldn't hide his shock. The sight overwhelmed him. Luckily, Becka was facing the stove and mumbling so she didn't hear him coming in.

The kitchen was in shambles. With a hand on his heart, he vowed never to let her in the kitchen again even if that meant he would have to cook well into his old age.

The woman had made a complete and total chaos. And that under fifteen minutes. The pristine kitchen from the night before looked now as if a hurricane had passed through it and turned everything upside down.

Now, he knew why her kitchen had looked untouched the night before. Probably she didn't cook at all.

"May I help you, Becka?" he asked and Becka shrieked and dropped on the floor the spatula she had in her hand. She had been so focused on what she was doing that he had scared the hell out of her.

"I'm sorry, baby," he rushed to her. "I thought you heard me coming. I was whistling so...," he said, reaching down and taking the spatula from the floor and throwing it into the sink.

"Not a problem, Bryan. You just gave me a heart attack," she said with all the dramatic flair she could muster, pressing her little hand over her heart. "I was just finishing up breakfast. Coffee is already on the table. Go and pour yourself a cup and I'll bring the rest, okay?"

He nodded, but the moment she turned back to the stove, he shook his head. He couldn't believe one person could do so much damage while cooking breakfast. It was unimaginable.

In her hurry to do everything, she had thrown the eggshells on the counter, next to the bacon package and carton of eggs, also forgotten there. There were breadcrumbs everywhere.

Something was burning and he guessed it was the toast. He was right. The fire alarm set off and he rushed to open the kitchen door to the garden so the smoke would dissipate sooner.

Then he went to the toaster in a hurry and took the bread out.

By then, Becka had started crying. She had tried her best and her best failed her. She had known she didn't have any cooking skills, but she had thought she could make breakfast, once in her life, without having everything go wrong and, more important, without setting off the fire alarm.

Breakfast was the only meal she was brave enough to try. Becka was afraid if she tried something more elaborate, her kitchen would go up in flames.

However, today she had wanted to impress Bryan. Well, she impressed him, all right. That was sure. But then, it was not the impression she had wanted to give him.

Becka was crying in earnest now, and as much as he wanted to, Bryan couldn't go to comfort her. There was no time for that. He had more pressing matters to take care of.

After turning off the toaster and taking the toast out, Bryan rushed to the stove where the eggs were slowly turning into a black-reddish mass. He was sure the fire alarm would soon rouse all the neighbors.

With efficient and measured gestures, he took the pan off the stove and threw it in the sink. A look at those eggs told him he couldn't save them anymore. Shaking his head, he returned to the stove and turned it off as well.

Bryan looked around and picked the eggshells abandoned on the counter and threw them in the garbage. The man wiped his hands with a kitchen towel and returned the bacon back in the fridge.

After a last survey of the kitchen, Bryan washed his hands and then, finally went to Becka and slid an arm behind her. He gathered to his chest and kissed the corner of her mouth tenderly.

He nudged her head up and brushed her tears away with his thumb.

"It's all right baby, it's not the end of the world, all right? Come on, stop crying now and let's eat the bacon and toast. I think they're okay. We'll have some coffee and everything will be fine. If you're still hungry after we finish breakfast, we can go to Timmie's and have something to eat there, all right?"

"I wanted everything to be perfect," she wailed, making him smile and kiss her once more.

"Everything's perfect, honey," he reassured her and hugged her again.

"How can you say that?" she shouted. "The eggs were a failure from the beginning and that stupid fire alarm won't stop..."

"It's stopped now. Look, no shrilling sounds. The room is aired, see? The smoke is gone. Look, it's stopped," he comforted her again after the last beep of the alarm finally died out.

"I wanted to make something nice for you," she sobbed.

Becka didn't understand why she was so emotional and why she couldn't stop sobbing. Come to think of it, she had never cried like that before the last few days and she had never been a mass of tangled emotions.

"Come on, stop crying, Becka," he shook her gently. "You did. You did something nice for me. No one has ever bothered to make me a cup of coffee at least so you've done more than anyone else in my life. Please, now, stop crying. It's all right," he patted her back to reassure her.

Becka hiccupped a couple of times and allowed him to lead her to the table and help her sit down. Bryan poured coffee and they started munching on the toast, which was thoroughly black, and on the bacon, which, happily, was only partially burnt.

Both tried to ignore the crunching sounds filling the kitchen. It was as if a battalion of mice was munching at the same time.

"I do appreciate your effort, sweetie, but from now on, I'll cook, okay?" Bryan told her in between two bites. "And I do want you to promise me you won't ever try to cook again. You want a homemade meal, I'm available. Anytime, day or night, I'm here for you. Just don't try to cook again. I wouldn't want to hear your kitchen went up in flames," he urged her, his mind filled with horrible scenarios.

Becka nodded, keeping her eyes down, but she didn't say a thing. She felt her failure deeply and she couldn't look him in the eyes.

She had never cared about her inability to cook before, but now her inaptitude in the kitchen felt like a failure and she was sorry she didn't take her Aunt Marjorie up on her offer to teach her how to cook.

Bryan nudged her head up and smiled at her. He leaned over to kiss her and then said, "You're a real treasure, baby, believe me. You don't have to feel ashamed. I'm sure you can do things I can't, so everything levels just fine."

She nodded again, but didn't reply. They continued to eat their breakfast in silence.

"Any plans for today?" he asked her.

"I haven't made any plans for days," she confessed shaking her head. "I didn't feel like it."

"I'm sorry I upset you so much," he apologized, but she waved his concern away.

"It was my fault as well, so… Anyway, tonight I'm forced to go to a family dinner. Would you like to come with me?"

Bryan suddenly felt a constriction in his throat. Going to a family dinner was a big thing. He couldn't say it was too soon because he already knew how he felt about her, even though they had known each other for so little time. The week and a half without Becka wasn't something he would like to remember or relive. Yet, meeting her family hadn't crossed his mind.

Bryan looked at Becka and saw the hope in her eyes. He felt like an ogre for wanting to say '*no*'. So, he agreed to go with her.

Hearing his answer, Becka jumped off her chair and directly onto his lap, peppering his face with kisses, and making him laugh. He was content she was so happy with his decision.

CHAPTER NINE

Bryan was sitting in his idle car in front of Becka's house. He'd been sitting there for almost fifteen minutes already, and still couldn't find his courage to get out and ring her doorbell to let her know he was there.

He was wearing his dress pants and a white shirt, although he wasn't very sure it was the right attire to meet her entire family. He had thought of wearing his best dress suit at first, but the evening was too hot and he didn't think he could wear a coat. Besides, he absolutely hated wearing a tie. It always felt as if someone had strangled him and he already felt his throat was a little too tight. He didn't want to add more to his discomfort.

That evening was a first for him. In none of his previous relationships, had he made it so far. Bryan had never met the parents of the women he had dated. Maybe because he hadn't been so much into the woman he was dating or maybe because it hadn't ever felt like the right moment. There had always been reasons and he had always declined to show up at such gatherings. This time, he knew he couldn't back out of that dinner.

The man wanted Becka in his life. He was positive about that. He knew having a real relationship with her meant that he, unfortunately, had to meet the pesky parents, as well.

Family was a pivotal pylon in Becka's life from what he had gathered from her, and he couldn't treat that with indifference.

Beside the thought of getting together with her family, which would have worried any man meeting the parents for the first time, he also worried he would have to go directly into a den of witches.

Witches had never crossed his mind before he witnessed what Becka could do. He had always written such things off as just a hoax.

That day, at the lake, he had been forced to reconsider his beliefs. Nothing else would have explained what had happened.

Had it not been for the icy swirls of wind gushing around him, he would have gone with telekinesis, which seemed to border on being a somewhat more scientific fact. He would have possibly thought of hypnosis, which also appeared a more valid theory, but then, considering the circumstances, that didn't make the cut. They were in the middle of a fight so Becka couldn't have hypnotize him no matter how good she might have been.

When nothing else worked, he had to go with what might have seemed unreasonable, yet the only possibility.

Becka had told him a little about each of her family members so he wouldn't feel he was plunging into the unknown with no information at all. Yet, that didn't assuage his worries.

The idea that someone could read his mind or could turn the entire meal into a bunch of frogs had the power to render him a little more skeptical about his wisdom to make that visit. A sane man wouldn't go into something like that if he hadn't been hit over the head with something first, and then dragged into the lair.

But then, he couldn't have refused her invitation if he had wanted to continue seeing Becka and have her in his life and he did.

Bryan glanced at the dashboard clock and saw it was almost time to go and ring the bell. He had arrived earlier because he knew he would need some more time to reconsider everything and make up his mind or, more precisely, to pretend doing that. His decision had already been made the day before when he came to convince Becka to give him a new chance.

With a deep sigh, he got out of his car and with resolute but resigned steps, not unlike the ones of the people on their way to guillotine, he went to Becka's door and rang the doorbell.

Bryan was positive her door would be unlocked given what he knew about her, but he didn't want to make her believe he considered he could come and go from her house at will.

The theme of *Jaws* made him smile again and he felt more at ease with his choice than he was a few moments ago. Her hurried steps sounded on the wooden floor of the hall and he imagined her running to open the door for him. That image in his head made his heart grow a little.

He wasn't wrong. At the sound of the bell, Becka had rushed down the stairs, leaving her hair down. She had tried to make up her mind about how to fix her hair for the last fifteen minutes. She knew it didn't matter how her hair would look in the eyes of her family, but she wanted to look perfect for Bryan.

Becka had thought her feelings for him were strong before he came back to her the day before, but then, after spending that night and half a day with him, her feelings had grown much stronger.

She was determined to make their relationship work because without him she had been miserable and life had been bleak. She didn't want to go through all that again.

Becka opened the door, a little out of breath, and beamed at him. Bryan pulled her into his arms and kissed her soundly as if he hadn't seen her for days, even though only a few hours had passed since they said good-bye.

She wrapped her arms around his neck and let herself feel his passion. His kiss made her forget about the dinner with her family and anything else she might have had on her mind. She didn't even care that someone could see them from the street.

It only mattered that she was in his arms and he seemed to love and desire her enough.

Bryan couldn't let go of her. It took him a few long kisses before he was able to pull back. Only then, he returned her smile. Every fiber in his body was alert, screaming for her.

He didn't understand how he had fallen so hard for that woman in such a short period of time, but he was in love, head over heels, a feeling he had never experienced before. Suddenly, a strange thought crossed his mind and he frowned.

"What's the matter?" Becka asked, seeing his frown, and concern shadowed her face.

Bryan watched her steadily, thinking how to frame his question, and only after a few seconds of pondering over the matter, he found his courage to ask her about what puzzled him.

"Don't take it wrong, Becka, okay, but I need to know something... Is what I feel for you the result of a spell or... the real thing?"

Becka scowled at him and pulled back with a gasp. Then she launched herself furiously forward and punched his chest as hard as she could with her fist.

"How can you ask me something like that? You... you... you're a jerk."

She punched him again for good measure and tried to slam the door in his face but his arm blocked her move.

"Becka, be reasonable, baby."

"I'll show you reasonable, you... you... you... ass!" she yelled and, turning her back to him, she stormed out of the hallway into the living room like a little fury.

Behind her, the hallway wardrobe opened with a resounding thump and all the coats hanging inside flew out and swirled to the floor in a rain of colors.

Bryan only shook his head with resignation and followed her inside, stepping carelessly over the clothes lining the floor of the hallway.

This time, he was prepared for her storms and didn't mind walking into the lion's den. He imagined he would be safe enough because she liked him sufficiently. He thought she wouldn't truly try to hurt him.

He did hope he wasn't wrong since he didn't know what a witch could, in fact, do. The thought that he should have researched the subject a little, to be more informed and prepared, crossed his mind, but it was too late to do anything about that.

He found her at the window in the living room with tears in her eyes and his heart ached to see her so desolate. He hated himself because he was the reason for her tears, yet again.

The day before, he had promised himself he would do his best not to make her cry anymore and not even a day later, he did it again.

"Sweetheart," he called out to her in a soft voice. "Come on, don't cry," he said putting a hand on her shoulder.

He tried to soothe her, although he didn't have too much experience with soothing. He would just go away whenever a woman started crying. This time, he couldn't walk away.

Becka shook his hand off her shoulder and rubbed her fingers over her face to dry the tears away. Then, she turned to him and looked at him sadly, but with determination.

After watching him for a few moments, she said, "You'd better go, Bryan. If this is what you think about me, then it's clear there's no chance for us to be together, so we shouldn't waste our time anymore."

Bryan felt an icy wall rising between them and for the first time in his life he felt scared. His mind raced to find a way to persuade her they still had a chance, but after struggling for a few moments, he concluded he would better go with the truth.

"All right, sweetie, here's the deal."

At his words, Becka looked up at him, but kept quiet, allowing him to continue. She seriously considered to deck him if he had said anything hurtful again. At least, she could try.

"I want you too much, baby, and I'm pretty sure my liking you so much means that I love you. It's a too strong feeling to be something else. Now, considering I've never been in love in my entire life, and I do mean never," he emphasized his words, "and this is happening so fast, I had to ask myself if it might have been something you did. It's not like me," he pleaded.

She was narrowing her eyes in anger and that foretold a new storm, so he rushed with his explanation.

"That being said, it doesn't mean I have any kind of bad thoughts about you. Far from that! I just wanted to make sure it was me who loved you.

Without any external interference. You understand?"

Becka didn't reply. She just kept looking at him, weighing his words. She could see why he would interpret things like that. A man at his age who had never been in love would have been bound to question the validity of his feelings, especially if everything had happened too fast. That was understandable. It hurt though that, even for a moment, he thought his feelings were induced by a spell.

She nodded to show him she could see the validity of his argument, and then said, "I understand what you mean. It's a valid reasoning, that's true. That doesn't mean it doesn't hurt, Bryan, because it hurts like hell... Listen to me, Bryan. Being a witch doesn't automatically mean you can do whatever you want. There are limitations and boundaries. You can't step over boundaries because there are consequences. And, besides that, who the hell would want to make someone fall in love with them and live with the knowledge that their love is not real? Tell me!" she asked him and slapped his chest.

He pulled her into his arms, kissing the top of her head and whispered to her, "I didn't mean to hurt you. I just wanted to be sure it was me."

"All right, then. What now? Do you want to break up with me or what? Because I don't know if there's a way to prove it to you. I can yell it from the top of the roofs but that doesn't prove anything."

He pushed her at arm's length and looked at her with disbelief.

"Are you serious? How would breaking up with you make it better? There's no doubt I want to be with you. Where do you find these ideas?"

Becka shrugged again and he thought he did find that habit of hers charming. She looked like a naughty schoolgirl and for a moment, the thought she was way too young for him popped into his mind and he struggled to fight it back.

Bryan didn't want to think of anything that might have worked against their relationship, but then, in a way, he felt like a thief, who was stealing her youth. He considered to tell her that, but decided against it. She enjoyed drama and quite a lot and he didn't want to use up all his resources to calm her again. He was sure he would need those while he visited with her family.

It wasn't that he didn't appreciate her dramas. Becka had flair for a good scene and she looked very authentic. It was ingrained in her.

Now, that he was thinking of that, he realized she was the first woman whose drama he had ever enjoyed. He used to walk out of the door whenever a woman tried her theatricals with him. If that wasn't a sign he was in deep, he didn't know what else to look for.

Bryan looked at her from the top of her head to her toes. He loved how the white dress hugged her curves. It stopped a palm over the knees, which left the better part of her beautiful legs in sight.

He appreciated the fact she would wear white. Most women would try to wear only black or other dark colors merely to entertain the illusion that they looked thinner. The man admired Becka because her originality was refreshing. He liked she felt well in her own skin and she was able to see herself as beautiful as he saw her.

"By the way, you look great, baby. Your family will be stunned to see you with me. I should have worn a tie or something. Your dress is elegant and I look like a slob. As if I'd had no knowledge about fashion or choosing clothes," he shook his head in regret.

"Be serious, Bryan," she waved his concerns away. "You look just fine. It suits you and I want you, not the replica of a playboy. Anyway, some of my cousins will be wearing jeans, if only to drive my great-grandma crazy. We all have a bone to pick with her and this is their way of rebelling, you know," she grinned at him.

"But not you?"

"I have the same bone to pick with her, no worries," she nodded. "However, I found out that wearing jeans at the dinner table would upset my mom as well so..." she shrugged. "Anyway, you look great and if Matt doesn't come in his business suit, you'll be one of the best dressed men at the table, so you have nothing to worry about," Becka patted his arm reassuringly.

Bryan nodded and pushed her toward the hallway so they could leave. When Becka saw all her fall and winter coats on the floor, she groaned. She hadn't realized what had happened when she stormed out earlier. He just grinned at her and patted her shoulder to show her it was not a problem for him.

"It's all right, Becka. At least now that I'm prepared to see things flying around, this isn't such a big shock to my system," he told her with the same grin on his lips.

She narrowed her eyes again. She was trying to discern whether he was making fun of her or not, but chose not to reply. She started picking the clothes up. Bryan helped her and they finished in no time, so they could finally leave.

***

Becka admired how he drove. Bryan was confident, but he wasn't aggressive. He didn't want to prove anything to anyone and he didn't care if others tried to overtake his car.

"Did you tell your parents you were bringing me to dinner?" he asked, glancing at her and taking in her posture.

She looked like a Madonna, all in white, with her hands folded neatly in her lap and serenity written all over her face.

She nodded, "I told them I'd come with my boyfriend but I didn't give them any details."

He glanced at her, surprised. In his book, women would give all the details, including the ones they shouldn't. That was something very new for him.

"Don't tell me they didn't ask any questions," he showed his scepticism to her words.

Becka fidgeted in her seat for a few seconds, but decided she'd better be open with him so she replied, "Well, all right. It seems you know already. Mom was very happy to hear I finally had a boyfriend, because she didn't think I'd ever get one. You know, I had that bad habit of chasing all the guys away... They were either too boring or too annoying, so... no big deal... Anyway, she asked just a minimum of questions and I gave her your name and a general description. That's all. Father wanted to know more, but I cut it short. He's overprotective and he can drive me crazy. Plus, he'd send my brother your way to make sure everything is all right for his little girl and that would be just too embarrassing."

Bryan laughed hearing her morose tone and glanced at her again just in time to see her pout. She had her moments when she resembled a teenager but he didn't mind that either, although until the moment he met her, he had never glanced at the teenagers that crossed his path.

"You wouldn't laugh if he'd sent Alex your way," she advised him. "Alex is a sweet brother, but he can be a pain in the butt all the same."

Bryan laughed harder. He had never imagined his sweet Becka would use such words and it was refreshing to see she could constantly surprise him. He wouldn't have enjoyed a linear relationship either.

CHAPTER TEN

Bryan felt stupid carrying his big bouquet of roses and waiting in front of Becka's parents' house.

Becka had insisted they could just go inside, but he had declined her proposition and told her to ring the bell as normal people would do when they went to visit someone. Becka mimicked a sign to show him she thought he was crazy, but seeing his steely determination, she gave in.

The woman rang the bell and waited anxiously next to him for the door to open. She wondered what her mother would say seeing her in front of the door since she had never rung the doorbell. Normally, she would just barge in.

Becka had been impressed when Bryan took a huge bouquet of roses from the back seat, after they stopped in front of her parents' house. She wouldn't have believed the tough guy would think of flowers.

Now, she was amused because she saw how uncomfortable he was standing there with those flowers in his hand. Truth be told, he didn't look like the type of guy who'd carry flowers. It was just not him. Suddenly, a thought crossed her mind and she frowned. She turned to him.

"You never brought me flowers," she accused him morosely.

At her unexpected outburst, Bryan turned his eyes to her and looked at her as if she had grown a horn right on her forehead. Her outburst had come out of nowhere.

For a moment, he didn't understand what had upset her and then, when the meaning sank in, with a puzzled frown between his eyebrows, he replied, "First of all, our dates have been a bit unconventional, baby. Coming to take you out for a sail or coming to apologize didn't seem to require flowers.... Okay, maybe when I came to apologize," he stopped for a second, reconsidering what he was saying.

Bryan suddenly realized that exactly when he came to apologize had been the moment when he should have brought her flowers, but that thought had never crossed his mind.

To cover his blunder, he continued in force, "Second, what flowers could I bring you when you have that garden? How could I compete with that?"

"It's not about competing, Bryan," she dismissed his excuse with a flutter of her hand.

"Look at you. You bought flowers for my mother. My mother has a garden as well, so… the question remains. Why wouldn't you buy flowers for me?" she asked showing that stubborn streak of hers, although she was aware she had chosen a man who could show romance in other ways, but wouldn't bring flowers. It was just not his type and that was just her luck.

Bryan shook his head as if he'd needed to clear his mind and then he decided to answer. Exactly when he opened his mouth to reply, the door opened and a beautiful woman, in her fifties, smiled at them both, saving him from an answer that might have upset her even more.

He glanced at the woman framed in the door and noticed Becka was almost the exact replica of her mother. Bryan smiled and thought she would look great in her advanced age considering her heritage.

"Oh, sweetheart, you're finally here," the woman cooed and hugged Becka, kissing both her cheeks after the European fashion.

She squeezed the young woman a little more and then she finally turned to Bryan with sparkling eyes.

"Who do we have here, dear?" she asked.

Hearing her talk, Bryan was happy Becka hadn't inherited her mother's voice, too. It was one of those voices he couldn't stand. It reminded him of his mother's constant whining and recriminations. Yet, he continued smiling since he couldn't do otherwise. He knew he couldn't wince. He had to keep that phony smile on his lips although it required a real effort. Yet, wincing wouldn't have marked a very good beginning for his visit and it might have had long-term bad consequences.

He stretched his hand and said, "I'm Bryan, madam."

He shook her hand briefly and offered her the flowers, which were still a reason for discontent for Becka. He made a mental note to buy her flowers and as soon as possible.

Women loved flowers, he remembered, and associated romance with them, although he didn't understand why. He believed in showing what he felt through what he did. Bringing flowers didn't come too high on his list.

Becka's mother, Emily, smiled at him in turn and invited both inside, constantly chattering and making him feel uncomfortable. Bryan was there for Becka, though, and he was decided to make every effort not to upset her or embarrass her in front of her family. If he had to listen to that woman's talking all evening, he would do that.

Becka's parents lived in a real mansion, given the size of the building. His house was big, according to his standards, but this one was much more than that. From outside, it was quite impressive and somehow intimidating, but then the inside of the house seemed much more imposing.

The size of the entrance hall was on the generous side and the floor sported tiles with a floral motive. Stunned, he noticed the left wall was lined with a beautiful table, which screamed that it had been made somewhere in the 18th century. It wasn't something he'd have chosen for his entrance hall. He was convinced that table had a place in a museum.

The hallway led to a circular room where he could see the same tiles but with a geometrical motive this time. That room seemed to be another hallway and that perplexed him. He couldn't understand the necessity of having two of them.

Once inside the circular room, he could hear several voices coming from somewhere on the left. The voices were mingling in chatter, but he couldn't make out any words. It was just a cacophony of gibberish.

Now, seeing her parents' house, Bryan was positive Becka never had any shrewd intentions on his wealth and her anger at the lake made more sense to him. His accusation must have come like a blow. He imagined she had felt hurt and insulted at the same time, and she had had all the right to feel that way.

He wasn't sure if he could compare what he possessed with her family's wealth. That was by far the house of a very rich family and he wondered how it was possible his Becka was living in that small house in town when her parents were living the way they did. It wasn't like they hadn't loved their daughter from what he had seen so far.

Bryan wasn't disappointed though, since he liked to think she was as unspoiled and real as she seemed. She didn't appear to be touched by the rich girl syndrome.

She wasn't demanding and she didn't ask for expensive clubs or restaurants and she had even enjoyed his cooking which, in his opinion, was nothing someone could find in the restaurants en vogue.

Emily led them to the living room, which was at least ten times larger than Becka's. It was a vast space covered by several Aubusson carpets, but it still seemed to have difficulty containing all the people inside.

Bryan had the feeling he had walked into the middle of a big party. He had thought he would come only for a family dinner, though.

Looking around, he noticed some of the faces he'd seen in the pictures displayed in Becka's bedroom the night before.

Becka sensed he was uncomfortable and took his hand, giving it a little squeeze to encourage him. The man glanced at her and she could see the questions in his eyes and squeezed his hand again to let him know everything would be all right. She was wrong, though.

"I told you I have a big family, Bryan. At least, you can meet them all at once and that is done. I see everybody is here," she smiled at him and, as always, her smile had the power to make him relax.

A middle-aged man, almost of the same height as Bryan, came to them with supple steps and hugged Becka.

"How are you, sweetheart? We haven't heard much from you for the last two weeks, I think?" he phrased his reproach in a mild way.

"Oh, daddy, I'm fine. And I've talked to you, how can you say I haven't?" she replied and her voice showed her love for the man.

"I've said *'not too much'*, Becka, not that you haven't talked to us at all," he corrected her gently, then turned his eyes to Bryan.

Bryan noticed the older man's dislike immediately. It wasn't very difficult to spot it, as it was there in his eyes for everyone to see. He didn't want to let anything ruin Becka's day, so he tried hard not to show any expression on his face. Becka was a smart woman and she would have seen immediately something was amiss.

"So who do we have here?" Gabriel asked with a grave tone.

"Daddy, this is my boyfriend, Bryan," Becka chimed in, her happiness evident in her voice.

Bryan shook the older man's hand and lowered his head respectfully. He didn't know what to say to him and he didn't want to get into any argument if it was possible to avoid it.

However, Bryan was as wrong as Becka. No matter what he wanted, things had a way of evolving without asking for his opinion.

More people came around them and he began to feel crowded. Although everyone was kind to Becka, almost all of them were throwing him dirty looks as if he had come out right from the sewer. They seemed not to like her choice in boyfriends at all.

Bryan told himself he didn't care and that, in the end, they'd have to accept his presence in

Becka's life. He didn't intend to let them chase him away.

Gabriel, Becka's father, decided he would be the first to begin the attack against him.

"So, what do you think you're doing with my little girl?"

"Daddy!" Becka gasped stunned by her father's outburst and turned to him with wide eyes and her little arched mouth opened in a perfect 'o'.

"I beg your pardon?" Bryan inquired with a cool voice, although the question had angered him.

He had a pretty good idea he wasn't part of their social class, but that didn't mean he was nothing.

"You heard me very well, young man," Gabriel repeated. "What do you think you're doing with my girl? First of all, you're far too old for a girl like her," her father reiterated his bad feelings towards Bryan.

"Father, I think I can choose anyone I want," Becka started in a quarrelsome tone, but she couldn't go too far because she was interrupted immediately.

"Yes, sweetheart, you can, but choose someone of your own age," her father replied conciliatorily.

"And maybe not a felon, Becka, if that's possible. Look at his scar," Ariel chose to interfere, turning her nose up at the scar lining his cheek.

By now, Bryan's face looked as if it had been chiseled into stone. He had thought about this meeting and he had known that those would be their concerns, but now that everything was real, there, he felt chilled to the bone.

The man didn't like how things were going because it seemed his relationship with Becka was on the line.

He chose not to reply to Becka's sister, but he judged her in a second. She was one of those uptight women who had the misfortune to have had a bad hand dealt in life and took it out on everyone else.

"Becka knows what she's doing," her cousin Jay jumped into the melee and gained Bryan's gratitude. "You all know she's the smartest of us when it comes to people. And I wouldn't talk if I were you," he turned to Ariel.

Bryan liked that man. He was on his side and even though he knew Jay was a gambler, that didn't matter at all then. The important thing was he took Becka's side and tried to cut Ariel down a notch.

"How dare you?" Ariel started shouting. "How dare you to say something like that to me? She's my sister and I have to look out for her."

"Yes," Alex got involved in the general discussion.

Bryan knew he was Becka's brother because she had showed him his picture the night before.

"You should leave Ariel alone. And you Becka should think a little better about the kind of people you get involved with."

"I should? I should think a little better?" Becka's voice increased in intensity. "How dare you talk about Bryan like that, you moron? He's ten times better than you."

By now she was shouting and Bryan could see a few knick-knacks took off and swirled to the floor, followed by a few pillows that were on a sofa. Nobody cared, apparently. Probably such scenes were usual occurrence around there.

"Becka, baby," he touched her arm and tried to soothe her, but she wouldn't have it.

She turned to the mob with her hands fisted on her hips and said, "This is my boyfriend, and I emphasize, *my boyfriend*. Mark my words: either you start treating him as he deserves and welcome him into our family or I'm out of here."

Jay intervened immediately: "Don't worry, Becka, I have your back. I support you all the line. Hey, man," he said and stretched his hand to Bryan. "Hope you're fine. This is a crazy bunch, to be sure. You just don't pay any attention to them and everything will be just fine. Becka knows what she's doing," he repeated his earlier comment, tapping Bryan's shoulder.

Bryan shook his hand smiling. Beside Emily, who might have just been playing the role of a good hostess, this was the first friendly face he had seen in that room.

His joy was short-lived though, when a very old woman with the whitest hair he had ever seen approached them with heavy steps. Everyone made way for her.

She seemed to be a very important part of the family. Everyone deferred to her. Bryan took in her stature and admired her posture.

She might have been old, but she walked like a general. The lines on her face showed she had had tragedy in her life. She didn't seem a pleasant woman, but she was certainly formidable for such an old lady.

"So you're the fortune hunter, I see," she said in a booming voice, piercing him with her eyes.

For a moment, silence reigned in the room. Most of them had thought of that, but up to that moment, no one had dared to bring the subject up into the open. They looked to each other in shock, but aside from the raised eyebrows and a few open mouths, no one moved or said anything.

Becka and Bryan looked at her with stunned eyes and then looked at each other. The irony was lost on the others, but not on them. Both of them burst into laughter and Becka tumbled in his arms, laughing like a lunatic.

Everyone was staring at them, thinking they had gone mad. No one understood what was so humorous in accusing someone of being a gold digger.

Becka pulled back a little and looking at Bryan, asked him through guffaws of laughter, "How does it feel to be at the other end of the stick?"

Bryan laughed again and kissed her mouth soundly which drew a few gasps from the crowd around. Apparently, that was not sanctioned behavior in that house. The two of them didn't care though.

All the tension Bryan had felt before was gone now. Becka could have that effect on him. He wrapped an arm around her shoulders and the two of them faced the audience.

"Well, ma'am," he said politely, watching the old woman steadily, and bowing his head for a second, just as a belated sign of respect, "here I am. Not a fortune hunter, but I'm still here and I intend to stay. Not necessarily in this house," he thought to specify so no one misunderstood him, "but on Becka's side."

The old woman narrowed her eyes dangerously at him and said in a crisp voice, "I don't like him, Becka. Throw him back into the pond."

Becka stared at her great-grandma in shock and shook her head. She expected some opposition, but she didn't expect to hear things like that. Any sense of decorum had disappeared and everyone was attacking Bryan as if he had been a lowlife.

"He's not a fish to throw back in the pond and he's not an object," she said in a steely voice, Bryan had never heard before.

He thought that now he had the possibility to see another side of Becka and this side of hers was as fascinating as the others.

"He's a human being, a man, and he is mine, regardless if you like him or not. You don't decide for me. I love him and he loves me, and that's it. Case closed," she stated with determination, waving her hand and tapping her right foot for good measure.

A young man, close in age to him, came forward and stretched his hand to Bryan,

"Welcome to the tribe, man, even if it's a loonie bin. I'm Matt. I think Becka chose well," he said in a serious tone.

Bryan shook his hand. The sincerity in Matt's voice impressed him. Finally, there was another one who welcomed him among them without taking shots at him first.

"Thank you, Matt," he said. "It's a pleasure to meet you. I can assure you of that," Bryan said smiling widely.

"Nonsense," the old bat retorted, taking a step forward. "Becka, end this stupid relationship right now. This is not the type of man with whom you should associate. If you do need someone, we'll find you a nice man from a good family."

Her voice carried far. She was the type of woman that expressed her opinions loudly and usually everyone listened to her. Not this time though.

Becka took his hand and said, "We're leaving, Bryan. If my family doesn't understand to accept you, then we'll go and that's it. I won't come to the next dinners, mother, I hope you understand," she said to her mother over her shoulder, heading to the door and pulling Bryan after her.

Emily was in shock. She whimpered and covered her mouth with a trembling hand. She knew her Becka and her stubbornness. When she decided something, then nothing could make her change her mind and she didn't want to lose her youngest child.

"Becka, please," she pleaded, but Becka didn't give any sign she had heard her and continued her way to the door.

"If you leave this house now, with him, I'll have the fund trust changed on Monday morning. You will get nothing," her great-grandma said in a categorical voice. "He'll leave you then, because there'll be no money to feast on, but it would be too late for you to get your money because I won't change my decision."

Everyone froze. No one had ever thought Rebecca could do such a thing. She hadn't threatened Matt when he came with Velma or Jay when he tried to pull one over her. They knew when she made a decision about something, she didn't revisit her decision.

Becka stopped and turned back to her, pulling always Bryan in her wake. He could feel her shake with rage and was sure everything would start flying around in a moment.

Becka stopped before Rebecca and in a clipped tone replied, "I don't need your trust money. They come with strings attached, strings I don't like. You can take it and do whatever you want with."

"Hmm," the old bat replied looking at her sharply. "And how would you live? And what about this one?" she pointed to Bryan. "Do you think he'll still stay with you once you're penniless?" she said looking at Bryan with scorn.

"First of all, dear great-grandma," said Becka in a falsely sweet voice, "people work nowadays and they earn money to live on. Few need trust funds to pay for their daily expenses. I'm young and I can work. And if you're willing, we can make a bet Bryan won't leave me," she ended triumphantly and Bryan loved her even more in that moment.

"You think so, girl? Go ahead then, leave this house. Let's see who'll pay for your school and for your house and clothes and food. You think he'll keep you?" she tilted her head to Bryan with disdain.

"As a matter of fact, yes," he intervened in their argument for the first time. His voice was calm and businesslike. "I can afford to pay both for her school and for her house. She deserves it. Actually, she deserves much more and I intend to see that she gets everything she wants," he concluded.

Marjory came forward and spoke for the first time, "Grandma, you've done a lot of things to all of us along the years and no one has ever said anything. I think it's time for you to think of others, not only of what you want and how you think things should be because, I must tell you that, you're not always right. Becka is a smart girl, maybe smarter than many in this group," she said, looking around at the people surrounding them, and continued, "She found someone she loves and it's clear to me he loves her, too. I think you'd better let them be."

Gabriel looked at his wife and saw how desolate she was at the thought of losing her daughter. He didn't feel too comfortable with that either. Becka was the apple of his eye and he hadn't taken into consideration he would lose her because of his stubbornness.

He still thought Bryan was a little too old for her and he was concerned about his scar. That scar might have been an accident, he couldn't know for sure, but it also might have been the result of a life outside the law and that worried him a lot.

"Son," he addressed Bryan, "I see my daughter is determined to be with you and I know very well that I can't do a damn thing about it. She has to live her life as she wishes and probably make her own mistakes. I don't want to lose my youngest child so… I think I'd have to welcome you in my house," he said extending his hand to shake Bryan's.

Bryan shook his hand, understanding how hard it was for Gabriel to accept him. In a way, he admired the man for putting his daughter first and for pushing his feelings aside.

He wasn't a naïve man and he didn't believe the man took a liking at him all of a sudden. He knew he would always be a reason for discord in their family.

Emily was so happy her husband had decided not to shun their daughter that she started crying in earnest now. She went and hugged Becka as if she had returned from a very long trip and she had been away for years. After she cried over her for a few moments, she also went and hugged Bryan, who was effectively shocked seeing such an expression of affection from her.

However, not everyone was happy. He could hear murmurs around them and see a few unfriendly faces. The old bitty, Rebecca, was watching everything with an evil eye.

The most unfriendly face, beside Rebecca's, was Ariel's. She didn't like how the story was evolving and she decided it was high time she had done something about it.

"Father, you can't accept that. Becka's a child and has no idea what she's doing. You have to make her see how wrong she is."

"And I say she does know what she's doing," Matt intervened. "Could you let your bitterness and jealousy aside for a moment, Ariel, and be happy for her? It's obvious she loves him and love is not something to trifle with," he admonished her.

"You can't know she loves him," she retorted. "Your gift is not refined, so you can't be sure of what she feels and if you tell me you do, then you're lying," she shouted pointing to him.

"I know how she feels and not because I've read her mind," Matt replied in a calm voice. "I haven't even tried to. But it's obvious. Doesn't anyone else see it?" he turned around to sweep the others with his eyes, because he didn't believe everyone was blind.

"What do you mean?" Adam, his grandfather, asked. "If you haven't read her mind, then you can't be sure she truly loves him. No one can. She might just want to rebel against the family, which is perfectly normal at her age," he added shaking his head.

"She was furious just now," Matt pointed out. "You could see her tremble with anger. Have any of you seen anything flying around? Have you?" he repeated more strongly, looking at each of them.

Everyone was astonished, including Becka. She hadn't even realized that, even though she had been extremely furious, nothing had happened. She had unconsciously controlled her gift. She was so happy that she had been capable of controlling her gift that she simply jumped, pumping her hand in the air, and shouting, "Yay me," and hugged Bryan, who was laughing, seeing her so carefree although he wasn't very sure why she was so happy and what Matt was talking about.

"I did it, Bryan, I did it!"

"Yes, baby, you did. You rock," he replied, still laughing and lifted her up and swirled around with her, kissing her soundly.

The others were watching them, unable to believe their eyes. Some of the people from the younger generation were jealous little Becka was the first one to beat the odds and get control over her powers. Jay and Matt were happy for her and simply watched the couple with wide smiles on their faces.

Once Bryan finally put her down, Matt hugged her, "You did it, little girl. More power to you," he said, kissing her cheek loudly.

Marjorie hugged Becka and turned to her grandmother, "Becka did her part. Now, you have to do yours. You have to give her the trust money. That's the right thing to do."

Rebecca smirked and replied, "In your dreams! She might love him and committed to him but he definitely doesn't love her. We'll have a meeting with the trustees and they will see what's what."

A few loud expressions of agreement were heard from the others who didn't like to be left behind by the youngest of the bunch.

Becka turned to Rebecca and told her, "I was serious when I said I didn't need your money, so the meeting with the trustees is unnecessary."

"Hmm, you're afraid of what they are going to say, I see. They'll see at once that he doesn't love you and you can't face the truth," Rebecca chuckled, satisfied to have been vindicated.

"No, it's not that. I'm not afraid because I know the truth and I don't need anyone's confirmation. I don't see the point in having Bryan paraded in front of them just to satisfy your sadistic pleasures," she replied.

"Baloney," Alex intervened with sarcasm. "If you don't want to meet with the trustees, it means you know he doesn't love you and you're afraid of what you'll hear."

"All right, everyone calm down," Bryan said with authority, when he saw that Becka was growing angrier.

He thought he had had enough of their drivel that evening and he wanted to end the discussion. "What are they talking about, sweetie?" he asked her.

"Really, it doesn't matter because I won't take her money," she answered with obstinacy.

"You don't need her money, Becka, and if you don't want it, then you won't take it, that's not an issue. But there's more to it than that, Becka. So, what is it?"

Becka looked down and didn't want to answer. She didn't know what to do, as a matter of fact. It wasn't she didn't trust his feelings and she wasn't afraid the two trustees would tell her Bryan didn't love her. However, she didn't know how Bryan would react to that meeting and she preferred not to find out.

"I'll tell him, sweetie," Matt put a soothing hand on Becka's arm. "So you understand better, great-grandma here," he said pointing to Rebecca, "thought it would be funny to get her revenge on her unfaithful husband by putting a curse on the following generations."

Rebecca gasped hearing his disrespectful tone, "I thought you loved me," she accused Matt.

Matt waved her concerns away, "I love you, that's not the issue here. It doesn't mean, though, I'm not upset being your Guinea pig, great-grandma," he told her and then turned to Bryan. "Anyway, Bryan, this is how things are. None of us can refine and control their powers until we fall in love for real and we commit to the person we love. Now, let me explain to you what's with the trust money. We can access the trust money only if the person we love also loves us in return and commits to us. And that's determined by a pair of trustees who are mind readers," Matt finished his explanation.

"Oh, I see," Bryan said nodding. "So, those trustees would be able to say if I love and commit to Becka, as well. That's the bone of contention here." He turned to Becka, "I understand you don't want her money and I agree with you. I don't want it, either. Is this the only reason you don't want to see the trustees, though?" he inquired.

"Well, not really… I don't know how you'd feel to have someone read your mind," she admitted.

"So it's not because you don't trust my love," he specified, staring into her eyes steadily.

"Of course not," she snapped at him.

"All right, then," he concluded and turned to Matt. "This mind reading, are there consequences to that?"

"Consequences?" Matt asked puzzled.

"Yes, you know like you could lose some of your mental capabilities or you might be persuaded to do something you don't want to…," Bryan specified.

"Oh, that," Matt dismissed his concerns, "no, nothing like that, don't worry. The only downside to it is that they can see what you think."

"Well, if they're not concerned I might swear at them, I don't mind," he said turning to Becka. "Sweetie, I know you don't want the money and I strongly advise you not to accept it. I have enough for both of us and we won't starve or have to cut down on too many things. However, if this will bring peace of mind to your parents, I'm willing to do it, all right?"

Everyone stared at him with disbelief. For a few moments, no one was able to do or say anything.

Only Becka hugged him and whispered, "For them, it would be great. But you don't have to do it if you don't want to. I trust you, and that's what is the most important."

"I know, baby," he whispered back. "But if we can make them feel at ease, why not?"

Becka nodded and hugged him with more force. She couldn't believe he would do something like that for her and he loved him more for his thoughtfulness.

"You think you can play them?" Ariel asked with contempt. "Jay tried and it didn't work, so you won't be able to, either," she told him.

Bryan looked at her like she had lost her mind for a moment, but then his eyes simply swept over her as if he had dismissed her, which made her angrier and she left the room furiously.

"Why don't we invite the trustees here, now?" Rebecca asked sweetly. "There's no better time than the present. They're two of my dearest friends and they won't refuse me… I don't want to wait until Monday and hear something happened and you couldn't make it to the meeting," she addressed to Bryan.

"That's just fine with me," he replied to her. "Invite them over. Maybe we can have a drink while we wait," he told Emily. "My throat is a little dry after so much talking."

He was aware he might have come across as being rude, but he did need a glass of something strong. There mightn't have been any kind of witchy things going on but he felt a little tired after all that commotion.

"I'll bring you a scotch," Matt said. "I'll take one for me as well. I do need one after this ruckus," he continued and left for the table where several bottles of alcohol were kept.

Becka took Bryan's hand and pulled him to a love seat. She didn't intend to let anyone come close to him after they'd behaved so horribly with him. They sat down, and Bryan stroked her arm to soothe her.

"It'll be over soon, love, and then we can go home," he said.

"Where's home, Bryan?" she asked him with wide eyes.

He took a moment to think, but there wasn't much to think over. He knew he needed her all the time and even though their relationship was so young, he didn't need time to see where it was going because he didn't intend to let her go.

"It's up to you," he answered. "I know what I want and that's being with you. Now, if you want to wait and see how it'll be, we can wait for a while and see each other every day. If you feel the same, then we can choose to live together, either in your house or in mine. Of course, mine is there on that island and it means we have to sail every day to town if you need to be in town…"

Becka squeezed his hand and replied, "I'd say wherever you want is fine with me, but I'd lie."

Bryan froze hearing her answer. He couldn't believe his ears. His hopes were crushed and his expression steeled once more.

"I knew you wouldn't continue with this charade, Becka," Ariel said with glee.

They had been so focused on each other they hadn't heard her sneaking up on them. Hearing her voice, they looked up at her. Her face shined with delight and she was looking at Bryan with triumph in her eyes.

"What's going on?" Matt asked returning with the drinks.

"Not much," Bryan muttered. "Probably, I'll have to go now," he said and tried to stand up, but Becka pulled him back next to her.

"What are you talking about? Why would you leave?" she asked him and her eyes were stricken with pain.

"You said that…" Bryan started to say and she interrupted him.

"I said I preferred to live in town. You know I don't like waking up early in the morning and coming all the way from your island to town in the morning would be awful. Of course, we can spend our weekends there. It is a wonderful place but I don't see myself living there permanently. That's what I said."

"No, it isn't," Ariel snapped. "You were very clear you didn't want to live with him," she pointed out.

"No, I wasn't. I might not have phrased my thoughts correctly, but what I meant was that I wanted to live in town so you should stop being so delighted," Becka snapped back at her.

Ariel put her hands on her hips and repeated stubbornly, "No, Becka, you said that…"

"Shut up for a second," Bryan barked at her and she stopped, too stunned by his rudeness to say anything anymore. "Now, Becka, let's clarify. Do you want me to live with you in your house?"

"Yes, of course, that's what I want. And you said I could choose," she replied stubbornly.

"Yes, you can choose, that's not the issue here. As long as you don't ask me to leave from your life, I'll agree to everything," he said, taking her hand with tenderness.

The icy block that had begun to form inside him started to melt. He was relieved he hadn't been wrong about her.

Becka hugged him and kissing his lips, she whispered, "Don't be stupid. How can I want you to leave when I can't function without you?"

Happy, Bryan hugged her tight and kissed her hair in relief. He didn't notice Ariel left in a huff and he didn't actually care what she was doing. After holding Becka tightly to him for a while, he let her go with regret and took the glass from Matt's hand.

"You don't know how much I need this now, man," he said to Matt.

"I can imagine," he mused. "You do look like a man in need of something strong, indeed."

Bryan took his glass and swallowed half of the whiskey at once, feeling less tense afterwards. He tapped Matt's shoulder saying, "Thanks, man. Good stuff, by the way."

"Yes, Uncle Gabriel always has good stuff handy. He's the most generous of the uncles," Matt said, elbowing Bryan, "Keep that in mind. If you go visit Uncle Michael, you're out of luck. He doesn't take out the good stuff for guests. It's just for him."

Bryan laughed and felt included in the inside stuff. Matt was indeed the good man Becka had described. Bryan thought Matt would make a good friend besides being one of his few allies in that house.

They chattered for a while, most of the time with Becka next to him, hanging on his arm, but some of the time she took off to talk to her cousins or aunts.

Matt was amused seeing Bryan, who looked quite impressive, as he was so tall and fit, looking around, so lost, trying to find Becka in the sea of people crowding his aunt's living room.

When the two trustees arrived, which didn't surprise anyone, as all of them knew Rebecca's reputation, the chatter stopped and the family's glances shifted between Becka and Bryan to the trustees. All of them were impatient to hear the verdict.

Yet, Bryan started to sweat. A thought had crossed his mind some time earlier and was still nudging at him. He had wondered if the old bitty had the trustees in her pocket because, in that case, they would say what she wanted to hear and he was convinced Becka would believe them. They were witches after all and they could read minds. His word against theirs might mean close to nothing.

Gabriel came with the two trustees to introduce them to Bryan. "This is Mr. Thompson and this is Mr. Jones."

Bryan shook their hands and expected to see what they had to say. Becka had come next to him and slipped her arm around him as if she had wanted to comfort him. He wrapped his arm around her shoulders as well and looked inquiringly at the two old men.

No one was talking anymore. Bryan glanced around and saw expectation on everybody's faces. Only Rebecca didn't show any. Her face was expressionless, even though she was trying to stare him down with her eyes.

Bryan shrugged and turned to the two men to see what they wanted from him. Once his attention was on them again, he felt a light probing in his mind and frowned.

"He can feel it," Mr. Jones whispered to Mr. Thompson. "Did you see?"

"Yes, I see he does," he replied. "Well," he said turning towards Rebecca, "You know I won't lie, Rebecca. I know what you want me to say, but the truth is he does love her and he's committed to this relationship."

Mr. Jones approved as well with a nod and Rebecca frowned. Everyone was waiting to see what she was going to do and they didn't have to wait for too long.

"Very well, Becka and Bryan," she said, "if this is the case, then you have my congratulations. I won't lie and say I like you," she said to Bryan squarely, "however, I'll welcome you to the family for as long as you're faithful to Becka."

Bryan nodded. He understood her feelings even though he didn't agree with her. He imagined it wasn't so easy to accept the fact that a man like him would date a young woman like Becka.

"On Monday morning, come to my office and I will make the transfer of your funds," Mr. Thompson addressed to Becka.

Bryan intervened right away, remembering her stubborn refusal of the money, "Do you want that money, Becka? Because I do have enough for both of us."

Becka took a moment to think. Finally, she shook her head, "No, I don't. I didn't like what happened here tonight because of that fund and I don't want to have anything to do with it."

"Oh, my God, are you stupid?" Ariel shouted. "How can you reject so much money? Didn't you want to open that stupid shop?"

"Calm down," Matt admonished her. "Becka, I understand your feelings in this matter, but the money is yours and you should take it."

Becka shook her head and Bryan gathered her to him.

"If Becka wants a shop, I'll take care of that," he said. "I think we can skip dinner tonight, Becka, what do you say?"

She nodded and said, "Mom, dad, we're leaving now and we'll talk later, all right?"

Emily teared up again when she hugged her daughter. She was happy Becka had found her love, but she was also sad her little daughter wasn't so little anymore. She hugged Bryan as well for good measure and he hugged her back with stoicism, although he wasn't very big on such gestures.

EPILOGUE

Eleven months later

"Gabriel, you have to come now. Now, I said," Bryan yelled into the phone.

"What the hell happened to you that you're in such a state?" Gabriel's voice boomed at the other end of the line.

"She's mad, that's what happened. She's lost her mind," Bryan yelled again.

"What are you talking about? What's going on there?" Gabriel snapped worried for his little daughter.

"She lied to me, you hear me? She lied and now, I don't know what to do," Bryan shouted.

"Okay, calm down, son, and tell me what the problem is. What could she have done to make you lose your calm like this?"

"She's giving birth now!"

"What do you mean *now*?" his father-in-law asked, scared witless.

"She didn't say anything all day and just now she told me she's ready. I asked her to go to the hospital and she said it wasn't time. That she planned it that way. She told me to call Marjorie, but no one's answering the phone at their place and I don't know what to do. I've never assisted in a birth. I haven't even watched a birth in a movie. Damn it! I've always walked away when there was a scene like that. What the hell am I going to do?" he lost his temper completely.

"Okay, okay, let's see. Calm down first! Marjorie is here. We'll come at once. I'll have her call you from the car so she can assist you by phone if… if… You know…" Gabriel ended in a weak voice.

"No, I don't know. I don't want to know. It's Becka we're talking about and I don't know anything."

A few murmurs came to him through the phone line. Gabriel was talking to someone.

"All right, Bryan, Marjorie said to calm down and she'll call you from the car."

"But…"

"No buts, man, just wait," Gabriel replied and hung up, leaving Bryan in silence.

***

"A girl and a boy, Bryan," Marjorie said. "Congrats to both of you. And you've done a good job helping Becka to bring the boy into the world. Have you thought of any names yet?"

Becka nodded exhausted and Bryan stroked her forehead lovingly. He turned to Marjorie and told her with pride, "He's Sean and our daughter is Lea." He looked at his wife again with love and kissed her, "You have to rest, baby."

She nodded and closed her eyes. The little ones were sleeping soundly, as well, but Bryan felt like he had climbed the Everest.

215

MATT'S DILEMMA
BOOK 2

To Simona and Andrei

THE WINSTONS FAMILY

Rebecca's children

Adam (m. Anna)

Evelyne (deceased)

Adam's children

Marjorie (Twin, m. Jonathan) – children: Matt (34), Maggie (28), Jay (28)

Michael (Twin, m. Amelie) – children: Josh (26), Lily (26)

Gabriel (m. Emilie) – children: Ariel (32), Alex (32), Becka (19; m. Bryan; twins: Lea and Sean)

CHAPTER ONE

"Becka, move your butt upstairs, now," Bryan's voice boomed and made Matt smile.

Matt knew Becka's policy of not locking the front door. He also knew Bryan didn't have much success in making her heed his advice.

That was why Matt didn't even bother knocking. He just came inside. After all, he felt there like at home. Becka and Bryan were some of the kindest in the family, although their couple was strange by far.

"I thought you liked my butt," Becka shouted from the study, and then stormed out of the room.

She missed Matt by an inch. She didn't even notice him and started taking the stairs two at a time.

"I love your butt, and you know it. But right now, bring it up here. She levitates, damn it, and she won't listen to me," Bryan's harangued voice came from somewhere above, and Matt burst into laughter.

Matt's imagination wasn't very strong, but at least, he guessed how stressed Bryan felt, having two gifted children.

As an outsider in the Winston family, Bryan had to put up with a lot of things. However, no one could say he shrunk his responsibilities.

Even if he didn't have a clue what to do in some circumstances, he dug his feet in the ground, and took everything in stride. Now, though, he seemed overwhelmed with his one-and-a-half-month daughter, who inherited her mother's family's heritage.

Only whispers came from upstairs, so Matt decided to go there, and visit with his niece and nephew. He knew his apparition would make Bryan roll his eyes. He'd understand Becka had failed to lock the door again, and he'd probably give her hell after Matt left.

He wouldn't say a thing in front of Matt. No matter how upset he was, Bryan never said anything to Becka in front of others. He thought they had judged her enough for marrying a man twelve years older, and she didn't need to hear any '*I told you*'.

Matt knocked on the nursery door, and Bryan looked up, concern edged on his face. When his eyes fell on Matt, his tension eased away, and he smiled, shaking his head.

"You haven't locked the front door again," he said in a resigned voice, glancing at Becka.

"I forgot," she shrugged, and patted his hand. "Don't worry, no one will come in, but Matt. Hi, Matt, what's up?"

Matt couldn't hide his amusement. His younger cousin was always a delight, and he enjoyed seeing Bryan struggle both with his concern for her, and his ineffectiveness in making her understand the dangers of the city.

"Just passing by. I've got an hour to kill and thought of coming and seeing you two. And the munchkins."

Matt came inside and went to Becka, who was holding Lea in her arms. He kissed Becka's cheek, and then, stroked the baby's head and put a kiss on the top of her head.

"She's already causing problems, I hear," he turned to Bryan, who raised an eyebrow inquiringly. "I heard you when I came in," Matt confessed, and a naughty smile appeared on his lips.

Becka blushed. She remembered what Bryan had shouted to make her come upstairs. She speared him with a pointed look, and Bryan just grinned.

Matt chuckled. He loved both of them and his heart burst with joy whenever he thought how good they were together. Yet, he was jealous of them sometimes, because he couldn't have the same thing.

"So, the problems started, I understand," he said, nodding to the little bundle in Becka's arms.

'Yep, and it scares me shitless, to tell you the truth. Thank God, Sean hasn't manifested any kind of powers yet," Bryan replied.

"He will… In time," Matt told him, putting a reassuring hand on his shoulder. "You'll manage, don't worry. You've never struck me as a man who can't handle everything."

Bryan scowled, but didn't reply. He glanced at Becka, ready to say something, but she shushed him, putting her finger to her mouth.

"She's asleep again," she whispered, and Bryan came to her to take his daughter and replace her in her crib.

Becka and Matt started to the door, expecting Bryan to follow. When Matt looked back, Bryan was still watching his daughter sleep, and his expression was priceless.

Matt had liked Bryan since the moment they met. Yet, once he got to know him, his respect and feelings for the man evolved.

Bryan was a devoted husband and father, and it crushed Matt to see that hulk of a man so deeply in love with his family.

Matt went downstairs after Becka and found her in her study. She was typing something at her computer, checking a pile of papers at her elbow.

"What are you doing?" he asked her.

"I have to finish an essay. Just two more lines, and I'm done," she replied, but didn't look at him.

Matt leaned on the doorjamb, crossing his ankles, and kept silent so she could finish her work. A minute later, Bryan came downstairs, as well, and waved Matt to come to the kitchen with him.

Even before stepping into the kitchen, the aroma of a beef stew reached his nostrils, and he inhaled with pleasure. His stomach growled and Bryan, who was close to him, chuckled.

"Ready for lunch?" he teased Matt.

"I suppose you cooked," Matt inquired in a dry voice.

"You suppose well," Bryan replied. "I wouldn't let Becka into the kitchen. She's a walking disaster," he shrugged, and, going to the stove, picked up a wooden spoon to stir the stew.

"Am I?" Becka bristled from behind Matt, and Bryan winced.

"Come on, sweetie, you know you can't boil an egg," Bryan replied, yet, there was no reproach in his voice. "And we're fine, aren't we? It's no need for you to cook when I can do it very well," he added.

He came to her, took her head in the cradle of his palms, and kissed her lips tenderly. Matt turned to look out of the window. The tender display touched a yarning in his heart, he thought he'd squashed long ago.

"Hungry everyone?" Bryan asked, turning off the stove and taking bowls out of a cupboard.

"I'll set the table," Becka intervened.

"What's there to set, baby?" Bryan wondered. "Just take a seat and I'll bring everything to the table."

"But I want to help," Becka retorted with annoyance.

Matt knew she didn't want him to think she wasn't doing anything around, but he knew better. Bryan didn't allow her to do much.

"You've had enough to do today, Becka," Bryan stroked the side of her face and kissed the tip of her nose. "You had to go to school – and forgot to lock the door, in the process," he thought to add, "and you worked on your paper for the last couple of hours…"

"Yes, and you cooked, cleaned and took care of the babies," she replied. "And in a couple of hours, you'll have to go to the dojo for your afternoon and evening classes, so…"

"I can do it, don't worry," Bryan waved her concern away, at the same time, leading her to the table and helping her to sit. "You're a new mom, and must rest as much as possible," he pointed out.

"I was a new mom a month and a half ago, Bryan. I'm perfectly fine now," she replied stubbornly.

"And that's how you have to remain," he pushed on her shoulder when she tried to stand up. "Come on, Becka, just sit. I can carry three bowls to the table myself," he said in a frustrated tone.

Becka just shrugged, but didn't try to stand up again. Matt, who always enjoyed their sparring immensely, watched her. She was biting her lower lip, annoyed with something.

"What's the problem, pumpkin?" he asked quietly.

"He won't let me do anything," she snapped. "As if I'm fragile."

"I never said you're fragile," Bryan's voice came from a few feet away.

Becka and Matt turned to him, and Matt immediately stood up to help Bryan to put the heavy tray on the table. He'd filled three bowls to the rim and sliced warm homemade bread.

"I can tell you, you cook as well as my mom," Matt sniffed the stew, and grumbled in satisfaction.

Becka smiled, proud of Bryan. Aunt Marjorie was the best cook she'd ever met, and Matt's praise meant something.

She dipped her spoon in the stew, and fidgeted a little in her seat, before carrying to her mouth.

"Out with it," Bryan said. "Something's bothering you," he asked, looking at her sideways.

Matt knew Becka couldn't even sneeze without Bryan getting concerned.

"Well, if you want to know," she started saying hesitantly, "I don't think it is right for you to do everything. It's already been a month and a half since I gave birth, so I am perfectly able to…"

Bryan stopped her, touching her hand.

"Don't worry about, Becka. You do more than enough. You have to wake up at night and breastfeed, and…"

"Huh!" she snorted inelegantly, and Matt had to hide his smile.

"Huh?" Bryan asked. "What does that mean?"

"Whenever I wake up, you wake up too, so don't try to sell me on that stuff," Becka shrugged.

"I might wake up, but I don't breastfeed," he retorted, miffed.

Matt couldn't hold it anymore and burst into laughter.

"You two are comical. The first couple I've seen quarrelling because the other is doing more," he shook his head.

"You eat and shut up," Becka snapped at him. "I'm serious, here. Yes, I breastfeed, and yes, I go to school. That's the sum of my accomplishments," she sulked.

"I wouldn't say that," Bryan murmured. "You keep me happy, Becka," he said, taking her hand, and squeezing it with tenderness. "And don't worry so much. Your mom will send Rosa's daughter here tomorrow. She'll clean and do the laundry, so I won't have much to do."

"Finally," Becka said relieved. "At least, you won't do those anymore."

Matt grinned. He knew Becka wouldn't accept Bryan's hard work for long. Now, at least, she knew there was someone else to take up the brunt of the housework, because Bryan would have never accepted her help.

It wasn't easy to hire help in their houses though. They needed to keep the family's secret and they couldn't hire just anyone.

Luckily, their hired help worked for them generation after generation. Rosa was Becka's parents' housekeeper and Uncle Michael's housekeeper's daughter.

"So, she'll start tomorrow?" Becka asked.

Bryan just nodded and spooned more stew. Matt knew he must have been exhausted. He'd started doing everything long before the birth of his children, and also kept his training schedule.

They savored the beef stew in silence for a few minutes, and then Becka looked at him inquiringly.

"What?" he asked.

"I was wondering if you had any news," she shrugged, and took another slice of bread.

"What kind of news are you expecting?" Matt asked and following her example, helped himself to another slice of bread.

Bryan did know what to do in the kitchen. He imagined Bryan knew what to do in almost every situation. His cousin by marriage was one of the most resourceful and talented men in the family.

"You know, Matt," Becka insisted. "It's May 19th already."

"And?" Matt asked with dismay.

He knew where the conversation was going and didn't like it. Only Bryan looked from one to the other with curiosity.

"In July, it's your birthday," Becka doggedly continued. "On 27th," she thought to specify.

"So?" Matt asked, feigning disinterest. "Are you planning a party for me or what?"

"Don't try to play games with me, Matt Winston," Becka snapped, and her small fist hit the table. Bryan's eyebrows shot up. "You know very well what I'm talking about."

Matt shook his head, scooped more stew and chewed.

"Not really," he replied. "I was thinking of taking a cruise or something, that's true. I haven't made my mind yet, though," he shrugged.

Becka stared at him with disbelief. Then, she took a breath, ready to launch herself in a lecture. Bryan touched her arm and calmed her.

"Matt," he said. "I see there's something the matter here and I really don't want Becka riled up. So what is it?"

"Why don't you ask her?" Matt asked stubbornly. "I don't know what she wants from me," he answered with indifference, and continued eating.

He didn't really regret coming to their house. He liked watching them interact and loved the little ones. Moreover, he always ate well in Bryan's kitchen.

"Okay, sweetheart, what is it?" Bryan asked her. He understood Matt wouldn't give in.

"He'll be thirty-five on July 27th," Becka pointed out.

"And?" Bryan insisted. He knew there must have been much more than Matt's birthday.

"He'll lose everything then."

"What will he lose?" Bryan asked again, feeling like he was pulling teeth.

"His powers, his trust fund…"

"Oh, I see, now. So that thing has a deadline," Bryan nodded when the truth dawned on him.

He turned to Matt and expected he'd say something. Yet, Matt just continued eating. He wasn't interested in expanding on that story.

"Come on, Matt," Becka said. "You still have a little over a month and a half."

That made him freeze with the spoon half way to the mouth. His stunned eyes locked on Becka. After a few seconds of deafening silence, he put the spoon back in his bowl and asked, "Are you for real?"

"Now, what?" she asked, throwing her hands in the air.

Bryan mused. Becka had a real talent for drama sometimes.

Matt pushed the bowl away with regret. He did want to eat that stew. A frown appeared between his eyebrows and he stared Becka down.

"I couldn't find a woman to love until now and you seriously think I could find one in a month and a half," he noticed. "Bryan, your wife has lost her mind. I'm really sorry for you," he said, turning to Bryan.

"Nah," Bryan replied. "Becka's smart and you should listen to her. It doesn't always take years to fall in love. It took me a day and a half, maybe less. And you still have over forty-five days, I think," Bryan shook his head, chastising him.

"Okay, I see it now. You're nauseatingly happy, both of you, and see everything through pink glasses," Matt concluded, and started to stand up.

"Maybe yes and maybe no," Bryan replied. "That doesn't mean you can't finish your stew. Both Becka and I," he said, with a meaningful look at Becka, "will refrain from talking about this matter anymore. Right, sweetie?" he asked her and reluctantly, she nodded.

Undecided, Matt looked from one at the other, and, in the end, his hunger won. He sat back on his chair and pulled the bowl back in front of him.

"So, how's your schedule these days?" Bryan asked. "You said you'd like to come by my dojo for some training," he observed.

"Not today, though," Matt said with regret. "I have a late meeting. An ugly divorce case," he specified. "Are you there tomorrow? In the morning, for instance? I have a couple of free hours then."

"Yes, I am. It's Becka's day off school and she'll be staying with the brats. See, sweetie, you do things, so don't complain anymore," he turned to her.

CHAPTER TWO

Tension filled the conference room, yet Matt didn't appear affected. He leaned back in his chair, his ankle over his knee, his papers forgotten on the table.

He never needed to refresh his memory. Files played the role of props for him. He used them to intimidate. He never checked them, either in a conference room or in court.

The man next to him, his client, Paul Willow, was a sleek man in his thirties. He didn't like him, but his partner, Joshua, had accepted his case and, with Joshua suddenly married and in an extended honeymoon, the case had fallen in Matt's hands.

Something didn't seem quite right with that Paul Willow, but his divorce case didn't present any difficulty for Matt. The facts didn't leave any loophole for the opposing council.

"So, let's recap here," he addressed to the opposing lawyer, Fred Rhoades. "Mrs. Willow signed a prenup before marriage. It is a straightforward document. We all agree with that. If she cheated, she'd get nothing. We have four men willing to testify that they slept with her on several occasions. They might not be outstanding citizens, but their bad reputations will make our case stronger. Plus, Mr. Willow is willing to pay for a DNA test to prove Mrs. Willow's son is not his," he said very matter-of-factly, and stopped to gauge their expressions.

The lawyer seemed annoyed and started cleaning his glasses. Her client, Nora Willow, soon to be Nora Barnes, had paled and the shadows under her eyes swallowed almost half her face.

Matt didn't feel any kind of pity for her. He couldn't stand cheaters and gold diggers, and, according to the file he had on the table, that woman was both.

Interesting though, although she'd paled and her fingers were shaking, she didn't flinch under his stern eyes. She returned his look squarely, as if she hadn't felt any remorse or shame.

"Now, we can go to court. We can't lose. Everything is cut and dry. Of course, by the end of the proceedings, we'll have your reputation in shreds, Mrs. Willow, and your son will find out the truth about his mother," he told her directly, his scorn obvious, both in his voice and eyes. "Or we can settle now," he turned to the other lawyer. "She gets nothing, as the prenup says. My client will not pay any alimony to his ex-wife and her child. But the child won't find what kind of woman you are," he concluded, his eyes returning to her. "So, what would it be?"

Matt's voice didn't raise, not even a notch, as if he'd just read dull instructions. He finished presenting the alternatives and waited patiently for their decision.

Rhoades tried to whisper something to his client, but the woman put up her hand and quieted him.

"I'll sign the agreement," she told Matt in a very calm voice.

Matt had never seen such a composed woman in a divorce case as the woman before him. She didn't react verbally to anything. She didn't attack or tried to push the guilt on her ex-husband's shoulders. The only sign she felt something was that tremor of her fingers.

"It's not like I'd have wanted a cent of his money anyway," she continued. "And it is true, his contribution to the house was much higher than mine, so, of course, I couldn't have asked for the house. I should ask for the money I invested in the house," she pointed out, and Matt became more focused on her.

No way she'd give up that money, if she knew she was entitled to it. His eyes narrowed, and he tried to use his mental abilities to read her, but he didn't succeed, and that puzzled him. His mental powers hadn't completely developed, but he still could read something here and there.

"What I want, though, and this is *not* negotiable," she warned in a steely voice, "is that he signs a document giving up any kind of parental rights. He stated my son isn't his. He must sign the papers," she concluded, and the inflexions of her voice warned Matt, she wouldn't budge on that score.

Matt lifted his left eyebrow, pensively. The woman had a lot of guts for a woman painted as a slut. She kept surprising him, and he didn't like it.

He turned slightly to his client with an inquiring look. The man just shrugged.

"I don't care about parenting the brat. You can prepare the documents, can't you?" he asked Matt.

Matt nodded briefly and stood up.

"I'll be back in a couple of minutes. May I hope you won't start fighting while I'm gone?" he asked.

The woman's behavior wasn't natural. She didn't reproach, accused or pleaded. He feared she'd explode while he was away.

Nora just nodded, and, completely disinterested in her future ex-husband or the lawyer next to her, she picked up her cell phone and started checking messages or emails. Matt shook his head imperceptibly. That woman befuddled him.

Then, he left the room to ask his paralegal to prepare the documents and bring them in the conference room.

He didn't dare to stay away for long. His instincts told him something was very wrong, and he wanted to avoid any kind of ugly events.

He returned to the conference room and silence greeted him. Only his client was drumming his fingers on the tabletop. Fred Rhoades was checking an agenda, and Nora was standing near the window, admiring the square at the back of the building.

She turned her head when he returned, but when he told them the documents would be ready soon, she preferred to remain near the window.

The following fifteen minutes felt like hours. Matt tried to make small talk with his fellow lawyer, but Rhoades's monosyllabic answers annoyed him.

His client started texting back and forth with someone, and seemed to have the time of his life. His soon to be ex-wife, didn't leave the window until his paralegal had come with the papers.

Then, she approached the table, took her reading glasses out of her handbag, and, after reading the documents carefully, dignified, she signed them.

When she finished, she collected her things silently, ready to leave.

"Mrs. Willow," Matt stopped her, but when he saw the mocking glitter in her eyes, he corrected himself, "I apologize, I wanted to say Ms. Barnes. My paralegal brought these papers for you. You have info about how to change your name and everything. As Mr. Willow renounced his parental rights, you can also change your son's name, if you want to," he specified.

"Do I have to?" she asked, and, for the first time, she sounded fearful.

"No, you don't have to," Matt answered softly.

"Thank you," Nora said and stretched her hand to him.

Matt shook her hand briefly. Her skin was freezing cold, but that didn't bother him. The brief electrical shock did. His eyes were focused on her face, and the surprise in her eyes told him she felt it as well.

Matt stepped back, bowed his head, and started gathering the files. The door clicked behind her, but he didn't even turn.

CHAPTER THREE

When his phone rang, he stopped under the overhang of the newsstand shop, a newspaper under his arm, and his umbrella in his left hand.

The weather channel had announced frequent rain showers and thunderstorms for that day, and he'd left the house prepared. They hadn't been wrong. It poured, and lightning lit the sky, covered with heavy clouds.

Matt took his cell phone out of his pocket and checked the screen. He frowned. Becka rarely called him so early in the morning, and he feared the worst. He'd seen her two days before and everything seemed fine.

"Hey, pumpkin, everything okay?" Matt asked Becka.

"I need your help," she said breathlessly, as if she'd run for her life.

"What happened?" Matt inquired, his heart beating frantically, and his fingers clenched on the umbrella handle.

The panic in his voice must have reached Becka's ears, because she hurried to say, "Oh, no, Matt, nothing happened. I've just run to take cover. It's pouring, you know. And I can't call you from home. I need your help to buy a gift for Bryan. Of course, I couldn't call when he could hear me," she chastised him.

Matt breathed relieved. He hadn't realized he was holding his breath.

"Thank God, Becka. You scared me," he confessed. "When do you want to buy that gift?"

"Are you free now? I'm in town, not far from your office," she replied.

"I'm not in the office. You know the shops across from my office? I'm there. I came to buy a newspaper and I was thinking to go for a coffee or something."

"Oh, Matt, it's perfect. Can you make it to the mall? I'm already there. Most of the shops will open in half an hour. We can have a snack together before that," Becka said with enthusiasm.

"Won't Bryan get upset if you eat now, and then, skip the lunch he cooked?" Matt asked her maliciously, his eyes wandering along the road.

"Nope. He'll cook dinner today, but not lunch. I'm supposed to have lunch at U of T, and he will be at his dojo. Mom came in the morning to spend time with the babies, until I get back at three," Becka explained.

"Okay, Becka, we have a deal. See you at Timmies, in about fifteen minutes, all right?" Matt gave in.

"Great, Matty. I knew you'd help me," she replied enthusiastically and disconnected the call.

Matt sighed and resigned to walk through the rain to the mall. He opened his umbrella, and started down the street, whistling a merry tune. At the traffic lights, he crossed to the other side of the road, so he could head right to the mall.

Few people passed by. Most people had found cover somewhere, so he could move at ease. Most of the time, that part of town was crowded.

Suddenly, the wind intensified and almost blew his umbrella away. He grabbed the handle better, and angled the umbrella against the rain pour, which came sideways now.

He pushed ahead mulishly, his head down, and mumbled to himself. Becka had chosen the wrong day to go shopping.

He heard an anguished cry and looked up. A few meters away, a woman with a toddler in her arms, was fighting the wind. Her umbrella had broken, and her bags had fallen to the ground. She shielded the child as much as she could, and now was trying to collect her things.

Matt rushed up and picked her bags fast. He started to hand them to her, and only then, he saw her face and practically froze.

Nora Barnes looked at him warily. The rain plastered her long red hair to her face, neck and shoulders. Her wet summer dress left little to imagination. It showed every single curve of her body and outlined her underwear. Her arms full of a fidgeting toddler, Nora tried to balance everything in the other hand.

"So, we meet again, Ms. Barnes," Matt drawled.

"Yes, it seems so," she replied in an indifferent voice, yet her eyes betrayed her nervousness.

She tried to take the bags from his hand, but he pulled them to him. She frowned. Her lips parted, and her entire face showed she was puzzled. His actions didn't make sense.

"What are you doing out with your child in this rain?" Matt inquired, his voice far from friendly. "This isn't the responsible action of a parent," he observed.

He closed the distance between them, so he could hold the umbrella above the toddler's head. Grudgingly, he protected her as well.

"Well, parents can't dictate the weather, Mr. Winston," she replied sarcastically. "And parents do need to go to work and leave children at a daycare, when there's no one to watch for them at home."

"Huh! I wouldn't have thought you'd get a job so soon," Matt said maliciously.

He didn't think that type of woman would look for work. Generally, someone like her would immediately look for another sucker to pay her bills.

"Not that's your business, but I've had this job for over seven years," Nora replied, peevishly.

She'd have preferred to keep her mouth shut and let him think whatever he wanted. Yet, she was afraid he'd consider she wasn't a good mother, and he had the means and power to make her lose her child.

Matt scowled. No way she'd had a job for the last seven years.

"I'm not one of your swains, Ms. Barnes, and I don't believe everything I'm told."

She just shrugged, and said, "That's your prerogative. I do apologize, Mr. Winston, but I do have to get Nathan to daycare. I have several things to do before my shift today, and I really cannot spend the entire day here in the street with you."

Long eyelashes shadowed her green eyes, and the raindrops hanging on them distracted him. The green of the pupils reminded him of the lush meadows he'd seen in Scotland a few years before.

"Mr. Winston," she repeated more forcefully, "We do have to go."

"Hmm, I apologize. I spaced there for a few seconds," he replied. "Where are you headed?"

"Just told you, daycare," she said through tight teeth.

Nora didn't understand what was going on with him, but she didn't have the time to ponder upon his bizarre reactions. She had too many things to do that day. She'd just cleared the appointment she had with Nathan's doctor.

"I got that," he snapped. "But where? What direction?"

"None of your business," she replied.

"I'm afraid it's my business, Ms. Barnes," he answered sternly, and his unnerving eyes disconcerted her.

Afraid, she pointed toward the entrance of the mall.

"We need to take the train."

"Good, I'll take you there," he said.

Without relinquishing her bags, he slid an arm around the two of them, and gathered them under his umbrella, to herd them to the entrance of the mall. A slight tremor crossed her body, and vibrated in his hand, which was also holding the umbrella over them.

Nora didn't protest, although she was very angry. She was angry because of the rain and because of him. She was angry because she was stupidly afraid he'd do something to take her son away.

"Why are you doing this?" she asked, frustrated.

"Because I can," he answered calmly, and when she stopped in her tracks shocked by his nonchalant answer, he just nudged her ahead.

***

When he arrived at Timmy's, Becka was seated at a table in the corner. She already had two cups of coffee on the table, and two breakfast sandwiches, so he didn't stop at the counter. The young woman seemed lost in her thoughts and didn't even notice his arrival.

"Hey, there, pumpkin. Why the long face?"

"What long face?" she smiled at him, standing up and giving him a warm hug. "I've got no reason for a long face. Just thinking," she assured him.

They attacked their sandwiches, and after the first bite, Becka started grilling him.

"Why did it take you so long to get here?"

He shrugged, "I met someone I knew, and we exchanged a few words, that's all."

"How come you're not wet?" Becka wondered, checking him out. "You don't have an umbrella. I got wet even with the umbrella," she observed, showing him the wet patches on her shirt.

"I had an umbrella, but I gave it to that someone," he waved her question away, as if not very important.

He'd foisted that umbrella on Nora. They'd fought back and forth for a few minutes for that darn umbrella, he remembered.

For such a small woman, she was very stubborn. In a way, she reminded him of Becka, but Becka had a sweetness, which Nora lacked.

Matt didn't know if it was the difference in their age, but the woman seemed hardened somehow. Becka would never be that way. With Bryan on her side, Becka would always keep her serenity and a certain innocence.

Becka sipped her coffee, her eyes on Matt, pensively. His dark hair, the shadow of his beard and his dark-blue eyes, as well as his impressive built, made him a favorite with the ladies. Yet, lately, he didn't even date. She had an idea why, but she hoped she was wrong. She didn't understand why Matt would sabotage himself.

"Are you all right, Matt?" she asked, touching his hand with hers.

"Yeah, why?" he looked up at her. For a moment there, he'd got lost in his thoughts.

"I don't know. It's something about you, you know. And you haven't even shaved…"

"Ah, that," he smiled, mischievously. "I don't have to meet clients today, pumpkin. So, I indulged. Don't read more into it than it is," he reassured her, patting her hand.

He finished his sandwich, drank his coffee almost in one go, and then asked her, "So, what about that present for Bryan? What's the occasion?"

"Ah, that," Becka said, starting to gather the wrappers. "On 23rd, it's Bryan's anniversary. I wanted to have a party for him, but he said no. I asked if I could invite at least a few of the cousins, and he said, sure, if I wanted the company, but not for his birthday. He doesn't seem comfortable with that. I think no one has ever celebrated his birthday, you know?" Becka said ruefully.

"Then, you could celebrate it with him. Just the two of you. A romantic evening, something to drink – oh, sorry, you can't drink, I forgot," he smiled at her remorsefully.

"I know, but I could just sip one drop of champagne, I think. Just to toast for him," she said, in an insecure voice.

"Yes, you could do that. It won't harm your babies or you, I am sure."

"And I want to buy a present for him. I was thinking of something practical, something he'd use, and something whimsical, just for the fun of it. But I don't want to buy a shirt or a tie," she shuddered. "Oh, gosh, imagine Bryan with a tie!"

Matt chuckled, although Becka was right. Bryan didn't wear a tie. Ever. He'd wanted to wear one for their wedding, but Becka had refused to have him uncomfortable that day. He was probably one of the few grooms who didn't wear a formal attire at a big wedding.

Matt thought a little, and then said, "I know what you could do for him. You could organize a small gym in the basement. In that room, next to the laundry. You can put a boxing bag, a treadmill, and a home gym – I saw one. It offers the possibility of thirty exercises. He'd be set for the days when he can't go to the dojo."

"You're a genius, Matty," Becka jumped off her chair and smacked a kiss on his cheek. "I was thinking on the same lines, but didn't know exactly what to do. You know I don't really have any experience with that," she admitted.

"Yep, I know," Matt grinned.

He remembered one of Becka's visits in his house, a couple of years ago. She wanted to try the treadmill. She simply fell and was almost thrown away. He had a hard time to explain her bruises to his uncle. For over half a year, he was forbidden to come to their house.

"I know where we should go to buy everything you'd need. Now, the problem is how we set everything up, without Bryan's knowledge, of course," Matt said.

"Well, if we hurry," Becka said, checking her watch, "we'd have about five hours per total. That means to do the shopping and arrange the gym. Would it be possible?" she asked, her wide, imploring eyes fixed on him.

"Yes, of course, we can do it. If we don't waste time looking for that whimsical thing you want to buy," he specified, standing up.

Becka waved her hand and then, she snatched the tray before Matt could take it.

"I'll take care of this, Matt. And no, I won't buy the whimsical thing today. I don't need advice for that, "she explained.

"Then, we can do it," he concluded and after she took care of the tray and wrappings, he took her hand to lead her to the shop he had in mind.

CHAPTER FOUR

When the alarm rang off, Matt woke up mumbling, then growled and stopped it with a violent slap. He sat up and rubbed his face, trying to dislodge the sand scratching his eyeballs. He ruffled his hair, running his fingers through it.

He glanced at the clock and scowled. He'd slept only three hours and the lack of sleep had left his brain in a dense fog.

He got out of bed and went to the bathroom, wondering where the days, when he didn't need more than an hour or two of sleep, had gone.

He leaned on the wash bowl and dared to glance at his reflection in the mirror. He regretted it at once. *Oh, man.* He almost didn't recognize the man staring back at him.

When, the heck, have I grown so old? Lines marred his forehead and black shadows outlined his eyes. His one-day stubble hid the civilized man, he liked to show to the world.

He shook his head in puzzlement. Not even six years ago, he could party all night, and then, go to the court the following day, his mind clear and focused on the case. Of course, he hadn't partied so hard ever since.

Pondering that mystery, he turned on the faucet, and picked up his toothbrush. Brushing his teeth, he thought he was fortunate enough that day. At least, he didn't have a court day that morning, and, if he remembered correctly – which could have been questionable, considering the blur in his mind, he didn't have any pressing appointments.

His eyes narrowed to slits. *Why, the heck, did I wake up? I could have slept a couple of hours more.*

Yesterday, Bryan had been so happy with Becka's present that he'd caved in, and accepted her party proposition. They hadn't invited many people, just Jay and Matt, and a couple of Bryan's friends.

Yet, they'd partied until four in the morning, and Matt got home and in bed only after four thirty, which accounted for his bloodshot eyes and the dryness of his mouth. The mirror didn't flatter him that morning, and his thirty-something body protested vocally to the lack of rest.

Matt remembered he used to feel that way only when he had a hangover. Yet, he knew he hadn't drunk anything else but a couple of beers and a glass of champagne the night before. He could drink a bit more without getting wasted.

Brushing his teeth refreshed his mood enough, so, he took a long shower, which made him feel almost whole again. He considered shaving, but pushed the thought to the back of his mind with disgust.

He didn't have anyone to impress, and didn't enjoy the thought of wasting ten minutes just for that. He could do with that beard for another day. *I heard beards are trendy again, so...*

His stomach protested and Matt opened the fridge, thinking he could use a sandwich or something. His eyes laid on a lonely tomato, forgotten on a shelf. *Worse than Sahara around here*, he scowled and slammed the door.

He didn't remember when he'd gone grocery shopping the last time. A quick search through the cupboards depressed him and made him grab his car keys, determined to head for the first Timmy he could find.

***

He'd been in the line for over fifteen minutes. The line moved slowly on, and the increased need for caffeine put a metallic shine in his eyes. With narrowed eyes, he willed the cashier to move faster.

Matt understood the guy was in training and had his own limitations, but he didn't understand the logic of using a trainee at peak hours.

What smart ass thought it would be good for business? A location to avoid in the future, he thought. He could find a Timmy not far from his office.

Everyone was irate. People were in a rush to get to work and lots of unpleasant comments flew around. The dissatisfaction escalated more and more, yet it didn't bother any of the employees milling around, without a specific purpose.

Matt's tiredness and hunger made him less charitable toward the young man, who moved with the lightning speed of a turtle. He still had two more customers before him, and started to jingle his car keys, impatiently.

After five more agonizing minutes, and a string of sweet words, addressed to the young employee mentally, Matt finally put his order in and got his coffee.

He moved to the side to wait for his sandwich, and relished the thought of tasting the black coffee, he'd waited for so long.

Matt had barely sipped from his coffee cup that the cell phone vibrated in his pocket. *What now?* he mumbled. They could have waited for him to enjoy that coffee first.

Resigned, he took the phone out of his pocket and checked the screen: St. Michael's Hospital. He frowned at first, and then, the implications hit him square in the chest. Someone close was hurt. He forgot about the coffee instantly.

"Hello, Matthew Winston speaking," his grave voice announced.

"Mr. Winston, I'm officer James Preston. Do you know a Nora Barnes, sir?"

Matt clenched his fingers on the phone. Yes, he knew Nora Barnes, but he didn't understand why the police would call him.

"Sir?" the officer's voice sounded inquiringly on the line.

"Yes, I know a Nora Barnes," Matt found his voice. "Why?" he asked.

"Would you be able to come to St. Michael's?" the officer avoided giving him a direct answer. "I'd be at the emergency room entrance," he specified.

Matt disliked the officer's underhanded manner, but couldn't refuse to go there. He had a bad feeling about the reason for that call.

"I should be there in maximum ten minutes," he confirmed and disconnected the call.

Matt was about to leave, forgetting about his sandwich, when his number got called. He shrugged, took his sandwich and coffee and left the coffee shop.

He hesitated in front of the shop for a moment, pondering the wisdom of taking his car from the parking lot. Then, he thought better.

I doubt there's any parking space there. Better I leave it here, he thought and went to add some more money for the parking.

***

Matt entered the hospital full of apprehension. He abhorred hospitals and made a habit not to visit any, if none of his family members was in there. Then, he didn't have a choice.

Officer Preston, a solid forty-something man, was waiting near the entrance, talking to the security guard. He'd probably made a joke because the guard was laughing loudly, with no respect for the sick people, waiting not even a few feet away from them.

"I'm Matthew Winston," he said, closing the space between him and the two men. "You called me," he said to the police officer, who was watching him as if he'd been an exotic exhibit. *It's probably the beard,* Matt thought.

"Oh, yes, Mr. Winston," the officer greeted him. "Let's go to that corner and talk without interference," he proposed pointing to one side of the waiting room.

Matt gritted his teeth. He wanted to hear why he was called and didn't give a fig if anyone had heard them.

"I understand you know Ms. Barnes," the officer stated.

"Yes, I do. I've already said so," Matt replied, his fingers clenching into fists.

He'd worked with police before, but that specific officer didn't have any consideration about wasting his time.

"You know she's a paramedic," the officer assumed, and Matt nodded.

He didn't know anything of the kind, of course. He hadn't been interested enough to check her background, but he wanted the officer to continue, and didn't think his denial would help.

"We were called to a scene this morning. The person who called said they needed the police, but also an ambulance, because people were hurt," the officer explained and rubbed his moustache. "Ms. Barnes and her colleague got there a few minutes before the police cars. The shooter hadn't left the scene yet, you see," the man continued, "and both of them were shot."

Matt's blood ran cold and he put his hands in his pockets. They were shaking, and he clenched his fists to control the tremor. His dark-blue eyes had turned metallic.

"Now," the officer continued, "Jack Nolan, Ms. Barnes's partner, wasn't hurt very bad. The bullet missed the artery. He was still conscious when we got to the scene, and was trying to get to Ms. Barnes. She wasn't so lucky," the police officer said flatly. "Two bullets in her chest, one in her left leg and one in her left arm. The shooter was furious because of a woman. That one had run away, so he took his anger out on Ms. Barnes," Preston said without inflexion.

Matt swallowed hard and brushed his forehead with unsteady fingers. He might not have liked Nora Barnes much, but only two days before, he'd seen her and she was fine. He couldn't imagine that young and composed woman, lying on a slab in the morgue.

"Has she died?" he managed to ask, through tightened teeth.

"No, don't worry yet. She's still alive. In surgery, but alive. They reserved the prognosis yet, but… Anyway, we spoke to Jake Nolan. And he mentioned two things. First, Ms. Barnes has a son," the officer said, counting on fingers.

"Yes, Nathan. He's about three," Matt replied in a hoarse voice, massaging the base of his nose.

"Yes, that's what Nolan said," Preston nodded in agreement. "Now, it seems Ms. Barnes is a valuable employee and has some leeway. She works some modified shifts, something like that. She'd arranged with her manager to leave at eight-thirty and take the kid to the daycare. She has a neighbour she pays to stay with the kid after she leaves at five thirty, but that woman must leave for work at nine fifteen or something like that," he said and looked at Matt meaningfully.

"I see," Matt replied, because the police officer seemed to expect an answer.

"Nolan says she has no one to help her out. In the past, she told him she must make it home in time because the neighbour was very clear she wouldn't wait. Nolan also says Ms. Barnes is adamant not to have the kid taken by social services, you see," Preston confided.

"Yes, I see," he replied dutifully, wondering where the man was going with all that prattle.

"We talked to Nolan, who, by the way, is with my partner right now," he thought to specify, and Matt just stared at him.

Why, the heck, would he think I'd be interested who's with Nolan? I don't even know that Nolan. Maybe one of Nora's conquests, he reflected with malice. He felt raw and mean, at the same time.

"Nolan implored us not to let the child go to social services, and the doctor said, if Ms. Barnes survived, it would be good if she didn't stress out, and this thing with the child would stress her, guaranteed," the officer nodded.

Matt kept staring at him. He didn't understand what the man wanted from him.

"So?" he asked, a migraine drumming in his temples.

"Nolan didn't know anyone close to Ms. Barnes. I understand her parents died. She's completely estranged from her ex-husband, who considered the child wasn't his, and didn't want to have anything to do with him."

"Yeah, so?" Matt asked more forcefully, his patience already at an end.

"Well, Nolan remembered she mentioned you, Matthew Winston, two days ago. He said she complained of your domineering demeanour and that you made her take your umbrella, and stuff like that. So, he thought you might be her boyfriend," the officer said and Matt's eyes widened in shock.

"We looked through her bag and found some papers with your letterhead and we called your office. They gave us your phone number, you see," the officer explained.

"Yes, I see," Matt said in a tired voice. "So, what do you want me to do?" he asked, in a matter-of-fact voice.

Yet, his heart cringed in his chest, and the air, suddenly, seemed in short supply.

"I knew we could count on you," Preston slapped him on the shoulder, and chuckled.

CHAPTER FIVE

This time, contrary to his custom, Matt didn't burst into Becka and Bryan's house. He didn't even think to check and see whether the door was locked or not. He was still in shock and he couldn't react normally. He pushed the bell, and waited patiently for someone to come and open the door.

His mind was in turmoil, and he couldn't focus on anything specific. His world had turned upside down in a matter of hours, and he could do nothing more but keep a façade of calm. He was far from being calm, though.

Bryan opened the door, a smile on his lips. His smile stopped when his eyes lay on the bundle Matt had in his arms. He could see only a mop of brown-reddish hair, sticking everywhere on the head of a toddler, whose face was hidden in Matt's shirt.

"Hey, there," Bryan greeted them in a soft voice and with a small smile, although he'd already noticed the storm brewing in Matt's eyes. "Would you like to come in?" he asked when Matt didn't answer.

Matt, unable to speak yet, nodded curtly and passed by Bryan into the house. Bryan shook his head, and then, closed the door behind him.

"Let's go out on the patio. We've decided on a brunch today," Bryan explained to him, just to fill in the silence. "Becka has no school and I took the morning and half of afternoon off," he continued.

Matt didn't seem to hear a word.

Bryan was aware of Matt's strange disposition, and he didn't want to push him. He'd always known Matt was very deep and his calm was a mere fabrication. He'd always believed Matt would explode one day, and he'd proposed himself to be far away when that would happen.

"Look who came to visit, Becka," Bryan told his wife in a cheerful voice, stopping next to Matt.

The toddler still held on Matt's neck and didn't dare to look around. Bryan saw the stuffed leg of a plush toy coming from between the child's body and Matt.

"Hi, Matt," Becka said softly, standing up and coming to him.

She touched his cheek, looked straight into his eyes and shook her head.

"Why don't you two take a seat?" she invited them. "And maybe you can introduce us to your little friend."

Matt nodded and sat down, the child always hanging on him. With a few whispers, he convinced the boy to sit in his lap and face his cousins.

"This is Nathan, Nat for short," Matt told them. "Nat, these are my cousins, Becka and Bryan. They're fine, don't worry," he said, stroking the toddler's head.

"Would you like a cookie?" Becka asked Nat. "Bryan bakes the best cookies in the land," she continued cheerfully, and made the child smile shyly.

When she presented a plate with cookies to him, Nat chose carefully, and started nibbling on the chocolate cookie immediately.

"You'd like some milk, too," Bryan guessed, and poured milk in a cup, which he handed to Matt.

Matt took the cup, but froze for a moment. Bryan held his look, and gradually, he got to something close to his normal self, and helped Nat to drink some milk. When the boy pushed the cup away, Matt chuckled – a white mustache rimmed the child's upper lip.

"How old are you?" Becka asked Nat.

The boy considered her carefully, and then showed her three fingers.

"Oh, you're already three," she exclaimed cheerfully, again. "You're a big boy, not a baby," she said with exaggerated wonder.

Nat nodded seriously, and Matt stroked his head.

"Do you want some more milk?" he asked the child who'd finished the cookie already.

Nat shook his head, and then looked around.

"Would you like to run through the garden?" Matt asked. "It is okay, isn't it?" she asked Becka.

"Of course, it is," she said. "It's all yours, Nat," she invited him to take control of her savage garden.

The boy's face lit with delight, and he squirmed in Matt's lap to be let go. Matt lowered him to the ground, and he shot as fast as his short legs allowed him to the first bunch of colorful flowers. On his haunches, he touched the petals with awe, yet he never let the teddy-bear under his arm go.

"Should we talk now or…?" Becka asked Matt.

Matt shook his head, his eyes on the boy.

"He has to sleep soon, I think. Toddlers sleep during the day, don't they?" he asked turning to them.

Bryan smiled at him and shrugged, "Not something I'd know. I haven't had any experience with any other children, but my own. And they have a long way till they become toddlers."

"We can call aunt Marjorie or mother," Becka proposed, but Matt shook his head.

"No way. I don't want them to know anything right now. If later it's necessary, I'll tell them, but not now," he repeated stubbornly.

"Then we can check the Internet," Becka said.

"That's a good idea," Bryan said. "I'll bring the laptop," he announced, going inside.

Becka and Matt waited for him in silence. Nat was muttering something to a flower, but no one understood what he was saying. The regular breathing of the twins came through the monitor, Becka had put on the corner of the table earlier.

Bryan returned with the laptop and a notebook to take notes.

"I imagine you'd like to know more, not only if he sleeps during the day," Bryan explained the notebook. "We can make notes of what's important. It's a good lesson for Becka and me, as well."

Becka and Matt nodded and the three adults started their research about a toddler's timetable and routines, all the time glancing at the child, who had a lot of fun talking to the flowers and insects he found.

Half an hour later, Nat came to Matt and nudged him.

"Yes, pal, what is it?" Matt asked.

"You read," the boy said.

Matt seemed confused a few seconds, but Becka intervened.

"I think Nat wants you to read to him. That's what you want, Nat, yes?" she asked the child.

Nat nodded vigorously, stretching his arms to be taken up, and Matt sighed. He stood up, took him in his arms and told Becka and Bryan, "He asked me to take a few books with us. They're in the car. I'll be back in a moment."

"Don't trouble yourself," Bryan stopped him. Give me the keys, tell me where the books are, and I'll bring them."

"That's a much better idea," Matt agreed and handed the car keys to Bryan.

He sat back with Nat on his lap.

"Bryan will bring the books and you will choose one. But only one," he said in an authoritative voice, when a greedy light shone in the toddler's eyes.

His eyes focused on the child, when Becka's musical laughter reached his ears. He looked at her. She had fun on his expense.

"Becka!" he warned her.

"Come on, Matt, you're so funny. And I can see you'd be a good daddy," she added seriously, and Matt paled at her words.

"Don't even joke on that subject, Becka. It's forbidden topic," he argued.

"If you say so," she shrugged.

CHAPTER SIX

"He's finally asleep. Thanks, guys, for lending me that monitor," Matt said, pointing to the second monitor on the patio table.

"Don't sweat it," Bryan answered. "No big deal. We bought four to be sure we had one working if anything happened, so…"

"Anyway…" Matt started, but Becka stopped him, touching his hand.

"Forget about that, Matt, and spill the beans," she insisted, and Bryan smiled.

He liked it when Becka reacted with authority. Her attitude was in such a contrast with her small frame that it amused him to no end.

Matt explained about Nora and what happened that morning.

"I had to go and get the child. That woman didn't have a conscience, man. I got there exactly when she was coming out of the door. She didn't care she left the boy alone," Matt said, and his voice shook with anger. "And she did ask me to pay her for the time she stayed there. What kind of mother leaves a child with someone like her?"

"Maybe a mother who had no other choice," Bryan replied softly. "Did she mistreat the child?"

"No, but…"

"And probably Nora intended to be back on time," Becka reminded him. "I understand she arranged her shift so she could have plenty of time to go and get Nat, before that woman would have left."

"But she should have thought she could get hurt," Matt insisted mulishly. "With her type of job…"

"Not necessarily, Matt," Bryan disagreed. "It's not like she's in the line of fire all the time. Probably, it was the first time something like that happened, you know."

"I think," Becka said thoughtfully, "you resent her because of the way her ex-husband portrayed her during the divorce."

Matt stared at her for a few seconds, and shrugged.

"It was true, you know. She didn't fight back and didn't say he was lying about her being a serial cheater."

"Serial cheater? Really?" Becka asked and her eyes narrowed. "Why? Because her ex, who apparently has enough money to buy witnesses, says so?"

"She didn't defend herself, Becka," Matt replied in a very matter-of-fact voice.

"What would have been the point? Does she have money to fight you?" Bryan inquired in a quiet voice.

"I don't know," Matt admitted. "But she could have said something."

"If it had been pointless," Bryan shrug, "I understand why she didn't. Did you verify the facts yourself?"

"No, of course not. Everything was on file when it landed on my desk."

"Then," Becka said poking him with a finger, "you can't know what's true or not, so don't throw rocks, Matt. I thought you were more ethical than that," she reproached.

"But she didn't defend herself," he bellowed, "don't you get it?"

"You have to figure it for yourself," Bryan shook his head, and slapped him on the shoulder. "We can talk till we're blue in the face, Matt, but only you can uncover the truth. Anyway, what now?"

"I don't know," Matt admitted. "There's no one who can take care of the child. If child services take him, she'll face some serious problems to get him back," he said, and his face darkened.

"So?" Becka insisted.

"So… For the moment, I'm stuck with the kid. The problem is they live in a very small apartment. One bedroom, a tiny living-room and kitchen. The bathroom has a tiny shower. I wouldn't even fit in there... I was thinking to move him and his stuff in my apartment," he said pensively.

Becka approved, nodding. Bryan just smiled, enjoying Matt's thinking process.

"I could take care of him," Matt said not very convinced. "I mean, I have the time. We have cases on the roll now, but I have three young associates who could handle them... I can lend them a hand now and then, without effectively going to the office... I'd have to take time off, you know," he told them, glancing from one at the other. "I don't know where his daycare is so, that's out... I will have to go grocery shopping... This morning, I discovered I had only one tomato in my fridge, and half a box of cereals in a cupboard. Nothing else, not even a box of coffee or tea," he opened his arms in exasperation, and the other two smiled.

He paused, and a frown appeared between his eyebrows.

"I don't know how to do with the cooking though," he admitted. "And I don't want to involve my mom. Would it be bad if I buy fast-food?" he asked, and both Becka and Bryan nodded vigorously.

"Don't worry," Bryan said. "First, did you check their fridge?"

Matt closed his eyes with a scowl on his face, and slapped his forehead.

"I didn't even think of that. I should go and do it, I think. God knows how long she'll be in hospital. She wouldn't like to find living beings in her fridge when she comes back home."

"Definitely," Becka said, laughing.

"We'll go check it together, all right?" Bryan said. "And then, knowing what's there, I can start making some food for you. It's no big deal," he put his hand up when Matt wanted to interrupt him. "I'll make enough for two or three days. When you finish it, just let me know and I start a new batch."

"Oh, my God, how long do you think she'd be in hospital? If she survives, I mean, because it wasn't very clear she would," he clarified in a bleak tone.

"Don't worry, she will," Becka stroke his arm.

"The boy should sleep at least two more hours," Bryan said. "Let's go and take his things from that apartment and check the fridge. We'll go grocery shopping on the way back here. Becka can take care of him if he wakes up and Marissa's here, if Becka needs help. Is it all right with you?" he asked his wife.

"Sure," Becka said. "I'll manage, no worries. Just go," she pushed them out of her garden.

***

"Smart of you to mention that fridge," Matt told Bryan. "All those vegetables and fruit would have gone to waste."

"Told you. From what you said, Nora seems a very devoted mother, Matt. I don't know how you can't see it. Anyway, I was sure she'd have a lot of good food for the child. We need to buy only a few things for you – coffee, tea, things like that, and you're set for a few days. I'll make you a few casseroles for today and tomorrow, at least, and you can just warm them in the microwave."

Matt shook his head and said, "You can't imagine how grateful I am to you right now."

"Matt, you are a smart guy, who can also read minds. Read mine, already, and stop bothering me with your misplaced gratitude. We're family, man. You were there for me when I needed you. I'm here for you now," Bryan said quietly, arranging the last things in the truck of his car.

He'd insisted on taking his car because he didn't like how shaken Matt was, and didn't want to risk him behind the wheel.

Matt, even shaken, decided to probe Bryan's mind. He avoided doing it, as a norm, because he didn't like to intrude in people's thoughts. Yet, he wasn't always successful in holding back. As he didn't have enough control of his gift, he picked random thoughts now and then, even if he didn't want to pry.

This time, though, he felt compelled to pry. Bryan's thoughts levelled him. The man really didn't think Matt should be grateful, and was willing to do everything in his power to help him.

The day had been a roller-coaster of emotions and shocks for Matt. The man tried hard to recollect himself when tears pricked at the back of his eyes.

He longed for his usual self, but it seemed more and more afar and difficult to reach.

The two men returned to Bryan's house just after Nat woke up. Tears welled in the little boy's eyes.

The thought Matt had also left scared him. He didn't understand why his mommy wasn't coming to take him, and he clung to Matt, as if he'd been his last resort.

"Come on, munchkin, let's eat a banana," Matt said, "and stop crying. I won't leave you. You won't get rid of me so soon. We'll go to my house to live until mommy comes home, all right."

"Mommy says no stranger," the boy replied, and looked at him with big eyes.

"I'm sure she did," Matt said, "and she's right, Nat, but I'm no stranger. You saw me talking to your mommy."

Nat rubbed his eyes and pondered over his words, then he nodded.

"Banana?" he asked.

"Yes, you'll have a banana," Matt confirmed and sat him on a stuffed pillow, he'd previously placed on one of the garden armchairs.

"Do you want me to slice it?" he asked Nat after he made sure the child was secure.

"I'm not a baby," Nat countered. "I can eat a banana," he added, and the mutinous expression in his eyes warmed Matt's heart.

He smiled and shook his head, "Yes, you're not a baby. Here you are," he handed the banana to him, and then watched him peeling it carefully.

The kid was focused on his task and didn't pay attention to them. Becka leaned toward Matt and whispered, "Have you noticed he doesn't talk like a small child?"

"Is that bad?" Matt straightened, with a glint in his eyes.

"No, don't be silly," she laughed. "He's just very intelligent. Someone took good care with his education. I'm sorry I have to point it out to you, Matt, but the woman you described wouldn't have done that. I do think you have to gather all the facts before judging her," she shook her head at him, disapprovingly.

Matt watched the child and thought Becka was right. His eyes turned pensive, and Bryan slapped him friendly over the shoulder, "You'll straighten everything up, I count on you."

Marissa came out with a fresh pot of coffee for the adults and filled their cups, making small talk with them. She left them with their coffees, and went inside, brushing her fingers through Nat's hair. Nat laughed.

"He's a very sociable child," Matt noticed. "I expected problems, you know. Especially because he saw me only once, and even then, I quarreled with his mother."

Bryan waved his hands, "All's good, Matt, you'll see."

He hadn't even finished reassuring Matt that Matt's cell phone rang. Taking it out of his pocket, Matt verified the screen and winced.

"What?" Becka asked.

"The hospital," Matt said, and took a few steps away from the child, so he couldn't hear what he was saying.

"Matthew Winston speaking," he said.

Both Becka and Bryan were focused on him. Matt paced, ran his fingers through his hair and then, pinched the base of his nose. He was frustrated and upset.

"I'll be there in half an hour, probably," he replied, and listened some more, nodding. "All right, I understand and, of course, I'll come," he added and turned off the phone.

"Guys, I have to go to the hospital. She's awake and frantic. She was told I have…" he said, pointing to Nat.

"Not a problem," Bryan said. "He can stay here until you come back, Matt."

Matt nodded and thanked him. Then, he knelt next to Nathan and told him, "I have to run an errand, Nat. You'll stay with Becka and Bryan here, and I'll be back in no time."

"No," the child said. "I won't stay. I come with you."

"I'm sorry, munchkin, but I can't take you in a hospital. I promise to be back. You'll have fun here. You can make cookies with Becka and…"

Bryan interjected immediately, "God forbid, Matt. Becka has red light in the kitchen. If Nat makes any cookies, it will be with me."

The alarm in Bryan's voice didn't sit well with Becka, "Come on, Bryan, is it really necessary to…"

Bryan stopped her with a finger on her lips, "Sweetie, you know it is. Imagine the fire alarm raging. The babies waking up… No, love, you won't touch anything in the kitchen. I thought we had an agreement," he said in a very serious voice, and Becka, reluctantly, agreed.

"Yes, Nat, you'll make cakes with Bryan, and afterwards, we'll draw something, okay?" she asked him.

The child stared Matt down.

"I promise to be back this afternoon," Matt repeated, seeing the mutinous expression of the child. "I won't leave you."

The boy considered him a few more seconds and then agreed with a nod. Matt hugged him, laughing, and turned to leave.

"Take a cab, Matt," Bryan suggested.

He feared the visit at the hospital would shake him. Matt had already had his share of shocks that day, and Bryan didn't think it was smart to let him drive.

"I'll call you one right now," he said and went inside.

Matt had to give in. Bryan's thoughts had been too loud for him not to hear. He understood the man's concern for him and he didn't want to repay his kindness with callousness.

CHAPTER SEVEN

The nurse buzzed him into the intensive care unit immediately after his arrival. Her stern and reproachful face made him uncomfortable, as if he'd been a teenager again, called to the principal's office for one of the pranks for which he'd been so famous.

"She's been frantic, but she refused a sedative. You need to calm her down. Her fever spiked, and that's not good," she explained to Matt.

Matt nodded and followed her to Nora's ICU room. He looked at her through the glass, before opening the door. The bed seemed to swallow her whole, and his heart cringed.

"Try to calm her down, not to agitate her," the nurse warned him again, in an authoritative voice.

"Of course," Matt replied, although he doubted he wouldn't agitate her.

The nurse left him there, and he gathered his courage to open the door. He knew his visit might cause her much more anguish and even though he didn't like her, he didn't want to cause her more problems than she had.

The moment he entered the room, she turned her head to him, and he felt the intense gaze of those green eyes right in his chest. She watched him with something akin to hatred.

He was only a few feet away, but even from that distance he noticed the tears clinging to her lashes. He felt the impulse to console her and balled his hands into fists to prevent any dumb move.

She looked paler than he remembered, even though the fever, which glimmered in her eyes, had flushed her cheekbones. The dark shadows under her eyes had expanded and swallowed almost half of her face.

Under his scrutiny, she made an effort to wipe the tears off her face, but one arm was hooked to the IV unit and she couldn't make use of the other, yet not for lack of trying.

She seemed determined, and afraid she'd hurt herself worse, Matt rushed to the bed, quieted her movements, and wiped off her tears with his thumbs. The gesture felt extremely intimate. Uncomfortable with that closeness, he hurried to step back.

She'd trembled under his touch, and his eyes searched her face to see whether she was afraid of him. The display of emotions didn't reassure him.

"I want my son back," she enunciated, and her voice was strong, far from the weakly form she presented.

"Don't worry about that right now," Matt replied quietly. "Just..."

"I want my son back," she almost shouted at him, interrupting him.

"As soon as you get out of the hospital you'll have your son back," he said, always patiently. "Right now, I don't see how you could keep him here with you," he waved his hand, showing the antiseptic hospital room.

"I won't let you take him away from me," she said, as if he'd never said anything.

Matt sighed, bowed his head resignedly, and ran his fingers through his hair. He needed patience with her, no matter what.

The nurse had already bad-mugged him, and he didn't want to be the recipient of her looks if he failed to reassure that woman.

"Look, Nora..." he began, but of course she interrupted again.

"I won't let you," she interrupted in a mulish voice. "You've attacked my dignity, insulted me in any possible way and made everything in your power to leave me penniless – and I'm talking about the money belonging to me, not to that sorry excuse of a human being that was my ex..."

Matt noticed she gathered more steam along her declaration, and the flush of her cheeks intensified. He worried her fever went up and decided to end that stupid sparring.

He stepped next to the bed and leaned over her. He hushed her with his hand, which covered half of her face. Her eyes widened, and again, he wondered whether he frightened her.

"Now, I want you to keep silent until I finish what I have to say. I don't want to hear one word from you, Nora," he warned her in a stern voice. "Do you understand?" he asked her.

He waited a couple of seconds, but she didn't answer. She just kept staring at him with those shimmering green eyes, which pierced him straight into his soul.

"I've asked if you understand," he repeat, sterner than before, trying not to think of what he felt.

After a second, she licked his palm, and he practically jumped out of his skin. He took his hand off her mouth immediately and watched her, shocked.

"You wanted an answer," she shrugged. "Well, with that shovel over my mouth, I couldn't have answered. So…" she explained, a quirky little smile in the corner of her mouth, and Matt had a glimpse of the naughty girl she must have been a few years back.

"But you'll keep your mouth shut and listen," he concluded, after taking a deep breath to calm his senses.

That lick had reached deep inside him, and all his nerve endings stood to attention. He didn't doubt she'd see the proof of his arousal if she looked closely, and he prayed she wouldn't. He'd have a hard time to explain that.

He tried to pry on her thoughts, but came back blank and that stunned him. He might not have had full ability, but still could read something from everyone.

"For the moment," she nodded slightly. "But make it fast," she warned him, and her eyes narrowed. "If I don't like what I hear, the entire hospital will know it, do you understand?" she finished in a menacing voice.

"Little girl," he smirked, "never make threats you can't carry on," he said, and tweaked the tip of her nose.

Nora huffed in indignation and opened her mouth to rebut him. Matt only touched a finger to her lips and shook his head, which made her keep quiet.

"Now, maybe I can speak in peace for a moment or two," he said. "So, that Nolan guy was concerned about the kid. By the way, you've found a *'great'* baby-sitter, Nora. When I got there, she was just getting out of the door and stopped just enough to ask for money. What kind of a woman leaves a small child alone in an apartment, huh?" he asked and a frown appeared between his eyebrows.

"I always..." Nora started, but Matt's finger was back on her lips to silence her.

"I'm talking now. And I wasn't talking about you. I imagined you'd have made it in time if the shooting hadn't happened. I wasn't accusing you. So, let me finish," he ordered.

"Where's my son now?" she asked, as if his finger hadn't touched her lips and he hadn't asked her to keep quiet.

Matt groaned, and bowed his head in mock resignation. He shook his head, and then looked back at her, a faint smile on his lips.

"You can't stop talking if your life depended on it, huh?"

"Where's my son?" she repeated doggedly. "I see you don't have him with you. Have you delivered him to child services?" she asked, and her voice shook. Now, fear was obvious in her voice.

"No, of course not. If I'd had that intention, I'd have let the police call child services in the morning and I'd have been done with it."

"So where is he?" she asked stubbornly.

"He's fine," Matt replied.

"Not what I asked," she retorted peevishly, and stared him down with a mean light in her eyes.

"Maybe not, but I thought to let you know he was fine. He's with Becka and Bryan," he replied.

"I don't know any Becka and Bryan," she observed and lifted an eyebrow interrogatively.

"They're my cousins," Matt answered. "At least, Becka's my cousin, and Bryan's her husband."

He took a few steps to the window to gather his thoughts. He had a few questions for her and didn't know how to ask them. He came back and observed her eyes had never left him.

"We couldn't determine if you knew someone who could take care of Nat. A relative or a friend…" he inquired mildly.

"I don't have relatives, at least not in Toronto," she admitted, and moved her fingers agitated. "I have a cousin and an aunt somewhere in BC… Friends…" she started to say and turned her eyes to the bed.

Matt waited a few moments, but she didn't continue.

"Yes, friends, Nora… Do you have any friends?"

She shook her head, and then looked up at him.

"Just a few people from work, but more like… acquaintances, you know… There's no time for friends… With work and a child…"

Matt noticed she avoided his eyes, and nudged her chin with his thumb. She looked at him, surprised, but he'd already seen she was uncomfortable admitting her loneliness to him.

"I understand things like that, Nora. You shouldn't be embarrassed."

A shadow crossed her face and she looked down again.

"What now?" he asked, turning her face back to him.

"It's not like you believe me anyway," she shrugged, and then hissed.

The movement of her shoulders had sent ripples of pain through her entire body, and she bit her lower lip not to yelp. Tears gathered in her eyes, turning their green in liquid intense glimmer.

"Calm, baby," Matt soothed her, tenderly stroking the side of her face.

Her puzzled eyes came back to him. Matt wasn't aware he'd used an endearment, but she'd felt his tenderness deep to the core.

"No unnecessary movements for a while, okay?" he told her and straightened.

Nora missed his touch immediately, and turned her eyes back to the utilitarian blanket, which was covering her up to midriff.

"I believe you don't have time to socialize," he reassured her, but noticed the ironic smirk appeared on her lips again. "What?"

"Mr. Winston," she drawled, "you thought I'm a femme fatale with a string of lovers to shame a call girl. I doubt that impression changed in the span of a few hours."

"My name's Matt," he replied in a sterner voice than he wanted, but her words had touched a sensible cord.

Bryan had sowed doubts in his mind about the file he was handed when asked to handle the Willows divorce. He was thinking of checking the facts again, although it was too late to do anything about the divorce.

"I think," she said hesitantly, "we lost the thread of conversation. You were telling me about my son…"

"Yes, let's get back to that," Matt conceded.

He wanted to return to safer ground. He didn't want to touch the matter of her divorce right then. He needed to find some answers first, and then he could either apologize or show her he wasn't a naïve young man.

"I took him with me," he said and put up his hand to stop her when she opened her mouth. "I'd have preferred not to take him from his environment, especially now, when he has to deal with your absence, as well. But I wouldn't have been able even to shower in your apartment. It's like a tiny doll house, for God's sake," he exclaimed. "We've spent the day with Becka and Bryan, as I've told you already, but we'll go back to my apartment tonight. Bryan helped me to gather Nat's things and empty the contents of your fridge," he told her and smiled. "I thought you wouldn't want to find it full of alien beings when you got back from hospital," he looked at her for confirmation.

"You thought well," she gave him his due.

"That's good," Matt grinned. "Anyway, we've done some research..."

"What research?" she narrowed her eyes.

"About toddlers, of course," he answered nonplussed. "It's not like I've been around many, and the two of them have only babies – twins, a month and a half old."

"Oh, my God, those people are so busy and you left my child in their hands..."

"As I said before, calm down, Nora," he snapped at her. "They're fine. Becka relates perfectly to children and Bryan is the embodiment of patience. Plus, Bryan will cook for us, enough for two days..."

"Bryan?" she asked, not sure she heard him correctly.

"Yes, why?" Matt looked at her inquiringly.

"Bryan will cook for you," she repeated to make sure she heard him.

"Yes, specifically for Nat. Our research showed fast food wasn't very good for him and I don't know to cook at all," Matt explained.

"But how come Bryan... Never mind..." she decided to drop the subject.

Matt finally understood why she was so astonished.

"I get it now," he laughed. "You wonder why Becka won't cook. It's simple. Bryan won't allow her to step in the kitchen... No, no, it's not like that," he rushed to explain when he saw her frown, "Becka's just a disaster waiting to happen in the kitchen. Even if she tries to boil an egg, freaky accidents happen. So, in their family, Bryan's the cook."

"Oh, he's a cook," she said relieved.

"No, he's not. He's a kick-boxing and Brazilian jiu-jitsu trainer," Matt said and, when her face fell comically, he grinned.

"You're pulling my leg," she accused.

"Nope, I'm telling you the truth," Matt shook his head. "Bryan is... a very interesting character, I'd say. I like him, you know... You'll like him too," he said quietly, and looked at her with a strange intensity, she felt down to her belly.

Matt kept quiet for a few seconds, and then, continued, "Look, I think we should do this. I won't bring Nat here," he said and, seeing she wanted to say something, he stopped her. "No, don't take it wrong. I won't bring him here, as long as you're in the ICU. I don't think you want him to see you like this," he said and looked at her inquiringly.

Nora shook her head, "Of course, not. He might not understand and he'd get upset."

"Exactly," Matt approved. "As soon as they move you into a reserve, I will bring him there to see you, all right?"

"I might get a semi-private room. I think my insurance covers that," she said thoughtfully.

"Don't think about that now," Matt waved her thoughts away.

He'd already decided to discuss the room matter with the hospital and cover a private room from his own pocket. He didn't want to bring Nat into a room with someone else he didn't know and might scare the child.

"Meanwhile, if you want, you could talk to Nat over the phone," he offered. "I think that would work for maximum two or three days, if you're good enough and get better," he grinned at her, and Nora scowled at him in response.

"It's not up to me, you loggerhead," she observed.

"Oh, yes, it is," Matt insisted. "It depends on your mind. You know, mind over matter," he explained.

"That's bullshit and you know it," she replied, crossly.

"No, actually, it isn't," Matt answered in a serious voice. "Your state of mind we'll help you recover sooner. Anyway, do you want to talk to Nat now or not?" he asked her, and tears welled in her eyes. "What now?" he asked with exasperation, opening his arms.

"Nothing, I'm just happy," Nora answered in a shaky voice. "So you won't take my son from me," she asked for reassurance.

"Don't be stupid," Matt's dry answer came, and he took out his phone and dialed Bryan's number.

He listened with half an ear to the conversation Nora had with her son. He was thinking how to organize everything and made mental notes to get in touch with his personal assistant that evening and rearrange his schedule for an entire month. Matt knew he had a few appointments he needed to keep, but hoped to get rid of everything else.

He was more interested in the conversation Nora had with Becka and Bryan. She surprised him by smiling a few times and even laughing heartily at something one of the two said.

When she finished her conversation, she handed him the phone back.

"Thank you, Matt. I won't ever forget that," she told him and her eyes shone with gratitude.

"No big deal," he replied with nonchalance, although he doubted he'd ever be at ease when she trained those eyes on him.

He couldn't understand how she could affect him when he didn't like or respect the woman.

"Does Nat have any allergies, something I need to know?" he asked her.

"No, no allergies. He's a very healthy kid," she smiled at him. "About the daycare… I know you could leave him there, but they won't give it back to you," she said with a brief hesitation and bit her lip. "Maybe, if I call tomorrow… and see what they need…"

"Don't bother with that," he waved her offer away. "Is it important for his development to go there?" he reconsidered.

"Not really… Well, he plays with other children…"

"But couldn't I take him to a park and have him play with children there?" Matt inquired, pushing his hands into his pants pockets.

"Yes, you could. But don't you need to go to work?" she asked him, and her voice showed her surprise.

"I'm the boss," he replied dryly. "I decide when and if I work," he explained. "I'll have to go to the office for some appointments, and I do have a couple of court appointments scheduled, but Becka and Bryan assured me they'd look after him when I can't, so don't worry about it," he continued, balancing on the balls of his feet.

They assessed each other in silence for a few seconds and then, Nora said, "I can't thank you enough, Matt."

"You don't have to," he replied, always in a dry voice. "Everything will be fine, and, no, you owe me nothing," he thought to add for good measure.

She looked at him with disbelief, and then huffed, "Yeah, sure. You rearrange your entire life around my kid and I don't owe you…"

"No, you don't," Matt repeated forcefully. "So, are we good now? Can you get back to sleep so you recover sooner?"

She closed her eyes, shook her head and said, "Yeah, why not?"

"Good, then I'll see you tomorrow," he hurried to say and left the room.

She looked after him aback. *That's one weird man, Nora. Something's not right with him.*

***

Matt left the hospital after he discussed the possibility of covering the costs for a private room, once Nora would be moved into a regular hospital room.

He made sure they understood he didn't want any kind of fuss about who paid the bill, and he persuaded them. He explained Nora was a proud woman, and it wouldn't do any good to her health to have her riled. He pointed out she'd be if they told her he covered the costs.

In a cab, going back to Becka and Bryan, he questioned his reasons for reacting the way he did. He was a rational man, and never did anything without weighing carefully the pros and cons.

This time, though, he didn't even stop to think. Something pushed him to do things he'd have refused if he'd given himself time to ponder about

285

them. It wasn't about the money, of course. He was far from wanting any.

Yet, his behavior was beyond his comprehension. He couldn't even say he'd been bewitched because he had first-hand knowledge about that. He knew a witch when he saw one, and Nora wasn't it.

Now, the question remained: what was about Nora? He behaved uncharacteristically whenever he was near her.

What the heck? I've changed my life for her completely in one day, and willingly.

When he realized that, Matt froze.

CHAPTER EIGHT

Matt woke up with a little bundle of joy bouncing on his stomach. He liked sleeping on his back and enjoying his king size order-made bed. Almost 6.2 feet tall, Matt needed all the space he could get.

He rubbed his face with one hand and steadied the kid with the other. It had become routine already. Every single morning, during the last four days, he'd woken up with Nat jumping up and down on him, and he wondered if the child did the same thing with his mother.

Matt thought about the differences in size and muscles between Nora and him. He wondered how she fared after such an episode. She was just a slip of a woman, no match for the energetic bouncing of the child.

His training with Bryan had defined his abs some more and he was in great shape, but it still felt like a mule kicked him in his stomach.

"All right, munchkin," he said, "I see you're up already."

Nat nodded vigorously, and showed him all his milk teeth. All in all, Matt observed with satisfaction, Nat was a very balanced and happy kid. He took everything in stride and didn't get riled easily.

"What made you so happy this morning?" Matt asked, setting the child aside and getting out of the bed.

"You promised I can go to Becka," the child enunciated correctly, almost jumping on the bed. "She promised we go to the park. She promised you'll take me on the lake on Saturday. And I can see my mom today again," the child talked a mile a minute, and Matt smiled.

"I see Becka promised a lot at my expense," he joked, but when the child glared, he hurried to add, "Now, don't worry, we'll do everything she promised, okay?"

Nat smiled happily again and jumped out of bed. He followed Matt into the bathroom, and, like every other morning, Matt helped him to clean his teeth, wash his face and comb his hair.

Matt had already found out the kid liked to choose his own clothes and get dressed by himself, so after he had his shower, he went to the kitchen to prepare breakfast for both of them.

He had a long day before him, starting with leaving Nat to Becka, so he could go into work. He had a court appearance in less than two hours, and it wouldn't do to be late.

***

Somewhat tired, Matt came to take Nat from Becka a little after three. By that hour, Nat must have finished his nap and, now, he was probably ready to go.

Matt also hoped to get some lunch from Bryan because he hadn't had the time for a bite since morning, and his stomach had been grumbling since noon.

He didn't bother to ring the bell. He doubted Becka had locked the door after he left their house in the morning. He knew Bryan didn't have any plans to go out that day, so he couldn't have discovered his wife's forgetfulness.

He went directly into the house and for a second there, froze. His great-grandmother raised voice came from the back of the house. When she wanted, Rebecca's voice boomed in a way that would have made a drill sergeant proud.

"I can't accept it, young man," she bellowed.

Matt immediately rushed through the kitchen and out onto the patio. It wasn't a stretch to think Rebecca was chastising Nat, and he couldn't allow it. The child was in his care and he wouldn't have permitted anyone to shout at him.

Rebecca wasn't a mean and unfeeling woman, but she did like to have her way every single time. Yet, this time, Matt couldn't let her.

Once outside in the garden, he stopped suddenly. Stunned, he stared at the scene before his eyes, and for a moment he was sure he hallucinated.

Rebecca held Nat in her lap, one arm around his midriff, and she pointed a bony finger to Bryan, who was sitting in a lawn armchair not far from her. Bryan tried to keep a serious face, but a stubborn smile fought to appear in the corner of his mouth.

"What's going on?" Matt asked in a voice far from mild.

Nat immediately turned to him and shouted, "Matt."

He held his arms up, so Matt could take him in his arms. Matt realized he'd become the child's anchor since his mother's shooting, and, curious enough, he didn't mind it. He actually enjoyed the pure joy on the kid's face whenever he saw him.

"Hush, now, young man," Rebecca told him with authority. "First, you must finish eating your snack, and then, you can go to Matt."

Obedient, Nat immediately snatched another biscuit off the plate on the table and stuffed it in his mouth. Everyone smiled, and Matt ruffled the boy's hair.

"Where's Becka?" he inquired, glancing at Bryan.

His great-grandmother waved her hand, "She's in the study. She had to take her mother's call," she explained.

"You see," Bryan intervened maliciously, crossing his arms over his chest with nonchalance, and stretching his legs in front of him, "Rebecca thought a double-front attack would be in order. Becka's mother would nag her, while Rebecca would bellow me into submission."

"Submission for what?" Matt asked. He hadn't heard any problems or complaints related to his favorite couple lately.

"For taking the trust money, of course," Rebecca snapped at him. "I've waited long enough. I've hoped they'd come to their senses sooner or later, but it's been almost a year. I won't take his refusal for an answer," she ended with obstinacy, and pointed the same bony finger to Bryan.

"Sweet great-grandma," he began but she interrupted him with a smirk.

"Don't take me with *sweet great-grandma*," she retorted. "I know you don't mean it and I won't have it."

"Don't mean it?" Bryan inquired with puzzlement.

"Of course, you don't mean it," she huffed. "I've seen you. I know how you think. You hate me and that's why you won't let Becka have the money," she explained in a bitter voice.

"Now, there, you're wrong. I do think you are sweet in your own way," Bryan replied.

When he saw she intended to contradict him, he stood up and put a hand on her shoulder.

"You don't show it, Rebecca, but you're not as mean as you want people to believe. About the money, sorry," he said and shook his head, "but I don't need it and Becka doesn't want it, that's all.

Don't take it personally. I won't say I'm sorry she doesn't," he shook his head and patted her shoulder, as if he'd wanted to sweeten the blow.

He thought a moment and leaned over her and kissed her parchment-like cheek, which stunned her. Then, he started back to the house, throwing over the shoulder, "I suppose you're hungry, Matt. I'll bring you something, just take a seat."

Pleased, Matt smiled and sat next to Rebecca. Bryan was always considerate, and if he'd told someone how domestic Bryan had become, no one would have believed him.

Matt shook his head, amused, when he felt Rebecca's eyes on him. He turned to her and met her assessing sharp eyes.

"How have you been, grandma?" he politely asked her.

He had to do some conversation with her. He couldn't ignore her forever.

"Don't grandma me, Matt," she retorted. "You've got some explaining to do, young man," she said, looking at him pointedly.

Matt shook his head, and said quietly, "No, I don't have to explain anything."

"I care to differ and the proof is in my lap," she snapped, and Nat looked up at her.

"Me?" he inquired shyly, and Matt wanted to yell at his great-grandmother for not considering the child's feelings.

It wasn't something new for Rebecca, but he still hoped. At least, her age should have mollified her enough.

"You're the proof, kiddo, but in a good sense," she ruffled the boy's hair. "Now, finish eating if you want to play," she ordered in a voice that didn't allow any more inquiries.

Nat immediately snatched a slice of orange and shovelled it into his mouth. Satisfied, Rebecca smiled at him and stroked his head.

"So, when were you going to tell me you had a son?" she brusquely asked Matt.

Matt just stared at her. He'd have liked to answer something, anything, but his mind went blank in shock.

"You're my daddy," Nat said in awe, and the adoration in his voice humbled Matt.

The glimmer in the child's eyes shook Matt and he came back to reality.

"Thanks, grandma," he said sarcastically. "How can I now..." he started but couldn't finish.

"You take care of him, you're his dad. I don't care who fathered him," Rebecca replied and shrugged, as if everything had been very simple.

"You're my daddy," the child repeated, and Matt groaned.

"Should I congratulate you?" Bryan's dry voice came from behind him.

Matt looked up and saw the stern expression on Bryan's face. He didn't need his mind reading gift to know what his friend thought.

He raised his arms helplessly and asked, "What should I do, now?"

"It's not for me to know," Bryan replied curtly, and set a tray with a bowl of soup and a sandwich before him.

"What kind of question is that, Matt?" Rebecca huffed, and lowered the child to the ground. "Now, you can go and play," she told Nat and slapped his behind jokingly, making him laugh.

However, Nat didn't leave immediately. He looked at Matt and said, "You promised I can see mommy today."

"Of course, you will," Rebecca answered at once. "We'll all see mommy today."

Matt chocked, and soup gushed out of his mouth. Bryan jumped back, but Rebecca wasn't so lucky. She was right on the path of the liquid, and both her face and her top took the brunt of the spray.

"Matthew Winston!" she shouted, throwing her arms in the air, exasperated.

She hadn't expected something like that from Matt, not in million years. Matt had proved the most balanced of her grandchildren and great-grandchildren by far.

Nat and Bryan started laughing like hyenas, but Rebecca gave them the evil eye, huffing. She needn't do more, because they smothered their hilarity at once.

Nat chose to run to Becka's flowers, which fascinated him, and where Bryan had set up his outdoor toys, while Bryan gathered napkins to help Rebecca clean up.

Matt just stared at her. His eyes had widened. He couldn't believe he'd sprayed his fastidious great-grandma. But then, he couldn't believe her gumption. She just invited herself somewhere she had no business to go, and he'd be damned if he'd just rolled with it.

Rebecca huffed again and snatched the napkins from Bryan. She started wiping her face vigorously, still frowning.

All the time she made use of the napkins, she muttered, "I've never... never... never thought you'd do that to me... How, the heck, am I going out now? Huh?" she ended her muttering, with a shout from the top of her lungs, and she bad-mugged Matt again.

Matt still couldn't say a thing. His tongue was in knots. He'd have liked to say a lot of things, but none was appropriate for his great-grandma's ears.

Bryan intervened immediately. He noticed Rebecca was ready to slap Matt silly. Although he'd liked to see how it would go, considering that Matt was much taller than his great-grandma and outweighed her by at least 80 pounds, he didn't think the show would have been good for the kid.

"I'm sure you can borrow something from Becka," Bryan tried to soothe her, in a quiet voice. "It isn't the end of the world, you know? I know, you are taller, it's true, but she's rounder and it will compensate," he explained.

"Are you saying I look like a scarecrow, young man?" she changed her target suddenly, and rallied against Bryan, gathering more steam.

"Far from me, Rebecca," Bryan replied.

His voice was always calm. He didn't need another shouting match that day. Rebecca had given him enough grief that afternoon.

"Then are you saying Becka is too round?" she snapped at him, ready to defend her great-granddaughter.

"She's perfectly round," Bryan observed very matter-of-factly, "so, let's not get into an argument here."

"I think I should go," Matt finally found his voice.

He thought he'd take advantage of the sparring match between Rebecca and Bryan and sulk away with Nat. Yet, he thought wrong.

Rebecca immediately turned to him and barked, "Eat your lunch and keep your mouth shut. Maybe, this time, you can eat your soup without spraying me again."

Matt's worry escalated. He thought he knew Rebecca, but he didn't understand her game now. He only knew he'd have had a serious fight on his hands if he'd wanted to make her remain there, at Becka's house, or go home, but not to the hospital with him.

"Grandma," he started, but she didn't have any of it.

"I said, have your lunch," she snapped more forcefully. "You'll have enough time to talk to me this afternoon and evening," she observed.

Her words had the effect of a cold shower for Matt and strengthened his resolve.

"What do you mean?" he asked in a dry voice, pushing the tray away, definitely not hungry anymore.

"I decided to borrow a top from Becka, so you won't get rid of me so easily, Matt," she scowled at him. "I'll be ready in no time at all."

Matt frowned at Bryan because he was the one who'd had the idea to offer one of Becka's blouses. Bryan just shrugged, disinterested in Matt's anger.

"This is your battle, Matt," Bryan said.

"What battle?" Becka's voice came from behind him, and he turned his head to her.

He smiled at his wife and informed her, "Rebecca needs one of your tops, sweetie. Matt showered her with soup," he grinned.

Rebecca slapped his arm, unamused with his antics.

"Try to find one that goes with my skirt," she ordered Becka. "How did it go with your mom?" she asked slyly.

"We had a nice conversation, grandma, and no, I didn't accept the trust money," she said. "How come Matt sprayed you with the soup?" she asked, sitting in her husband's lap with fluidity.

"Don't change the subject, young lady," Rebecca snapped at her. "I want you to reconsider," she slapped her palm on the tabletop, vexed that the young woman hadn't bent down.

"Sorry, grandma, I can't," she shrugged, and her voice showed no contrition. "If you hadn't conditioned that money, things might have been different," she observed.

"You know why I did it," Rebeca defended her decision.

"I know and I understand your reasons, truly," Becka replied, and leaning forward, stroked her grandma's arm. "But that doesn't mean I agree with you. The way you treated Bryan..."

"Sweetie," Bryan intervened, but Becka hushed him, with a shake of her head and a finger firmly put on his lips.

"What did you expect me to do, when I saw a man like him with you?" Rebecca countered, waving her hand in Bryan's direction.

"A man like him?" Becka jumped off Bryan's lap, ready to do battle, and the air vibrated all around them.

Becka controlled her fury now, and things stopped flying around all the time. Yet, the air still vibrated whenever she grew angry, and her husband knew he had to do something.

Bryan attempted to intervene and pull her back in his lap, but she slapped his hands away.

"No, Bryan, she won't get away with insulting you once more," Becka said ferociously. "Once it was more than enough," she observed, and her eyes thundered to her great-grandma.

"But I didn't insult him, Becka, don't be stupid," the old woman said in a very unemotional voice, which contrasted with Becka's white fury. "I just said he's so imposing and serious and... I couldn't see you with a man like him... At that time," she thought to add when Becka practically growled. "I thought he'd stifle your exuberance and youth. Now, I know better," she shrugged. "You don't have to get in a huff, young lady. People, make mistakes. Just wait until you get to my age. Then, tell me you haven't made any," she challenged Becka.

Becka didn't have the time to answer because Matt chose that moment to stand. He braced his palms on the table, and reclaimed Rebecca's attention.

"I want to know what you plan to do," he demanded with authority and watched his grandma with steely eyes. "You've played enough with me already," he raised his voice.

He slapped the table top, finally losing his temper, and making a few eyebrows raise. Matt never showed if he was rattled or furious, and his outburst was uncharacteristic enough to astonish them.

'Now, I'm starting behaving like a loony bin', he thought, his eyes always fixed on the old woman. He knew she plotted something, and he didn't like the direction of her actions.

If he could have gone back to the early hours of the morning, he'd have made different plans for Nat that day. He'd have never taken the chance of letting Rebecca know what was going on.

"I'm planning to see your young lady, Matt," Rebecca said very straightforward, unimpressed with his temper. "With or without you," she pointed out.

Matt's eyes flashed with anger. He even had to step back so he wouldn't be tempted to knot his fingers around the old bird's neck.

"There's no such thing like *my young lady*, grandma," Matt said squarely, unwilling to attract Nat's attention.

"Who are you kidding, Matt?" Rebecca mocked him, waving her fingers to him. "Humph! No man takes over the care of a child just out of the kindness of his heart," she waved the assumption away, with a flutter of her hand.

"There was no one else, that's all," Matt groused.

"Sheesh!" Rebecca puffed. "You have enough money to pay someone, Matty. You are a kind man, I'll give you that, but kindness only goes so far. So, I want to meet the woman who…"

"You won't meet anyone," he snapped, interrupting her in a rude voice. "You'll stay here or go home, whatever you want, but you won't interfere in my business. Is it clear?" he practically growled at her.

"I don't like your tone," the old woman straightened her back and looked him down.

"I don't care," he answered. "You don't know when to stop. You tried to control everyone's life from the beginning, and it simply killed you that you couldn't control mine. Well, I don't care," his fist made contact with the tabletop. "I won't have it," he thundered to the old woman. "You can do whatever you want, great-grandma, but do it as far as possible from me and my business," he said in an icy voice now, aware he'd lost his temper and made a show of himself.

Then, he turned to Nat and stretched his hand toward the boy, "Nat, we're leaving to see your mom, now. Come on, munchkin."

Nat ran to him, forgetting about the yard toys he was playing with. Matt had bought him a crabbie sand table three days ago and Becka and Bryan had set it next to the flowerbed the child liked most.

"You promised Becka and Bryan can come too," he took Matt's hand.

"I know, but they have guests. They'll come with us tomorrow," Matt smiled and ruffled the child's hair.

"No, need," Rebecca intervened. "We can all go with you now. I just have to change my top, Nat, and we'll be on our way."

She'd already understood Matt didn't want to say anything wrong before the child and she took advantage of his weakness. She knew how to play her hand and succeed in her plans.

She didn't have any notion of pity. Sometimes, people needed a steely back to survive, and she had learned early not to show kindness when she shouldn't, and not to back down when she wanted something.

This time, Matt effectively saw red. He let go to Nat's hand and turned to Rebecca. His expression showed he was now ready to say everything he wished to say, no holds barred.

Becka whispered fearfully, "Bryan, do something."

CHAPTER NINE

Bryan's intervention spared both Matt and Rebecca of a total fallout. Matt left their house with the kid and Becka in tow, and Bryan remained to deal with the old witch, as Matt was thinking of her now.

Matt rarely had bad thoughts about his great-grandma. He understood why her heart had grown cold and why she wanted to control everything and everyone, even though he didn't like it.

They'd butted heads over the years, sometimes more, sometimes less. The worse had been when he brought Velma with him to introduce her to the family. Yet, even then, Rebecca hadn't made him see red, ready to lash out at her and spit out all the resentments he'd gathered over the years.

This time she hadn't just stepped over boundaries, she'd blown them up completely.

Matt was more furious because she'd made all those comments in front of the child. If the child had repeated any of them to his mother, which was a strong possibility, Nora would have been convinced Matt wanted to steal her child from her.

And just like that, they'd be back to square one. Over the last few days, they'd found a common ground somehow. Nora was less circumspect and fearful of him, and a few barriers had come down, which he loved.

When they moved her into a reserve, he'd brought Nat to visit. The child had helped their interactions and she'd opened more to Matt.

The glimmer of resentment and hatred had disappeared from her eyes, which relieved him. That now she was also well on her way to recovery added to his satisfaction.

He'd told himself he was satisfied they'd part ways soon, but he knew he was lying to himself.

There was something there, although he wasn't sure what. He'd never been so muddled in the head when it came to a relation with a woman. He didn't know whether he wanted to see more of her in the future or not.

Their conversations had become less strained, and he'd learned she was an interesting woman, far from the materialistic and cheating female he'd thought her before.

He still couldn't glimpse into her mind. He didn't belabor over his inability to read her thoughts and took everything in stride.

He'd discovered things about her in the same way a regular person with no paranormal power learned about the people around, and that seemed to be more satisfying than just reading someone's mind.

He'd also hired an investigator to dig into her past and her ex's past and present. He couldn't forget what Bryan had told him and he wanted to see whether he'd been duped.

It saddened him to hear she'd been on her own for most of her life. Her parents had moved to Florida when she was barely eighteen. They died there, in a break-in, a few years later.

The investigator researched the divorce evidence and came back empty. He'd established beyond any doubt that it was impossible for the four witnesses to have had an affair with her. Not only had they never met her, but at the times of the alleged dates, Nora was always working.

What he found was evidence against the ex-husband, though. Apparently, he'd had two girlfriends on the side and for some time already.

Matt had sworn never to accept a file again without checking the evidence himself. He knew Nora had been doled a terrible injustice and he'd been the instrument of her humiliation. Whenever he remembered how he'd talked to her, he gnashed his teeth in frustration.

"Are you alright, Matt?" Becka touched his arm.

He glanced at her for a second and then checked the child in the back seat.

"Yes, I'm fine. Just a little raw after… Well, after, you know."

Becka just nodded and glanced out of the window.

"You know, I don't think anyone has ever stood against her and that's why she thinks she can do everything she wants," she remarked pensively.

"I don't give a… fig," Matt censored his language, both for Becka and Nat's sake. He felt raw and mean and needed to swear. "I've had enough with her meddling and her demands," he slapped his hand on the driving wheel.

"I know. But… she's old… and… in her way, she does love all of us. As a matter of fact, everyone knows she loves you more than anyone else," she pointed out to him.

"Like I care," he shrugged, a scowl etched on his face. "I'd prefer she didn't love me at all."

"I like her," Nat's voice came from the back of the car, and Matt's eyebrows climbed on his forehead.

"Really? How come?" he asked the boy.

"She barks. She doesn't bite," Nat replied.

"Where did you hear that?" Matt asked him, surprised the boy could say something like that.

"Mom says so… About dad…"

"Your dad shouted as well?" Becka asked, turning in her seat to look at Nat.

"At mom," the child said. "He doesn't see me."

"How the… how come he doesn't see you?" Matt asked with disbelief, editing his words again.

"He says… I don't exist," the boy explained, and both Becka and Matt snarled.

"Maybe you didn't hear correctly," Becka tried to console him.

"No," Nat replied. "He said so. Many times."

"Bastard," Matt grumbled. "Someone should teach him a lesson. With their fists."

Becka heard him and smiled. Matt had always been willing to protect the underdog and dole the necessary punishment.

"Mommy needs flowers," Nat suddenly said.

"I bag your pardon?" Matt asked surprised, stopping at the traffic lights.

"Flowers. She needs flowers," the child insisted.

"How do you know?" Becka asked.

"Yesterday, I saw people with flowers. People bring flowers in a hospital," Nat repeated stubbornly.

"Okay, don't get your pants into a twist, pal," Matt laughed. "We'll buy flowers, buddy. Right there," he said, pointing to a flower shop. Then, he signaled to the right and changed lanes.

***

As Matt had allowed Nat to choose what flowers he liked, they made their entrance in Nora's room with a big basket. To Becka's delight, the toddler had chosen a basket full of Alstroemeria, which signify devotion, prosperity and fortune.

Nora's eyes widened when they fell on the basket, which supposedly Matt and Nat carried. Matt had convinced the boy they should both carry the basket. He doubted the boy had had the strength to hold it in his tiny hands.

She accepted the flowers gracefully, although she shook her head to Matt, chastising him for spending so much. She'd seen such baskets while window shopping and knew they were over $150. She couldn't believe the man would spend so much money just to humor a child.

Only then, she saw Becka. Her eyes had been riveted on Nat and Matt and almost missed the short, blond woman next to Matt. For a second, her heart cringed, but she chased away any sadness and smiled widely at Matt's companion.

"I'm Becka," she said, "Matt's cousin. I bear fruits," she showed a bag, where she'd stuffed a few oranges, bananas and apples. "Just stuff you can eat without the need of cutlery," she specified and placed the bag on the night stand next to Nora's bad.

"Becka's my friend, mom," Nat boasted. "She plays with me every day. She let me touch her babies. They're funny. No hair or almost no hair. And they sleep all the time or they cry," he rushed to say, tripping over his own words.

The adults smiled indulgently, and then, Nora turned to Becka.

"You can't imagine how grateful I'm to you for all the help…"

Becka interrupted her by touching her arm and shaking her head.

"You don't need to be grateful. It's good experience for my husband and me. My babies won't be babies forever, you know," she laughed.

Nora nodded and laughed, as well, "Don't I know it! It's like now they're in the crib, just sleeping and asking for food every few hours, and, suddenly, you have a small typhoon on your hands."

"Should we put the flowers on that stand there?" Matt asked, suddenly unwilling to be left out of the conversation.

"Yes, I think it's perfect there," Nora replied, a strange shyness in her voice.

Matt's left eyebrow went up his forehead. He'd never seen her shy.

Nora invited them to sit. She had two chairs in the room and she took Nat on the bed with her. She kept touching him and brushing his hair, a sign she'd missed him terribly.

"So, you're good with Becka, Nat, yes?" she asked the little boy.

"Yes, and with Bryan. And I met their great-grandma today. And she is funny," the boy announced with exuberance.

Both Becka and Matt looked at him as if he'd lost his mind. There were lots of things one could say about Rebecca. Being funny wasn't one of her traits, though.

"What?" Nora asked, noticing their puzzlement.

"Great-grandma is anything but funny," Matt replied in a dry voice. "Not even when I was of Nat's age I thought differently," he explained.

Becka just nodded. She agreed wholeheartedly with everything Matt said.

Feeling Nora's inquiring eyes on her, she explained, "Great-grandma is… let's say, special. And she's good to take in very small doses. Today, both Matt and I had a little too much of her presence," she laughed.

Matt just growled and ruffled his hair with his nervous fingers.

"She said Matt's my dad," Nat announced proudly, jumping on the bed.

All three adults froze. Matt looked at him with widened eyes, Becka covered her mouth – she didn't know if she wanted to scream or laugh, and Nora watched Matt in shock.

"What did she say?" Nora asked in a small voice, afraid she'd hear the same thing again.

"Matt is my dad," Nat repeated, nodding vigorously. "And I agree," he let them know there was no doubt in his mind about Matt's identity.

"Say something, darn it," Nora snapped at Matt.

He shrugged, "I am at a loss of words."

"How can you be at a loss of words?" she rebuked him. "You're a lawyer, for God's sake. You don't do anything but talk all day long."

He scowled at her and groused, "That's what you think lawyers do all day? And what the heck do you want me to tell him? He's three. What will he understand?"

"I don't know," she threw her hands in the air, "but you need to say something, and soon," she pointed out.

"Why me and not you?" he retorted furiously. By now, his eyes glinted and he spoke through tight teeth.

When Nora didn't have anything to say, Becka intervened, "If you two don't mind, maybe it's better to leave it like this for the moment. There's enough time to…"

"When? After he's convinced Matt's his father?" Nora pounced on her.

"Hey, I'm not the enemy here," Becka thought to mention and put her hands up. "Yet, Matt still has to take care of Nat for a while and I don't think antagonizing…"

"He's my father," Nat interrupted her furious. "Great-grandma said so," he said, and everyone noticed tears in his eyes.

"No one says differently, kiddo," Becka replied, ruffling his hair. "Just adult talk," she laughed.

"Becka," Nora said, staring at Matt. "Would you mind taking Nat with you to the coffee shop downstairs and buy me a latte or something? I'd owe you one."

"Buy one for me too," Matt said taking money out of his pocket. "And Nat, they have cookies, I hear. See what you want."

"I have money, Matt Winston," Nora tried to push his hand away so Becka couldn't take his money.

"And so do I," Becka said and exhaled loudly. Then, she took Nat's hand and pulled him with her. "We'll buy you some cookies and me some white chocolate," she explained to him.

"I want white chocolate too," the child scowled.

"Then you shall have it," Becka laughed. "Nothing wrong with that, once in a blue mood," she told him in a conspiratorial voice and left the room.

Nora looked after them. Matt didn't need to be a mind reader to know she was furious.

"Look," he started, but she stopped him, shaking her head.

"You need to straighten things up. When they come back," she insisted.

"You're right, but your timing sucks," he explained and she glared at him.

"I know you're upset, but the child must live with me for at least another week if not a little more. I won't have him upset. In time, he might transfer his wish of having a father upon someone else or... I don't know, okay? I know, though, I can't upset him now. It's enough he misses you, don't you think?" he tried to soothe her, stroking her arm, but she jerked away, and he tightened his teeth in frustration.

"Yes, but when I get out and he won't see you, he'll think it's my fault, and I have to live with him for much longer time than you do," she said and poked him in his chest with a finger.

"Is it absolutely necessary that he doesn't see me anymore?" he asked her.

His question came like a blow and stunned her. Nora just looked at him.

The silence stretched for almost a minute. Matt ran his fingers through his hair agitated, and then said sarcastically, "I see you glow with glee at my proposition."

She shook her head, and replied, "You just... stunned me. I thought you couldn't wait to get rid of me and Nat."

"Nat is great," Matt pointed out. "Why would I want to get rid of him?"

"Me, then," she groused, hurt by his words.

"I've never said that. I... like you... I think," he shrugged. "I thought... we should try at least... I mean... we should see how it works... if it works... We haven't seen each other in the best light until now, you know. We might be surprised with what might be..." he continued wishfully, and his eyes swept over her.

The day when she moved into the private room, he'd brought her a set of sweats at her request. They hang loose on her, but didn't hide much of her shape.

Nora's eyes glimmered, taking him in. Then, she closed her eyes for a couple of seconds, clenched and unclenched her hands a few times, and then looked straight into his eyes.

"Right now, I have a phobia about any kind of relations with a man."

"I know you've just divorced and I don't want to pressure you..."

Matt took a step toward her, but she stopped his words and his advancement with a gesture.

"It's not the divorce, Matt. The divorce was the end. It's been about a few years of resentments and upset... and... I know I'm unfair right now, but I lump all men in the same category – unworthy, untrusty, and better gone from my life."

"I see," Matt said quietly. "I think… I won't bother you then. Once you've recovered and can take care of Nat, I'll remove myself from your life, don't worry," he replied bitterly.

Nora watched him carefully, and then came to him and touched his chest, "No, I don't think I truly want that. Maybe… we can try and see how it goes… But you know Nat goes where I go… I don't have anyone to leave him with and…"

"Don't worry," Matt replied, taking her hands in his. Hope glimmered in his eyes and his tone didn't have the same resigned and bitter sound. "I don't mind having Nat around. And maybe, now and then, he can stay with Becka and Bryan for a couple of hours, to give you some respite," he smiled at her.

"Definitely," came Becka's reply from the door.

They turned to her, both surprised, and not a little guilty, and Becka smirked.

"I think it is a great idea, Matt, and I am sure Nat thinks the same, don't you Nat? Don't you like spending time with me and Bryan?"

Nat nodded vigorously, and then said, "And Bryan even cooks. Like you, mom. His food is very good," he said and licked his lips, making them laugh.

"So, you're a good cook," Becka concluded. "That's just perfect. Matt can't cook anything," she shrugged. "A lot like me. Matt, do you think it's a gene missing in our genetic code or what?"

Matt chuckled, and nudged her chin with his thumb, "Oh, kiddo, you're so funny."

"By the way," Becka told Nora, "on Saturday, Matt will take Nat sailing."

Nora frowned and turned to Matt, "I don't think it's safe."

"Oh, yes, it is," Becka contradicted her and patted her on the shoulder to smother any upset. "Matt is the best and most careful sailor you'll find, plus he insists on guests wearing the life saving vests, so Nat will be in no danger."

Nora seemed a little reluctant, but the imploring face of her son made her turn to Matt, "Are you sure you can take care of him while sailing?"

"Of course, I can," he responded, offended by her lack of faith.

"And if I can convince my mom to take care of the babies, Bryan and I can accompany them," Becka chimed in.

"And we'll come to you in the afternoon, so you'll see Nat is in one piece," Matt joked, which he regretted immediately when Nora scowled at him.

"By the way," Becka said, "I am sorry, but tomorrow, Nat won't be able to come to visit. I bought tickets to a puppet show and it's exactly after his nap," she apologized. "I hoped you wouldn't mind…"

Nora shook her head, immediately, "No, it isn't a problem. I can survive without visitors for one day," she smiled, but her smile was sad.

"You'll still have me," Matt rushed to say.

Becka burst into laughter at the look on his face when he realized what he'd said.

"I mean, I'll still come," he rephrased his statement, bad-mugging Becka.

CHAPTER TEN

Matt couldn't wait to have a visit with Nora just for himself. He'd enjoyed watching her interacting with Nat, and he'd been very pleased to see Nora getting along with Becka.

However, he longed to be alone with her. He wanted to further the relationship he'd told her about, and that wasn't going quite smooth when there were witnesses in the room.

He drove and left Nat and Becka at the puppet show, promising he'd be back for them before it ended. He hurried to the hospital afterwards and, on the way there, he stopped to buy her a potted orchid.

He remembered Nat's words. People brought flowers when they came to visit someone in the hospital.

Matt thought a little further ahead, and decided to buy her some cookies to nibble on, a couple of magazines and a new book. He'd already brought her a couple of books the day before, but he didn't think she had too much to do in that hospital room. He'd have crawled on the walls, had he been in her place.

He wasn't very sure about the magazines, but he decided he couldn't go wrong with a National Geographic and a Reader's Digest.

***

A knock on the room's door brought a smile on Nora's lips. Matt was early, but she wasn't sorry he was there already.

She'd been thinking about that visit since the day before. Once he'd planted the idea in her head, she'd been thinking of nothing else.

She left the book she was reading on her pillow, and said, "Come in."

The door opened and, to her surprise, it wasn't Matt the one coming into the room. An old woman, well in her eighties if not older, entered her room with the gait of a general. Her white hair rendered her black eyes more compelling, and those eyes zeroed in on Nora, as soon as she entered and closed the door behind.

Although she could see some resemblance with Matt, especially in the way the woman carried herself and the shape of her eyes, nose and mouth, Nora remarked, "I'm afraid you have the wrong room."

The woman gave her the chills. Her piercing look and the smile perched on her lips didn't reassure Nora at all.

"I've got the right room," the woman said and advanced into the room. "I'm Rebecca, Matt's great-grandmother. I think it's high time we met," she observed stretching her hand to Nora.

Nora politely shook her hand, but replied, "I haven't even thought it was the time to meet each other. I'm just a passing acquaintance of Matt and…"

"Balderdash," Rebecca retorted, and Nora's eyes widened. "Passing acquaintance, my foot. My great-grandson doesn't make a habit of caring for people's children. I don't even think he'd spent more than a couple of minutes with a child before meeting you," she waved her hand dismissively.

"Probably, he had his reasons," Nora said softly, and indicated a chair to the old woman to sit down, even though she'd have preferred to send her on her merry way.

Rebecca sat on the chair while Nora perched on the edge of the mattress. Rebecca's visit made her anxious and her nervousness increased with every second.

Nora supposed the old woman had come to tell her *'shoo away and leave my great-grandson alone'*, and she wasn't sure how she should react.

She'd pondered everything carefully since the previous afternoon and felt she wanted to get to know Matt better. She didn't welcome Rebecca's interference but, for the moment, she decided to wait before reacting.

"I brought you some chocolates," Rebecca said, and took a box of chocolates out of her huge handbag.

Nora thanked her with half a voice and put the chocolates on the night stand, next to the flowers she'd received from Nat and Matt.

Both women assessed each other in silence for a couple of minutes, and then, Rebecca began her attack.

"So, you're the woman who bewitched my Matt," she said, and her voice implied she'd already judged Nora and found her wanting.

A warning light shone in Nora's eyes. She proposed to herself to be polite with the woman – she was old, after all, and Matt's great-grandma, but she wasn't willing to let her humiliate her.

She knew she was somewhat average. Her hair was just a touch too fiery, her skin extremely pale and her green eyes too prominent on her face because of the paleness. Even her height was average, barely 5.4. What wasn't so average was the roundness of her hips and thighs and the size of her bust.

"I must say I was dying of curiosity to meet you," Rebecca continued, not bothered with Nora's attempt to warn her off. "Matt has never been unkind, but he's never gone so out of the way to please someone. He'd arranged his personal and professional life around you and your son," she noticed.

"Let's leave my son alone," Nora asked in a mild voice, yet the underlying steel was there, and Rebecca chuckled.

"Let's not," she retorted and Nora's eyes flashed with storms. "I like the little imp. He's smart and energetic – a good child. Someone took good care of him," she gave Nora her due. "Anyways," she fluttered her hand, "the idea is there's something with you and you reeled my Matty in," the old woman continued.

Nora looked at her with disbelief. Yes, Matt showed some interest, but he didn't seem hooked on her. He just expressed some interest in exploring a possible relationship. That didn't mean he was bewitched, as Rebecca claimed.

"Don't look at me like that, young lady," Rebecca snapped. "I know my boy and I know he's infatuated with you."

"If he's just infatuated, you don't have anything to worry about," Nora remarked very matter-of-factly.

She was sitting, her back ramrod straight and her hands quiet in her lap. Yet, inside, she seethed.

How dare you come here and judge me? What makes you think you're above me?

"I'll worry if I want. Now, I want what's best for my boy," Rebecca continued, as if she'd discussed the weather. "You're good, probably, given how Nat turned out, but..." she paused for effect, "you're not the best."

For a second, Nora couldn't breathe. She knew the old bat would say that, and yet it surprised her.

"Why are you here again?" she asked with nonchalance, as if she hadn't been insulted already.

"It's very simple girl," Rebecca replied. "You need money. That's no doubt there," she continued, and irony sounded in her voice. "I already know everything about you. That's how I traced you here," she waved her hand, showing the hospital room. "Now, you need to tell me how much you'd need to let Matt go. His future is somewhere else," the woman concluded in a demanding voice.

Nora looked at her in shock. She'd expected a dress down, more insults, threats, possibly. She didn't expect a demand to name her price.

She needed only a few seconds to recover, though, and then, she jumped off the bed and started bellowing.

CHAPTER ELEVEN

An icy fog claimed Matt's mind when the nurse told him Nora had an older woman visiting with her. He knew who that woman might be.

He needed a few seconds to react, and gather his thoughts. Then, in a hurry, he threw a *'thank you'* to the nurse over his shoulder, and practically ran to Nora's hospital room.

He perceived a raised voice coming from the room just before opening the door. He didn't waste time with knocking, but threw the door open. He stopped in the threshold, his nostrils flaring and his eyebrows almost knotted in a terrible frown.

Nora was looming over his great-grandma, and he couldn't stop admiring how good she looked in warrior mode.

"Is it clear?" she continued, without noticing his arrival. "I don't need your money or your approval. You can shove both where…"

"Young lady," Rebecca stopped her. "Your language is deteriorating," she observed with an icy contempt.

"So what?" she replied back. "I don't care for your opinion about me and you cannot buy me."

"Of course, not," the old woman remarked. "It's not like you'd accept less when you know Matt's financial worth now. You wouldn't, would you?" she sneered.

"I don't need his money or yours," Nora stressed out. "I make what I need. What I want is for you to get out of here and never come back," she shouted.

Then, she turned to the door to open it and throw the old bat out. She went cold all over when her eyes fell on Matt.

He was watching her with impenetrable eyes. He looked good, although slightly harassed, and regret nested in her heart.

She was a practical woman, though, so she squashed any regrets and feelings, and said, "You're just in time to show your great-grandmother to the door. I'll ask for a discharge tomorrow morning, so, yes, I apologize, but I do need you to watch Nat for me tonight. Tomorrow, though, I'll take him out of your hands." By the end, her voice shook, although she had started calm enough.

Matt didn't answer at first. Her flat voice sounded strained to his ears. He looked into her eyes and found them dull. The light he'd seen there yesterday was gone.

"Yes, I'll show great-grandma to the door, and yes, if you want to leave the hospital and it's safe to do so, I'm all for it. What won't happen is to make me go away," he pointed out.

Closing the distance between them, he touched her faintly rosy-colored cheek with his fingers. Anger had powdered her skin and her lips were trembling.

Without thinking, he leaned down, and lightly touched his mouth to hers. His fingers lingered on her face for a few more moments, and then, he straightened.

He stared at her a little more, and then, handed her the bag with the things he'd brought her, "Hold onto this, Nora. I have to take care of my great-grandma," he mentioned sarcastically.

He turned to Rebecca and asked, mildly interested, "Are you going out on your own steam or do you need my help?"

Both women gasped. Nora couldn't believe her ears. She'd actually thought he'd leave and that would be the end of it.

Rebecca was even more stunned. She'd never imagined Matt would actually take action against her. He'd grumble, yes, but, in time, he'd resign to her way of thinking.

She'd tried to wedge a rift between Nora and Matt the day before, when she told the child Matt was his dad. She liked the boy well enough, but she didn't think Matt should be with someone just because of his sense of duty. She wanted something more for him.

"How dare you talk to me like that?" she pounced on him.

"I asked whether you leave by yourself or I needed to have you removed," he rephrased his previous statement and stared Rebecca down.

The old woman huffed, and the color raised in her face. Nora felt sorry for her when she saw her lips quiver.

"Matt," she touched his arm hesitantly. "Maybe you shouldn't…"

"I should have long ago," Matt contradicted her in a steely voice. "Excuse me, honey," he said, and moved her hand from his arm.

He stepped closer to Rebecca and, unnervingly, he asked her again, "So what'll be, great-grandma?"

"If you think Marjorie won't hear about this…" Rebecca threatened, but Matt put up his hand and stopped her.

"I don't give a… fig," he blue-pencilled his language. "Mother will understand," he shrugged. "Now, I want you to leave," he said in an even sterner voice.

Rebecca had had enough. She straightened and in the most authoritative voice, replied, "You understand you'd never get your hands on the trust money."

Nora gasped lightly. She hadn't intended to make Matt lose his money or put him in the cross hairs with his family because of her.

She rushed and touched his arm again, "Matt, I don't want you to…"

"But I do," he replied, always watching Rebecca with flinty eyes.

Rebecca realized he wouldn't back down, and she glared at him. She turned on her heels without a word and left the room.

Matt made note of her glare and knew what she'd do first. He turned to Nora, caressed her face with his fingers, and said, "I'm sorry, but I need to let mom know that Rebecca will park on her doorstep."

"Oh, my God, your mom will hate me, if only for that," Nora cried out with dismay.

Her chances with Matt became thinner and thinner, and she admonished herself for not listening to her reason.

She knew she shouldn't have gotten involved with anyone. She had other priorities in mind and again, she'd set herself up for disappointment.

"Be serious," Matt replied. "Mom's not like that," he explained to her and helped her sit on the bed.

Then, he took the phone out of his pocket to call his mother. He intended to call Jay afterward and ask him to go and take Becka and Nat from the theatre and bring them to the hospital.

CHAPTER TWELVE

Nora watched Matt talking to his brother, Jay, over the phone, and envied the easy camaraderie between the two. She'd never had such an open and warm relationship with anyone in her family.

The conversation with his brother relaxed Matt. He'd been enraged before.

She'd felt his tension – the man was hopping mad, and all that made her nervous. Now, though, he slowly came back to something close to his normal peaceful self.

Matt had surprised Nora a second time that day when he called his mother in her presence. She'd assumed he'd leave the room so she couldn't hear his explanations.

The call hadn't lasted long. Matt had succinctly explained to his mother that he had a girlfriend, which stunned Nora even more. She hadn't known he was thinking of her in those terms. Not that she minded. She might have been a realistic woman, but still liked to dream now and then, and she'd fantasized about Matt a lot, and in a very short span of time.

He'd also confessed to his mother that his choice didn't meet his great-grandma's expectations and, consequently, she had done her best to sabotage him, which he couldn't abide.

He hadn't gone into details, but warned her that Rebecca was probably on her way to her house. She'd definitely want to complain about the ungrateful brat, he'd turned out to be.

Nora hadn't been able to hear his mother's replies, but Matt's words and behavior had astonished her. He'd even chuckled a couple of times and in the end, he'd resignedly accepted an invitation to dinner on Nora's behalf for when she would leave the hospital.

Jay needed much less explanations than Matt's mother. Matt just told him he'd quarreled with Rebecca, who'd interfered in his relationship with Nora, and asked him to go and take Becka and Nat from the theatre and drive them to the hospital.

He didn't want to leave the hospital before he had a chance to speak to Nora, and Bryan was watching the babies that afternoon.

When he'd organized everything to his liking, he shoved the phone into his pocket and turned to her.

"I think I need to apologize for my great-grandma's behavior," Matt said, and his posture showed he wasn't very sure about what to say.

Nora had been standing all that time, and now, exhausted after all the commotion and the roller-coaster of emotions and thoughts, she walked with difficulty toward the bed and sat down. Her stiff and painful legs barely supported her.

The doctor had advised her to use crutches, but if she limped, she didn't put much weight on the injured leg. She preferred not to be encumbered by the crutches, especially because her chest hurt whenever she tried to use them.

She looked at him thoughtfully and replied, "You know she thinks I refused her money only because I thought you'd have more."

"And why would you care?" he asked her. "You didn't seem so concerned with what people thought of you a few days ago," he alluded to the day in his office.

"I didn't care about what you thought then," she admitted with a shrug, "but I seem to care now."

"And why do you care now?" Matt closed the distance between them.

He sat on the bed next to her and took her hand in his. He felt the light shake in her fingers.

'She's not indifferent to me. Far for it.' A satisfied smile perched on his lips and he squeezed her fingers carefully.

"Because it matters," Nora replied quietly, staring into his eyes. "It's impossible for you not to think I'm a fortune hunter, especially with everything you know about me," she continued ruefully.

She remembered very well what had been said in that conference room in his office. She didn't forget what he told her when they met in the street, either.

"I know better now," he said, and brought her fingers to his mouth.

Nora glared at him and reclaimed her fingers, "What do you know better now?"

Matt heaved a deep sigh. He knew he'd have to tell her one day, but he'd hoped that wouldn't be the day.

There had been enough turmoil for an afternoon, and he was afraid she wouldn't respond well when she found out the truth.

He needed emotional distance to do it, so he stood and sauntered to the window where he leaned on the windowsill. His eyes roamed over her, a strange light shining in his dark-blue pupils. He lingered over some choice spots, and his nostrils flared. Then, he turned serious and looked straight into her eyes.

"I've done what I should have done before you'd signed those divorce papers," he finally confessed.

She drew a long breath. She felt like she couldn't get enough air. She couldn't look away from him. Matt's eyes were very compelling.

"What does that mean?" she asked for clarifications.

"It means I hired an investigator," he replied quietly, watching her carefully. He didn't want to miss any of the reactions playing openly on her face.

"What for?" she flashed out at him, and her eyes narrowed.

She had some suspicions and she didn't like them at all. After finding out that Rebecca had checked on her, hearing the same thing from Matt made her seethe.

"Because, during the last few days, I got to know the real you, and what I read in that file before that meeting didn't match what lay before my eyes," he shrugged, to excuse himself.

"So, you wanted to make sure I didn't try to dupe you," she replied in a quarrelsome voice.

Matt didn't say anything for a few seconds and just looked at her. He just knew that what he was going to say might spoil his chances with her.

"Wouldn't you have done the same?" he asked quietly. "I mean I read that file, and I thought I had the correct information before my eyes – for which, by the way, I'm going to kill my partner when he comes back from his honeymoon," he groused out. "He should have done his homework and not accept such a case. I mean, we're lawyers and, sometimes, we do defend people who don't deserve it, but not in such situations, like yours," he said furiously, clenching and unclenching his fists.

He took a few seconds to calm down, and then continued, pointing to her, "Then, there you were. I got to know you, and nothing I saw matched the image I already had in my head. Wouldn't you question your instincts, Nora?" Matt inquired softly.

'*Especially when you've already been burnt,*' he added in his mind caustically, always his steady gaze trained on her.

"Maybe, yes," she admitted with a noncommittal shrug.

She understood in a way, although she wasn't very comfortable with him knowing so much about her when she knew almost next to nothing about him.

"You know, we're not equal in anything," she pointed out.

"What the… heck, do you mean?" he groused, finding himself again in the situation of changing what he said in mid-sentence.

His language had worsened during the last few days and he knew where to place the blame.

"Well, let's see," she tapped a finger to her lips, suddenly feeling mean.

The day had strained her and it wasn't over yet. She needed to release some of the pant-up pressure, and she chose him to be the recipient. She knew she wasn't fair, but, that very moment, being fair seemed overrated.

"You seem to know everything about me, while I know next to nothing about you," she pointed out.

"You know plenty," he said, pushing away from the window.

With heavy steps, he came toward her.

"Come on, Nora! We've spent together a good part of a few days already. You must already have some knowledge about me. I know there are other things you need to find out and you will," he said.

Matt inhaled deeply to calm sudden doubts. Few people would accept his loony bin family, and especially their special skills.

"There might be things you'll dislike or which will make you run for safety, I know, but I won't hide anything from you," he stated with determination.

Now he loomed over her, not very comfortable with his decision of being completely open with her. That was something he'd never tried before. He'd always kept something secret, even from his parents and siblings.

"You have money, I have only a paycheck," she pointed out. "Even my savings have been lost when I contributed to the advance for the house," she explained in a disheartened voice.

"Yes, I know. It was the money you should have received after the divorce, and I made it impossible, I know," Matt nodded, in a bleak mood now, his nervous fingers running through his hair.

"Don't gloss over what I'm saying here, Matt," Nora snapped at him. "I didn't say I lost money because of you. I said you have money while I don't."

"Unimportant," he waved that argument away.

"How can you say it's unimportant? Rebecca already labelled me, and the remaining part of your family will soon follow suit," she said with exasperation.

"Some will," he admitted and sat next to her.

He took her hand in his again. Now, a smile played on his lips, and drove Nora crazy.

"How can you be so unconcerned about that?" she cried out. "Matt, I'm talking to you," she poked him, when she saw he was more concerned with her palm than what she was saying.

"I know you are," he looked up into her eyes, suddenly very serious. "I can guarantee there will be family members who will try to undermine your position and say vile things about you. It would have happened even if you'd had a fortune, or blue blood or whatever. Bryan went through all that, you know. If Becka and he survived, in the end, we will too, I promise you."

"I have a child," she reminded him.

"So? I can't see any problem there. The little imp is smart and sweet. And he is yours, so I have no issue with that."

"But others will," she replied quietly, and touched his face. "I might not be the best choice for you, Matt, even for a brief affair."

"First, I don't need a brief affair, Nora," he replied dryly. "If I wanted an affair, I wouldn't be here. Second, I don't care about the best choice," he said, watching her intensely. "I care about my choice."

He leaned and kissed her lips briefly and then stood up to walk his frustration.

"All right, we might have a fall out, today, tomorrow or next year. Or we might end up together," Matt said. Nettled, he turned back to her. "What will be, will be. We can't change it, Nora. But I'd be damned if I let some hypocrites dictate my actions and my choices," he boomed, and Nora's eyes opened wide.

"Very well said, son," a melodic voice came from the door.

CHAPTER THIRTEEN

Shocked, Nora and Matt turned like one. Someone had entered the room, and they hadn't noticed. A hushed cry flew off Nora's lips, but Matt's hand on hers, reassured her that everything was fine.

Marjorie Winston, and her husband Jonathan, stood just inside the door, holding hands, as always. Pride for her first born had brought tears in Marjorie's eyes.

Jonathan smiled at the younger couple with delight. Once, in the past, he'd been in the exact sore spot where his son stood now, and he understood better than anyone what Matt felt.

"Mother," Matt exclaimed with exasperation. "I thought we arranged to see each other when Nora was discharged," he reproached to her.

"I know, I know," she waved her hand. "I also know you'd have found a way to keep me away, afraid I'd try to meddle in your business, like grandma," she admonished him, waving her finger under his nose. "You should know me better than that, my first born," she chided him. "Plus, I needed a reason not to talk to grandma. She came just when we were leaving. We apologized because we were in a rush, and left her there," she said, and then, pensively, she continued, "I hope she won't still be there on the door stoop when we get back home. She didn't take it well, I must say."

Nora glanced at Matt, and the blush spreading on his face and neck surprised her.

"Care to make the introductions, Matty?" his father asked, amused, and his smile reflected in his dark eyes.

Curious, Nora studied Matt's parents. Matt didn't take after only one of them. He had his mother's eyes and father's coloring.

His mother seemed very serious and his father easy-going. Matt's temper was a combination of the two.

Matt sighed and glanced at Nora. He shrugged, took her hand and brought her in front of his parents.

"This is Nora, my girlfriend," he introduced her. "Nora, this is my nosy sweet mother, Marjorie Winston, and this is my father, who, if I know him well, and I do, has definitely been dragged here. He's Jonathan Winston."

Nora barely kept her laughter, however his father chuckled and slapped his son over the shoulder.

Marjorie scowled at Matt, and then took Nora's stretched hand. Yet, instead of shaking it, she pulled the younger woman into a hug.

Now, that astounded Nora. She'd expected a different welcome from Matt's parents. They certainly must have had higher expectations for their son, not a single, almost broke, mother.

She didn't even know what her financial situation was right then. Matt had helped her to fill in the forms for a disability claim two days before, but she still had to wait for an answer.

She awkwardly hugged Marjorie back, and no sooner had Marjorie released her, that Jonathan enveloped her in a bear-hug. As tall and well-built as Matt, Jonathan didn't bother to control his strength, and she yelped at the sudden pain.

Immediately, Matt pulled her in his arms, and, with a ferocious scowl, bellowed to his father, "She's hurt, damn it."

Then, he led her to the bed as if she'd come unglued before them, and nudged her to lie down.

"I don't want to lie down in front of your parents, Matt," she hissed. "I'm fine, it was just a twinge, really," she attempted to convince him, but he didn't have any of that.

"Who are you kidding now? If I didn't know the extent of your wounds…" Matt shook his head.

"I'm very sorry, Nora," Jonathan came and caressed her arm. "I haven't realized you were hurt," he explained.

"Why would she be in hospital if she weren't?" Matt growled, and everyone looked at him, as if he'd lost his mind.

"It's not like I knew the circumstances of her hospitalization," he reproached to his son.

"Don't worry about," Nora waved Jonathan's sincere concern away. Then, she turned to Matt, and, in a soft voice, she said, "It was just a twinge, really. I'm fine. I'll even talk to the doctor to discharge me in the morning," she explained, stroking his arm to soothe him.

"Allow him to worry, pumpkin," Marjorie told her.

She came to the bed as well and wedged in between the two men. Gently, but with steel determination, she helped Nora lie down, which made Matt very happy.

"You have to give a man his due, now and then. Their pride is a fragile thing, I'm afraid, and you need to placate them," she said, brushing Nora's hair away from her forehead.

"Hey!" an entire chorus of male protests came from around the room.

Nora peeked past Marjorie, and chuckled. Both Matt and Jonathan were scowling. Then she noticed the scowl of a third man, who'd come with Becka and Nat. It was a darn convention gathering in her room.

Unruffled, Marjorie patted her hand and turned to the others. She said with nonchalance, "It's true, you know."

Then she noticed the new people in the room, and greeted them, "Hi, Becka and Jay. I haven't seen you there."

"We've come just in time to hear you, auntie" Becka grinned. "And I absolutely agree with you," she nodded vigorously.

"Not you too," Jay complained.

"Who do we have here?" Marjorie looked at the toddler, who was clinging on to Becka's hand.

Nat hid behind Becka shyly, and Nora tried to jump off bed, only to be stopped by Matt.

"Easy, honey. My mom won't have him for dessert," he attempted to joke, but her glare told him he wasn't funny.

Then, he eased her up, in a sitting position.

"Stay here," he ordered, and she frowned.

Matt didn't pay attention to her frown, but called Nat to him. The boy came from behind Becka and launched himself at him, hugging his legs.

"Easy, Nat," Matt said, in the same voice he'd used with Nora. "Look, these are my parents," he turned the boy around, and pointed to Marjorie and Jonathan.

That was all it took for the boy. He forgot his shyness and greeted Matt's parents with a smile.

Marjorie showered him with compliments and made him feel important, and Jonathan shook his hand. Nat beamed with pride.

After a few minutes of inane chatter, Marjorie turned to Nora, "So, tomorrow, you want to be discharged. You know you can't go at home alone, especially with Nat. I doubt you could manage by yourself."

"I will, don't worry," Nora dismissed Marjorie's concerns.

She didn't want Marjorie to believe she'd be a burden, and she'd be clutching at her son.

Matt didn't even bother to tell her she was wrong. He just rode rough-shod over her words.

"Of course, she won't be alone. She and Nat will stay with me until she recovers. I understand it might take a few months."

"Matthew Winston," Nora glowered at him and pushed him, so she could stand. "I won't have you tell me what to do," she poked him in his chest with her finger.

"She has the same bad habit, mother, like you. She likes to poke," Matt chuckled.

Jonathan and Jay joined in his hilarity, which didn't endear them with the two women.

"Yep, that she does," Jay said and came next to Matt and elbowed him, a grin on his face.

However, neither Nora nor Marjorie were amused with them. Nora raised a brow and stared Matt down, while Marjorie just gave them the evil eye.

Becka thought she'd better save what was left of that visit. The men seemed unaware of the bad currents, and the other two women were seething.

"I think Nora's correct if she wants to decide her own recovery, Matt," she said, and Matt glinted his eyes at her. "And I'm very sure she'll decide to live with you, and take advantage of your help with Nat. After all, we all know she loves Nat above all."

Nora knew she'd been trapped by Becka's words. She couldn't stubbornly insist she'd live by herself. She knew she had physical limitations for the moment, and didn't want to endanger her son. Yet, it didn't seem right to just move in with Matt.

Nat kept looking from an adult to another. He was confused because of their behavior, but he understood just fine that Matt wanted them to live with him.

"We'll go home with Matt, mommy, right?" he asked Nora, putting her on the spot again.

She sighed deeply and said, "We'll see, sweetie. Mommy will have to think it over, all right?"

CHAPTER FOURTEEN

Nora sat on the cushy pillow laid on the wide window sill, watching the marina. Matt's apartment had a superb view of the harbor and Nora had already learned to enjoy it.

The morning after meeting Matt's parents, Nora persuaded the doctor to discharge her. She promised she'd take it easy and start physiotherapy after two weeks.

Matt supported her and assured the doctor he'd make sure she'd not overtax her body. Of course, he took her to his apartment directly, and started doing just what he'd promised.

During that afternoon with Matt's parents, for Nat's sake, she'd accepted to go home with Matt, although she wasn't sure it was a smart move.

Whenever she thought of the encounter with Marjorie and Jonathan, she shook her head with dismay. That had been one of the most confusing afternoons she'd ever lived, and she wasn't sure she'd entirely understood what had happened.

Nora feared everything would crumble to her feet in no time. She'd had her doubts when Matt came to take her from the hospital the morning she was released. Some of those doubts didn't disappear during the following two days, although Matt had been very considerate, in his own way, ever since.

Matt offered her the third bedroom available in his apartment. That brought some relief. She'd feared he'd nurtured certain expectations, and she didn't think she could live up to them, not so early in their relationship anyway.

Her ex might have painted her in harlot's colors, but at heart, she was an old-fashioned woman. Aside from her ex-husband, she'd been involved with only one other man before her marriage. That relationship had lasted for almost three years.

She wasn't completely at ease in Matt's house, though, in spite of Matt's efforts to make her feel welcome. Not used to be underfoot and waited hand and foot, she worried that, one day, he might feel crowded or view her or her son as an imposition.

Living in the same house with him gave her more insight into the kind of man he was. She found out new things about him all the time, and she liked more and more the man she discovered.

Yet, one thing distressed her: Matt was overbearing. He didn't allow her to do anything, not even to carry her cup to the sink or dishwasher. He'd jump to his feet at once and nudge her to sit or lie down.

He expected her to obey his edict of not lifting a finger and rest as much as possible. If she didn't, discussions aroused.

Even when it came to Nat, they had arguments. She couldn't complain he tried to separate them. He was all for her to spend as much time as possible with her son, but only if she didn't try to take care of the boy's bath, for example, or prepare his food.

Bryan still supplied them with meals, and that embarrassed her to no end. Yes, she had a hard time standing and walking, but she could do most of the cooking sitting, in her opinion. Of course, Matt was deaf to any argument.

The thought he was so domineering drove her crazy. As result, they butted heads all the time, and they hadn't spent seventy-two hours together yet.

Every time a discussion aroused, Matt would lecture. He'd speak in a calm voice, as if he'd tried to pacify her. That tone of voice riled her more than if he'd shouted at her.

She had eyes and could see the twitch in his jaw or the flash of his eyes when she turned to be very stubborn. Yet, he pretended he wasn't upset, and left the impression she'd overreacted, as if he'd had to calm a child's tantrum.

The buzz of the intercom interrupted her ruminations. She glanced at the door surprised. Matt had left with Nat for ice-cream half an hour ago, but Nora doubted he didn't have the key.

For a moment, she thought to ignore the intercom, yet the person calling was stubborn enough and kept punching the code in. With her heart in her boots, Nora tiptoed to the door.

The intercom went finally silent, and she sighed satisfied with the respite. She turned to go back to her favorite spot, when the beeps began again and she jumped up. The sudden move jarred her leg, and she hissed at the piercing pain, tears welling in her eyes.

Now, her temper flushed, she pushed the key and asked in a belligerent voice, "Who's there?"

"Finally," Marjorie's melodious voice came and Nora froze. "We were concerned something happened to you. I've just spoken to Matt and he said you were alone at home," Marjorie said, and then, sighed with relief. "Buzz us in, Nora, dear," she asked.

Nora closed her eyes in defeat. She didn't even want to know who that 'us' was. Far too many people were around Matt all the time. During the last few years, she'd learned to content herself with Nat's company. She didn't have family or a string of friends to visit her.

She pressed the button to open the door downstairs, and unlocked the apartment door. Then, she leaned on the wall, waiting for the group to come upstairs.

A few minutes later, a knock sounded on the door and she opened it. Stunned, she looked at the people crowded on the landing. She knew most of them. At least she's already met most of them.

Marjorie and Becka beamed at her and came in, leading the way for the others. Marjorie took one of her arms, and Becka the other. They both helped her to get to the sofa without allowing her to put much weight on the injured leg.

The others followed, chatting with each other, and carrying bags in their hands.

Nora couldn't understand that family. They baffled her. Ironically, she understood Rebecca. Her behavior was predictable. Theirs wasn't. She couldn't believe they'd visit with her and not berate her for laying her hands on their golden boy, Matt, as Rebecca said.

Marjorie sat next to Nora with a whimsical smile on her face, and patted her hand, as if she'd known what thoughts crossed the woman's mind.

"This is my husband, Bryan," Becka motioned a tall, well-built man to come and make Nora's acquaintance.

Nora's eyes swept over the strong shoulders and prominent cheekbones. She noted the scar on his left cheek, but didn't react. She beamed at him, grateful for everything he'd done for her son and herself.

"Nice to meet you," he said, shaking her hand. "I'm going to put the food in the fridge," he winked at her. "You'll have enough for about three days, now. Some of it will go into the freezer, but Matt is capable enough to microwave it," he grinned.

"Jonathan, take our bags to the kitchen, as well," Marjorie asked her husband, in the voice of a general.

He just saluted her jokingly. First, he came to Nora, kissed her cheek and asked, "Is everything fine? Does my boy treat you right?"

Taken aback, Nora couldn't formulate an answer and just nodded.

"Good, then," Jonathan approved, patted her shoulder, and sauntered in the direction of the kitchen.

"Have you cooked as well?" Nora asked Marjorie with dismay.

"Of course, dear. I mean I knew Bryan cooked for you, but I had to contribute with something," Marjorie explained with a shrug. "What kind of mother would I be if I let others take care of my children, huh?"

Nora didn't know how to answer and wide-eyed, she just stared at her. For a moment, she thought Marjorie had taken a pot-shot at her because she did let someone else take care of her son. Marjorie rubbed her arm, and beamed at her some more, until Nora thought she'd simply scream.

"Now, let's see... You know Jay already," Marjorie continued, as if she hadn't noticed Nora's confusion and distress.

Jay waved at her, and the grin on his lips told Nora he knew what she was thinking. She wondered what he'd say if she wiped that grin off his lips with a well-aimed fist. Those Winstons played with her mind.

"This is our daughter, Maggie. She's Jay's twin," she specified, the ghost of a smile in the corner of her mouth.

Nora understood why. Maggie and Jay looked anything but alike. Jay had inherited his father's eyes, and his hair was dark blond, while Maggie had her mother's eyes and her father's coloring, like Matt. Anyone would have guessed Maggie and Matt were siblings. Jay was more difficult to place in the family, if one didn't know his mother, as well.

"Hey, there," Maggie greeted her with exuberance, almost hopping in place, her curls going this way and that way.

At the tone of her voice, Nora winced inwardly. She just knew Matt's sister was one of those women with excess of energy, who were busy all the time and never stopped to rest or smell the roses. Nora wasn't a slacker herself, but people like Maggie exhausted her just with their presence.

Nora merely waved back with a shy smile, and Maggie, her dark hair bouncing in thick and silky curls, tucked her legs under her on the carpet, next to the armchair Jay had already claimed.

"This is Lily," Marjorie presented the other young woman in the room. "Lily is my niece, and Matt's cousin," she explained.

Lily shook Nora's hand with warmth, but she didn't have Maggie's enthusiasm. Nora's eyes took everything in - the tall and slender silhouette, the short curvy red hair and dark blue eyes. Lily was exactly what she wasn't, and she seemed of the same age or maybe a couple of years younger.

"I'll take the cakes and snacks out of the bags," Lily said, looking at Marjorie, and then she attacked the bag close to her.

The bags, with the exception of the bags Bryan and Jonathan carried into the kitchen, had been left next to the coffee table. Nora had imagined they'd been shopping. The thought they'd brought cakes and snacks for the visit didn't cross her mind.

"I should be the one offering you some coffee or cakes," she suddenly realized.

She tried to stand up and go search Matt's kitchen. It wasn't her house, true enough, but she lived there for the time being and she had to play the hostess role.

"Don't be silly," Marjorie stopped her. "You may hold with ceremony when you have friends or acquaintances in the house, but we're family. Matt would never talk to me again if I'd let you go through all that trouble," she shook her head at Nora.

"You only have to get used to having a large family," Becka laughed.

"Not easy, believe me," her husband, who was just coming back from the kitchen, carrying two platters with hors-d'oeuvre, replied. "By the way," he said to everybody, "Jonathan is making coffee. I boiled some water to make some tea for you, Becka," he told his wife, who thanked him with a nod.

"But you're the guests in the house... I mean... I...," Nora started stuttering.

The idea that they might think she was actually the guest in that house swiftly dawned on her. She couldn't contradict them - they were right.

"We are the guests, that's true," Maggie said, "but you are in convalescence, and that gives us the right to change roles," she waved her worries aside.

"I didn't mean..." Nora tried to explain, but Jonathan, coming with coffee and cups, interrupted her.

"But you should," he said putting everything on the table. "If I know my Matt, you have the right to think you're in your house and we're just guests."

"No, no, no, I didn't mean..."

"Don't trouble yourself," Marjory took her hand. "Matt will be here in no time and I don't want to explain to him why you're agitated and how we upset you."

"Matt's stubborn enough not to talk to us for a year," Jay remarked and Nora stared at him. Disbelief and shock marked her face, for everyone to see.

Matt and Nat chose that exact moment to arrive.

CHAPTER FIFTEEN

When Nat learned they had guests, he didn't want to linger in the ice-cream shop anymore. He insisted on going back home at once.

Matt didn't argue with him. He needed to be there as well, and shield Nora from any possible attacks, so they rushed back home.

Now, Matt glanced at Nora and saw the shock on her face. He'd already worried, but now he became livid, and his ire narrowed his eyes and his nostrils flared.

He asked in a stern voice, "Now, who upset Nora and how? What did you say to her?"

Much to his dismay, their reactions to his words weren't what he'd expected. He'd expected excuses or explanations, but none came.

Jay and Maggie burst into laughter and howled like hyenas. Nora tried to say something, opened her mouth, but nothing came out. His mother glared at him and shook her head in disapproval.

"Now, Matt, is this a way to talk to your parents?" she chastised him.

"If you distressed her…" Matt started saying, but his father came to him and slapped him on the shoulder.

"Call back the troops, son," he said with a chuckle. "Nobody declared any kind of war here. Nora simply can't believe we take care of our people and we consider her part of the family now. No need to blow a fuse over that," he shook his head to his first born.

Matt looked around and felt ashamed. He picked a thought here and there and realized his father was telling the truth.

He'd assumed a lot of wrong things. No one was guilty of anything and were openly making fun of him.

"Come on, brother," Maggie said from her spot near Jay, "lighten up. We're not here to upset Nora, but the opposite. And we brought gifts, by the way," she mentioned and pointed to the snacks Lily was still setting on the table.

Lily knew Matt and took his outburst in stride. Matt always jumped to defend people who couldn't defend themselves. She imagined he'd seen Nora as the sacrificial lamb when he found her in the middle of his close-knit family.

"So you're all right," he said to Nora, although he didn't sound very confident.

Nora just nodded and stretched her hand to Nat who came to her immediately.

"We bought ice-cream for you too, mommy. Matt asked what you liked best and bought you pistachio," he said, although his tongue knotted around the word '*pistachio*'.

Everyone smiled and Nora kissed the top of his head, "That's awesome, baby. I can't wait to taste it."

"Not before you try my pastries, I hope," Marjorie intervened.

"You're in for a treat," Lily said, finally finishing fussing with the food. "Aunt Marjorie is the best when it comes to baking."

"I wouldn't sell Bryan so short," Becka contradicted her, a scowl on her face. "His pastries are heavenly, so that you know."

"Thank you, sweetheart," Bryan said with a self-deprecating laugh. "That's what a man wants to be praised for -- his pastries."

"Come on, Bryan, everyone knows how macho you are," she blew off his concerns.

"That's true," Jay noted. "You have nothing to worry about. One look at you, and no one would give a thought to your pastries, Bryan."

"What do you mean?" Becka asked in an icy voice, measuring him.

"Becka, Becka, Becka," Jay shook his head. "The man rivals a mountain. One look coming from those steely eyes of his, and no one would dare to say anything to him."

"But Rebecca," Bryan corrected him, and another round of laughter burst out.

"Oh, man, I won't ever forget what happened when she met you that first time," Jonathan slapped his knee. "Matt, you need more seats around here. How come I haven't noticed that before?" he wondered.

"Because you've never come in groups," Matt observed dryly. "I'll make sure to add more furniture in the near future. Now, let's borrow the chairs from the breakfast table and…" he frowned, thinking what else to bring in.

He thought of the bar stools in the kitchen, but they weren't very cozy for a chat in the living-room. He also had a chair in his den, but nothing else.

"I'm okay," Bryan said.

He left the tea he'd brought for Becka on the coffee table, and then, pulled Becka up. After he took her seat, he lowered her in his lap.

"Nat will seat in my lap," Marjorie demanded.

She waved to the boy, calling him to her, which he did immediately -- another surprise for Nora.

"I'm good," Maggie told Matt from where she sat on the carpet.

He knew she was. Maggie rarely sat in an armchair or on a sofa, if she could sit on the floor with her legs tucked under her. Many made fun of her, calling her the gypsy of the family.

"So, you need only two chairs," Lily made the math for him. "One for me and one for you," she waved her hand around to the others who were all seated.

"Right, two chairs coming up," Matt attempted to joke.

He wanted to lighten the mood because he felt awkward after accusing his family of nefarious endeavours. Then, he brought the chairs from the breakfast table.

***

Nora lay down on her bed, sated with food and laughter and fun. She'd felt out of her element when Matt's family came to visit, but that changed once everyone was pushing food on to her and recounted stories of a much younger Matty.

She'd felt included. She was the centre of attention, although sometimes, either Matt or his mother fanned too much over her.

A couple of times, she even rolled her eyes, which amazed her. She hadn't done that since her high-school years.

Some of the stories they told had been either very touching or very rambunctious, but she enjoyed them all. She also enjoyed seeing Matt blush a few times.

He couldn't touch her because he was seated across from her, yet, she was aware of his intense gaze all the time. She even felt the caress of his dark-blue pupils all over her skin, whenever his eyes swept over her.

Sometimes, her heart would trot faster and she wondered how Marjorie didn't hear it. At the same time, she got hotter and hotter under that intensity and the waves of desire coming from him. Those raw sensations, which she didn't want or afford to feel right then, bothered her a lot.

Despite Matt's opposition, Marjorie and Jonathan shared their memories about Matt as a toddler. Sometimes, she laughed hearing about his antics, but mostly, her feelings for Matt grew a little more.

His siblings and cousins told stories about him as a teenager. They were so good in recounting those times, she could almost see Matt, as a teenager, always chased by girls or ready to play an inoffensive prank, which would land him up in the principal's office.

Maggie's stories were the most outrageous. Some of the things she related shocked her parents. Apparently, they were completely unaware such things had happened in their children's life during their adolescence. Jonathan laughed heartily, but Marjorie had to fan herself a few times.

Once, Matt growled and threatened his sister, promising serious payback if she didn't stop. Maggie just laughed at him, and high-fived Jay, who supported and contributed to all her stories.

For Nora, it had been a magical afternoon and evening. She'd never experienced so much camaraderie between family members. Her family had never shared such joyful and touching moments.

Yet, something bothered her. Sometimes someone would begin to tell a story, and, suddenly, all eyes turned to them in warning. Immediately, they'd changed their story in mid-sentence. She even surprised a few imperceptible shakes of the head. Every time, Bryan mused, and an ironic smile appeared on his lips, as if he'd been in on the secret.

She was sure they hid something from her. She didn't know what, but intended to find out. She felt as if it were something very important and decisive for the evolution of her relationship with Matt.

Light knocks on the door drew her back to the present. She hesitated a fleeting second, but then she softly said, "Come in."

Matt opened the door and stopped. He'd mussed his hair again, undoubtedly by running his fingers through it. She'd noticed that habit several times and found it charming.

Dressed only in dark slacks and a white shirt, which defined his shoulders and was open half way down, he looked good to eat. Too bad she was on a strict diet.

He looked her over, his dark-blue eyes getting darker while sweeping over her sleeveless nightie. The cotton hugged the curves of her body in the right places, and, unaware, he licked his lips.

He looked his fill and then, said, "I saw you still had the light on… I imagined you were still awake so… I thought we could… talk, maybe. I don't feel like going to bed already," he explained with some difficulty.

Matt massaged the base of his nose. It wasn't like him not to find his words, but his world had changed dramatically lately, and he felt like walking in a haze.

"Yes, of course," she said.

She sat up carefully. Her movements didn't pain her so much now when most of the soreness was gone.

She leaned back on the headboard. His eyes followed the fall of the thick red mass of hair over her shoulders.

With a pat on the bed, she invited him to sit. He hurried to do so, after closing the door. It was more than he'd expected when he decided to come to her room.

"I hear if Nat wakes up, don't worry," he thought to assure her. "Are you very tired?" he asked, concern showing in his eyes. "I know a lot of people visited tonight and you're still in convalescence. I saw it on your face, you know. The exhaustion, I mean. It was obvious you were tired."

"Oh, that's why you rushed everybody out," she guessed, and he nodded.

"You shouldn't have," she said, shaking her head. "Yes, I felt a little tired now and then, but that's because I'm not used to such gatherings, Matt," she stroked his strong forearm with a featherlike touch, and a shiver ripped through his body. She thought she'd imagined everything and continued, "But everybody had fun, including me."

"I'm glad you enjoyed their company, Nora. I love the others in the family, even Rebecca sometimes, but the people who were here tonight are the ones I love the most. If you feel good in their company, then it's perfect," he said, half-facing her, playing with her fingers and looking intently into her eyes.

He'd touched her fingers several times by then. The first time, his touch had surprised her. She'd have thought the skin on a lawyer's fingers and palms was smooth, yet Matt's wasn't. His skin was rough and, every time he slid his fingers over hers, she felt the touch deep in her core.

"You do some physical labor, don't you?" she asked before she was even aware she'd opened her mouth.

She cringed when the meaning of her own words dawned on her. He chuckled when she closed her eyes with dismay.

"You know you can ask me anything," he said softly, his fingers touching her wrist and sliding up on her forearm.

She shook her head and licked her bottom lip. Then, she opened her eyes and said, "You're touching my hands and arms all the time."

"I'd love to touch all of you all the time," he admitted, and her eyes rounded. "Don't worry, Nora, I know you need time, and not only to recover physically. I know you're not ready to open yourself to me emotionally now," Matt said very matter-of-factly, and touched the side of her face. "But a man still can hope," he chuckled with self-deprecation.

"What if I'm never ready?" she inquired in a whispered voice.

He shrugged and bowed his head, his eyes following the finger he slid up and down on the inside of her arm. Then, he looked up at her, a strange light in his eyes.

"I'm a grown-up, I'll survive," he shrugged again. "It wouldn't be like I could blame you or force you to like or love me," he pointed out.

"I like you just fine, Matt," she said, and brushed the hair off his forehead.

Matt, always watching her intently, leaned over her and touched his mouth to hers. She sighed and cradled his face in her hands, opening her lips for him.

Matt braced on one arm on the bed and then, kissed her softly, his lips learning hers. His kiss was hesitant at first, but became more confident.

He didn't hurry and kept his kiss sweet, taking his time to savor her taste. He didn't want to arouse her, but to help her recognize his body as her mate. Yet, he could feel her tremble next to him, and his male ego felt satisfied.

His fingers slid over her right arm, in a hypnotic rhythm, leaving goosebumps on her skin in their wake. He changed the angle of his kiss and his fingers reached to her waist, resting on the roundness of her hip for a few seconds.

"Would you lie down to be more comfortable?" he asked, his lips almost touching hers.

The heat inside her spiked when she felt the words forming over her lips. She shimmied down, almost without thinking.

Her fingers burrowed into his forearms for support. Her nightie hiked up on her thighs, and

Matt breathed deeply when his eyes swept over her legs.

Braced on his elbow, he stretched next to her, his head in his palm. His other hand lazily stroked the side of her face, and then cupped her chin.

He leaned down and when his mouth was a hair's breadth away from hers, he whispered, "I'd love to kiss you some more, Nora. But only if you're comfortable with that."

He searched her glimmering eyes, but they didn't reveal anything. Then, he tried to read her mind, and see for himself what she thought, and as always, came out blank.

"Yes, please," she replied softly, and he felt her breath on his lips.

Now, he needed to kiss her, more than anything. His hand slid from her chin and caressed the side of her neck.

His lips settled on hers, and he sighed. She swallowed the sound and answered with a sigh of hers, and he felt a jolt of awareness in his lower body.

While his lips molded hers, his fingers stroked her shoulder and arm, down to her wrist. His fingers intertwined with hers, while his kiss became more daring and deeper.

He stopped only when both of them needed to come up for air. They breathed hard, and Nora's lips were rosy and slightly puffy. His fingers were still closed on hers, and his thumb stroked the inside of her wrist.

Matt's eyes were locked on Nora's face. She still had her eyes closed, but then, when her respiration quieted, she opened them slowly. The heat in her pupils kicked Matt squarely in his chest.

"I'd love to touch you everywhere, Nora, but I don't dare. I think I'll try not to think of that for at least another week, baby," he confessed.

Nora didn't do anything more than look at him. After a few seconds, she blinked and licked her lips.

"You know you're killing me here, honey," Matt said with a chuckle, yet his voice wasn't as confident as usual. "You never say anything and I don't know what you think."

"Oh, I think plenty, Matt," she replied in a dry voice. "The problem's everything is confusing. I know I want you and I can see you want me, but I don't know if it is all right, or it is too soon or if you want just that," she shrugged.

"Wow, all that," Matt laughed. "You know you don't have to make up your mind right this moment. About anything," he assured her, smoothing her hair.

Then, he took a thick lock between his fingers. He lifted to his face, and brushed it to his cheek.

"No, I can't make up my mind now," she replied ruefully. "I need time, probably more than a week," she warned him.

"Sweetheart, you can take a month or two, or as long as you need," he said and kissed her forehead.

They lay in silence for a few minutes, Matt always braced on the elbow, and his other hand stroking her arm, her hip, and, in a very daring moment, her thigh. Nora kept watching his face. The emotions playing on his face and in his eyes captivated her.

"You want something from me," she suddenly said, and his eyes came fast back to hers.

"How do you know?" he frowned.

"I can see it on your face," she replied. "It's hard to miss it."

"I see," he said. "I thought you've read my mind," he replied mildly.

She giggled at his words, and that surprised him. He'd never heard her giggle and didn't think she'd be the woman to do that.

"Come on, Matt, I'm a grown woman. I don't believe in fairy-tales and paranormal things. I do believe there's an explanation for everything," she stressed out. "Like now," she said. "I knew you wanted something because I could see it in your eyes. No one's capable to read minds," she shook her head with determination.

"If you say so," Matt accepted her explanation, although he felt a sort of hurt. Yet, he couldn't come out and say, *Hey, I can read your mind*. Quite inaccurate. He couldn't read her mind.

"So, what do you want?" she asked again.

"I don't know what you'd think," he started hesitantly, "but I was thinking..." he said and stopped.

"Come on, Matt, don't be shy. You've been anything but shy until now," she laughed.

"I was wondering if you'd like to sleep with me," he snapped, uncomfortable with what he had to say and annoyed with her amusement.

"Smooth," she said gingerly, and touched her upper lip with her tongue.

"I'm not talking about... I'm talking about sleeping, you know, that activity people do at night, to regenerate or whatever," he clarified his idea, miffed by her comment.

"Oh, I see," she smiled. "Really? Just sleeping? Why would you want that?" she suddenly frowned.

"Because I want to feel you next to me," he admitted. "And because we might feel more emotionally comfortable afterward, or... I don't really know why," he admitted. "But I know I do."

"So, to be clear," she said, turning on one side to face Matt, and held her head with her hand, copying his posture. "You want to sleep next to me, to hold me in your arms, and nothing more," she said, and her voice showed her bafflement.

"Yes, that's what I want. I told you I wouldn't touch you otherwise, even if you wanted it. You wouldn't enjoy anything right now, anyway, considering your wounds."

"Probably not," Nora conceded. "Do I have a minute or two to think?" she asked him, in a playful tone.

"Take as long as you need," he murmured, and his hand rested on her hip.

Nora closed her eyes and touched his chest with her palm. He knew she was pondering the pros and cons because a serious frown formed between her eyebrows. He wanted to reach out and smoothen the frown away, but resisted the impulse. He knew it wouldn't have been fair to touch her and muddle her mind, but for a moment there, he didn't care about what was fair.

Her fingers drummed on his chest and each touch drove him mad. Blood pulsated in his temples, and his arousal increased tenfold. He clenched his teeth, and thanked God her eyes were closed.

After something that felt like hours, she opened her eyes, smiled at him, and said, "All right. Nothing wrong if we share a bed and body heat," she explained her decision.

"Romantic," he noticed dryly. "I don't know about the body heat," he continued. "It's summer already, if you haven't noticed."

"Yes, I noticed, Matt," she snickered and patted his chest. "I was just joking. I hope you know that," she suddenly looked up, straight into his eyes, and he saw genuine concern.

"Yes, I know," he grinned at her.

"And how do we do that?" she asked.

"I thought you'd never ask," he joked. "Let's take my bed," he proposed. "I had it order-made and I am comfortable in it. This one here is only a regular king."

"You mean to say you've offered me the low-quality bed?" she pretended to be affronted.

Matt laughed and flicked her nose.

"You're a laugh a minute, you know that," he replied. "No, smarty-pants, your bed isn't low-quality, but you're tiny and it's big enough for you. Anyway, you'll share my bed now, so you can't complain anymore," he said and in a fluid move, he stood up and took her hand. "Come on, let's see how you like my giant bed," he grinned at her and helped her stand.

Then, Matt knelt and finding her slippers, slid them on her feet. She giggled again. Although he'd abhorred giggles before, he liked how she sounded. Now though, he put a finger on her lips, "Shush, you'll wake Nathan."

Nora pretended to zip her lips and he chuckled. Their fingers intertwined, and he pulled her after him. They moseyed to his bedroom, Matt always taking care to match her slow gait.

When he opened the door, she stopped and looked around in awe.

"My God, this is much more than a bedroom," she whispered.

His bed was wide enough for at least four people to sleep without touching each other. The thick carpet, in warm autumn colors, stretched from wall to wall, and two armchairs and a small table nestled inside an alcove in one corner of the room.

"I gather you like it," he said dryly.

"You could say that," she nodded with enthusiasm. "Much better, more colorful and with more personality than the other one," she added, and grinned at him.

"Now, you share it, as well," he shrugged. "The ensuite bathroom is that way," he showed her a door on the right. "Tomorrow morning, I'll bring your things from the other bath so you could use this one. After Nat, of course," he grinned. "He always uses my bath in the morning, sorry."

"Yeah, I noticed," she said. "I expected him to come to me in the mornings, and to be honest, I felt somewhat betrayed when I noticed he came to you instead," she replied.

"Better me than you," he remarked and her eyes widened.

"What do you mean?" she glared.

"I imagine he likes to jump on you in the morning. I haven't had a morning without him bouncing up and down on me. With your wounds, that wouldn't be what your doctor recommended," he pointed out, an eyebrow hiking up his forehead.

"Oh, I forgot about that habit," she laughed briefly, and then grimaced. "How could I forget?"

"You've had enough to deal with. Let's hope he continues to choose my body for his morning amusement," Matt said and stroked the side of her face with the back of his hand. "Now, are you ready to turn in?" he asked her.

Nora nodded hesitantly, and then, shyly, she headed to the bed.

"What side do you prefer?" she asked without turning to him.

"Any of them is good for me," he replied.

Matt helped her climb onto the bed, and then, after she lay down, he covered her with the bed linen.

Matt turned off the light and crept into bed next to her. He slid his arm around her and, gently, pulled her to him. Once they settled, he opened his fingers on her abdomen and a satisfied sigh sounded in Nora's ear.

Nora felt her skin burning under his fingers, and long-forgotten sensations ran through her body.

It felt good in Matt's arms. His body almost surrounded her completely and, to her surprise, she discovered a sense of security and protection in his arms, which she'd never felt before.

"If you need to sleep more tomorrow, you can," he whispered, his lips nearly touching her ear, and she shivered. Matt pulled her closer, thinking she was cold.

"Becka said you'd promised we'd go sailing tomorrow," she whispered back, and her hand rested on top of his on her belly.

"I know, baby, but that will be at eleven. We won't stay long on the lake tomorrow," he promised her. "Just a couple of hours. We'll spend more time when we go to that get-together to Bryan's house on the island, okay? I don't want you to overdo it right now," Matt explain and his concern touched her.

"That's fine with me," she replied, and caressed his fingers.

"Good," Matt said. "Now, sleep baby," he asked her, and his lips touched her face.

CHAPTER SIXTEEN

That was Nora's fourth outing on Matt's yacht and she'd started to wait for those trips with impatience. Nora loved the feel of the wind in her hair and the smell of the water. Everything was different there – the light and sounds, the air and silence.

She couldn't wait to see Bryan's house on the lake, which Becka had praised so much. She was as giddy as Nat whenever she thought of that Saturday.

Maggie and Lily had taken an exuberant Nat to the bow. They chatted and laughed together. The boy kept asking questions, barely giving them the time to answer any of them, and that amused the women to no end.

Nora smiled. Those days, Nat could ask questions faster than anyone could answer. More than that, the lake fascinated him and he was curious about everything. He'd already expressed the wish of becoming a sailor one day. She was just thankful that day was far away.

Before the shooting, Nora had taken him on a stroll on the shore now and then, but she'd never had the time to linger. She'd always had too many things to do, and she didn't have the luxury of longer strolls or outings. She always felt guilty because she couldn't offer Nat such luxuries, but she'd promised herself she would one day.

Now, with the lake always in sight from Matt's windows, her son had become crazy about it. She couldn't deny she had also fallen in love with the lake.

Marjorie and Jonathan sat next to her on the benches shadowed by a huge colorful canopy. After they chatted her for over a quarter of an hour, now, they whispered between them and let her be.

Nora contented herself with watching the men man the yacht. Her mouth watered at the powerful display of muscles on their backs and arms.

Jay and Josh looked good enough, but they wouldn't hold a candle to Matt. He was taller and brawnier than the two other men. His dark coloring made him look very dashing, and she couldn't take her eyes away from him.

A seagull speared the sky and cried out, and startled her from her reverie. She shadowed her eyes and looked in the direction of Bryan's power yacht, which was also full of people.

His in-laws had joined them for the get-together. They were on the deck, fanning over the babies, and the corners of Nora's mouth lifted in a crooked smile. Nothing like a baby to make grown-up people sappy.

Nora had met Emilie and Gabriel a few days ago when they came by Matt's apartment for a brief visit. It was obvious they'd come to ogle her, and that had made her very self-conscious.

She should have got used to it by then. Lately, it had been a constant parade through Matt's house. One evening, Matt even observed dryly that his apartment had never seen so much traffic in years.

Beyond Bryan's yacht, the sail of his friend's yacht was visible. Bryan had invited Max to spend the day with them, not only because he needed another boat for all the people coming to his lake house. Max was his partner in the dojo and his best friend, and they got along very well.

Nora caught a glimpse of Ariel's straight blond hair, flying into the wind. She stood alone at the bow, looking into the distance.

Nora had noticed Ariel was slightly uncomfortable with Max, and she suspected Max was making Ariel jumpy and all too aware of her being a woman.

Alex and Max worked together, manning the yacht, and Michael and Amelie huddled on a bench on the deck.

Nora liked all of them, although Ariel and Alex had seemed somewhat cold and reserved toward her. She didn't know if they didn't like her or they were simply more reserved than the others. She shrugged – she didn't really care one way or the other.

She'd got to know Maggie and Jay better, and she'd made fast friends with Becka and Bryan. They were warm and friendly, so it wasn't hard to relate to them.

She'd already spent over two weeks in Matt's apartment. Although she felt better now, and she'd even started her physiotherapy, she found it hard to broach the subject of her leaving his house. She'd got used being around him, and the thought of not seeing him again made her sick.

Not that Matt seemed willing to give her an opening to discuss her imminent leaving. Whenever he asked about her health, he always changed the subject before getting to the point where she would claim she'd manage by herself and had to move back home. She didn't know how, because her disability pay covered only the rent, but she had to find a way.

Nora had spent all her nights in his bed. Matt would hold her, always careful not to give her any reason for discomfort. Yet, he always seemed to envelop her completely.

She didn't recall she'd ever had such a restful sleep in her entire life. Matt made her feel protected and cherished.

He never asked anything from her and never went beyond a few kisses -- all right, quite hot kisses. He truly intended not to rush things and demand anything from her, and his consideration baffled her. It was obvious he'd wanted more, but he never pressured her.

Nora turned around and brushed her hair off her face. She sighed deeply. She knew everything would change once she moved out of his house. That feeling of well-being and security would disappear. She also wondered if he'd still take the trouble to come around when she wasn't underfoot.

"Anything the matter, Nora?" Matt asked, sliding his arms around her from behind and brushing his lips on the side of her face.

"No, not really," she smiled, looking up at him and covering his hands with hers. "Just enjoying the surroundings."

"Yeah, sure," he replied in that dry voice she loved so much. "That's why you're sighing, right."

"No, really. I do enjoy being on the lake," she said, leaning her head back on his chest, her eyes always on his.

"That I know," he said.

He stared intently into her eyes first. His eyes always seemed to harbor mysteries and secrets she couldn't imagine. Then, he looked at her lips, and his fingers burrowed unconsciously in her midriff.

"How come you know?" she said lightly.

"It's on your face, baby," he answered pushing his chin forward. "It's not like I can read your mind," he mumbled, and she laughed.

"Good to know," she said. "You might run for cover if you read my mind," she teased him.

"I doubt that very much," he said and leaned over her to steal a kiss.

It was almost over before it started, but her lips still tingled and her fingers quivered on his hands.

"Later, baby," he whispered. "We're almost there," he explained, kissed her again and left.

Nora turned to see if they'd arrived at their destination, and her eyes fell on Marjorie and Jonathan, who were smiling at her with deep satisfaction. She'd completely forgotten about them, and now a blush spread all over her face.

Jonathan laughed heartily, and Marjorie, smacking him for his lack of subtlety, told Nora, "Don't mind us, Nora, dear. We just love to see you and Matt like that."

She patted Nora's leg and left it at that. She turned to her husband and began lecturing him in an undertone.

Nora couldn't understand Matt's parents. They should have been furious she'd insinuated herself into their son's life.

Matt was a renowned attorney and had amassed a fortune. She was just a paramedic, who, right then, was paid a little over half her salary, because of her health issues, and that would continue for at least half a year, as her doctor warned her.

Nora shook her head and gave up understanding their reasons. She went back to watching the men, busy with the approach maneuvers.

CHAPTER SEVENTEEN

The party had been going strong for several hours already. Nora wondered how they weren't exhausted yet. She'd sat on a blanket most of the time and felt a little tired.

They'd arrived at Bryan's house a little after ten and the food was arranged on a few folding tables. They spread blankets under the trees, in the shadow, and ate heartily, laughing, talking and teasing each other.

Nat had his nap inside Bryan's house. Marjorie and Jonathan, but also Michael and Amelie, and Gabriel and Emilie, rested in the house with the children, while the younger generation played volley.

Jay invited them to a card game, which made everyone throw something at him. They laughed while egging him, but Jay still seemed somewhat hurt.

Nora didn't understand why and no one offered to explain. Feeling bad for Jay, she told him she'd play with him, but Matt stopped her.

"You know I don't like to say you can't do something, baby, but, in this matter, I have to. You'll never play cards with Jay," he said in a stern voice.

"But why?" she asked with exasperation, taking exception with his haughty manner. "Why everyone is reacting like this? Does he cheat?" she asked.

Jay groaned loudly, as if she'd just stabbed him in the back, and covered his face with his hands, bursting into laughter.

Matt smiled whimsically and shook his head.

"No, he doesn't cheat, but you still won't play with him. I know you're probably bored out of your mind, but if you want to play cards, you can play with me," he offered her, a crooked smile on his lips.

"I'm not bored," she replied through tight teeth. "You can go and play," she shooed him away.

"You won't get rid of me so easy, sweetie," Matt countered and lay down next to her on the blanket.

He noticed she was peeved, and he'd already spent too much time away from her. He'd been painfully aware of her, and kept her in his sight all the time, but he had to play with his siblings and cousins for a while. Otherwise, he'd never heard the end of it. They'd have mocked him he was besotted, which was the truth, of course, but he didn't feel like being the butt of their jokes.

Nora shrugged and turned her head to the group of young people resuming their fun. Ariel took off her shirt and shorts. Underneath she wore a black one-piece swimsuit, which hugged her body like a glove. Nora snickered when she noticed Max's eyes bulging out.

"What's so funny?" Matt asked and looked in the same direction.

He immediately saw Max's reaction and scowled.

"Ariel will make mincemeat out of him," he grumbled, unsure if he liked Max's attention for his cousin or not.

"Why?" Nora turned to him curious.

"Ariel is fastidious by far. She doesn't even like Bryan. She just tolerates him," Matt shrugged. "Imagine how she feels about this guy."

When he saw she didn't like how it sounded, he hurried to explain.

"Don't take me wrong, honey. I love Bryan. He's like a brother to me, you've seen it. And I have nothing against Max. I know him well. Hell, I've sparred with the man and we went out in a group a few times. I like him just fine. He's steady and honest. But Ariel… I don't see her going for his ponytail or his goatee," he shook his head. "And that might be her loss," Matt remarked. "Max might be the right man to mollify her a little. She's too stiff by half."

Nora leaned on him and he enveloped her in his arms.

"Maybe she'll try to know him better," she said quietly, watching Ariel heading for the shore to swim.

Matt observed Max taking off his shorts, and following her. Max's thoughts were loud enough, and Matt snickered.

"I think I'll put my money on him," he said, and his fingers burrowed underneath Nora's shirt.

Everybody had carped at her to take it off. It was a very warm and sunny day, and it must have been uncomfortable to wear it. Yet, self-conscious, afraid her scars would draw eyes, she'd refused.

Her abdomen quivered under his palm, and a smiled lifted the corner of his mouth. His mouth found the hollow between her neck and shoulder and kissed her.

"Matt," she panted for breath, and tried to still his hands. "We're in the open. Everyone can see us."

"So what?" he groused.

His lips trailed the column of her neck up, until they found the sensible spot he'd already discovered behind her ear.

"I don't care. They've guessed we're together by now, and if they haven't, then I've been wrong about their intellects all along," he whispered.

His tongue touched her earlobe and she shuddered. A faint moan reached his ears, and satisfied, he nibbled at her.

His fingers gently touched and massaged the skin on her abdomen and up until he reached underneath the soft curve of her breasts.

He didn't dare to continue his journey. He'd been continuously aroused for two weeks now, and he didn't think he could behave himself if he went into forbidden territory.

Matt breathed deeply and put his chin on the top of her head. He could do with holding her for the moment.

Not even five minutes later, Nat ran out of the house like a tornado, and came to them.

"I'm up, mommy. Hi, Matt. You said we swim when I wake up," he rushed to say.

Matt chuckled, kissed the top of Nora's head, and told her, "Sorry, honey, duty calls."

"You'll take care of him, Matt," she said, but her voice sounded inquiring.

"You can trust me. I won't let anything happen to him," he replied in a serious voice, and kissed her mouth briefly. "He'll also wear a safety vest, so don't worry."

"I should come too," she said nibbling at her bottom lip.

"And do what?" Matt asked irritated.

It wasn't as if she could jump into the lake and save Nat if anything had happened. However, seeing how irked she was, he changed his mind.

"All right, I'll spread the blanket right there on the shore, so you could keep an eye on us," he offered.

"I can spread the blanket myself," she retorted, but he didn't want to hear a thing.

He pulled her up, picked up the blanket and moseyed with her to the shore. Nat was hopping, happy to get into the water at last.

Sitting on the blanket, her legs tugged underneath her, Nora watched them. Matt was teaching Nat to swim and she wondered at his patience.

She hadn't heard him raise his voice once. Sounds carried on the lake and she heard his patient instructions, repeating things several times. He never tired.

From farther away, Ariel's harsh replies to Max's words clashed with the quietness of the lake. Apparently, everything Max said rubbed Ariel the wrong way.

After almost an hour, Matt took Nat back to the shore. The boy still had energy, but Matt knew he needed to have his afternoon snack.

They returned to the others and Nora noticed the food on the tables had been refreshed. New things had appeared, and her mouth watered when her eyes fell on the famous pastries both Marjorie and Bryan had baked. Apparently, a quiet competition was going on between the two of them.

Lily had already filled her plate with everything in sight. Nora suspected Lily's metabolism was very fast. She'd seen her eating and she couldn't have been so slender otherwise.

Nora smiled until her eyes fell on the cup with hot chocolate, which Lily had left on the table. Her eyes widened when she saw the tea spoon stirring the liquid. Lily didn't handle the spoon, and that shocked her.

Nora gasped and blinked hard. Matt immediately noticed what she'd seen and grumbled, "Lily."

Lily looked their way and suddenly, the tea spoon stopped moving. Nora looked from the spoon to Lily, and then to Matt who pretended to watch his brother, who was teasing Alex. She thought she'd imagined things and decided to let the matter drop.

"I might have a sunstroke," she said in a faltering voice.

She couldn't find any other explanation for what she'd witnessed. She rubbed her eyes with shaky fingers.

Matt took her hand, kissed it, and then said, "Let's take you to the shadow, all right. I'll fill a plate for you with everything," he assured her and spread the blanket under a tree.

He helped her sit, and, to his astonishment, he discovered he could read her thoughts and feel her turmoil now. He'd tried to read some of her thoughts during the last few weeks and couldn't.

Matt probed her mind a little, happy to be able to do it. Then, he blocked her thoughts, feeling like a voyeur.

He shook his head, overwhelmed with the significance of the event, and, after making sure she was comfortable, he returned to the food with Nat, to fill plates for all of them.

Nora still looked suspicious, unsure she'd imagined things or not. However, her rational mind didn't allow her to dwell on such impossible things. Probably, Lily had stirred her hot chocolate before, and inertia pushed the tea spoon to move. *'This is the only reasonable explanation'*, Nora nodded, and decided to leave it well alone.

CHAPTER EIGHTEEN

Everybody gathered on blankets, close enough to carry a conversation. They talked about everything and nothing.

Marjorie mentioned a few fundraisers she organized, and everyone offered their time and money to help out. Apparently, Matt's mother was a good organizer and she chose the neediest causes to support.

Ariel spoke about a few experiments she'd made with grafting some different species of plants. She was passionate about horticulture, yet, she didn't like her present job. She felt smothered and unchallenged. Nora understood she'd have liked to have a nursery one day.

Becka spoke about her classes and Bryan seemed to know everything about. Nora couldn't believe such attentive husbands existed. In her experience, men were egocentric and narcissistic.

Everyone shared something and they tried to make her share as well, but she didn't have anything to share.

She was afraid to let them know about how things had evolved with Matt and nothing else had happened in her life lately. She just recounted something Nat had done and they seemed to be content with that.

After a while, they broke into groups and moved a little farther. Becka, Ariel, Maggie and Lily were playing with the babies and entertained Nat.

The older generation gathered on one blanket and shared their concerns about their children in hushed voices. Yet, now and then, something reached Nora's ears, and she wondered why all of them seemed concerned about a specific task the young people had to complete. She intended to ask Matt later, hoping he wouldn't mind her nosiness.

The men started playing football. Just Matt remained with her, always holding her in his arms and whispering some nonsense words in her ear.

The afternoon trailed along. The sun was bright and a light breeze ruffled Nora's hair. Everything was just perfect.

She might have dozed for a while, lulled to sleep by Matt's endearments and the heat coming from his body. She breathed the salty smell of his skin, and her body reacted immediately. Yet, she still fell asleep.

When she woke up, her eyes searched for Nat immediately, and she smiled when she found him. He was still with the women and the babies.

Maggie played hocus-pocus for children and Nora had to admit she was very good at it. She'd produced a little bird out of thin air, and Nat almost laughed his heart out. Then she snapped her fingers, and a small chocolate bar appeared in her hand. She handed it to Nat and he looked at her adoringly.

Nora was in awe. She'd seen shows before, but Maggie was smoother than any other magician she'd seen. As a rule, Nora could guess how they did what they did, but there was no way to say with Maggie.

Nat turned to Ariel and said something, and Ariel smiled. She snapped her fingers and a red apple appeared in her palm.

Nora frowned in confusion. The apple was big and she didn't see where Ariel could have hidden it. She still wore her swimsuit only. Just a few moments ago, Nora had wondered how Ariel didn't melt under Max's hot stare. The man's eyes zeroed in on her and he practically didn't blink.

The baby in Lily's arms raised his arms, and the toys on the blanket beneath them floated in the air.

That was too much. Scared now, Nora jumped out of Matt's embrace and shouted, "What the heck's going on here?"

Her words stopped all activities. Even the men, who were playing football, forgot about the ball, which kept rolling to the edge of the water.

No one paid any attention when it went under the surface of the lake.

Nora felt all eyes were on her, but now, she didn't care. She was scared. She couldn't find any reasonable explanations to what she'd seen and her fear escalated. Her chest heaved. She was breathing hard and her head felt light. Then, she fainted.

"Damn," Matt grumbled, and rushed to catch her.

"I am sorry," Becka said, coming toward them.

Bryan followed her with his eyes, and then asked Max to follow him inside the house.

Max understood something was happening and his friend didn't want him to witness it. He respected Bryan too much not to heed his call.

Becka sat on Matt's blanket, and stroked Nora's hair.

"I still can't stop the babies whenever they choose to play," she explained to Matt. "Sean has just discovered he can move objects. Imagine how titillating it is for him," she apologized. "They're too young to understand when they may do some things and when they shouldn't. I imagine it will take a few years…"

"Don't worry, sweetie," Matt said. "She had to find out somehow. She's a very rational woman and I'd have had a hard time to make her belicf if she hadn't witnessed everything by herself," he pointed out.

He brushed his lips over Nora's, and then, whispered, "Come on, Nora, come back, baby. Wake up."

After a couple of attempts, Nora opened her eyes. Confusion glimmered in her green pupils, and her eyes searched Matt's face for an answer. She sat up in his arms, rubbed her eyes, and then turned to him.

"I think I'm hallucinating, Matt," she confessed with a small voice. She still sounded scared.

Matt shook his head, his eyes on her face.

"What do you mean?" she asked breathlessly.

"You aren't hallucinating," he answered very matter-of-factly.

"Impossible, Matt. Do you know what I thought I saw?"

"Not really, but I can imagine. Although, if you give me a second, and allow me to read your mind, I can answer."

All color disappeared from Nora's face. Her lips quivered and her fingers shook on Matt's forearm.

"What do you mean?"

"I mean I can read your thoughts, baby, but I won't do it if you don't allow me," he answered quietly.

She scowled at him for a second, and then she taunted him, "All right, read away."

He looked at her intently for a few seconds, and then chuckled.

"First of all, I didn't know you had such a colorful vocabulary, Nora," he jokingly chastised her. Then, he became serious, "Right now, you're thinking I'm playing with you, but in the back of your mind you still wonder what's going on. I understand you saw Sean lifting the toys off the blanket, Nora. It's no big deal," he started to say, but she interrupted him.

"What do you mean it's no big deal, Matthew Winston?" she asked in a very strong voice. "And how come you knew what I was thinking?" she thought to ask when the reality dawned on her.

"What Sean did is called telekinesis. If someone has the gift, it is no big deal. So far, Becka, Lily, Alex, Josh and now Sean have that gift," Matt explained, and her eyes widened in shock.

"What Maggie and Ariel did?" she remembered their exploits and asked in a fearful voice.

"That's just… witchcraft," Matt said and winced, imagining how that would sound in her ears.

She pushed away from him, scrambled a little farther and stared at him. Then, she looked around at everyone.

"What do you mean?" she bellowed now.

"Well, I'd say…" Matt started to say, but Alex beat him to the punch.

"Come on, Matt, you're a wuss. Things are simple, Nora," he turned to her, although Matt tried to stop him.

"We're witches. Well, most of us. My mother isn't, Matt's father and Becka's mother aren't, and, of course, Bryan. The rest of us inherited several talents. Some have one talent, others have two or three. Some of us cultivated them, and others didn't. That's all," he shrugged.

Nora just looked at him at a loss of words. She couldn't accept what he said.

"What?" she inquired, dizzy already.

"By God, Matt, you said she's a smart woman," Alex grumbled with disgust.

"Shut up," Matt bellowed at him. "And leave, now."

He was furious with his cousin. He didn't have any tact at all and he didn't care if he insulted anyone.

Marjorie came to Nora and took her hand.

"Pumpkin, it's not like we're a horrible family. We just have a few gifts, that's all. There are people who can play an instrument. I can do automatic writing and read people emotions, for instance. Matt can read minds and emotions and so on, Nora. It's nothing to be afraid of. Ask Jonathan, if you want. We've been married for thirty-seven years now, and he's never had anything to fear. Right, Jonathan?" she turned to her husband.

Jonathan approached her. He took Marjorie's hand and kissed it. Now Nora knew where Matt had learned to do that.

"I had only one fear, my love," he said, a whimsical smile on his lips. "That I won't give you the happiness you deserve."

Marjorie's eyes shimmered with joyful tears. She turned back to Nora, patted her shoulder and said, "You'll see you have nothing to worry about. Just think of what you know of Matt, and you'll do the right choice, pumpkin, I'm sure of that."

Nora stubbornly looked away, and Matt sighed.

"I think we should go back home," he suggested, and everybody agreed.

They started to pick up everything, when Nat came to Matt and asked, "What's a witch, Matt?"

Nora froze in place.

CHAPTER NINETEEN

Nora felt frozen inside. The cruise over the lake didn't calm her, as it had happened before. When Matt transferred everything in his car, she just waited aside, her thoughts churning in her head.

Everyone came to say their good-byes, but she seemed aloof, and they didn't linger.

Matt helped her in the car, after he secured Nat in the child's chair in the back. He leaned over her and locked her seatbelt, when he noticed she just stared through the windshield.

Suddenly, she turned her eyes onto him, and said, "I want to go home."

"We're going home," Matt nodded quietly.

Her hand grabbed his, and she said through tight teeth, "My home, not yours."

He shook his head, and instinctively, leaned over her and kissed her hard.

"I'm sorry, sweetheart, I can't drive you to your apartment. You're not hundred percent, and you can't take care of yourself and Nat the right way," he denied her requests, shaking his head.

When he saw she wanted to interrupt him, he touched his fingers to her mouth, shaking his head again.

"I know you'll try, Nora. You're strong and stubborn enough to try. But your body won't let you. I have to take you home with me," he repeated mulishly, and the tone of his voice didn't leave room for arguments.

"I won't sleep with you," she lashed out at him.

He remained still, hurt visible in his eyes, but then, he nodded, "All right, you'll sleep in the other bedroom, if that's what you want."

"That's what I want," she replied meanly. "You lied to me and…"

"I've never lied to you," he answered quietly. "I just haven't revealed everything."

With those words, he closed her car door and jogged to the other side to get them home.

The drive home didn't take more than five minutes. When they got upstairs, Nora wanted to take Nat with her in the empty bedroom, but Nat didn't understand why he couldn't spend the remaining of the afternoon with Matt, and started crying.

Emotionally exhausted, she left them alone and left. Regardless everything, she still trusted Matt to take care of her son.

Lying in bed, she kept turning things in her head. The shock hadn't worn off yet, and she still couldn't believe the Watsons were witches. She knew there wasn't such a thing as witches.

She considered paranormal abilities, although, in the past, she discounted them. She still didn't reach any conclusion, and, after a while, worn out, she fell asleep.

Matt's fingers, skimming over her face, woke Nora. She blinked and looked at him confused. He'd turned on the lamp on the night table, and she realized it was already dark outside.

"Hey, there," he said softly. "I didn't know whether I should let you sleep. It's late though, and you haven't had any dinner yet. Do you want me to bring it here or do you think you could stand having dinner with me?"

His eyes showed his insecurity, and her heart cringed. Matt was a kind man and she didn't want to hurt him. However, she couldn't just gloss over what had happened.

"I could have something to eat," she mumbled.

"Do you want me to bring you a tray here?" he offered again.

"No," she replied sitting up. "I'll be in the kitchen in a couple of minutes."

"Do you need my help for anything?" he asked, straightening up.

"I'm pretty sure I can go to the bathroom under my own steam, Matt," she answered back.

"I don't need your paranormal powers to support me."

Her voice sounded spiteful. She felt cruel and raw and she didn't feel like cutting him any slack.

Matt took in her bad mood, nodded, and left the room, locking his hands at the back of his head. The feeling of defeat was gnawing at him, and he didn't know how to stop that train wreck.

***

When Nora came into the living-room, Matt was seated at the breakfast table, watching the lake. He'd already laid everything out on the table.

Sensing her arrival, he turned to her and stood up. *Always the consummated gentleman*, she thought, and then, she chided herself. Matt had always been considerate and respectful, and she was just lashing at him now, because of what she'd uncovered that afternoon.

She moseyed to the table and sat down. Matt held her chair and then, he took his seat again.

He started serving her with salad first, and then, he added a large grilled chicken breast and stir-fried vegetables on her plate. Always in silence, he filled his plate and with a gesture invited her to eat.

They ate in complete silence for a few minutes, and then, Nora looked up at him and asked, "Did you intend to ever let me know?"

"Yes," he answered.

She didn't like his brief answer, and scowled at him.

"Yeah? When? Sometime in the next twenty or thirty years?"

She sounded like a shrew, and Matt's left eyebrow hiked up his forehead. She blushed slightly, but her expression didn't change.

"Actually, no, Nora. I knew I had to let you know before we'd become more involved."

"Really?" she asked mockingly. "How more involved should we have been for you to spill the beans?"

His eyes turned hard. Matt had hoped they could discuss things reasonably, without attacking each other.

He understood she felt betrayed somehow. He didn't try to read her mind. He didn't feel he had the right of doing it without her knowledge. But her emotions were very strong, and no empathic person could have stopped the emotional waves.

"Definitely, before taking you into my bed and before asking you to be my wife," he replied silently.

To mask his concerns, he cut a piece of chicken and stuffed it in his mouth. He didn't taste it, but chewed carefully before swallowing.

Nora's eyes widened and a faint blush colored the top of her cheeks. Her fingers shook on the fork, which clanked on the plate. The sound resonated in their ears and she put the fork down. She leaned back and measured him.

"You've already taken me into your bed," Nora observed with sarcasm.

"Not the way I want to," Matt replied with a shrug. "I love cuddling with you, and I need sleeping with you," he admitted. "But I do need much more than that."

"I see," she said quietly and crossed her arms over her chest.

Nora looked at him a little more, and then said, "You know you could have had something more for some time now."

"Maybe," he shrugged again and forked some vegetables. "Eat your food, Nora, it's getting cold."

"How, the heck, do you think I can eat now?" she scowled at him.

"The same way I do," he replied, and nodded his head toward her plate to nudge her to eat.

"I'm not as insensible as you are," she said through her teeth, and Matt stilled.

She realized what she said, and recalling how careful and attentive Matt had been with her, she wanted to slap herself silly.

Nora reached out and touched Matt's hand, "I'm sorry, Matt. You don't deserve that. I'm just very upset and scared, you know."

"I can imagine," he groused.

"No," she replied with a self-deprecating laugh, "you can read my mind. You don't have to imagine anything."

"Actually, I do, Nora. As I said, I'll never read your mind without permission. Your emotions though…"

"What about them?" she inquired.

"I can't block them. I'll always know what you feel. I mean I know if you're happy or sad, or if you're scared or hurt, you know. I don't know if you love or hate someone… I'd have to read your mind for that," he explained to her, and waved his hand to her, again, inviting her to eat.

This time, Nora took her fork and played around with her vegetables, pensively.

"When you didn't allow me to play cards with Jay," she said and looked up at him, "was it because of his talents?"

Matt nodded and continued to chew. It took him a few seconds to swallow.

He reached out to her and interlocked their fingers. Then, he turned her hand, palm up, and his thumb started drawing circles on her smooth skin.

Nora felt his caress everywhere inside her body and swallowed hard.

"Yes, Jay has extra sensorial perception, ESP, if you want. He can see what cards you have in your hand. For the moment, he can't really control the gift and as result, he can't stop using it. Playing cards with him is… a farce, if you want," Matt shrugged.

"I see," Nora, said. "Outside the family, does anyone else know what you can do? I mean you and your cousins… you understand what I mean."

"No," Matt answered. "There are people who'd consider us freaks. Others would want to take advantage of what we can do. So, no, only the people in the family know about. Of course, the ones marrying into the family are told beforehand so they could choose… So far," he said in a very soft voice, "none of them backed out."

They looked at each other intently.

"You said," Nora started in an hesitant voice, "that you wanted to have me in your bed and marry me."

"Yes, I do. Both," Matt nodded.

"Why me?" she asked, and Matt blinked.

"Come again?" he asked confused.

"Why me? Why would you want to marry me?" she repeated more forcefully. "Because I found out what the Winstons can do?"

"Don't be stupid," he replied in a harsh voice. "I wouldn't marry for such a trivial reason, Nora."

"Then why me?" she repeated stubbornly. "Why would you be interested in marrying me?"

His eyes rounded, and the intensity of the dark blue took her breath away. Matt shook his head and stood up to pace, lost in thought.

After a few minutes, he came back to her.

"I can't understand. You're a smart woman. I've seen proof of your intelligence in many occasions. How can such a smart woman ask such stupid questions?" he asked, shaking his head.

"Look here," she stood at her turn. "I'm not stupid."

"That I know," he agreed with her. "I don't know how you can't see it, though."

"See what?" Nora asked with exasperation.

"That I love you," Matt replied.

He registered the shock on her face. Nora fell back on her chair looking at him with disbelief.

"Yeah, I can see you're crushed with joy," he said dryly.

He took his plate and the platters on the table into the kitchen. He cleaned them and put them into the dishwasher. She was still watching him with incredulity.

"Finish your dinner, Nora," he invited her, quietly. "Leave everything on the table. I'll take care of the dishes later. Good night," he added and left the room.

Nora remained at the table, looking out of the window, yet her eyes didn't register anything. On one hand, Matt's words elated her. On the other, they scared her, because she didn't know whether she loved him too.

Late, she realized her food was cold and her body stiff, because she'd been sitting in the same position for too long. With difficulty, she stood and slowly made her way to her room.

CHAPTER TWENTY

Nora was sitting on the window sill bench, watching the lake, when the intercom beeped. She grimaced and abandoned her place to answer the door.

Being Canada Day, Matt had taken Nat to see some shows on Harbor Front, together with Marjorie and Becka.

Although she had some apprehensions about the abilities running in the Winston family, she trusted Matt and his family with her son.

The last two weeks had been awkward. Matt had always been polite, but withdrawn. She'd been reserved.

They took their meals together, and Matt took Nat to visit Becka and Bryan regularly. They went together in the park, but Nora always refused to go out.

She didn't know how to react around Matt anymore. She knew she'd been mean and spiteful and she didn't know how to take her words back. Her former marriage had left her unprepared to fix the situation.

Nora was exhausted. Her mind churned around her feelings for Matt and what he'd told her.

She also worried about returning back to her apartment. As she suspected, her disability pay covered the rent, and she had only about two hundred dollars left in the bank after paying it.

She could solve that problem only if she'd returned to work, which seemed out of the question. The doctor didn't want to sign off. She had asked him just that when she had her medical appointment the other day, and he refused.

Yet, she knew she couldn't take advantage of Matt anymore. He was surly now, and she assumed he allowed her to stay in his apartment just because of his chivalrous up-bringing.

Nora pushed the button to the intercom and unlocked the door without asking who it was. She didn't really care. Her loneliness had become so acute that she'd have welcomed anyone, even Alex, who didn't seem to like her much.

When she heard the knock on the door, she opened it immediately and found herself before Bryan.

She sketched a shy smile and waved him to come inside. She knew she'd feel awkward to see someone after the fiasco at the lake, but she didn't expect to feel so bad.

Bryan entered, watching her carefully. He leaned over and kissed her cheek.

"You seem awfully tired and depressed," he noticed. "Is everything fine?"

"You flatter me, Bryan" she replied dryly.

"Not my intention, Nora," he shook his head. "I've brought something for us," he told her, showing the bag in his hand. "Go and take a sit on the sofa. I'll put everything on a platter and come to join you."

"I can put everything on the platter," she replied stubbornly, and snatched the bag. "Now, you can go and sit on the sofa," she said and give him a push in the direction of the sofa.

Bryan didn't budge at first, then he laughed, put his hands up to show he surrendered, and sauntered to the sofa. He could see Nora in the kitchen, trying to locate the platters.

He chuckled and told her, "Try the last cupboard down on the left. That's where Matt keeps the platters. He still doesn't let you in the kitchen, I see," he observed.

"You know he doesn't," she replied ruefully. "Either you or Marjorie provide the food. I'm not allowed to do anything around here and it drives me crazy," she confessed, arranging the pastries on the platter.

"Have you told him that?" Bryan inquired mildly, always watching her, judging her reactions and emotions.

Nora shrugged, but said nothing. She carried the platter to the coffee table and asked, "Would you like some coffee, coke or beer?"

"A beer would be good," he answered with a shrug. "Don't bother with a glass, Nora. I don't need one," he thought to mention. He never bothered about etiquette.

She returned to the kitchen to bring him the beer, and he noticed with satisfaction that she moved easier. She wasn't completely healed, and from what Matt had told him, he knew she might remain with a slight limp for her entire life, which didn't bother Matt at all.

It was important that she was on the road of recovery. Now, only if he could help to heal her other wounds.

Nora returned with a beer for him and a coke for her. She sat in an armchair and sighed.

"Tough day?" Bryan inquired.

"Tough couple of months," she replied with a nod.

"I can see that. So, why haven't you told Matt that you'd like to do some work in the kitchen?"

She looked away. Then, she leaned forward and picked a piece of pastry.

"You're avoiding my question," Bryan observed.

"Of course, I'm avoiding your question," she snapped at him.

"Why?" he insisted.

She sighed deeply, and then, she gave in.

"Because Matt and I are not really talking, you know. He asks if I'm okay and if I want to eat something or watch a movie. He asks permission for taking Nat with him... But nothing else," she shrugged.

"Since when?"

"Like you don't know," she scowled at Bryan. "Since that blasted day at your lake house."

"So, you're upset with Matt for what had happened there and what you found out," he concluded.

"I was. Then," she thought to specify. "Come on, Bryan, don't tell me you wouldn't have been surprised if something like that had happened to you," she lifted her eyebrows in disbelief.

Bryan shouted with laughter and slapped his knee. His eyes sparked with amusement.

"What's so funny?" Nora frowned, not understanding how he could laugh in such circumstances.

"You, Nora, you're funny."

"Because I was surprised and scared when all that happened?" she asked with dismay.

Actually, she hadn't expected that coarse behavior from Bryan. He didn't seem the kind of man to make fun of someone just for the sake of it. *'How wrong can I be sometimes,'* she thought.

"Of course not. I wouldn't laugh at you for that, Nora," he scowled at her.

He'd hoped she knew him better by then.

"I'm laughing because you assume I've never been in that position," he hooted again, shaking his head.

Nora just looked at him, her eyebrows up her forehead. She'd never seen Bryan in such a state.

"Imagine," he said, "I took Becka exactly to the same spot. We made love for the first time, one of the most beautiful moments in my life, by the way.

And then we quarreled," he said. "You'll certainly hear why," he added with a wave of his hand. "I won't waste our time going into those details. Pretty soon, someone will find a great joy relating the events to you. I've been the butt of their jokes ever since," he flapped his hand with disgust. "Anyway, at the time, I didn't know anything about her family and, to be perfectly honest with you, I didn't believe in such things," he explained.

"I know what you mean," Nora said. "I had the same ideas and everything came as a shock."

"Yes, I know. It was the same with me. Anyway, at the time, Becka couldn't control her powers, you know. She got so upset with me that the wind started gushing around us, and things flew into the air," he shook his head, chuckling. "Imagine, a big cooler just flying around, past your head. Oh, boy, that did scare me," he confessed, although he was laughing.

Nora listened to him with astonishment.

"What did you do?" she asked breathlessly. She'd have run for cover and waited there until the coast would have been clear.

Bryan ran his fingers through his hair, gulped from his beer, and then, looking straight into her eyes, said, "I was an ass. The biggest possible ass. I treated her as if she'd been a freak. I hurt her, and deeply."

"Oh, my God. How did she accept you back?" Nora asked wide-eyed. She wouldn't have been able to forgive something like that.

"I was lucky, I think. I went by her house a few days after. I had in mind to beg, grovel... You know -- do everything possible to make her forgive me. But she forgave me immediately. She didn't feel the need to punish me."

"I see," Nora murmured, yet she found hard to believe that a woman could just push something like that aside and forget about it.

"Now, let me tell you something, Nora. If I could accept things flying around and winds and storms, believe me, you can accept Matt's talent. His, at least, doesn't scare you. You know he can't hurt you. Like by hitting your head with a cooler, for instance," Bryan said, laughing.

"Matt has asked you to come and talk to me," she concluded, clenching her hands together.

"Oh, no, Nora. Don't even tell him I talked to you about this. He'd skin me first. I'd love to remain in good relations with Matt. He's one of the good guys, you know. I don't want to lose his friendship, Nora. But I know he pines over you, and if I were to guess after seeing you today, you pine over him too. Why don't you cut a slack to both of you, and try to talk to him? I understand he's afraid you don't want to listen to what he has to say and he hurts," Bryan said, finishing off his beer.

"I'd like to talk to him, but I don't even know where to begin. I'm also afraid he'd think I'm only trying to take advantage of him because of my present situation and that's the worse," she confessed, leaning forward. "He knows the doctor won't sign me off for work and I'm in a bad financial situation."

"Then just give him permission to read your mind. That should banish any kind of doubts and suspicions. I assure you, the process is painless, I tried it," Bryan said in a matter-of-fact voice.

"Easy for you to say," she snapped.

"I know it's easy for me to say," Bryan nodded. "It's always easy to give advice, I know. But if you don't do something, you'll both lose. Matt won't ever pressure you. And if he thinks that's what you want, he'll leave you alone, no matter how much he hurts," Bryan explained to her.

Nora closed her eyes and bit her bottom lip. Bryan could almost see the little wheels turning, round and round.

"May I ask something more from you, Bryan?" Nora suddenly opened her eyes and trained her shiny green eyes on him.

"Of course, you can," Bryan nodded.

"Would Becka and you keep Nat over the night? Today or maybe tomorrow, if you can't today," she rushed to say.

"We can keep him with us today, not a problem. It will be fun," he grinned. "Let me call Becka and tell her. She's with Matt and Nat right now. She can take Nat directly home, and you and Matt can have the apartment to yourself tonight," Bryan winked at her and took his phone out of his pocket.

He dialed Becka's number and explained everything as fast as possible, warning her from the beginning not to say a thing to Matt.

CHAPTER TWENTY-ONE

Matt dreaded an entire afternoon and evening alone with Nora. He longed to be with her, and yet, knowing she didn't want to talk to him, simply made his chest ache.

Becka had asked to have Nat with her until the next day. She assured him she'd cleared it with Nora.

He still checked with Nora, and that made Becka growl at him, which cheered Nat considerably.

They were just about to go home and the boy didn't really want to go inside. He'd have preferred to run along the harbor.

Marjorie had wanted to accompany Matt at home. He'd sensed it. Yet, Becka took her hand and invited her to see the twins.

Matt couldn't compete with the twins those days. Soon, his mother sauntered to Becka's car and left with her.

Matt resigned himself to another afternoon of silence. The thought that Nora was in the same apartment with him, so close, and yet, so far away, killed him slowly.

He groaned, but he didn't have anything else to do. He drove back home.

To his dismay, he didn't encounter any traffic stops, any traffic jams, anything. He got there in no time. With a sigh, he parked his car and leaned his head on the driving wheel for a few seconds.

'Start cracking, scaredy-cat,' he mumbled and got out of the car.

His apartment was on the twenty-seventh floor, and sometimes, the trip by elevator seemed to take forever. Of course, not that day. It felt as if the elevator had transported him to his floor in the blink of an eye.

He headed to his door with dread. He breathed deeply, preparing himself for another silent treatment, and then unlocked the door.

As expected, the apartment was silent. He knew she wouldn't welcome him, as she'd done in the past.

Suddenly, a painful thought popped into his head. Nora had left, and her request to Becka was just a decoy. She'd be waiting for Nat at Becka's house, and head with him to her own apartment afterward.

"No," he bellowed, and his fist punched the wall with all the force he was capable.

Matt wanted his chance and he couldn't just lie down and have it slip through his fingers. He couldn't let Nora go without a word.

He practically tore the door down when he pulled it open. He didn't care his knuckles were bleeding or he might destroy the door.

He'd barely got out of the door with a purposeful stride, when Nora called him from behind, "Matt, where are you going? What's happened?"

Matt staggered on his feet. He slowly turned around, and his eyes fell squarely on Nora.

Wide-eyed, she looked from him to the hole in the wall and back. She paled when her eyes zeroed in on his bloody knuckles.

"That's what I heard," she whispered. "You punched the wall," she said louder, shaking her head.

She couldn't believe he'd done that. Matt was always calm and composed. He wasn't a hothead and she couldn't reconcile the image she had before her eyes with the Matt she knew.

She stared at him and bellowed, "Are you out of your mind? Why, the heck, would you do that?"

Matt flapped his hand, tried to say something, and then scowled at her. He didn't find the courage to admit why he'd done it.

"What's the matter? What made you so angry?" Nora asked again, in a calmer voice this time.

She'd have never thought there was anything that could make Matt lose his temper. He was constantly so patient and understanding that his present behavior astonished her.

'What made me so angry? The woman is clueless, damn it! She's just torn my heart apart and she's asking what's the matter,' Matt shook his head.

Then, he cleared his throat, looked away for a few seconds. Reaching a decision, he closed the door behind him. He threw the keys in the bowl on the table near the door, and only then, he looked back at her.

He felt stupid for what he'd done, and he knew he had to say something and explain his behavior. Lying to Nora wasn't a choice.

"I thought you left," he said with a sigh.

"I beg your pardon?" she replied, wide-eyed.

"I thought you left the apartment. You left me," he repeated, "and you asked Becka to take Nat, so you could go to her house and take him with you," he explained louder, his tone of voice rebellious.

He sounded like a petulant child explaining why he'd done a stupid thing. For a few seconds, Nora couldn't answer. Her green eyes showed bewilderment at first, and then anger.

"Really? Do you really think I'd be so callous, Matt?" Nora asked, hardly keeping her temper in check.

He sensed his words had offended her and tried to apologize, "I'm sorry, baby. I didn't think. I just reacted," he opened his arms, at a loss of words. He didn't know what to say and make her hurt less.

"You should know me better than that," she said, morosely.

"I know you better," he admitted. "I've just lost my common sense for a moment."

Nora looked him over, and then, she took his hand and pulled him after her.

"Where are we going?" he asked, and again slapped himself in his mind for asking stupid questions. As long as she wanted him with her, he didn't mind where they were going.

She turned her head toward him and smiled, "Just in the living-room for the moment. Right after we've cleaned those knuckles and stopped the bleeding," she thought to add.

"The bleeding's stopped, don't worry about it," Matt waved the matter away, as unimportant.

"Come on, Matt, humor me. Let's clean those knuckles first, and we'll see afterward."

Matt gave in and let her fuss over his knuckles. When she finished, she led him into the living-room, and invited him to sit on the sofa. Satisfied that he was doing her bidding, she moseyed to the kitchen.

"By the way, Bryan passed by this afternoon," she said disappearing into the kitchen. "He brought some pastries for us. I asked him first if Nat could go to their house for a sleepover, and then he called Becka," her voice came from the kitchen and Matt leaned sideways, to see her through the alcove.

"Why did he come?" he asked, and suspicion rang in his voice.

Nora returned with a tray in her hands, and Matt immediately jumped to his feet and rushed to relieve her of the burden.

She tapped her foot on the floor furiously.

"I'm not frail, Matt Winston. I'm able to carry a tray," she grumbled at him.

"No, baby, you're not frail. But you won't carry a tray before another month or two. We'll see how it goes," he shrugged, without promising anything.

"With you, I won't be allowed to carry anything for the rest of my life," she glared at him, putting her hands on her hips.

Matt shrugged, and grinned at her. He was smart enough not to go into an argument with her right then.

"Come on, here, have a sit," he invited her, laying the platter on the coffee table in front of the sofa.

Nora decided to choose her battles and let that one go. She didn't see she'd win it anytime soon.

She sat on the sofa and, leaving her slippers on the floor, she tugged her legs under her. She leaned forward to take one of the plates on the tray and a pastry, but Matt immediately stopped her and prepared a plate for her. She huffed, but didn't comment.

She waited until Matt also helped himself to a pastry and sat in an armchair, not far from her.

During the last couple of weeks before the event at the lake, he'd bought two more armchairs and a few ottomans and pillows, he'd spread through the living-room.

It seemed necessary. They'd had guests almost every day at that time. They used to come in groups, and always commented on the lack of enough furniture.

After her melt-down at the lake, the group visits ended, and some visits stopped completely. Probably, people were wary of her.

"I think we should talk," she said, after biting into the pastry.

Matt was about to carry his pastry to the mouth, and his hand froze in mid-movement. His eyes darkened, and he didn't dare to blink.

"You don't need to worry," she said, with a small smile. "Or better said, I hope you won't worry. You said you could read my mind, if I allowed it," she continued in an inquiring voice.

Matt just nodded. He put the pastry back onto the plate and left the plate on the table.

"I allow it," she said softly. "Knock yourself out," she tried to lighten the mood, but Matt didn't feel so relieved.

"Are you sure?" he asked falteringly.

She nodded with determination and closed her eyes. She didn't know what reading her mind involved, but she'd already decided to take Bryan's advice and didn't want to back out.

Matt stared at her, and then, seeing that she didn't change her mind, closed his eyes and let himself immerse in her thoughts. He didn't need more than a few seconds to have tears in his eyes.

He left the armchair, and pulled her in his arms, forgetting about his earlier worries, and hugged her tight, until she said a soft *'ouch'*.

"Oh, baby, I am so sorry. I didn't mean to hurt you," he said in a rush and pulled himself at a distance.

"I know, Matt. You just held me too tight. Otherwise, you, touching me, that's not a problem," she said, and touched his face with her fingers, tracing his stubby beard.

Nora closed the distance between them, and slid her arms around him. She leaned her head on his chest, and breathed contentedly.

Matt hugged her again, not so tight this time, and kissed the top of her head.

"I'm ready now," she whispered.

Matt became so still, she feared he'd stopped breathing.

She looked up at him. She felt as if the intensity of his eyes had swallowed her. The dark-blue of his pupils turned darker.

"Do you mean, you're ready for me?" he asked, unsure of himself.

"Yes, if you haven't changed your mind, of course," she replied.

In a second, he scooped her up in his arms, and with huge strides headed to his bedroom.

"Not in this lifetime, Nora. Sorry, baby, not in this lifetime."

Once in his bedroom, he laid her on his bed and stepped back. He just stared at her, happy to see her lying in his bed once more.

Then, he turned back and closed the door, as if he'd been afraid the world would intrude upon them.

CHAPTER TWENTY-TWO

When they arrived at Marjorie's house, Nora couldn't believe her eyes. Her future mother-in-law hadn't spared any expenses.

Flowers covered every corner and every surface available. The buffet was decadent and in an array of colors that caught people's eye and watered their mouths.

Matt held her hand and chuckled at her surprise.

"Mom always knows how to give a party, baby," he brushed his lips on her cheek.

"I can see that," she replied in awe. "I've never seen anything like that. But she needn't have gone to so much trouble…" she shook her head.

"Honey, you have to winderstand something," Matt whispered in her ear. "I'm her first born. She's been waiting for this moment for thirty-four years. We must let her have her way," he advised, and Nora nodded.

Nat, who was holding her other hand, shouted, "Mommy, look, Becka's here."

Immediately, he pulled his hand out of hers and ran to Becka, his most favorite person in the world after Nora and Matt.

Becka welcomed him with a tight hug and a kiss on the cheek.

"Wow, you look so handsome," she praised him.

Matt had refused to have him dressed in a suit for the party. He'd insisted he was a child and needed to feel free to move around.

In the end, a compromise had been reached between all parties involved – Nat wouldn't wear a suit for the engagement party thrown by Marjorie for them, but he would wear one for the wedding.

Once the word they had arrived spread out, everybody came to congratulate them. Marjorie and Jonathan beamed with pride, and hugged both Nora and Matt several times.

People admired Nora's dress, and she blushed. Matt had weakened her resolve with a constant attack for a week and made her accept it. He bought it himself, and presented it to her as a gift, together with all the necessary accessories.

The emerald sleeveless silky dress hugged her body, without being snug. It stopped just at her knees. Her eyes shone stronger, reflecting the color of the dress.

Considerate, Matt bought low-heel shoes for her, so she wouldn't overtax her leg, and a small bag. He was already concerned she'd overdo it during the party, and he'd lectured her about not standing for too long and let him know when she got tired. By the end of the lecture, she'd rolled her eyes several times, but she promised to let him know if it became too much for her.

She remembered what Marjorie had said, about giving a man his due. Matt was always attentive and attuned to her needs. The least she could do was to respect his wishes in that concern.

They moseyed through the guests, holding hands, chatting about inconsequential things and answering questions.

They had to go different ways when men took him aside to discuss the bachelor's party, which he'd initially refused.

Nora had convinced him to accept it. It was like a coming to age ritual and she didn't want him to miss out on anything.

She went outside onto the patio with Lily for some fresh air. Marjorie had outdone herself, but Nora still felt smothered in large crowds.

"I understand the wedding will be at Bryan's house on the lake," Lily said, sipping from her glass with champagne, and eying Nora's dress.

That color would have worked for her too, but she needed it in another model. She didn't have Nora's curves.

"Yes," Nora smiled at her. "Becka will be my matron of honor, you know. We decided to have only a matron of honor and a best man. Otherwise, we wouldn't have had any guests or almost any," she laughed, and Lily shared her hilarity.

"Yep, you're right. I remember Becka's wedding. Only the old generation played the role of guests. We were all bridesmaids and groomsmen. It was hilarious," Lily giggled.

"What was hilarious?" Maggie sashayed to them, and toasted Nora.

"Becka's wedding," Lily explained. "With all of us part of the wedding party, remember?"

"Oh, yes," Maggie made a face. "I hope you won't do that to us," she implored Nora.

"Don't worry," Nora replied, laughing. "Just Becka and Bryan. Everyone else will be considered guest."

"Phew, thank God, Nora!"

She wiped off her forehead, theatrically, and the other two women laughed at her antics.

"So, I see you grabbed him, eventually," Rebecca's voice came from behind Nora.

Nora turned stiffly to the old woman. She hadn't seen Rebecca since the day when she came to the hospital. She couldn't say she'd missed her.

Rebecca sneered at her, and, suddenly, Lily turned on her heels and rushed to the house.

"Hello, Rebecca," Nora replied calmly. "I don't remember to have ever grabbed a man," she said and sipped unhurriedly from her glass.

She tried to hide any sign of distress. She knew Rebecca would pounce on her if she saw any weakness.

"Great-grandma," Maggie intervened in a bored voice, "I think Matt did all the grabbing, in the end. I can vouch for that, actually. I witnessed almost everything," she flapped her hand.

"I'm sure you have something else to do, young lady, so get lost," Rebecca snapped at her.

Maggie seemed to reflect a moment, then she shook her head, "No, sorry, grandma. Nothing to do. I was actually doing something," she pointed out. "I was talking to Nora. But it's not a problem," she patted her grandma's arm. "We can include you in our conversation. Right, Nora?" she asked and winked at Nora, who couldn't stop a crooked smile in the corner of her mouth.

"Girl, your manners are lacking," Rebecca snapped at Maggie again. "You don't know when you're not wanted somewhere. Now, get lost."

"Actually, Nora wants me here, don't you, Nora?"

Nora assessed the old woman before her eyes. Her annoyance with Maggie was escalating, and Nora didn't want to be the instrument of a rift between the two of them.

"It's okay, Maggie. Rebecca seems determined to tell me something, so we'd better let her do it. Meantime, would you mind filling me a plate with desserts? I saw them earlier and couldn't take my mind off them," she asked Maggie and stroked her arm.

"Are you sure?" Maggie asked unconvinced.

"Yes, I am," Nora replied, smiling.

Yet, Maggie read a fierce determination beyond that smile.

"All right, grandma, the scene is all yours," Maggie bowed mockingly, and Rebecca's eyes thundered at her.

Maggie glided toward the house, giggling.

Rebecca watched her leaving, and then turned to Nora. She stared her down with hard eyes, but then, Nora didn't back down either. She squared her shoulders and looked straight into Rebecca's eyes.

"Do you know you ruined all chances for Matthew?" Rebecca asked in a haughty voice.

"I don't know what you mean," Nora shook her head.

"He could have had everything," Rebecca threw her hands in the air.

Nora heard the sudden rustle of leaves and felt the gushes of cold air surrounding her. Her heart skipped a beat, remembering Bryan's story, but she told herself Rebecca couldn't kill her in Marjorie's house. She matched her look for look.

Rebecca scowled and threw her fist into the air. A black cloud appeared and rain started to pour over Nora.

Nora didn't move or show distress. *'A little rain didn't kill anyone'*, she thought.

Suddenly everyone was out on the patio. They were thundering at Rebecca, and Matt's voice was the loudest. He ran and hugged Nora to his chest.

"If you ever, and I mean ever, touch her, even with your thought, I won't recognize you as part of my family," he bit Rebecca's head off, and she gasped.

"You'd do that for her?" she asked with outrage.

"She's the woman I love. She'll be my wife in a week. You either respect her and my decisions and wishes, or you can forget I exist," he glowered, and took Nora with him.

Passing by his mother, who looked completely shocked, he asked in a mild voice, "Could you help Nora with something to wear, mother?"

She nodded and joined them on their way inside.

Everyone looked at Rebecca with astonished eyes. She'd been vocal in the past, but she never attacked anyone.

"Why?" Bryan asked her quietly. "You weren't so malevolent to me, and I, at least, did look like a ruffian," he said.

"Bryan," Becka shouted at him. "How dare you to speak like that about yourself?"

"Calm down, sweetheart. We need to know why she hates Nora," he stroked Becka's arms to soothe her.

"You hate my mommy?" Nat's voice interfered, and the grown-ups groaned.

"If Matt finds out he knows, it will be hell," Jonathan whispered to Amelie, who was closest to him.

Amelie immediately came forward and took Nat's hand. She said soothingly, "No one hates your mommy, Nat. You saw we all love her."

"But she doesn't," the boy said stubbornly.

"I don't hate her," Rebecca replied to the child. "I hate that plans were ruined, that's all," she said and tried to ruffle the child's hair, but Nat stepped back.

He looked at her for a few more seconds, and then looked up at Amelie, "May I have another slice of cake, auntie?"

Amelie nodded and smiled relieved that the crisis had been averted. She loved it when the boy called her auntie.

Nat had been told Matt would marry his mommy and, consequently, would become his daddy. That news made him happy. He already loved Matt, who always made time for him and never berated him.

Then, everyone told him to call them auntie or uncle, and, suddenly, he found himself in the middle of a huge family. More important, everyone tried to make him happy and paid attention to him.

***

Nora, Marjorie and Matt returned after fifteen minutes. Nora had refused a dress, but accepted a pair of pants and a shirt.

She had to explain to Matt several times that she didn't hold him responsible for what happened, and no, she didn't change her mind. She would marry him the following Saturday.

Matt was seething. He'd always known his grandma was a cold woman, who put her wishes and thoughts above everyone's. Yet, he'd never imagined she'd truly use her abilities to hurt someone, and especially the woman he loved.

Rebecca was still there when they arrived on the patio, and Matt simply saw red before his eyes. His stride lengthened, determined to get to her and throw her out, but Nora squeezed his fingers and, gently, pulled him back.

He looked at her over the shoulder, and she shuddered at the black intent in his gaze.

"No," she quietly said. "You won't do anything to tear your family apart."

"She hurt you," he growled.

"Not really. She just doused me," she shrugged. "It's no big deal, Matt. A little rain never killed anyone."

"I don't care," he barked again.

"But I do," she replied quietly, and he closed his eyes.

"All right, I won't throw her out, but she must not touch you. Ever."

She nodded, and both joined the others.

Rebecca pierced them with a black look. She fisted her hands and advanced toward Matt.

"You're making a mistake, Matt."

"It's mine to make," he replied in an icy voice. "And I don't see any mistake from where I stand," he pointed out.

"You won't get all your powers and your money," she snapped.

"Sorry to disappoint you, grandma, but I do have the powers. And the money… you know I have no reasons to complain," he snickered.

"You can't," she stepped back horrified. "You're with her just because you're a kind man and feel sorry for her."

"I told you not to insult her again," he started toward her with angry steps, but Nora, pulled his hand and he stopped.

"Nora, she's maligning you," he complained.

"So what?" she replied. "It's not like I care."

"But do you care you cost him his abilities and his money?" Rebecca asked her in a mean voice.

"What is she talking about, Matt?" Nora asked, a frown between her eyebrows. "Have you lost something because you're with me?" she raised her voice.

"No, baby, quite the opposite," he assured her. "Because of our love, I finally have all the abilities I was supposed to have."

"I don't understand," Nora complained.

"Let me explain," Bryan said, striding toward them, a smile in the corner of his mouth. "As an outsider, and once in your shoes, I might make more sense, Nora," he told her and came closer.

Rebecca gave him the evil eye, but he just smiled at her.

"You see, because of two tragedies in her life, great-grandma cursed all generations to come. They can't reach their full potential and use their abilities, until they've fallen in love and committed to someone," Bryan explained.

He stretched out his hand to Becka, and she immediately linked her fingers with his.

"For instance," he continued, "Matt's love for you helped him to control his mind reading skills and other extra sensorial perceptions," he said.

Nora looked at Matt, and he nodded, then leaned over her, kissed her lips and whispered,

"You see, you brought me much more joy that I could have ever dreamed."

Nora blushed and Bryan chortled.

"Now, to continue, Nora. Rebecca also set up trust funds for her grandchildren, and later for her great-grandchildren. But they couldn't or can't get that money until they fall in love, commit to someone and that someone commits to them. Of course, there's a set of trustees – mind readers, you see, who can check if someone tries to cheat. I understand someone did, in the past," he chuckled, looking at Jay, who scowled at him.

"Why everyone has to bring me into this discussion?" he asked with disgust, throwing his hands into the air.

"Because your story is funny," Bryan answered, and winked at him.

"Then," Nora said hesitantly, "I don't see what Matt has lost by being with me."

She looked at Rebecca inquiringly and then at Matt.

"That's the idea, love. I lost nothing, but I got everything," he said and lifted her hand to his lips and kissed it.

"Yeah?" Rebecca snickered. "Then prove it."

"The only thing we have to do is prove it to each other, grandma," Matt shook his head. "We don't have to prove anything to you."

"You're afraid," she said with an ugly laugh. "You know the trustees will see through this sham, as I have already seen."

"You wear blinds, grandma, so you actually don't see anything that's not directly before your nose," Matt replied.

"The children love each other, Rebecca," Marjorie intervened. "Leave them be," she urged her.

"You're stupid, Marjorie," Rebecca lashed at her.

"You won't talk to my wife like this. I told you so in the past, and I won't repeat it again," Jonathan came to support his wife.

"I see," Rebecca said. "They fooled you all. They thought I'd hand in the money immediately if they came and gave me a teary story about love. I'm made of sterner stuff than that, Matty boy," she snickered at him.

"Maybe I wasn't clear," Matt repeated dryly. "I don't want the money. I already have here what I want," he said lifting Nora's hand.

"You know what I think?" Rebecca said with satisfaction. "I think you are afraid. If you weren't, you'd accept to have her checked by the trustees."

"She offered me her thoughts, so I know very well what she thinks and feels," Matt replied unconcerned. "I don't need your trustees to tell me what I already know," he shrugged.

Bryan put a hand on his shoulder, "Matt, in the long run, it helps that thing with the trustees. I've been there, done that, you know."

"I don't want them to read her mind," Matt dug his heels in the ground, glaring at Bryan.

"But I do," Nora replied calmly. "I know you know how I think, but maybe it's better if everyone is convinced that we don't try to pull the wool over their eyes," she told him, stroking his arm.

Matt closed his eyes in defeat.

FINAL CHAPTER

The sun shone over the island the day Nora married Matt. She wore a princess white dress, with little pearls all over the bust. The sleeveless dress hugged her bust and waist, but flared around her legs.

Nora had had some reservations at first. She'd been married before, after all, and it didn't seem right to wear a white dress.

But then, she'd discussed it with Marjorie, who, together with Becka, Lily and Maggie, insisted on going with her to buy the dress.

Her future mother-in-law patiently explained to her that she was wrong. Nora hadn't had a white dress for her first marriage. She'd married at the Town Hall. Besides, that was Matt's first and only marriage, and he'd love to have his bride dressed all in white.

Matt's eyes shone with unshed tears when she started moseying to him. His eyes roamed all over her face and body. Pride flashed in his dark-blue pupils.

He surveyed her advancement toward him, but, for the first time in his life, Matt lost his patience.

He dashed down the aisle, Marjorie had fashioned throwing a white carpet between the row of chairs. He didn't stop until he reached her, entwined his fingers with hers, and kissed her lips lightly.

"What are you doing, Matt?" Nora whispered, and her wide, bemused eyes zeroed in on his face.

"I made a mistake, baby. We should have had this ceremony in our living-room, under five minutes flat, and then leave for our honeymoon immediately. I don't know if I have the patience to go through all this. I want to be alone with you right now," he whispered back, and for the first time since her accident, he didn't think of the wound in her leg, but urged her to hurry and get before the pastor faster.

His action shocked everyone and they couldn't react at first. Marjorie covered her mouth and tears trailed down her face.

Becka and Bryan looked at each other, Becka taken aback, but Bryan with a wide and knowing smile on his lips.

Nat, who'd been told what was going to happen, didn't understand what changed and kept asking his aunties, "What's going on?" Yet, no one was able to give him an answer.

When Matt slid his arm around Nora's waist and rushed her before the pastor, they recovered and burst into laughter.

Jay and Maggie high-fived each other, as they were known to do, and the others elbowed one another. Even the old generation chuckled.

"He's got it worse than I had," Jonathan whispered to Marjorie, and she nodded, a smile on her lips, despite her tears.

Nora blushed to the tip of her ears, but Matt had only one care in the world. He simply wanted to get married and be on his way to the cottage he'd rented on the shore of a lake in north Ontario.

They'd already arranged and discussed things with Nat, and the child had declared he'd be happy to live with Becka and Bryan for a couple of weeks, while his mommy and Matt enjoyed a brief honeymoon.

Everyone enjoyed the brief service – Matt's stipulation, because he didn't want to waste the time before the *I do's*.

Rebecca had been invited as result to extensive interventions from all the women in the family and, especially, because of Nora's constant lobbying. Matt had turned ice-cold toward her and didn't want to talk or see her.

The engagement party had ended with inviting Rebecca's trustees so they could ascertain whether the young couple was really in love.

Matt had been completely against that, but Nora, who didn't want to be the cause of any discussions between Matt and his family, had insisted.

When the trustees acknowledged Nora and Matt's love and commitment, Rebecca had felt like fainting. She'd been wrong once more.

She'd tried to approach Matt, but he didn't bother to discuss anything with her. He just announced the trustees he didn't want or need the money, and then, he gathered Nora and Nat, said their good-byes and left.

Rebecca watched the couple making their vows and a shadow crossed her face. She knew Matt and she knew it wouldn't be as easy to get back in his graces as it had been with Bryan.

Matt was a kind man, yet he wasn't given to forgiveness. He'd already told her in unequivocal terms to stuff her money where the sun didn't shine. Nora had supported his decision, although she asked him to express it in more polite terms.

Some of the family members still talked to her, but not all of them. She didn't really need their pity, but that fiasco had decided her to find another way to get what she wanted.

Her eyes fell on Ariel, who tried to fight off the insistent invitations of Bryan's friend, Max. Rebecca shuddered. That was a man she didn't want in her family. Thank God, that girl seemed to have brains!

AUTHOR'S BIO

Rowena Dawn writes romance, reads thrillers and watches comedies. She likes walking through the woods, but insanely loves the sea. She has a love - hate relationship with her writing and drives her dog crazy whenever she doesn't stop writing to take him out.

OTHER BOOKS BY ROWENA DAWN

Becka's Awakening – Book One in the Winstons series

Jay's Salvation – Book Three in the Winstons Series (forthcoming)

Ariel's Dream – Book Four in the Winstons Series (forthcoming)

Leap of Faith

Double-Edged – Book One in the Perfect Halves Series

Eyes in the Dark – Book Two in the Perfect Halves Series

Pulled In – Book Three in the Perfect Halves Series (forthcoming)

Mr. (Almost) Right

Thank you for taking the time to read *The Winstons Book One*, the second book in the series *The Winstons*.

If you enjoyed it, please, consider telling your friends or posting a short review.

Word of mouth is an author's best friend and much appreciated. Thank you,

Rowena Dawn

Contents

BECKA'S AWAKENING..5

   THE WINSTONS..8

   PROLOGUE 9

   CHAPTER ONE...22

   CHAPTER TWO..35

   CHAPTER THREE 73

   CHAPTER FOUR..94

   CHAPTER FIVE 109

   CHAPTER SIX...132

   CHAPTER SEVEN 148

   CHAPTER EIGHT 161

   CHAPTER NINE 170

   CHAPTER TEN 182

   EPILOGUE..211

MATT'S DILEMMA...215

   THE WINSTONS FAMILY 218

   CHAPTER ONE 219

   CHAPTER TWO..231

CHAPTER THREE 237

CHAPTER FOUR 247

CHAPTER FIVE 256

CHAPTER SIX 262

CHAPTER SEVEN 272

CHAPTER EIGHT 287

CHAPTER NINE 302

CHAPTER TEN 316

CHAPTER ELEVEN 322

CHAPTER TWELVE 327

CHAPTER THIRTEEN 336

CHAPTER FOURTEEN 343

CHAPTER FIFTEEN 352

CHAPTER SIXTEEN 370

CHAPTER SEVENTEEN 376

CHAPTER EIGHTEEN 384

CHAPTER NINETEEN 392

CHAPTER TWENTY 401

CHAPTER TWENTY-ONE 409

CHAPTER TWENTY-TWO 417

FINAL CHAPTER 430

AUTHOR'S BIO 435

OTHER BOOKS BY ROWENA DAWN 436